T0274617

STONE

Cold

SECRETS

NANCE NEWMAN

About the Author

Nance Newman lives in upstate New York with her two rescue dogs—Ela and Misty. Ela was a rescue from the Puerto Rican hurricane and couldn't bark a lick of English when Nance took her home. After she figured that out, she taught Ela English and Ela taught her some Spanish. Misty was rescued from a puppy mill and after seven years in a crate, she is experiencing everything life has to offer. She loves her sister, Ela, and has become her mirror. They are the truest of companions.

Nance recently retired—from work, but not from writing because it's one of the things she loves most to do. She's had wonderful employment opportunities, from teaching physical education to being a researcher at Eastman Kodak in the Motion Picture Film Department that increased her love for movies and storytelling. She was on a team that won an Oscar for the development of a new intermediate film for moviemaking.

Nance has been writing stories since college, as well as music (she sings and plays guitar). She loves a good movie, especially if it's fantasy or science fiction. She also loves to walk, bike, hike, garden, travel and to learn. Most of all, she loves to write and is excited to be able to devote more time to these passions.

She'd love for you to check her out at her website—nancenewman.com

STONE
Cold
SECRETS

NANCE NEWMAN

BELLA
BOOKS
2024

Bella Books, Inc.
P.O. Box 10543
Tallahassee, FL 32302

First Edition - 2024

Editor: Ann Roberts
Cover Designer: Kayla Mancuso

ISBN: 978-1-64247-584-5

PUBLISHER'S NOTE

Acknowledgments

Thank you to De and Marsha for taking road trips with me to scout out places I'm interested in using in my books. We've had lots of great adventures and I hope to have more!

Thank you to Genine and my sister-in-law, Debbie, for being two of my greatest fans and reading everything I write.

Thank you to Ann Roberts, my editor, for doing such a great job getting this book in shape. I've learned a lot from you and I'll try to remember it all for my next book so the editing might be easier!

Most of all—thank you to readers everywhere, especially to those who have picked up this book and read it. It's because you love to read, that I continue to write because I love to write!

Dedication

I dedicate this book to my mother.
I wish you were here to see this!

CHAPTER ONE

Would the small town of Endonford in the middle of Nowhere, New York, be small enough to hide us? Sitting in the front seat of a used Chevy truck, studying the placid scenery that resembled landscape paintings in paint-by-number kits, I hoped we'd done enough.

I glanced at my wife. M.E. (short for Mary Ellen), who had been driving the past six hours. I yearned to take over. My butt hurt from sitting, and I was way past bored. I was reminded of the time I had to suffer through a psychology course at Stanford University. Every humdrum two-hour class made me want to tear my hair out by the time the professor announced, "Class dismissed."

Whoever decided students needed a psychology course for a degree in interior decorating needed to be drawn and quartered. At least, that was what I used to think. Then my first client turned out to be a narcissist. I found myself reaching deep into my brain cells to recall my notes on that chapter. It served me well. The client loved the finished product, which of course, was all about him.

I'd hung portraits of him in different styles ranging from Surrealism to Abstract (I decided abstract art clearly defined this man's psyche), on almost every wall. The furniture I suggested could only be approved by him sitting on it or lying on it followed by, "This feels good on my ass," or, "Anyone laying down here beside me on this sofa (or bed) could not refuse me."

I gagged at that one. What I put up with to satisfy my clients…

"M.E.," I said, noticing the different shades of greens in the passing landscape of hills, grass, and trees as if an artist had carefully chosen the colors for this landscape. They weren't as vivid as the Irish countryside, but the multiple landscapes appeared to have their own hue, as if Mother Nature herself assigned each color to the sprawling vistas. Wooded areas had trees boasting darker green leaves, almost Christmas green, that fluttered in the breezes traveling in and around the branches. The subdued greens of the corn fields were a stark contrast to the golden greens, blanketing areas where there were no forests, lawns or plantings. On these sections of land, brilliant wildflowers pushed through the yellowish weeds and grasses.

It had been calming relaxing at first, but now I felt that if I saw one more stalk of corn, I was going to scream.

"M.E.," I said again, this time in my "If you don't answer me, you will regret it" tone.

M.E. shook her head. I knew the look she was trying to knock off her face. It was the same one she had when she was fired from her professorship position at Stanford University. It was where we met—both in college pursuing different careers. I smiled, remembering I almost turned down her advances when I discovered she was pursuing a degree in none other than, psychology. At the time I thought, Who does that? What would you even do with it?

It wasn't until our third date when she told me what could be done with a degree in psychology, that I began to look past the uninteresting course of study. I was not impressed with the first part of her list, that included jobs in business, education, research, and criminal justice. But when she got to the medical field, I became interested. With that little tidbit, I went home with her for what ended up being the best mind-blowing sex I had ever had. I was hooked despite the fact she told me afterward that she wanted to teach.

It wouldn't bring in the money I'd hoped, but she wanted to teach at the college level, her dream job being at Stanford. The university paid well enough, and if you combined the salary with the very intelligent and attractive woman, and the best intercourse I'd ever had…well, I decided I could work with that. And I did. For ten years.

Until she blew it.

"I'm sorry, what is it, Addy?"

"My turn to drive. I can't sit here any longer."

"We're almost there. Just a little more time in the platitude seat." She shot me a sideways smile at the word I had come up with halfway through our trip to describe sitting in the passenger seat for longer than a few hours.

I sighed heavily as I let my head fall back against the seat. "Fine, fine, fine. But you owe me. Big time." I adjusted my body, hoping to direct the ache in my bottom to either leave or find another body part to annoy for the remainder of the trip.

M.E. reached out and took my hand, caressing my fingers with her thumb to placate me. "More than I can ever repay you, but I promise I will spend the rest of my life trying to do just that."

I managed a weak smile.

"So, where were you?" I asked, my tone edging on apprehension most likely sounding as if I didn't really care where she had been.

"I'm right here. Driving."

"Ha, ha, ha. You were deep in thought."

"Did you ever think that driving might be just as boring as sitting in the platitude seat?"

"If that's the case, what does it matter which seat you're sitting in? Let me drive. Please?"

"Look!" M.E. pointed at the windshield. She was bouncing in her seat with the enthusiasm of a little girl who had to go potty and was just told they were turning into a gas station with a bathroom.

We passed a worn sign I couldn't read because it blurred as we drove by at a higher rate of speed than the following speed limit sign imposed.

"Slow down, babe. We don't need a ticket on our first day in our new town. We're also in the backcountry. The cops look for people like us."

M.E. glanced at the speedometer and then hit the brakes so fast, my seatbelt snapped in response to the vehicle thinking we had been in an accident.

"Sorry," she said sheepishly.

"I will be so happy to get out of this truck," I moaned, rubbing my shoulder and chest.

"Are you okay?" my wife asked, as she glanced back and forth between me and the road.

"I'm fine. Just keep your eyes on the road."

It wasn't the fact we were in a car that made me miserable, but it was more the type of truck we were in. Our jobs in California gave us the luxuries and stability I had hoped for when I married her. After she lost her job, we had to sell both our Infiniti SUVs and our trendy San Francisco townhome in the upscale Pacific Heights neighborhood. We used the money to buy a home in Endonford, New York, purchase a ten-year-old Chevy Silverado to drive across the country, and pay for the subsequent move. The rest was put into stocks and bonds in hopes it would pay off and one day get us back to San Francisco, where I really wanted to be. I wasn't so sure about my wife.

If it wasn't for the Endonford Stone House built in 1822, one year after the teeny, little town of Endonford was established, I wouldn't have chosen New York as a place to settle. Taxes were way too high, and I wanted nothing to do with the rest of the state. Except for the big city. The only saving grace in my eyes was that New York City could rival San Francisco. We would be approximately a six-hour drive from there or a short plane ride from the minuscule airport outside of Ithaca. It was doable on a long weekend. It would have to do.

For now. Thank God my father was able to help M.E. land the job in Ithaca.

Too many changes had assaulted us in the last few months and sitting in a ten-year-old truck only solidified the real truth: I was now a country dweller (a much-preferred title over country bumpkin or hick). We had lost so much, and I had to accept the path our lives had taken. Because of that, I had to make this work.

"So, what did the sign say? I didn't see it."

"Endonford. Ten miles."

"Oh, thank God. Well then, you might as well drive the rest of the way."

She flashed her million-dollar, perfect, white teeth and full-lipped smile at me. A few strands of her soft, dark-brown bangs swept across her forehead, accentuating brilliant blue eyes outlined by thick velvety lashes. At thirty-three, her striking features were still enough to draw in any woman of any age. I not only knew this first hand, but I had seen it happen over and over again, and it was often a thorn in our marriage. But the feature that sealed a woman's fate in my wife's presence was her childlike dimples that softened the sharp lines of her jaw and cheekbones. Any woman subjected to those dimples became a drooling mess.

God, I did love her despite her indiscretion that almost ruined us. I loved her broad shoulders and concrete ribbed abs. I would lay next to her and count the "six-pack," and then boast to my friends that they were more like an eight-pack. I loved her slender hips and strong muscles that shouted to be seen when she wore tight shirts and pants that hugged her physique. And then there were the parts of her body that made sex with her more pleasurable than…well, there really was no describing it.

But it wasn't just the physical being that kept me chained to a relationship I probably should have left after her recklessness. She was often a kind, caring, thoughtful, and extremely romantic woman, and I knew with every fiber of my being that she loved me with all her heart. Then again, I was becoming mistrustful of my being's fibers. After all, if she really loved me that much, why did she feel the need to have sex with one of her students?

That thought stared me in the face more times than I cared to admit, forcing me to examine myself in the mirror. Who was I kidding? My biggest flaw was that I overlooked her biggest flaw that should have sent me packing—she was a flirt, and she was hormonally cocky about it because she was totally aware of how women responded to her flirting. She pretended to be oblivious to her shenanigans. She wanted to believe she could be friends with all women including the ones she made what she thought to be innocent sexual advances toward. It didn't help that the women in turn always wanted more. Again. Who was she kidding? Me? Herself? The women she flirted with? More than likely it was all of us.

M.E. was a woman who enjoyed feeling good. Flirting did that for her, but she never did it to pursue more than a fun, sexually suggestive friendship. That's all she expected and wanted from her female friends: that every one of them would be her friend despite her improprieties. That made her stupid in my eyes. I tried to tell her that, especially after her infidelity. Flirting with a woman who didn't know her libidinous ways always led to trouble. She insisted the definition of friendship was a carefree connection with someone with the capacity to sexually tease yet remain absent of sexual emotion. No matter what I said and the following arguments that ensued, she just couldn't get it through her head.

But when Raeann, a pretty third-year student in one of her classes, requested help with the unit on Human Behavior, M.E. learned that lesson the hard way. M.E. never told me the specifics of how it happened, but from what she said, Raeann wanted more than a passing flirtation. M.E. said no, making one naïve student a very angry woman who reported M.E. to Human Resources at the university. She got caught violating the Code of Conduct, and we both suffered the consequences of her continual actions she maintained were innocent.

I wanted to say "I told you so" so bad, it took everything I had to keep my mouth closed. Deep down, I knew that saying those words to her would only add salt to an already festering wound. I couldn't do that to her. For whatever reasons, I still loved my wife.

So, here I was, still married to her, with the worst ache in my butt ever. And here we were, void of our cushy San Francisco life, driving cross-country in a big ole truck, hoping to start anew. It was a chance she convinced me to take.

Nine miles later, we came to a flashing yellow light at a crossroads. Fields covered three of the corners, but the plants pushing up from the dirt were unrecognizable to me because I had never been on a farm. I ordered meals online that came in boxes with the ingredients already cut and diced and measured. I never cared where the produce came from or what it looked like before it found its way onto my dinner table. Cooking was not one of my strong suits or lifelong desires. It wasn't even on my bucket list. I just knew we had to eat. So, for me, a meal in a box was one of the best things that had come to the Internet.

On the fourth corner, a dirty building with two run-down fuel pumps sitting on a lot of cement-like dirt stood out like a sore thumb. Pocket ruts larger than a car's tire threatened to swallow your vehicle if you weren't careful when pulling into the parking lot. Despite the sign on the building that advertised there was not only gas available, but in fact, a store inside, the beat-up appearance of the business was not very welcoming.

However, it made me happy I wouldn't have to travel too far to get creamer for our coffee, but I fretted about the brands. They most likely didn't carry Nut Pods, Califia Farms or Starbucks creamers. God, I loved Starbucks creamers. I would most likely be stuck with cow's milk.

I sighed as M.E. completed a right-hand turn. The first thing I noticed was Endonford Elementary School. It looked new, built out of red bricks with big windows and paved parking lots and drives. A simple playground stood off to the side, consisting of a few swings, two slides and a monkey gym all built from metal and plastic. Okay, the school bordered more on city than backwoods town.

More farmland followed by—you guessed it—more farmland. And…well, you get the picture. Finally, more signs of possible life came into view. A long building with identical doors and windows running the length of it sat close to the road. It appeared to be some type of housing. There were ten units, each looking as dismal as the one next to it. A filthy white façade faded into the dirt-and-stone parking lot sparsely filled with dated vehicles. I frowned.

A few hundred feet down the road, a public building sat atop a small hill. It housed the Grange, the fire department and the town hall. Next to it was a church built in 1822, the same year the Endonford Stone House was built. The church was in bad shape much like the home we would arrive at shortly. Must have been a bad year for building. Chipped and fading paint, moss-covered front steps that were crumbling announced it was in desperate need of repair.

I cringed, keeping my nose pressed against the window so my wife couldn't see the distaste that I knew was surely written all over my face. The reflection of my downturned lips, squished nose, and dipped eyebrows in the window stared back at me as if to taunt me with the wrinkles the past year of stress had added to my thirty-four-year-old skin. I looked online for every miracle wrinkle cream, but deep down I knew no cream could erase what had happened or the path our lives were about to take.

Why did I have to love her as much as I did? Was she worth giving up my elite job as a top interior decorator to the important people of San Francisco? Or my luxurious life in a plush townhome I had so lovingly enhanced and garnished to make my own? Did she really learn her lesson? She promised— no, she swore to me that she had—over and over and over again. She made me believe that this new start would be good for us. We could carve out a place where I could start my own upscale decorating business, keeping all the profits for myself and not for someone else. This could make the move remunerative at the very least.

From the looks of this town, they needed some upscale decorating. I wasn't blind to think I would get rich from it. But a woman could dream, couldn't she?

So, I accepted that even though her new position at Ithaca College in the psychology department didn't pay like her previous job, it did have possibilities. It could open doors to the more prestigious Cornell University, and from there, maybe back home. That was my hope, and I hoped it was hers.

A few more miles on my tired ass and I recognized the simple, large, rectangular, two-story stone building that came into view. I had looked at the pictures at least five times every day since I spotted the country residence on the real estate website. I smiled at the large red-and-white SOLD sticker plastered across the For Sale sign still on the front lawn, announcing a closure on the two-story home that was really in need of a makeover.

I felt a twinge of excitement fighting its way through the negative emotions that had become my normal. I had only seen pictures of the house until now. Yet seeing it in all its decayed and shabby state, the positive feeling it gave me wove its way through the trepidation that had taken hold of me since M.E.'s dismissal had upturned our very prestigious and comfortable life.

When we realized the only position she could secure was the one at Ithaca College, I began to search the surrounding area for a home or condo. One day, I stumbled onto the stone house while browsing real estate sites on the Internet. Possibilities immediately flashed through my mind. For the first time in my life, I could have something of my very own. I could turn it into a showplace for a new business. My business. A world-class interior decorating establishment excelling in vintage home styling décor (that would be antiques). What better place to forge this type of decorating enterprise than upstate New York where antiques were still a reputable business? And the stone house was most definitely an antique. The potential instilled a new hope in me.

I marked the webpage and continued to search Zillow and Realestate.com for possible homes, but nothing caught my attention. That was because my thoughts kept floating back to the stone house. There was something about it that intrigued me. It was plain and simple, yet regal and mysterious.

As I stared at the laptop screen, I began to imagine the changes I would make. I even printed pictures of the interior so that I could pen in these renovations that took form in my mind, like an elegant wallpaper in rich colors to enhance the dining room. I might even take out a few walls for a more open floorplan, but when I found out it was a historical home, I knew I might be constricted to their regulations in refurbishing a historical building.

When M.E. caught me mulling over the photos several times, most likely catching the intrigue on my face, she suggested we look into it. Upon hiring a realtor in San Francisco to sell our townhome, we set her to work with the realtor for the antique home on three-and-a-half acres in Endonford.

New York was complicated when it came to closing on property, but we made our way through it with the help of our realtor and an inexpensive lawyer. Soon, we became the proud owners of a historic stone house born in the 1800s. I still couldn't believe it was ours despite the fact I carried the photos with me in my purse, taking them out every opportunity I got—just like a proud parent with a newborn. They were a reminder of what I had lost and now the possibilities of what I might find.

The home and its acreage sat on a corner lot with a rutted dirt driveway on one side. M.E. steered the truck into the driveway and shut it off before facing me. "Are you ready?"

"I don't know if I'll ever be ready," I replied, my eyes focused on the grandiose structure standing like an age-old king.

She took my hand. "Babe, we've talked about this. It's a new beginning for us. We can make it what we want. We can *do* anything, *be* anything. Let's go into our new home and start this next chapter."

I smiled at her and nodded. Then we got out of the car. She walked around to stand next to me, and as she put her arm around my shoulder, she said, "I can't wait to see what you do with this place."

Neither could I.

While we gazed at our new home, that would require an enormous amount of work that was beginning to feel overwhelming, we heard a car approaching. M.E. kissed me before we turned to see it slowing as it passed by our property. A middle-aged man and woman sat in the front seat, and there was no denying the disapproving looks on their faces: Disgust filled their expressions. We'd seen it before, just not in San Francisco. There would always be those who reprehended what they didn't believe was right in their own minds.

I wasn't quick enough to stop my wife from waving, smiling, shouting hello, and making a fool out of herself. I knew it would aggravate a burgeoning situation because my wife had a habit of acknowledging bigots with intentional satire.

The couple's vehicle nearly stopped, making their wretched stares painfully evident, more so than they would have been if M.E. hadn't goaded them. Then they turned into the driveway of the house across the street as the garage door opened.

When the ugly faces in the car windows were out of view, I stepped away from my wife and faced her. "Was that necessary?"

"Absolutely. No one has the right to treat us that way."

"You need to remember one thing," I said as I walked toward the front door.

"And what's that?" she called from behind me.

"We're not in Kansas anymore."

CHAPTER TWO

We stepped into our new home hand in hand. The front door creaked like it had been closed for decades and forgot how to open (which wasn't far from the truth). I was prepared for what we'd see. I had looked at all the inside pictures online over and over again—planning, dreaming, rebuilding and reshaping the battered and broken-down interior of the magnificent stone structure.

I hadn't realized how unprepared M.E. had been until her jaw dropped and she took several full breaths as her eyes took in the peeling wallpaper, trying—and failing—to cover holes in the plaster, light fixtures hanging from the ceiling by one single wire, rotten trim on windows, not to mention all the dirt and dust.

I jumped in front of her and smiled as wide as my cheeks would allow. "You just wait! It will be the most beautiful home you've ever owned, let alone lived in."

"Great," she said sarcastically. "What do we do till then?"

* * *

It seemed the following two weeks flew by faster than one of the several airplanes that passed over our home every day to and from the small airport. The first few days were spent cleaning, cleaning, and then more cleaning followed by shopping, shopping…and more shopping. We had set money aside for groceries, cleaning supplies, tools, and a few pieces of furniture that would suffice until our belongings arrived from California. We needed a bed, sheets, blankets (we brought our own pillows with us), and a few more chairs for our lone card table. We made sure we picked out a bed that would match the décor of our other furniture arriving in a few weeks.

This was the only time I was grateful for the ten-year-old truck because it enabled us to load up the purchases and take them home. Despite the fact we saved on delivery costs and wait time for the arrival of our purchases, my appreciation of the truck vanished when we had to carry everything inside. After lifting, tugging, and swearing at the mattress all the way up to the second floor, I swore I would never move another mattress.

When the bed was set up in the master bedroom (we didn't know if it was the master bedroom, but it was the largest one so we dubbed it the master bedroom), I opened the package of sheets.

"Really?" I looked at my wife and then at the bright orange sheets. "You couldn't pick out white? Or a subtle blue? I told you I wanted everything about this place to mesh with my vision of it being a showplace for high-end interior decorating. Orange does not go along with that vision."

"I hope no one other than us will be looking at our sheets." She slipped her arms around me. "Besides, orange is the new blue."

"No that would be *Orange is the New Black* and that's a television show." I shook the sheet to open it, tossing M.E. backward.

She tackled me to the bed.

"Hey! We've got a ton of work to do. We can't be messing around," I said through giggles resulting from her tickling me.

Then she kissed me. It was slow, moist, and oh, so pleasurable, and when I opened my eyes, her blue eyes twinkled and her dark hair tickled my cheeks. How could anyone resist that?

"Shall we christen our new bed?" I purred.

"I thought you'd never ask." She kissed me again and gently lowered her body onto mine.

Over the next two hours, we got reacqauinted with each other's curves, soft skin, limbs and faces. We touched every inch of skin, caressing the spots we remembered as being sensitive. We lathered kisses on each other's neck, cheeks, chin, forehead, and lips, lingering there, wanting to remember the feelings that enveloped us before things fell apart.

Undressing each other was still awkward, but we removed each piece of clothing slowly, as if hoping it would stir up the memories of how wonderful it felt to be naked in each other's arms—to feel the skin of our breasts touching, nipples growing hard. I remembered the overwhelming need that would run through me every time I saw her glistening, satin skin. But part of me was afraid it wouldn't be the same.

M.E. was poised above me, breathing hard. Her eyes drank me in and a smooth smile melted my insides. I watched her watch me as her hand skimmed my stomach and nestled between my legs.

She lowered her head and whispered, "Do you still want me?"

How could I say no? "More than anything," I forced out between heavy intakes of air.

And with my acknowledgment, she slipped her fingers inside me. I felt the moistness suck her in, the emptiness that had been within me for months being filled by her presence as I moved with her thrusts.

I clung to her, not wanting to let her go just as I didn't let her go after our world fell apart. When she started to slow, I placed a hand on her arm. "More, I want more."

I opened my eyes again to see a wide smile. "Keep them open," she said in a hoarse voice that was barely a whisper.

I did so, my eyes locked on hers as our love crescendoed into a frenzy of long-lost need and want. When she was too tired to go on, and I was all but spent, we collapsed side by side on the bed and started laughing.

"We still got it," she said, sounding relieved.

"Maybe we never lost it," I offered.

"We did lose it. You know it. I know it." She turned on her side and placed a hand on my stomach. "But thank God, it was only for a while."

I kissed her. Despite the fact we were recovering from a bit of exercise, that feeling deep inside that ran from my vagina to my brain wasn't ready to be done. I ran my fingers over her breasts, not having forgotten the caresses and squeezes that made her moan. I kept my lips on hers, pushing my tongue against them, encouraging them to open, to accept me.

She did.

I moved my hand down her stomach to that small patch of soft hair that was moist and mixed with drops of sweat and desire.

"You don't have to, babe," I heard her say, and despite her words stabbing at my heart, I didn't stop. For some insane reason, it only made me want her more. So I took every bit of her, and when I was done, when the screams of ecstasy quieted, I rolled off her and out of bed.

"Where are you going?" she asked, surprised.

"We have a lot of work to do. Come on, you lazy thing. Off the mattress so we can put on these god-awful orange sheets."

After pulling on my clothes, I turned to see her still on the bed. I put my hands on my hips. "Well?"

"Are you all right?"

"That's an odd question. Of course I am. I'm better than all right. We just had a sexual liaison that could be one for the record books."

A grin spread across her face. "What record books?"

"The one for the loudest screams during intercourse."

She threw her shirt at me. "I was not that loud."

"I think we both were and I wouldn't be surprised if the nosy bodies across the street called the police because they think someone is getting murdered or something."

She grabbed her undergarments and began dressing. "I think even backwoods nosy bodies can tell the difference between screams of ecstasy and those of someone getting killed." She jumped off the bed and put her arms around me. "Besides, it's natural and none of their business."

I handed her shirt to her and she put it on. Then I slapped her butt. "Get to work, you lazy bum."

* * *

M.E. worked with me to clean the rooms we would be using. We set the bed up along the front wall of the room, but decided after making love for the first time in our new home, it might be better on the other side of the room away from the road. We placed the table and chairs in the middle of the dining room. The card table with four metal, collapsible chairs blended in well with the dining room's scratched and dented wood floors, crumbling plaster walls, and worn ceiling.

One of our stipulations in purchasing the home was that we had some leeway with decorating. I actually liked the layout of the house and I had lots of ideas. The realtor assured me I would be able to do what I wanted. I was aware of the Endonford Historic Society and I was willing to follow their guidelines as long as they were willing to work with me.

The kitchen was bare, and I mean literally bare, but that never bothered me before. To my chagrin, we had chosen to save money by cooking instead of purchasing ready-made meals on the Internet. Someone would have to cook. That would be difficult to do since there was no working kitchen.

So, back to the store we went and bought ourselves a microwave, a college dorm-size refrigerator, and a toaster oven. Those alone still limited our dining options, and we often found ourselves driving the streets of Ithaca looking for less expensive takeout.

By the end of the first two weeks, M.E. was ready to go to work. After attending some training sessions, she would begin preparing for fall classes. Despite my plea to take more time off and help me start the renovations, she insisted that we needed the money to pay for the renovations. She also pointed out that if she didn't agree to start in the fall, as well as teach a few summer classes, they wouldn't have hired her.

Even though we had agreed I would take a set amount of our condo sale to start on the modernization of the antique house, I knew it wouldn't be enough for everything I wanted to do. I starred at the worn and scratched wooden plank floors. They would be beautiful when finished. There was nothing like solid wood floors that shone from several coats of stain and polyurethane. What I loved about this house was its character, its history and its lifeblood that was embedded in the stone and wood fibers of the building. Restoring each piece of floor plank, chair rail, crown molding, frames, and decorative wooden ceilings would bring it back to life bit by bit. I hoped in doing so, it would do the same for me.

But first, I had to attend to the staples, one of which was getting Wi-Fi. After the nightmare of waiting on hold for hours just to speak to a customer representative and trying to get them to understand what I needed (apparently houses built in the 1800s didn't have Wi-Fi), I was successful in getting it installed.

I was finally able to use my phone and computer to search out qualified contractors. I hadn't had much success until there was a knock on the front door that startled me. We didn't have many neighbors, but not one of them attempted to approach us or stop by and introduce themselves. There were no welcome baskets with homemade cookies or sage advice on where to buy the best fruits and vegetables.

Sighing, I got up from the table. I strolled to the double doors and unlocked the deadbolt on one side. When I opened the door, I found a tall, rugged woman waiting patiently with her hands in her overall pockets, her green eyes wide. Her red hair was tied back in a ponytail and her skin had all the signs of years working outdoors. Despite the rough appearance, she was quite attractive. I guessed her age to be late thirties judging by the smooth skin on her face with only a tiny hint of laugh lines.

"Can I help you?"

"Hi, my name is Amelia Lakin, and I heard you were looking for a contractor."

I studied her. "How did you hear that?"

"Ithaca is a small town and Endonford is even smaller. People talk. I'm an independent contractor with my own business, but if I need help, I have no problem finding capable people to hire. I have a portfolio if you'd like to see my work. I know most of the contractors in the area and I know for a fact they're all booked out through the winter. Besides"—she smiled—"I've had my eye on this baby for a long time, waiting for someone to come and bring her back to life. I'd really like to be a part of that."

"And you aren't?"

"I'm not what?"

"Booked throughout the winter?"

"I could be, but I really would like this gig, so I've been putting off jobs waiting for you to arrive and hoping you'll give me a chance."

Gig, I thought. Who said *gig* anymore? But then the second part of her sentence stuck with me. "Why would you be waiting for me to arrive?"

"Oh, this isn't going very well. Can I come in?"

Thoughts of being alone in a big, empty stone building in a small podunk town ripe for a robbery—or worse, a murder—raced through my mind. But there was something about her that convinced me to open the door and let her in.

Her eyes went wide as they roamed the vast emptiness and dismantled the once prestigious home. She smiled at the card table in the middle of the dining room cluttered with my computer, phone, writing instruments, pads of paper and files. Then she set her eyes on mine.

"Years ago, I did a little work for the previous owner," she said out of the blue. "We became friends. Lots of good memories here. I'd stop by and Mrs. Edwards would be waiting for me with cookies and lemonade. Gosh, it looks so different. It's sad that she wasn't able to keep up with it. She really let it go. When I heard it was sold, I asked the realtor who bought it. He told me someone from California and he suspected they were going to live here because they requested information on New York State regulations, like for driver's licenses, insurance. You know, all that crap. They also inquired about the historical society and what they might require to renovate it."

"Why did the woman sell?" I asked, hoping to find out more history on the place than what I read in the meager articles I'd found online.

"Her kids grew up and moved away. Her husband passed a few years ago and she couldn't take care of it anymore. She's in a retirement home. You have to understand, this is a real small town. You've probably noticed that even though the main part of town is not far from here, people are pretty spread out around the township. It covers a lot of area, but most are connected through the church. So, it makes this a perfect example of where everyone knows everyone and their business.

"Anyway, she wanted to give it to the historical society, but they couldn't afford to renovate it. Everyone was excited to hear the new owners were from San Francisco. That spelled money to them, so they hope the renovation will be done right." Amelia leaned forward. "That means to their expectations, rules, and regulations." She waited for my reaction.

My heart sank a little. I was afraid the historical society might be a problem. "I am well aware of how, um, particular, historical societies can be. I think they will be pleased to know that I am an interior decorator. One of the best. I was well-known in San Francisco and I plan on making my niche here in vintage home styling décor."

"Antiques," Amelia mused. "That could work."

"How versed are you in restoring old homes by their directives?" I asked knowing her answer would mean the difference between hiring her on the spot and looking for someone else despite the fact she told me there was no one else. I just wasn't sure whether to believe her or not.

"Very," she answered. "I've done quite a few of the bed-and-breakfast mansions. Like I said before, I can give you my portfolio. It's in my truck. But what I can tell you right now is that you'll need to think about updating the heating system before the winter. It can get pretty cold up here since you're on higher ground. It's really old—uses propane. But it's a boiler system and they're not bad except that you can't use it for air-conditioning. For that you should consider the wall units. There are some on the market that are really efficient and cool very well. But keep in mind, there's a lot of good summer breezes if you don't mind opening your windows."

I motioned to a chair. "Would you like to sit? I actually have some lemonade," I offered, smiling.

"That would be nice." Amelia sat down and I went for drinks.

"Sorry, we don't have much else here right now. I just got word our truck is coming this week," I said as I placed the glasses on the table. "On the one hand, I'm excited to get our stuff. On the other hand, it will put a wrench in starting the renovations if I have to move everything around to get things done."

Amelia took a sip and then asked, "I assume you've got ideas on what you want to do?"

"I do. I'll be honest with you. I hope to make this a show place. I know it's far from major thoroughfares, but if I do it right, market it right, I think I can grow a really solid interior decorating business here."

"Did you have your own business in San Francisco?"

"No, but I was the number-two person at the top interior decorating company. I'm tired of bringing money in for someone else. I'm ready to make a go of it on my own."

"Well, if you show me your plans, maybe I can help convince you I'm your person. I'm sure we can develop a good working relationship. I've got a few connections with the historical society as well." She winked.

I sipped my lemonade and sat back. I looked at this red-headed woman. I had known a few redheads in my life and every one of them was as bold as her. I didn't know a thing about her, where she came from or if she really was a contractor, but there was something about her.

"Why don't you get your portfolio, your credentials, license, and a business card for me?"

"I carry them with me everywhere I go."

"If I can look them over, maybe we can talk."

Amelia got up and started to walk out.

"Amelia."

"Yes?"

"Why do you want to help me renovate this house so badly, especially if you've done so many others? I'm sure there are many more out there that need contractors."

"Like I said. A lot of good memories here. I want to see it done right. For Mrs. Edwards." She turned and left before I could say anything else.

For the next ten minutes, I poured over Amelia's information. When I was satisfied, I pulled a red folder out from under a pile and opened it. "This is full of my ideas that I've been working on since we decided to buy the stone house."

"We?" Amelia's green eyes looked at me with curiosity.

I came from a large city where gay was a second language. Here, I wasn't so sure how we would be accepted, especially after the close encounter with the nosy bodies across the street. Now I was finding out this was a rather religious community. I had no idea which religion, and I wondered if a system of high morals and values would make a difference to her in accepting me and M.E.

"I, um, my spouse and I moved here."

I knew if I were to hire this woman, she would find out sooner or later exactly what I meant by spouse. In San Francisco, telling anyone you had a spouse of the same sex was no different than discussing one of the opposite sex, but I wasn't familiar with smaller towns. I grew up in Los Angeles then moved to San Francisco, and lived there since I entered college. I was all about the big cities.

"So you and your wife moved here from California. I have to ask…"

Oh God, here we go. She knows. Everyone is already talking. Here it comes.

"Why would you move from a place with such great weather to here where you're sure to freeze your ass off in the winter?"

I stared at her for a moment and then broke out into loud laughter.

Amelia watched me intently as if wondering what about her question made me laugh uncontrollably.

"I'm sorry," I said when I finally stopped laughing. "It's just that, well, I thought...I wasn't sure..."

Amelia sat back in her chair. "Oh, you weren't sure how you and your wife would be accepted here in small town, US of A," she said in a very southern accent.

I chuckled. "We were getting a little nervous because no one has extended a greeting to us and a rather rude couple were driving past our house...Let's just say they could star in one of those movies where the neighbors turn out to be psychopaths and murder everyone on their street with an ax."

"Were they in a gold 1964 Chevy Impala with a black top and do they live across the street?"

More and more, Amelia was surprising me. Pleasantly. "Honestly, I wouldn't know the make of a car unless someone held up a really large sign with that information. But..." I thought a moment. "Come to think of it, the car was gold with a black top. And they did pull into the driveway across the street."

"That would be the Johnsons. What's that saying? Their bark is worse than their bite." She smiled. "It's not who you are that has the townspeople a bit put off. It's that you bought a beloved landmark and they're afraid you'll turn it into a den of sin."

"A den of sin? Are you kidding me?"

"I'm sorry. That's a poor analogy. They just don't want to see the stone house be less than what it could be."

I picked up my glass and tipped it toward her. "You should have said that first."

She leaned forward. "I can have a wicked sense of humor."

I was really beginning to like this Amelia—not that I had met other Amelias, but this one was just what the doctor ordered. I much preferred working with a woman, so her sexuality was a plus. I knew she would understand my vision. But now, I knew she would work with me to make sure it came to be without pissing off the town.

"Shall we go over what I would like to do? Then you can give me your suggestions. I think, Amelia, that together we just might make this work."

I took out drawings of the interior of the home, explaining where to put my office and showroom. I told her I wanted an open concept but I realized that taking down walls would have to be approved by the historical society.

She explained where the scant plumbing was and what would be needed to bring the bathrooms and kitchen up to date and to code—which was a lot. Really a lot. I was so into our discussions about literally renovating the rooms from the basement up—walls, ceilings, and floors that needed to be reinforced, and then refinishing floors and all woodwork—that I was surprised when I heard the front door open. I hadn't realized that Amelia and I had been talking about the renovations for hours and we hadn't even gotten to the outside of the house when M.E. walked through the front door.

I quickly wondered which M.E. we would get—the skeptical one that would be suspicious and probably a bit jealous of another female sitting with me and laughing, or the one that would take the opportunity of an introduction to an attractive woman to form another one of those coquettish relationships.

I decided not to wait for one or the other to appear and jumped out of my seat. I went to her, drawing her close and placing a sensual kiss on her lips.

She pulled back and look around me. "Who have we here?"

The lilt in her voice told me which M.E. Amelia was going to meet. Without turning around I answered, "This is Amelia. She's a contractor interested in helping with the renovations. Amelia, this is my wife, Mary Ellen. If you'll both excuse me for a few minutes."

I didn't wait for either of them to say something. I trotted up the steps to the upstairs bathroom—the only one working in our new home. I shut the door and took several gasps trying to slow my breathing so as not to hyperventilate. My reaction to their meeting confirmed I was still not over my wife's indiscretion and the destruction it brought to our lives.

I sat on the toilet and looked around the rather spacious, yet far from satisfactorally functional bathroom. It had one toilet most likely from the fifties. There was a claw tub with a shower, but no curtain or rod to hang it on. Both M.E.'s face and mine had dropped when we saw it. So much for sensual showers. There was no counter space and no medicine cabinet behind the worn mirror that hung lopsided on the wall above a small pedestal sink.

Yeah, if I hired Amelia, the bathroom would be the first thing to update—even before the kitchen.

If I hired Amelia.

And if I was the wife I was supposed to be, that decision would have to be made by both of us. I headed back downstairs. Listening to them as I descended the stairs to the living room, I knew that wouldn't be an issue. They were getting along just as M.E. wanted them to.

I took a deep breath before I entered the room. M.E. sat in my chair engaged in a very animated conversation with Amelia, whose gaze was intently fixed on my wife's. She appeared to be concentrating on every word that came out of M.E.'s mouth. To my chagrin, Amelia was totally being allured by my wife's flirtations, almost as if she was starstruck.

I sighed and walked over to the table, putting my arm around M.E. "So, what do you think? Should we hire her?"

My wife looked up at me. "We'd be a fool not to. She knows the structure. She knows the town and city. She knows competent people that will work for her if needed. Her portfolio shows expertise. The only thing we haven't talked about is cost. Once we know that, if it's in our price range, then my vote is yes."

I crossed my arms. "Well, Amelia, you've seen what I want. I'm sure there will be suggestions on your part and changes on mine. My last question is will you be able to sell my inspiration to the historical society?"

Amelia swallowed hard. I knew this would be the ultimate test.

"From our brief meeting, I believe you have a pretty good understanding about how historical societies want their historical buildings renovated. That being said, I know them well. I've worked with them on many structures in the area and every owner has been thoroughly satisfied. Their testimonials are in my portfolio. I can't, however, guarantee that they will accept every inspirational change." She air quoted with her fingers when she said, inspirational change. "But if we work together, I promise you'll have a good chance for most of them to come to fruition. I've always been able to come up with an acceptable compromise."

I waited a moment before answering because I wanted her to know that I was the boss and not my wife. "I can work with that. How long will it take you to put together an estimate?"

"Can you give me a few days?"

"Yes," I said, "I think we can do that. The truck is supposed to come soon, so we'll be busy with unloading."

M.E. looked up at me. "Do we really want to fill this place with everything and then have to move it again to work on something? You know we'll be the ones moving the furniture all over the place. I'm not so sure that's a good idea for several reasons."

"She has a point," Amelia said.

"I don't think we have the money to hold them off for the length of time it will take to finish everything." I picked up my papers and pretended to study them for an answer.

"I could clean up the basement, bring in a few dehumidifiers, and make some temporary pallets that we could put the boxes on," Amelia offered. "The furniture that you don't need right away could be stored in one of the rooms on the first floor that can wait until its refinished. Then as we finish, I have a few guys who could move the stuff to where you want it for a very reasonable price."

I smiled at her thinking she was just too good to be true.

"Just put up here what you definitely need or want." She looked at me and winked. "And make sure the movers stack things so that I can get to the furnace, electrical wires, plumbing, and the walls. I can show you the areas I need access to if you'd like. How long did you say before the truck gets here?"

"In about a week," I answered.

"Give me a day or two to calculate an estimate and make some drawings to reconfigure plumbing, heating, and electric. Then I can tell you where to put your belongings."

M.E. stood. "Where did you find her? I'm not sure we're going to be able to pay you what you're worth."

Amelia got to her feet. "I think we can work it out. I'll call in a day or two." She proceeded toward the front door and then turned. Stepping toward me, she extended her hand. I took it. "And thank you for giving me this opportunity. If you have any questions, comments, et cetera, just call me. We'll be in touch."

When she closed the door, M.E. stepped in front of me. Her face was filled with concern. I didn't think the reason was the hiring of Amelia because they were practically drooling over each other. If anyone needed to be worried, it was me.

"What is it?" I asked her.

"I received a phone call from the San Francisco police before I left work. Raeann is missing," she answered in a low voice.

Great. That's all we needed.

CHAPTER THREE

"What do you mean, missing?"

M.E. pulled a chair out for me and sat facing me.

"What did they say? When did she go missing?"

She put her fingers to my lips. "Shhh. Let me explain it. When I'm done, if you have more questions, I'll answer what I can." She sighed heavily. "She was staying on campus over the summer for an internship. She had a few weeks off before it started, so no one noticed she was gone until she didn't show up for the first day. That was two weeks ago. A friend of hers said she was taking a vacation before her internship started but had no idea where she went. Raeann told her she was going to drive up the coast. She didn't have a destination in mind. She left three weeks before she was supposed to show up for work.

"They checked her apartment and there was no sign of distress. Her car is missing too. The police are retracing her steps. Because she didn't have a plan for where she was going, it's going to take some time to figure out when and where she went missing."

M.E. paused.

"Why did they call you?"

It was a stupid question, I knew, because with everything that happened, the police would refer to my wife as a person of interest once they found out about their affair and the aftermath that included her firing from Stanford.

"You know why."

"But that was dealt with. The case was closed."

"Except she wasn't missing after the case was closed. She was still going to classes while we sold everything and packed up to move here. As far as we know, she wasn't missing when we left California. She is now."

I stood up and put my hands to my face as if hiding it might make all this go away. "Oh, my God. This can't be happening."

I felt my wife's hands on my shoulders. "Addy, look at me." When I didn't remove my hands, she gently pulled them away from my face. "Look at me."

I fought the tears that were preparing for the possible crisis to come—kind of like a track runner placing their feet in the blocks waiting for the whistle. When the whistle blows, everyone starts running like hell.

"I didn't do anything. I never saw her again after, well, after she accused me. They can't do anything to me because I haven't done anything. We're just going to have to ride this out." She put her fingers on my chin and lifted it so I had to look at her. "Can you do this with me?"

I wrapped my arms around her. "Of course. You're my wife. You promised me it was over. I believed you. I still do."

She kissed my forehead, my nose, my cheek, and then her lips lingered over mine, brushing them ever so lightly with a ticklish, but sensual touch, leaving only air between us.

I moved away abruptly, interrupting what could have ended in a pleasurable, before dinner appetizer. "What if they come here?" I started pacing, wringing my hands together.

"Addy, calm down. What if who comes here?"

"The police? What if they want to question us? Oh, my God, we just moved in. Our neighbors will run us out of town. Then where will we go?" I must have sounded like a raving lunatic because my wife hurried over to me and took me in her arms.

"This is not the Wild Wild West. People don't get run out of towns anymore."

I looked up into her eyes. They were passive, dull—something I had never seen before. The brilliant blue that dazzled everyone when they met her was dull like dirty water.

"You're worried," I said.

"Well, yeah. I'm worried they'll make our life a living hell. But I'm also not worried because I honestly did not do anything wrong. I haven't seen or heard from her since the last time she thrashed out at me at the dean's office."

"That was pretty ugly, wasn't it?"

"It wasn't pleasant by any means. We're lucky she didn't have me arrested."

"She was of consensual age. No way she could have had you arrested unless…" I turned away from her.

She walked over to the window. Planting her body against the frame, she stared out as if contemplating when she would have to mow the expansive lawn. "It wasn't rape if that's what you're going to say." M.E.'s voice was hard.

I wanted to kick myself. "No. No, no, no. I was going to say she could've fabricated something like that. But she didn't—that we know of."

M.E. relaxed. "That we know of," she agreed. She folded her arms. "Maybe that's why they called. The police, I mean."

"You think she might've told them something different than what really happened?"

"Maybe not her. But she's missing. If they talk to her friends, family…God, I didn't even know if she had family. But if they knew about our…our…"

"Tryst?" I offered.

Her smile was biting. "They could be telling the police right now that it was something more than what I was accused of."

"Don't you think Raeann got enough revenge by ruining our lives?"

"For some people, it's never enough." She shook her head. "God, I wish we could just put this past us."

I walked over to the window and faced her. "We left three weeks ago. According to what the San Francisco police told you, Raeann has been missing for two weeks."

"That they know of," she said.

"Okay. Still, you've been with me the last three weeks and before that, we were driving here. That took us a week. There's no way they can pin this on you. You were working during the day. You were with me every night. You couldn't fly to California, meet her at the park and then fly back in the eight hours you were working. So, we're good. You're good."

M.E. pushed off the wall. "That's right. We've got nothing to worry about." She drew me into an embrace. "I knew there were other reasons I loved you and not just for the mind-blowing sex." She held me out at arm's length. "That brain of yours is not to be rivaled."

I bowed. "Thank you. Now, I expect payment."

She kissed me. I kissed her back. We skipped right to mouths opening and tongues exploring. I felt the familiar butterflies play with my stomach, telling me desire was tugging at my sexual core. I took her hand and led her to the bedroom.

Our clothes found their way to the floor in a messy heap of material. Kisses and long caresses continued while each piece of clothing was unbuttoned and unclasped before it found its way to the floor, making the foreplay last deliciously long. And when we finally entered each other, teasing our orgasms to come again and again, it was early evening before we collapsed onto each other, breathless.

"The mind-blowing sex is still the number one reason I love you so much," she whispered to me.

"I wouldn't have expected anything else from you." I tucked my head into the crook of her arm and pressed against her. Regardless of what we had just done for each other, to each other, and despite how warm and comforted I felt in her arms, a tinge of hurt ran through my veins. I loved her for many reasons other than sex. And when she said she loved me most for the sex, it hurt, because she interacted with everybody as if the sexual prospect that she presented to herself was possible with anyone she wanted it to be. Loving me for the mind-blowing sex, in my mind, made me a whore.

I rolled over and the image of Amelia's soft features accented with emerald-green eyes that looked at me with such tenderness flashed before me.

Rather than wonder why I was still with her, I got up and put my clothes on.

She propped herself up on one arm and patted the bed. "Where're you going?"

"We kind of missed dinner and I'm hungry. So, I'm going to get something to eat. Wanna come?"

She grabbed my hand and pulled me back. Hard. Hard enough that I tripped over the edge of the bed and found myself lying across her. She sat up and planted another warm, wet, wanting kiss on my lips. "Yes," she purred. "I want to come."

The true act of our love started all over again, and when we were done, she fell asleep with her arms holding me close.

This time, I slipped quietly out from her hug, dressed, grabbed my keys and purse and got in the truck, but not before I left a note on the table. I was hungrier than the last time I tried to get something to eat, and there wasn't much in the tiny fridge. I would get takeout and bring it home. If she wasn't hungry, there was plenty of room for her dinner in the small, college-size fridge.

I drove into Ithaca and found a Thai restaurant along the main drag. Feeling more than sexually satisfied, but emotionally in turmoil, I decided to eat in the restaurant. I ordered my meal and takeout for M.E. I also ordered a vodka and 7 Up with a lemon twist. I was nursing my drink when I heard a familiar voice behind me.

"Hey there. What are you doing here all by yourself?"

I looked up to see Amelia. For whatever reason, my consternation dissipated from my mind, replaced by her smiling face and sparkling green eyes.

"Amelia. Hi. I came to get takeout, but since M.E. is sleeping, I thought I'd indulge myself with a drink, dinner, and a restaurant atmosphere. It's been a while since I've sat in a restaurant other than to wait for takeout."

We stared at each other, no words passing between us until I finally said, "Would you like to join me?"

"You sure that's okay? I don't want to intrude on your solitude."

"Oh, I get enough of that every day while my wife is at work."

Amelia sat down. "But"—she leaned forward—"if you hire me"—she sat back—"you'll have my remarkable company every day and then you'll have to come to a restaurant alone for some solitude."

I laughed. "I'll keep that in mind." I signaled to the waitress to take Amelia's order. The whole time Amelia scanned the menu and gave her order, I watched her eyes move as she read, her mouth form the words while a strand of her bright-red hair fell across one cheek, accentuating her deep, sea-green eyes. She was sturdy with delicate features, strong yet graceful.

But, there was a mysterious quality about her. She showed up on our doorstep without being searched out, and I hadn't decided if she had an agenda or she just really wanted to refurbish the stone house. On a good note, it was very possible that she would be helpful in making my dream come true.

For a brief moment, I got lost in my dream—refurbishing the beautiful stone house, creating my own business and making it all my own. Nowhere in my dream was my wife. Strangely, I didn't feel bothered by that, and a moment later, I was shaking my head to remove that thought.

When I looked up, Amelia was watching me. "Are you all right?"

I smiled through my embarrassment. "Um, yeah. Sorry. Listening to your order, I was just thinking how hungry you must be."

"Oh, that wasn't all for me. I also ordered takeout for my roommate."

"Roommate?"

"Yes. I have a roommate."

"Is it a friend mate or a significant mate?"

Amelia chuckled. It was a sweet sound, sort of melodic like a soulful ballad.

"I never heard it put that way before. He is a friend mate."

"Ohhhh." My voice went from low to high, giving the impression I assumed he was more than a friend.

Amelia's eyes dipped and her lips thinned. "Though dost assume."

"I think it goes 'though dost protest.'"

"Yes, but I'm not saying you're protesting, just assuming. David is a friend. A gay friend."

"Ohhhh," I said the same way I did before. "See, that kind of oh can mean different things."

"Ohhhh," she mocked.

"Nothing like a gay friend. I had one in San Francisco. It was hard saying goodbye to my bestie, but he promised he'd visit."

"A city gay boy coming to the backwoods of New York. He'll be appalled." She smirked.

"Yes, he will," I laughed.

"There's a great, gay nightlife in Ithaca. That should smooth it over."

"Well, if I ask for suggestions on where he can find the nightlife…"

"David will be happy to accommodate that."

"Ohhhh," I said again and she burst into an uncontrollable giggle. "You know what? I believe you'll be fair in your pricing, so I'm going to hire you right now."

"Really? That's fantastic. But you really should wait for my quote. You might not find it as reasonable."

"You don't seem like someone who would take advantage of us or cheat us. So, you're hired."

"Oh, my God. Thank you. I'm so excited to work on that house. It's definitely a love project," she said, her green eyes twinkling.

"A love project. I like that." I leaned forward. "So do you think you could come over tomorrow and do something about our bathroom?"

"I can come over and take a look."

I smiled. Talking to Amelia became easier as the evening wore on. Two hours of pleasurable conversation, nothing about the house, ended with an irate phone call from my wife.

"Where are you?"

"I left you a note. It's on the table downstairs. I ran out to get some food. I've got takeout for you. I'll be home soon."

"You've been gone a long time. Is everything okay?"

"Yes, of course. I just decided to eat here and have a drink. I've been mulling over project ideas for Amelia to start."

"Hurry home," she cooed.

"Leaving shortly."

"I love you."

"Love you too."

When I hung up the phone, I noticed Amelia staring at me. Again.

"We didn't talk about any ideas for me to start on, unless you call taking a look at the bathroom an idea for me to start on."

"It kind of is. Sorry about that. I don't normally lie."

"Then why did you?"

I sat back and folded my arms. "I'm not sure. No, strike that. My wife said something that bothered me and I left after she fell asleep—mainly because I was hungry and also because I needed to think about it."

"Is everything okay?"

I barely knew this woman and it seemed to be getting kind of personal. I answered anyway. "The move took a lot out of both of us. I think we're just tired. We have a lot of work to do to settle in and little energy to do it with."

"You do seem a bit stressed. I don't have to come over tomorrow."

"No, I need you to get the bathroom functional. I can't take a shower. I also need to get the basement settled before the movers come."

"You said your truck was coming in a week. I need you to know I'm not sure I can get the basement ready and make your bathroom functional in that amount of time."

"I understand, but I can help you with the basement. For the shower, all I really need is some type of shower rod and a curtain. It's a claw tub."

Amelia smiled. "Oh, I can fix that easy. Okay, boss. What time would you like me to show up tomorrow?"

"How about nine o'clock?"

"Sounds good. You do realize that a good part of the day tomorrow will be planning and going to stores to get the supplies I'll need, including that shower rod and curtain. So that will take a day away from the actual work."

"Being an interior decorator, I've…What's that saying? 'Been there, done that,' so again, I understand."

Our takeout orders arrived with the checks. A few minutes later we were standing in the parking lot next to my truck.

Amelia nodded toward my vehicle. "Do you like driving that?"

I looked at the monster truck. "Not really. But until we get a second vehicle, I've got no choice."

"Are you in the market for a second vehicle?"

"Yes and no. I would love a car of my own. I just don't have a lot to spend on one right now."

"I've got a Honda Fit I've been thinking about selling. If you're interested in taking a look, I'll drive it over in the morning. I won't be bringing all my tools until I know more of what you want me to do. I can fit what I need in the Honda. For a little car, it's got a lot of room."

"A Honda Fit," I said, looking at the truck. I never thought I would be driving a large truck. Then again, I really never thought I would drive a Honda Fit. Going from a Lexus SUV down to a tin can was so demeaning. But the thought of the freedom in having my own car… "That would be great. Thanks." I looked back at Amelia. "Well, I'll see you tomorrow?"

"Great, see you tomorrow. And thanks for the company at dinner."

"My pleasure," I answered. I got in the truck and drove home. On my way, my mind replayed the dinner over and over and over again. And every time I replayed it, my smile got bigger. Amelia had me laughing. Something I hadn't done much of in the last few months. It was liberating, especially when I was a firm believer that laughter was the best medicine.

However, I wasn't stupid to think laughter would fix M.E.'s and my predicament. But it made me feel better than I had in a while. I looked forward to working with Amelia. It made me happy to know that I would be creating my dream with someone who thought of it as a love project and would make the process enjoyable.

Maybe things were beginning to look up.

When I walked through the door, that thought flew right past me and back out the door and fluttered away at the sight of M.E. sitting at the table, arms folded. Her face was taut and she didn't look like a woman who just woke up after extremely satisfying sex. Maybe I wasn't as good as I thought I was. Nah, I really was that good.

She was angry about something. Before she could light into me, I spoke quickly. "While I was having my drink and a bite to eat, Amelia showed up. She sat for a bit and I hired her. We talked about what we needed to do tomorrow to get started. I'm sorry I was so long, but I brought your favorite Thai dish." I opened it so she could get a whiff. "It's peanut sauce." I moved the bag back and forth under her nose. "I missed you."

Her arms were still folded, but her facial features softened, except for her lips that were struggling not to smile. I set the bag on the table.

"I got fortune cookies. You can pick first. Or have all the fortunes." I leaned forward and kissed her on the lips. The first one landed on the cheek as she turned away from me. Just as I was about to walk away, she grabbed my hand and pulled me back for the next kiss that landed on her lips. It was strong, demanding, but not in a sensual way. It was more like she was making a statement.

"Don't do it again," she whispered when the kiss was over. And there was the statement. Her fierce eyes pierced a tiny hole in the armor I had built over the years for occasions such as this. There weren't many, but when they happened, it put me on edge.

I wanted to shout that I was hungry. I'm an adult. I can go out to eat if I want. There was no food in the kitchen. In fact, the only things in the kitchen were the few small appliances we purchased, which I found humorous because neither of us cooked. Even so, I worked hard to hold back a smile. Instead, I responded, "I promise."

Her demeanor changed in an instant like Clark Kent running into an alley and coming out the other end as Superman. Now she was the loving, sweet woman I first fell in love with.

"So," she purred. "Care to join me while I eat?" she asked as she took out the cardboard containers of food. "You can tell me what you and Amelia talked about."

"I'm kind of tired," I replied, but when I saw the warning look on her face, I sat down.

"You know." She waved a chopstick in my direction. "She's kind of different looking."

"What do you mean by that?"

"Well, that scruffy red hair, white complexion. She's muscular and rough-looking." She smiled at me. "Not like you."

"Okay," I drawled out. We definitely weren't speaking about the same woman. I found Amelia attractive—the way her green eyes lit up when she laughed, the bright, bold red hair that made a statement of happy and feisty. It was different than the reasons I found my wife or a movie star attractive—like Angelina Jolie. Everyone was different. Everyone was attractive in their own right. M.E. and I had discussed this many times before. She had always agreed with me. In fact, M.E. had always found all women attractive, especially the ones who flirted with her.

So, what was my wife getting at?

I watched her watch me, definitely waiting for my answer. "Thank you. I'll take that as a compliment."

"It was meant as a compliment. I think you're beautiful."

I waited for more—like smart, funny, interesting, good travel companion, anything other than sex and beauty. But nothing more came. Not that sex and beauty were a bad thing. I was flattered and happy she was with me for those reasons. When we first met, she pointed out my attributes that had nothing to do with sex and beauty all the time. But as the amount and intensity of her flirting increased, it seemed the other reasons she loved me shrank into the background.

It wasn't until much later into our relationship that I realized when she told me she loved me for my brain, it was only for her sake. I had built a very successful clientele list that brought in loads of money. I had come up with her alibi and defense in the disappearance of Raeann. I understood that my intelligence wasn't attractive to her, it just…worked for her.

"How's the dinner?"

"Delicious. Now tell me. What did you and the contractor talk about?"

I filled her in on the conversation between Amelia and me, but only the parts that pertained to making plans for the next day. I explained how Amelia would get the shower working and the basement ready for our belongings. Amelia would also try to complete as much of the plumbing and electrical needed for all the changes before our belongings showed up. I didn't tell her that we would be traveling around together for the day as Amelia picked out supplies and I paid for them. I also didn't tell her about the car—the Honda Fit—I was considering purchasing.

Why, you ask? Because after her off comments about Amelia, I was afraid she wouldn't let me hire her and say no about the car. Not that I needed her permission. It's just that what I really didn't need were her objections. I would figure out how to broach the subject of purchasing a smaller, used vehicle later. I was exhausted and just wanted to go to bed.

When M.E. finished her dinner, she picked up the boxes and tossed them in the trash. Then she took my hand and led me to bed. Without a word, she undressed me, put my nightshirt on and laid me down under the covers. Then she crawled in next to me and tucked herself against my side.

I waited for her eyes to close. When they did, I was relieved. Sleep found me quickly but it was haunted with nightmares of infidelity.

On both sides.

I woke sweaty and breathing hard, but it wasn't from sexual satisfaction in a dream. It was from fear and guilt. I had never cheated on my wife or on anyone for that matter. But my wife had cheated on me. Was my dream telling me that I would betray my wife?

I got up and dressed. I sat at a small table we brought with us for the bedroom, preparing for the day's work with Amelia, fully convinced that I would never have an affair. It wasn't in me. Besides, revenge sex might be satisfying when you had it, but after I could only imagine the guilt would eat you up. And the phrase "Two wrongs don't make a right" kept running through my mind.

The nightmare nagged at me until I heard M.E. stir. I was getting angry at myself. Why were my feelings about our situation showing in my dreams? Was the appearance of another woman, regardless of why she showed up in our lives, affecting me as well?

I wouldn't let it. I loved my wife as the saying went—to the moon and back. Despite the issues that now plagued our marriage, I was confident we would find our way through it. We were starting over. New beginnings always took time, but I hoped here in the stone house, she would begin to see me as more than a sex partner.

"Good morning, love. I was just about to wake you. How did you sleep?"

"Must be better than you. How long have you been up?"

"Not long, but there are things I need to get done before Amelia gets here. I want to prioritize all the projects that I want completed."

M.E. got out of bed, her naked body glistening with sweat from the warm night. "I hope central air is first on that list." She walked over to me and sat on my lap.

"Maybe not. If it means you'll get dressed before you walk over to me, then no, it's at the bottom." I put one hand on the back of her head and gently pulled her face to mine. While our lips locked in a full, heady, and very wet kiss, my other hand massaged her breasts and toyed with her nipples. I felt the tingle in those parts of my body that desired to be touched, stroked and entered.

She pulled back with a devilish smile. "Are you trying to get me back into bed?"

"No need to go back to bed," I whispered in a husky voice as my hand slid to her thighs, finding her sweet spot.

"I can't be late," she whispered, panting in between words.

"You drive fast. You'll be there in plenty of time," I answered, increasing the speed of my caresses.

Her head fell back. I kissed her neck, and then pulled her lips back to mine. They were so swollen and moist and it made me want her more. Having her naked body so close, feeling the wetness that spread between her legs and the kissing, oh, the kissing was so erotic.

Yet I struggled between wanting the sex and wishing I had the unconditional love to go with it. I envisioned a life where I was in control and it wasn't just me who was defenseless to her way of loving. I wanted it to be her who wanted, craved, and loved *me* with everything she had.

Only me.

CHAPTER FOUR

After our morning lovemaking, M.E. had to speed dress to get ready for work. She kissed me goodbye in a way she hadn't for a while, in fact not since the whole San Francisco thing. Ten minutes later, she was out the door, vowing to find a shower in the physical education building at work. I giggled as she walked past me totally flustered, with the smell of sex following her out the door. We were finding our way back to each other and that fact alone brightened my day.

I was feeling like I was on a marijuana high when I sat down at the card table with my computer. As much as the younger generation had turned its back on antiques, I still loved the quality, the personality, individuality and the beauty of each and every piece, no matter its size—as large as a stone house or as small as a silver spoon. I was researching pieces that I might want to use in the office and display room of my business. New York had a lot of antique stores so the options were plentiful. I was particularly looking for a desk, and after some intense searching, I had one in mind.

So, when Amelia showed up, I excitedly showed it to her followed by my plans and my Excel spreadsheet with the order of projects to accomplish.

While she sat at the table opposite me, reading, and writing things down in a small notebook that she carried, I pulled up the desk I had spotted on an antique furniture store website.

"Found it," I said, interrupting her train of thought.

"Found what?"

"The desk I told you about. It's in a store called Found in Ithaca. It's really beautiful. A large walnut rolltop desk. It will be perfect." I looked up at her. "Can we stop by there today so I can put it on hold?"

"We can bring it here in my truck if you want."

"I thought you didn't want a lot of stuff in your way right now. By the way, we're getting a reprieve. The truck won't be here for three weeks. Good for you. Ugh for us."

"That's good. It gives me more time. So no, one desk in here won't get in my way."

"Perfect! Hey there's another shop. I'm sure you know of it. Significant Elements? We can probably find a lot of things there to replace whatever we need to—like doorknobs and other hardware."

"That's the architectural salvage store. I'm very familiar with it. I do a lot of business there. The great thing about Ithaca is people here are still into antiques and restoring old homes."

"Great. Let me know when you're ready to go." A thought suddenly struck me. "Hey. I thought you were driving the Honda Fit today. The desk certainly won't fit in the hatchback of that little car."

"Actually, I brought my truck. After our talk last night, I went home and started making my own lists. I decided I was going to need the truck after all. I'll bring the Honda tomorrow when I don't have to cart anything here."

"Okay. Sounds good. Would you like some coffee? I'm going to make myself a cup before we go."

"I don't want to inconvenience you."

"Nah, not at all. It's one of those Keurig coffee makers. I'm not a cook. Or a coffee maker/perker or whatever you call a coffee maker."

Amelia laughed. "Keurig coffee is fine with me."

I started for the kitchen.

"So, that's why you were eating in a restaurant. You don't cook?"

"Nope. I don't like to cook. For me, it was a waste of time that I didn't have in San Francisco. I had so many other important things to do. Even so, I never would have bothered to cook home meals because there are *so* many wonderful eateries."

After a few minutes, I returned with our coffee, creamer, and sugar. I sat down and while I fixed my coffee, noticing she drank hers black, she asked, "Did you go to a restaurant for every meal?"

"Don't forget there's takeout. However, after a few years of takeout and restaurants, we both really wanted some homecooked meals, but without the cooking and the burning, and the spilling, and the cleaning up afterward. We pooh-poohed the idea of hiring a cook and gave in to one of those Internet meal services—the kind where they deliver fresh ingredients packed in separate containers. You mix them together and then cook them."

"Isn't that cooking?"

"It was for me. So M.E. was in charge of preparing those. I only heat things up in a microwave if I have no other choice. That's the extent to which I cook."

"Who did the dishes?"

"Dishwasher. We took turns. I was always miserable on my days to load it."

"And you want a full kitchen?"

"Me? Hell no. I'm kind of like Carrie on *Sex and the City*. I would use the stove for a closet, but, M.E. used it once in a while to heat things up. She insisted the microwave wasn't a healthy way to heat food—you know, plastic and all that stuff. We also used the oven when we entertained, but let's face it, I'm an interior decorator. That includes decorating the kitchen. So I have to have one here that is not only respectable, but out-of-this-world desirable."

Amelia's smile was warm and pleasing. She stood up and bowed to me. "Then you shall have it. Are you ready to go?"

Giggling, I grabbed my purse. "Lead on," I said. "I am in your hands for the day."

Her expression changed and she looked a bit confused as if she wasn't sure how to answer that. I imagined a joke or a sarcastic remark entered her mind. Instead, she smiled and responded, "They're good hands. I already promised your wife I'd take good care of you."

"You did? When did you do that?"

As we walked out to her truck, she said, "Okay, don't get mad at her. She called me on her way to work. We talked for a few minutes. She wanted to make sure I would do whatever you requested and to take good care of you while we roamed Ithaca today."

"Huh," I said, opening the door to the cab of her truck. Damn, I thought while hoisting myself into the passenger seat. Another truck. *I really hate trucks.*

Amelia navigated down a windy, hilly road. I didn't realize that Endonford was at the top of one of those hills and the town of Ithaca, or city as they liked to call it, was in a valley. Any way in or out of Ithaca meant you had to go uphill or downhill.

While she drove, she carried on about the beauty of the area, emphasizing the multitude of waterfalls and gorges. The largest, Taughannock Falls, was a flat, one-mile hike to one of the prettiest and tallest waterfalls in the area. Buttermilk Falls, Roger Tremon Falls were others she mentioned and suggested M.E. and I visit to experience the true beauty of the natural world of Ithaca.

I wasn't a hiker. I didn't like bugs, especially mosquitos. So, walking in the woods to see water didn't thrill me. Still, I promised her we would, all the while keeping my fingers crossed behind my back. It was so childish, but I wanted Amelia to like me, if for no other reason than to make the working relationship easier.

After several stops, I suggested we get some lunch since I'd only downed a cup of coffee for breakfast and my stomach was growling. *So embarrassing!*

She maneuvered the truck into a parking spot on a city road.

"Where are we going?" I asked.

"Moosewood. Very famous vegetarian place. They even have cookbooks out on the market."

"I'm really not a fan of vegetarian."

"Trust me. You'll find something you like. Their food is scrumptous."

Not wanting to venture too far into the vegetarian world, I chose a pasta primavera with fresh vegetables. True to her word, my meal was delicious. "God, I wish I could hire their cook to work for us. This is so good."

"Told you so," Amelia answered, delving into her tofu salad.

"I'm going to have to bring M.E. here. She'll love it."

"If she hasn't been here already. A lot of the professors from the university and the colleges come here for lunch."

"How do you know that?"

"I've done a lot of work at both. I can't tell you how many times the staff recommends this place to me." She chuckled before she took another bite of her lunch.

"She hasn't said anything, but you never know, I usually don't ask her what she has for lunch." I looked up at Amelia, intrigued by her information. "Sometimes you think you know everything about your spouse and then someone shows up and shows you otherwise."

"I'm sorry. I don't want to cause any trouble."

"No, not at all. It's just interesting that you said that. I never thought about what she ate for lunch. Even in San Francisco. We were just always too busy to ask, I guess."

There was an awkward moment of silence. I really hated unpleasant situations, so I asked, "So, Amelia, where do you live?"

"On the outskirts of town. I have an apartment in Newtonfield, just south of Ithaca."

"And where did you grow up?"

"In the slums of Ithaca."

"This tiny city has slums?"

"I think all cities have slums."

"I'm sorry."

"For what? It's not your fault my parents were worthless specimens of the human race."

"Ouch. Tell me how you really feel."

"I just did. Next subject. How about where did you grow up?"

"I grew up in Hollywood."

Amelia looked at me and her eyes popped. "Hollywood. You lucky dog."

"Not in the beginning. My mom had me out of wedlock. She was in a bad way as a teenager and she didn't know who my father was." I shifted in my chair. "She said that when she saw me for the first time, she vowed to straighten out. It didn't happen at first. Finally, she got a job at Universal Studios cleaning bathrooms. She moved up to soundstages and then to the administrative offices, where she met my stepfather. He was a bigwig at the studio with a very large salary. They fell in love and he moved us into his mansion."

"How old were you?"

"I was eight. I had a really great life after that. I wanted for nothing. They sent me to the best schools."

"How did you get into interior decorating?"

"My stepdad would take me to the movie and television sets with him. I was fascinated with the set designers. They created places and sometimes worlds that you really believed existed just by decorating. My first set was, I hate to admit it, *Star Trek*."

Amelia sat back. "Oh, I love *Star Trek*."

"I don't know why that doesn't surprise me." I giggled. "Anyway, my stepfather looked for the best university for me. I ended up in the design program at Stanford. I think my stepfather hoped I would do something other than interior decorating, but I was set on what I wanted to do. More technical than I would have liked, but I believe the program was the reason I became one of the best interior decorators in San Francisco. That's where I met M.E."

"How lucky were you?"

I noticed her smile was forced and I immediately felt bad for boasting about my wonderful life. Here was someone who grew up poor. Who knew how bad her life might have been?

"Tell me about your childhood."

"Yours is much more interesting. Are your parents still alive?"

I swallowed hard. "My dad is. But we don't speak anymore."

"I'm sorry. What happened?"

"My mom got cancer. Too much drinking, smoking, and drugs that led to her pregnancy and promiscuity. It also led her down a road to cancer. She was truly remorseful that her lifestyle as a teen and young adult would keep her from watching me live out my life. She told me that just before she died."

"Wow. I'm sorry."

"It's okay. She was a decent mother while I had her. She loved me the best she could. My stepdad's money made up for the rest." I grinned.

"So, where is your stepdad?"

"Probably screwing his young slut somewhere on Bora Bora."

Amelia was taking a drink of water and spit it out when I answered.

I laughed. "Again, it's okay. I've learned to live with it. When my mom died, my stepfather was despondent. He just didn't know what to do. He was a prime target for all the young women at the studios looking to climb the ladder. Looking at it now, I find it kind of ironic. That was my mom. She was always looking to climb the ladder. I just hoped my stepfather wouldn't fall for it again because they really did love each other." I sighed. "Anyway, I realized he lives on the dark side where women are concerned because he found himself another gold digger. So maybe it wasn't my mother he loved, just her opportunist ways."

"So, why didn't you try to talk to him? Maybe try to help him."

"I did. Many times. But it was useless. I think he felt so lonely, he screwed the first woman that came along and surprise, she was another money grubber. Or maybe he was trying to find another woman like her." I shrugged my shoulders. "Then he struggled with the guilt of what he was doing. No matter what I said, he refused to listen. He started to spiral out of control. We argued a lot and eventually I left.

"It was M.E. who gave me a good reason to leave. I wanted love in my life and she gave it to me. My stepfather could no longer do that. So, that's my life story and I'm sticking to it." I looked at my watch. "We should get going. We have a few more stops before we get my desk."

"Oh, not yet. You have to have dessert."

"I'm not so sure vegetarian dessert is my idea of sweets."

"Do you like chocolate?"

"What real woman doesn't?"

The waiter appeared and Amelia ordered two pieces of their vegan chocolate cake. When it arrived, I gave her a big smile. The chocolate treat was mouthwatering and left me wanting for more.

"Have you ever heard anyone say that chocolate is better than sex?" Amelia asked me. "That's how I feel about this dessert."

"I'll give it a close second."

We took a leisurely stroll back to the truck, enjoying the cool breeze and blue summer sky. Topped off with a very satisfying meal and great company, I found myself in the best mood I'd been in in a while—except of course when M.E. and I were making love. Nothing rivaled that feeling.

And then darkness rolled over that thought. It was true at the beginning of our love. Now, I wasn't so sure.

When we finished a stop at the local big box, home improvement store, we headed to the antique shop. I moved down the aisles, finding pieces that spoke to me. There were so many, making me decide to contact the owners in hopes of developing a relationship with them for my business. As I searched out Amelia to inquire as to who that was, I heard her speaking to a woman in a very animated way. It was light and happy. Hands were flying as stories were told and the laughter could be heard throughout the store.

"Hey there," I said, approaching the duo.

"Adalynn, this is Joan. She owns this fine establishment. Joan, this is Adalynn Pious."

I glanced at Amelia. I didn't remember ever telling her my last name. She leaned toward me, as if reading my mind. "It was on all the credit card bills you signed today," she whispered.

"No one can ever read my handwriting," I said, astonished that she could read my signature. Everyone always told me it was as unreadable as a doctor's.

She simply smiled.

Joan extended her hand and I took it. "Nice to meet you. You have a great store here."

"If you're into antiques. Not many people are anymore."

"But I read on the Internet that antiques are still alive and well in this city."

"That's true, but once the Ithaca clientele has bought what they want or need, there's no more clientele until the next wave of antique lovers comes along or the first wave needs something else. We do get outsiders now and then, but not always enough to support several stores. That's why we're down to four."

"Well, I'm an outsider. I'm also a prominent interior decorator from San Francisco. I was the number one decorator at Niche Interiors. I plan on opening my own business here. Maybe if we work together we can bring in more business to the area? I specialize in rich interiors with rare antique pieces."

"I'd be very interested. How soon before you open?"

"I'm in the building stage. Amelia here will be doing the contract work to get my store up and running. It'll be a few months, but I'll keep you posted."

Joan glanced at Amelia. She put her hands on her hips. "You didn't tell me you were working again."

Amelia's embarrassed expression said there was a story there, but I didn't press it. At least not right at that moment.

"Didn't get a chance. You were too busy telling me about your customer. Ms. Pious bought the Endonford Stone House."

Joan looked at me with her mouth open wide in surprise. "You did? Now that's an undertaking, but it's a beautiful building."

"Yes it is, and it will be a huge undertaking, but I'm up for the task. I plan on doing it justice. It will be even more beautiful when I'm done."

"Well, with Amelia doing the work, I'm sure it will be."

"Joan, I'm also interested in the large Victorian rolltop desk you have in the back."

"Wonderful. Follow me and we'll talk."

We walked to the back of the store, where the more high-end items were displayed. We haggled over the price, and twenty minutes later, all three of us were loading it into the back of Amelia's truck. I got into the passenger side and noticed Joan whispering to Amelia before she got in. Joan hugged her and went back into her store.

"So what did she say?" I asked when Amelia joined me.

"You'd have to ask her. Are you ready to head back?"

I looked out the front window, a little put-off, but decided whatever Joan said to her was none of my business. "I am. It's been a long, but very enjoyable day."

"It ain't over yet. We have a lot to unload."

"By the time we get there, M.E. might be home. She can help us."

"So, how did you two meet?"

I was amazed at the ease with which she slid back into casual conversation that had seemed to be about me and my wife all day. I decided to go with it. "She was at Stanford. I met her at a sorority party." I glanced at Amelia to see if she would roll her eyes. She did. "I wasn't in one, but I had a friend who was and she invited me to go. M.E. was there, and we literally just hit it off. The rest is, as they say, history."

"What drew you to her?"

Now, I decided to address her inquisitiveness. "You're asking a lot of personal questions. Do you have an ulterior motive other than working on the house?" I tried to sound as if I was joking, but there was something that nagged at me in the back of my mind. "I would think sharing histories should work both ways."

"I just like to know who I'm working for."

"And I like to know who's working for me."

"Noted." She grinned. "I went to trade school to learn my craft. I liked working with my hands. My parents didn't have money for me to go to college, but they never would have given it to me even if they did. The loans I would've needed were daunting. So, I didn't have the princess life you had."

"Wow. If you're going to work for us, I would suggest you take the chip off your shoulder. None of that was my fault."

I felt anger boiling in my veins and I was surprised at the turn the conversation had taken. I liked Amelia. I didn't want our working relationship to end before it began.

She sighed heavily. It was several minutes before she spoke. "I'm really sorry. I didn't mean that. I had no right to say what I did. I guess sometimes my sucky life gets to me and jealousy rears its ugly head when I talk to someone who was lucky in life."

"That bad, huh?"

"That bad."

"Maybe we might become friends at some point and you'll feel comfortable enough to tell me about your sucky childhood. But for now, let's not worry about who we were, but who we are. How's that sound?"

Amelia looked at me and smiled. "That sounds great. Thank you for understanding and for not firing me on my first day of work."

"You're welcome. I expect great things from you where my house and business is concerned. You can blame that on Joan." I grinned.

"And I promise to deliver."

"Good."

We drove the rest of the way in silence. I was still trying to figure Amelia out. It was possible she was embarrassed about her outburst, but whatever the reason, it made me wonder if she was someone we could trust. Someone *I* could trust.

Except for her momentary lapse in judgement, I really enjoyed being with her. She had great ideas and seemed to know what she was doing. Besides, it might be a while before I could find another contractor, if I believed what she said to be true—that most of them in Ithaca were already booked.

M.E.'s car wasn't there when we pulled into the driveway. A bit disappointed, I helped Amelia unload everything, but we left the desk in the back until my wife came home.

Inside, we piled the supplies in a corner of the living room. Amelia asked me to pull out the plans for the layout of the rooms. She grabbed a box of chalk out of one of the bags and began to measure and draw on the floor where walls needed to be repaired, taken down, or added.

We had agreed that all the wood floors were beyond refinishing. Therefore, I was to pick out flooring that I wanted to use with each room. I was actually happy about that. I loved restoring old buildings to their early glory, but this was going to be my home and my showroom. It had to be perfect. I would choose wood flooring that was rich in grain and color and spoke to me about the design I wanted to portray. Yet, I was no fool. It had to fit with the style of flooring used when the home was built. I could work with that.

This was the exciting part of interior decorating—when everything came together to produce the desired final look you were trying to achieve. Nothing excited me more than taking a project from the bare bones, picking out flooring, wall and trim colors, draperies, furniture, and most of all, the accent pieces that would mold it into the completed picture that started as an idea in my mind.

I watched Amelia work. She was dedicated, I'd give her that. Her lips pursed and her nose scrunched as she stood with her hands on her hips, evaluating a line she'd drawn. She moved with grace despite her height and muscular limbs. I wondered if her abs would give M.E.'s a run for their money.

Realizing I was about to drool, I got a soda. I held it up. "Would you like one?"

"Too much sugar and chemicals."

"I've got beer."

"I'm working."

"Not really. It's past five o'clock and you should be done for the day. We didn't discuss overtime." I smirked.

She put the piece of chalk in the box and tossed it into the bag. "I'll have that beer."

I handed it to her, noticing the white dust all over her fingers. I don't know why, but it was kind of sexy, and I had to turn away.

"We can sit outside on the steps if you want. Take advantage of the breeze. It's kind of warm in here," I said, putting the cold bottle to my cheek.

Just then my phone rang. M.E.'s name appeared on the screen. "Hey, babe. As you can guess, I'm still at work. I'm going to be a while. Do you want me to bring home dinner?"

"That would be great. When will you be home?"

"A couple of hours. Can you wait that long?"

"Yeah, sure. See you then." I ended the call and stuffed my phone in my pocket. Then I turned around. "M.E.'s not going to be home for a few hours. Do you think we can manage that desk on our own?"

"Do you think you can?" She winked.

I flexed a muscle. "I'm no slouch. No muscle girl either, but I can hold my own."

"I'm sure you can. We can give it a try on one condition."

"What would that be?"

"That you listen to my instructions."

"You're not one of those who likes to have all the control, are you?"

Amelia laughed. "No, I've just moved a lot of antique furniture from trucks to inside buildings and often up and down stairs. Not just from one side of the room to another."

"Oh, very funny," I said sarcastically as I followed her out of the room. "You better wait to finish that beer until the desk is safely inside."

She put the beer down and said, "See? I followed your instructions. I'm not a control freak."

"I knew we'd work well together," I said, slapping her on the back as I walked past her and out the door.

"Oh yes, we will," I heard her say from behind me, but it was so quiet, I didn't think she meant for me to hear it.

I couldn't quite distinguish the tone of her voice. It could have been teasing sarcasm, but it felt a bit off…sinister-like. I shook it off. Amelia was anything but that.

Still…

CHAPTER FIVE

Sitting at the table going over the next day's work for Amelia, my stomach growled. It had been two hours since Amelia left and three since my wife called and offered to bring dinner home.

My hunger pains were getting the best of me and I was about ready to call for takeout when I heard the truck rumble into the driveway. Several deep breaths helped me keep my unresolved feelings in check. M.E. had only been working a few weeks at the college, but it was beginning to feel like déjà vu.

This was how it started before. One day a week late at work turned into five days a week. Then she had to work weekends. But she promised me. She promised me she had changed and that she loved only me. She would make it up to me.

I wiped all emotions off my face except for the one that would show my wife how excited I was for her to be home. I ran to the makeshift closet and put on a sexy maroon camisole with a touch of lace and a low-cut front that accentuated my jean shorts. I kicked off my sandals and walked to the door barefoot.

I stood waiting for it to open.

When M.E. walked in, her smile was wide. But she wasn't looking at me. In fact, she almost walked right into me.

"Hey!" I shouted.

M.E.'s head perked up in my direction, and she looked at me wide-eyed. "Oh God, you surprised me. I thought you'd be sitting at the table immersed in the plans for our home." She held up the bag. "Dinner." She continued to the table where she opened the bag and pulled out the containers. Then she got silverware and glasses from the makeshift kitchen, ignoring my presence.

I stood and watched her, dumbfounded that she acted totally oblivious to my outfit. I shook my head and sat at the table. Without speaking I started eating a bowl from Chipotle.

M.E. poured two glasses of white wine and brought them to the table. "You must be hungry. You didn't even wait for me."

I hoped the look I shot her was one as deadpanned as I felt. I studied her face to see if I could figure out where her head was. She was a blank slate. "I didn't think you'd care."

She stopped opening her container of food and looked me up and down. She put her hand through her hair. "Oh, man. I walked right past that." She pointed to my chest and smiled. "No wonder. I'm sorry, babe. It's been a tough day. I was going to tell you about it while we ate."

I didn't reply and continued to eat my dinner.

"I really am sorry. You look pretty sexy, you know."

"I know," I replied.

She laughed. Then she leaned forward and spoke in a quiet, but very sensual voice. "Leave room for dessert."

I already decided I wasn't going to have dessert. Or be dessert. It was late and I was exhausted. I was also mad at her. Just a little. Okay, maybe it was totally my anger toward her. I chose to try a different route. "So, tell me, why was your day so difficult?"

"I got a call from the police again."

I stopped eating and met her gaze. A very unnerving thought passed through my head. Why would she have been smiling (and I mean her smile was one of pure pleasure) when she walked through the door, especially when she was facing more questioning from the police?

"What did they want?" I asked, worried they were beginning to suspect her.

"They had a lot of questions that were making me late for my class. Plus, I didn't feel comfortable speaking to them without representation. It felt like they were accusing me of something. So, I told them to speak to my lawyer."

My mouth dropped open. "A lawyer? Do we even have a lawyer? The last one only did real estate for us. Do you think you really need a lawyer? Will you use the one you had before?"

M.E. put her hand on mine. "Slow down, wife." She waved her fork at me. "I don't need a lawyer since I've done nothing wrong. I have no knowledge of where Raeann is, where she went, or what she's doing. Nothing. I haven't been in contact with her since we signed the agreement in the dean's office. Just like I said." She took a bite of her food.

"Then why do you feel you need a lawyer?"

"Because you know how the police can be. They can take your plain, simple, and truthful answers and read everything into them that is illegal. I want to make sure I have protection."

I looked down at my dinner. Suddenly, I wasn't hungry anymore. "I get that. So, have you called Arnold and Porter?" They were the law firm we used during her tangle with Raeann and Stanford. They were also the reason we were shorter on money than we would have been if she hadn't needed an attorney to protect our assets—and her ass.

"No, I haven't. One of the professors in my department was in the breakroom when I got the call, Ms. Wendall. She said she had a son who'd had a bad breakup and the girl disappeared not long after. She gave me the name of a lawyer who not only kept her son out of jail, but kept his name clear. Diane Kensington."

"Diane. That's a name you don't hear much anymore. She must be older."

"Why do you say that?"

"Because the name Diane was used more in our grandparents' generation. So, she's gotta be what, in her sixties?"

"More like in her forties. Her parents must have been old school."

"Hmm. When do you meet her?"

"I already have. I went to her office after my classes. That's why I was late."

And there was the reason for the big smile on her return home. It definitely had not been for me. Diane Kensington must have been quite the looker.

Quietly and hesitantly, I asked, "Are you sure you need her? Do we have the money for this?"

M.E. looked hurt and offended. "I won't use any of the money for the refurbish, if that's what you're asking," she answered harshly, stuffing food in her mouth. Then she looked out the window.

"I didn't mean that. It's just I was thinking about getting a car."

"A car? You know how tight things are."

I said nothing more. But I wanted to say that things couldn't be that tight if she had enough money for another lawyer. They weren't cheap. Everyone knew that. Unless she planned on paying in another way. And now I was fuming because all the money we had given to lawyers and we were about to give to another was because of *her* indiscretion. Would this ever end?

I abruptly got up from the table, almost knocking my container of food to the floor. I closed the lid and put it in the refrigerator. "Well, I'm glad you've got it under control. I'm tired. It's been a long day and I need some sleep. Thanks for bringing dinner home."

"Addy. What's wrong? Don't you want me to be protected?"

"And don't you want me to have some freedom? I gave up a lot for you. The least you can do is be supportive of me getting a car. It's not like I'm going to buy another Lexus or something outrageously expensive. It's just a used Honda Fit, for God's sake," I practically shouted.

M.E.'s face twisted. I couldn't tell what was happening for the first few seconds, but then I realized she was fighting to hold back a grin.

Finally, she said, "You didn't tell me it was a used Honda Fit. I know your tastes. Of course, my mind would go to a Lexus. And of course, we can find money for a Honda Fit."

"It's used," I said again as if it would seal the deal. "See? I'm thinking of us." I folded my arms and realized I was pouting.

"Oh, baby, I'm so sorry. Here I go thinking about myself again." She came to me and took me in her arms. Then she stepped back. "So, where did you find this car?"

"Amelia said she was going to sell it and would offer us a good deal if we were interested."

"Seems like a good thing this Amelia dropped out of nowhere on our front doorstep, don't you think?"

There was a hint of doubt in her voice, but I ignored it because she'd come around. She was either really thinking about me or knew she had better start thinking about me.

When I didn't answer, she asked, "So what's the car like?"

"No idea. She's going to bring it tomorrow since she won't need her truck." I pointed to the pile against the wall. "We brought all that home today. There's more in the basement. Copper pipes, PVC pipes, wire, all the stuff she'll need to get us hooked up. And then…" I grabbed her hand.

"Where are we going?" She giggled as I pulled her down the stairs and over to the desk.

"Voila."

She ran her hand across the top of the smooth wood, fine-grained desk. "That's beautiful. Where did you find it?"

"I went on the Internet and researched antique places. They have a few stores in Ithaca and I found it in one of them. I also spoke to the owner and I think I'll be able to form a working relationship for my business. Believe it or not, antiques are still big down here so I have to make sure to include that in my portfolio and showroom." I shrugged. "Maybe I can get into restoring historic homes and buildings. That would greatly expand my business," I said, feeling the excitement in my voice and knowing it had to show in my face. I was smiling so wide at the prospect of once again being on top in my field that I felt giddy. "Amelia knows a lot about historic restoration, so I'm making sure I learn as much as I can from her."

I realized she was staring at me. Her eyes were soft and her smile was gentle, smoothing out the barely visible lines on her gorgeous face.

"What?" I asked, a bit embarrassed by my outburst of enthusiasm.

She drew closer to me. Her hands caressed my back, slow and suggesting. "I like it when you get so excited, even if it's about your work and a used Honda Fit."

She kissed me. It went right from my lips down to my toes and at that moment dessert seemed not only feasible, but necessary.

I was hungry once again.

The next morning, I woke before M.E. Lately it seemed to be the norm. My dreams continued to be a mixture of reality and nightmares. Unsettling thoughts created scenarios that were disturbing yet had underlying truths.

I made a cup of coffee, hoping the caffeine would cast the visions out. I needed to believe in my wife. I wanted to believe in her. Last night, despite the fact she had hired a lawyer without consulting me and come home late from her office with a big smile on her face, she had shown me that she loved me. She was supportive of me getting a car. She loved the desk and she was totally in where my business was concerned.

Yeah, she seemed a bit apprehensive about Amelia, but I could convince her that Amelia was no one to be worried about. I had good feelings about her. She was going to be a big help in getting my life back on track.

We had also made love. Not just sex. She loved me with everything she had and I felt it in every fiber of my being. So, maybe my doubts were fading with each overture M.E. made, even though they were coming a bit slower than she had promised.

One could only hope.

Amelia showed up before M.E. woke. True to her word, she pulled into the driveway with the Honda Fit, a very white and very small Honda Fit. White was not my favorite car color, but if the price was right, I'd even consider taking violent orange or over-the-top neon green.

When I walked outside, I was greeted with a great big smile and her hand resting on the hood looking like a model from *The Price is Right* television show.

"What do you think? She's a beauty, huh?"

I chuckled. "For a tiny car, she's not so bad." I walked around the vehicle. "You called her a she. Does she have a name?"

"If she becomes yours, you can call her anything you'd like." Amelia leaned toward me. "But I named her Bertha."

I laughed out loud. "Oh, my God. Bertha? That's a name for a backwoods, big ole rusty truck." I pointed to our Silverado. "Kind of like that one."

"Bertha is a strong name with a lot of heart. This little baby has both."

"Okay, if you say so. Let's go inside. You can tell me what you want for Bertha, and then I'll talk it over with M.E. She's on board as long as the price is right."

"Let me get my bag and tool kit."

I led her downstairs where she'd work for the day—cleaning and preparing areas for us to store our belongings. If she finished early, she said she would rig an acceptable shower for us to use (yay!) and then start on the utilities in the basement. Right now, M.E. and I needed a home, and not just because living in a rundown stone house with falling walls and ceilings could be a little unnerving and definitely rustic. M.E. and I needed to feel normal again, especially since nothing about our situation was normal. A working shower would go a long way toward that.

While we talked, I heard footsteps coming downstairs and I knew my wife had woken. She carried two cups of coffee.

"Good morning," she said with a lilt to her voice. She gave me a kiss on the cheek and then walked past me, handing one of the cups to Amelia. "I see my wife hasn't made you a cup, yet." M.E. winked at me just before she took a sip from the other. "Hers is still up on the table. I'm afraid a bit cold by now, but luckily, we do have a microwave."

Amelia took the cup held out to her. "Thank you. I haven't had my morning dose of caffeine yet, not that I need it. But on big projects like this, it helps to keep me going."

"Well then, we'll have to make sure Addy keeps you supplied while you work." She walked over to me and put an arm around me. "Isn't that right, sweetheart?"

I looked at her and she burst out laughing. Then I pulled away and slugged her shoulder. "You can be such an asshole."

"I know, but it's one of the things you love about me." She kissed me lightly on the lips. "Now, I've got a bag packed. I'm hoping this will be the last shower I have to take at the college gym. Have fun, Amelia." Then to me she said, "Walk me outside?"

I did as she asked, basking in the morning-after-sex feeling that made me light and happy and…Usually I would say "secure" next, but we were working on that.

I walked her outside to show her the small, white car waiting to be mine. "She wants ten thousand. It's a 2019 and has forty thousand miles on it. No rust. She also said it was undercoated to resist rust from the salt used on the roads in the winter. Never thought about winter," I mused.

"Will you feel safe enough to drive this in the winter on these hills? I hear it can get a bit icy and there's often a lot of snow. This thing probably won't be able to maneuver in more than six inches. It's pretty low to the ground."

"You're right about the snow, but she said she has a new set of winter tires. Used only last year. With those, she said I'll feel like I have four-wheel drive. Besides, I don't plan on going anywhere if there's more than a few inches of that white nasty stuff on the ground." I walked over to the driver side and opened the door. "It's actually pretty cute inside. Oh, look!" I picked up a bottle of red wine with a white bow on it that was on the front seat.

M.E. looked skeptical. Then she checked out the label on the wine. "Goes right along with the car." She scowled.

I ignored her dig toward Amelia's tastes. "I trust her. She's lived here all her life so she's seen lots of winters. Besides, she wouldn't want to be the reason for my accident. I think she's afraid you'd sue."

"I would. For everything she owns."

She didn't smile like she was teasing or joking. I had to hope she was. It made me a bit uneasy.

"If you trust her, I think it's a good price. Go for it, but only as long as you feel it's right for you. It's a big change from that monster of a Lexus SUV you had. We could look for a used SUV. Something a little more robust for the winter."

"I think I'm good with this. But rest assured, as soon as I make my first profit, I will be purchasing a vehicle that is up to my standards. A brand new one. I do love the smell of new cars."

"I wouldn't expect anything different." She kissed me once again. "Last night was wonderful."

"Yes, it was," I replied, kissing her back, then I moved away from her when I noticed the neighbors' curtain pulled back across the street.

"What's wrong? We were having a really nice moment."

I smiled at her. "We were, but we weren't the only ones involved in it. The neighbors were watching."

M.E. turned and looked in the direction of my gaze and waved. Then the curtain fell back into place. "Peeping Toms," she said. "Screw them if they don't like seeing two people in love."

I studied her face. "Is that what we really are?" I asked like a foster child who was unsure where their love came from on a daily basis.

"Why would you even ask that?"

"It's just been so crazy, you know? And I guess I'm just a little unsettled about this crap with Raeann missing. I thought she was out of our lives when you signed that paper."

"That's why I've got Diane. She'll make sure Raeann is out of our lives for good this time. Okay?" She leaned forward and looked into my face that was downcast. She took her fingers and lifted my chin so my eyes met hers. "Okay?"

"Okay."

"I love you, you know?"

"I know."

She turned and walked toward the truck. "Have a good day and lots of fun getting our place up to snuff." She climbed in. "I can't wait to take a shower at home. Just hope I'm not disappointed." She winked.

"You won't be. Have a good day too," I replied and I shut her door. Then I stepped back and waited for her to drive away in the ugly truck that I believed she was beginning to enjoy. I smiled as I walked back inside.

Amelia was in the living room rummaging through the pile of materials. She looked up when I walked in.

I held up the bottle of wine. "Thanks for this. It was sweet of you."

"You're welcome. Is everything okay?"

I plastered a big smile on my face. "Yes. After I put this bottle away for another special occasion, I'm going to write you a check for Bertha."

She stood. "That's great! For you and me. I don't want to keep two cars anymore and I need my truck."

"I totally understand. So how do you want to do this?"

"I brought the paperwork with me. We can go downtown to the DMV if you want. We don't have to make an appointment anymore, so we can go whenever you want and transfer everything."

"Don't you have a lot of work to do?"

"I'm on a schedule. My boss is tough that way." She smirked.

"I can give you the check and we can sign a bill of sale. Then I can drive down there myself. I don't mind. It's time I try to find my way around."

"Or," she started, "I'm going to have to get lunch at some time. I need food. We could go during lunch and grab some takeout to bring back. I know a great sandwich shop."

"Okay. That sounds good. Do you need any help right now?"

"Nope, I'm all set. I'll be in the basement for a while if you need me."

"And I'll be here working on some plans if you need me."

"All right then. See you at lunchtime." She picked up her supplies and trotted down the steps.

I put the bottle in a box holding my work papers. I wanted to save it for a celebratory drink with Amelia when we finished the house. Then I sat at the table. Things were looking up. I opened my computer and pulled some files over. We just needed to get rid of this business with my wife's ex-whore. Then it would all be perfect.

I practically jumped out of my skin when I felt a rough hand on my partially bare shoulder.

I turned to see Amelia with her hands up.

"I'm so sorry. I didn't mean to scare you. I thought you heard me."

I laughed. "When I'm working, it's like I have noise-reducing headphones on. I'm totally immersed in what I'm doing. I hear nothing."

Upon hearing my stomach growl, I realized why she had come upstairs. I looked at her, feeling a warm flush ride up from my stomach to my face. "It must be near noon."

"Actually, it's almost one o'clock. Are you ready to get some lunch? We can eat first because I'm famished and then go to the DMV." She held a set of keys out to me.

I squealed as I held the check out to her. "I can't wait to drive it."

CHAPTER SIX

After a quick shower in the women's locker room in the fitness center, Mary Ellen made her way to her office at Williams Hall. It was her favorite part of the day. She loved strolling down the walkway around The Commons where many of the students congregated in the morning with their cups of coffee from the Express Café.

The coffee shop was across from the fitness center, and her building was another short walk from the café. She was happy not to have to walk the length or width of the campus to get to her office and classrooms. That would leave her no time to appreciate the sights—mostly the young female students that she had the liberty to take in every morning.

After she got her cappuccino with a sprinkling of chocolate powder, she made her way to a bench that she'd claimed the first day she arrived at the campus. This particular bench provided her with the best views of the students hurrying to get breakfast and make their early morning classes on time.

It was the best place to continue the research she had started at Stanford.

While she sipped her drink she watched the female figures, assessing each one in several categories she'd devised for her studies, including general classifications she used for the baseline of her research. All her subjects were female and all attended her lectures. Thus, she could observe them and have better access to their records. In a semester, she often had close to one hundred beautiful data points.

Under the umbrella she titled "scientific studies" were the categories of weight, height, hair color, eye color, physique, and intelligence. The first five were easy to assess just by sitting on her bench and observing. But she had to know the names of the subjects to access their records in order to obtain any information in the intelligence category.

She further examined her subjects with details regarding sexual preferences, personality (for example, type A or B), marital status, boyfriend/girlfriend status. For these groupings, she needed to interview the subjects—get to know them. She didn't mind that part of the study at all, because gathering this information was solely based on personal opinion. That opinion, of course, would be hers.

In the first category, she took all of the scientific physical appearance information and rated each one on a scale of one through ten with ten being as close to perfection as one could get. Of course, she had to allow for some bias because there was no scientific proof as to what female perfection was. That came more from television, movies, and commercials. Still, she kept it as empirical as she could.

From there, she factored in their actual IQ as well as her opinion of their intelligence. Did the female subject qualify as a dumb blonde, or a dark-haired brainiac? Of course, she had met her fair share of dark-haired, half-witted females.

After taking into account all of these qualities, she refigured a new scale for a final numeric result—again on a scale of one to ten. She chose the women for more in-depth study with a value of one to three. She didn't have any biases or prejudices, but she did have her likes and dislikes, and all her likes could be found in the women who received a score of one to three.

From there, she researched the students with as much data as was available to her, and then she would seek them out. Never did she approach any of them during her classes. She always sought them out in The Commons, the fitness center, the dining facilities, or if they came to her office for reasons such as extra help or missed classwork.

This morning, she kept her eye out for Melissa Blaken. A blond-haired, blue-eyed, perfect female specimen, she scored high in every category including intelligence. She topped the scale at one and Mary Ellen was excited to get to know this beauty. She had watched her for a few days and never saw her with a boyfriend, not that it meant anything, but Mary Ellen was hopeful.

As she sipped her cappuccino, she noticed Melissa out of the corner of her eye. This was the tricky part. She had to get the subject's attention so she could engage her in conversation without her thinking Mary Ellen had actually initiated it. Sometimes it worked; sometimes it didn't.

Mary Ellen pulled out a folder from her soft leather briefcase and pretended to thumb through it as she sipped her drink. When Melissa was approximately fifteen feet to the left of where she sat, Mary Ellen looked up as if taking a break from reading. She looked forward, then to her right and…wait for it. There. She turned her head to the left just in time to meet Melissa's gaze.

"Good morning, Professor Montgomery."

Hook, line, and sinker. Mary Ellen smiled to herself. "Good morning…" She paused for effect. "Melissa. Right?"

Melissa stopped in front of her and smiled a bright white smile. "Yes, that's right."

"How are you liking my class?" Melissa had chosen Mary Ellen's Research Methods in Psychology class.

Mary Ellen procured her position at Ithaca College by giving them a proposal to increase attendance in their psychology program with her course of study in Psychology of Human Sexuality. She put together a program that would include courses on sexual arousal, sexual orientation, love and attraction, and coercive sexual behavior. To the department's delight, she included an outline for teaching research methods to students in these areas.

The Psychology Department was intrigued with her proposal and gave her one year to prove her program. She was grateful, but extremely surprised when she got the call because despite the decent recommendation from Stanford University, it still came with the slap on her hand for her indiscretion with her student—Raeann Wilson.

Mary Ellen never stopped being angry about Raeann's betrayal. It cost her a lot—her prestigious position at Stanford and a large sum of money Addy didn't know about and Mary Ellen hoped to keep it that way.

The other agreement Addy was oblivious to was a gag order that her lawyer worked out with Stanford and Raeann. The files on Mary Ellen's indiscretion as well as her research was closed. They could not offer any of that information to prospective employers. Mary Ellen had hoped it would last long enough for her to get another position and prove herself but people talked. She knew it would come out sooner or later. She just hoped it didn't for the year it would take to procure the college administration's acceptance of her and her research. If she was able to finish her work and publish it, she would be revered in the intellectual world of psychology and the college wouldn't be able to afford to let her go. This would open doors for her to major universities.

"Oh my, God, I love it. In fact, I just signed up for your class on coercive sexual activity. I thought that would be a fun topic to do my research on."

Mary Ellen studied her. Fun. This young woman thought sexual coerciveness was fun. She grinned at Melissa and patted the bench next to her. This was her kind of woman. Excitement stirred in her belly at the possibility that she'd found her next primary subject. "I'm so glad that you're finding my classes interesting and beneficial to your degree."

Melissa sat down and Mary Ellen couldn't help but notice her long ankles and dainty toes in brown leather sandals, the nails painted in bright pink. She was nothing like her blond-haired, exquisite beauty that was back home waiting for her. She smiled to herself as the image of her wife's silky, shoulder-length hair with a bit of curl framing a face with high cheekbones, luscious lips and bright blue eyes passed through her mind. Her wife had curves where curves should be on a beautiful woman and lean muscle everywhere else.

She looked down at Melissa's pink toenails. Her wife, however, never painted her toenails. Mary Ellen's gaze traveled up the young woman's body to her face. She smiled. "I'd like to discuss my research project with you."

"By all means. I have time now." Mary Ellen looked at her watch for effect. "My first class starts in an hour. Give me your ideas."

Melissa's blue eyes sparkled and she tossed her blond hair.

Definitely a flirtatious move on her part. This shouldn't be too hard.

Mary Ellen spent the next excruciating ten minutes listening to Melissa's idea on researching BDSM as coercive sex. The excruciating part was that Melissa had no idea what she was talking about. The intriguing part was that Melissa had no idea what she was talking about.

Mary Ellen had a hard time holding back her excitement for her latest prospect, but by the time she and Melissa finished their conversation, Mary Ellen had her eating out of her hand. Back at her office readying for her first class, she knew she had to be careful this time. She had to make sure Melissa wouldn't become a turncoat if she was able to recruit her for her own study. The young college student seemed to have all the right credentials. She flirted with Mary Ellen, so there had to be sexual interest to some degree. She was fascinated by the subject of coercive sex, despite the fact she didn't understand what it really was. But her ideas on the subject worked in Mary Ellen's favor.

So, Mary Ellen convinced Melissa to meet her after their classes. They would get something to eat and further discuss Melissa's project. It would be at a bar where they could drink.

If all went well, Mary Ellen would convince her to go to her apartment—the one she rented a few days after she and her wife arrived in Endonford. It was a small one-bedroom loft in an old building at the east edge of town.

Addy thought Mary Ellen was working the summer school program. Part of that was true. It just wasn't a full-time position. She spent the rest of her time setting up her research project in the secluded apartment. The company that owned and resided in the rest of the building had closed, leaving only the vacant apartment until the rest of the space was sold. That would give her enough time to finish her research. Then she would write her paper and submit it to the seven top prestigious psychology journals, including her primary target, *American Journal of Psychology*.

They had scoffed at her proposal when she wrote it fresh out of college ten years ago. Angry and hurt, she began her research and had been doing it ever since. Another year and she would be ready to submit her work, proving them all wrong. It was too bad she couldn't finish it at Stanford, thanks to Raeann. Ithaca College would have to suffice.

Raeann Wilson. Her long, true black hair and deep-green eyes had intrigued Mary Ellen, reminding her of a wolf in the wild. Raeann's sexual prowess was her feral spirit and Mary Ellen was a slave to it. It shocked and upset her because it turned the tide of her research. Mary Ellen had become the coerced.

Then, the unthinkable happened. Mary Ellen fell hard for Raeann. She was everything Mary Ellen wanted in a woman, and she actually entertained thoughts about leaving her wife for the dark-haired beauty. But she never told her wife because just when she thought they were developing something more than a sexual relationship, Raeann turned on her.

Mary Ellen was devastated. And angry. And hurt. But more important, her research had been interrupted because of her own stupidity and lust for the perfect woman. Not that her wife at home wasn't close to perfect. It was just that…Raeann was Aphrodite.

Mary Ellen sighed and unlocked the cabinet where she kept her research. She began to write notes about Melissa and her plan for Melissa's part in her research. She let her excitement grow, hoping that this time she might be on the right path to recognition as a top scholar in her field of study.

She was well aware that Addy didn't think much of her career. With this research, she would prove to her wife that her degree in psychology could provide more for them than her silly decorating. It would make her famous and bring her financial success. People in the scientific field would recognize and respect her.

And she would never give up on her wife again.

CHAPTER SEVEN

I convinced Amelia to stop by the college so I could show M.E. my New York registration and hopefully take my wife for a short spin in my official new, albeit used car. The Honda Fit was not a Lexus GX, but it allowed me freedom, and to me, at this time in my life, it meant everything. What happened to us in San Francisco changed me. My wife changed me—the loss of my career and our home changed me. The fact was, both our lives changed because of her idiocy and betrayal, but at times, I wondered if I had handled things differently, would it have turned out this way?

For me, having my own car made a statement. "If you fuck up again, I can drive away." Not that I couldn't before. I could, but I didn't. So, I needed to amend that statement. "If you fuck up again, I *will* drive away."

When we arrived at the parking lot next to the fitness center, I texted M.E. to let her know we were there. I had no idea if she would be able to meet us. She hadn't given me a copy of her class schedule. In fact, she hadn't told me anything about her job other than she was teaching classes in psychology. Duh, I already knew that.

Only minutes after I contacted her, my phone dinged with a reply. She was on her way.

"Why don't we walk and meet her halfway?" Amelia suggested.

"Well, because I'm embarrassed to admit this, but I have no idea where she's coming from."

Amelia pointed past the building. "The Commons is right there past the fitness center. The psych building is a short way past that. I imagine she'll take the most direct route and that would be through The Commons."

I looked at her, astonished. She had told me she went to trade school, not college. "How do you know that?"

"I have my ways," she teased. "Remember at lunch I told you I do a lot of contract work for the college, so I know my way around the campus."

I looked at the clear blue sky that added to my happiness. "It's a beautiful day. Let's go for a walk." I put my arm through hers and we strolled down the sidewalk.

When we reached halfway around The Commons, we spotted M.E. coming toward us. I saw her eyes glance at our linked arms and I immediately dropped my hand. I waved and jogged up to her, taking her in my arms.

"I'm so happy you could meet me," I exclaimed.

"Meet us."

I stepped back and noticed her looking past me. "Excuse me?"

Her eyes found mine. "You meant to say meet us." Then she said to Amelia who caught up, "So, you really sold my wife that tin can? You know, it better be a good one."

"Oh, it is," I answered for Amelia. "I've been driving it all around town and it's like a little jackrabbit scooting in and out of bushes. Except, I'm scooting in and out of traffic." I laughed. "It's loads of fun. I can't wait for you to drive it."

"Oh no, no, no, no, no. That's not something I need to do in my life. I'll stick to the bigger vehicles, thank you very much."

The insult sank in and my shoulders sank with it. "Will you at least take a ride with me?" I asked quietly, noticing that Amelia was trying to act inconspicuous, her eyes roaming the campus, checking out its inhabitants.

M.E. leaned toward me and whispered in my ear, "Babe, things are going so well for both of us, we'll be in our big SUVs before you know it. You won't need a sardine can to drive around in. Besides, it wouldn't look good for my image when I make professor at a prestigious university."

"Okay, then," I said, a bit put out. "We need to get back to work. I have a list for Amelia to complete before the truck arrives with our stuff. We should get going."

I started to walk away, but M.E. grabbed my hand and pulled me back. She kissed me with that flirtatious, sensual, and very moist kiss that she used when she wanted to make sure she had my attention. "Remember, I'll be late. I have that appointment with the lawyer."

"Any calls from the police?"

"Don't you worry your beautiful little head."

Nothing like my wife ruining my good mood by making me feel belittled.

"No calls, and if there are, I'll refer them to Diane." She smiled and patted my shoulder.

Diane. She was already on a first name basis with the lawyer. Would there ever be a time when things like this didn't make me suspicious? I sighed. "I'll see you at home."

"Yes, I'll see you at home," she purred.

But this time, I didn't let it get to me. Normally, I would lean in for another goodbye, seal it with a kiss. Instead, I backed away with a smile on my lips and said to Amelia, "Come on, girl, the work won't get done without us."

As I scurried away from my wife with Amelia hurrying to catch up to me, the doubts of our move to Podunk Town tried to pierce my M.E. armor once again.

I felt a hand on my arm gently pulling me to slow down. "Hey, what's wrong?" When I didn't answer, Amelia said, "Sorry your wife wasn't happier about your car."

I slowed my pace. "Oh, it's all right. Neither of us have ever wanted or even been in a small car. For her, it's a change she won't ever be able to accept. For me, well, I'm beginning to like change." I looked at her and smiled. "Some changes."

She took my arm once again and picked up her pace. "Then let's get back to that stone house and make some awesome changes."

Leave it to Amelia to give me a pick-me-up.

When we got home, she went upstairs to the bathroom. An hour later, she came down searching for my approval.

"It will work until I get to the bathroom. Come up and see if you like it and then let's sit down for a bit and talk about your plans. We can discuss how I would like to approach things."

"Okay. What about the historical society?"

"Actually, I've done a little research. Did the realtor tell you this was designated as a historical home? What were their exact words?"

"They said it was designated as a historic home."

She sat down opposite me with a big "you're gonna love this" smile on her face.

"What is it?" I asked, now totally intrigued.

"The stone house is in fact a historical home. It's a federal-style home that was built in 1822 by the Woodward family; however, it is not an *officially designated* historical home."

My mouth dropped open. "You're kidding. Then why did they tell me that?"

"Probably to sell it. If you were interested in it as a historical home, telling you it was got you to buy it. And probably to keep you from getting any off-the-wall ideas about changing things."

"They lied to me. Isn't that illegal or unethical or something like that?"

"Not really. The stone house is historic in the antique old-home sense of the word, just not in the officially registered as a historical home sense of the word. It *is* eligible for federal and state historic designation. That's what they should have told you. But they didn't, hoping you might not find out. It was agreed upon to advertise it as a historic home because they didn't want…

how did they say it? Fancy, schmancy, rich outsiders coming in and making a mockery of it. The historical society contacted the realtor when they heard there was an offer. They hoped if they led you to believe it was officially designated, you'd adhere to their rules because you would believe you had to."

"Oh, my God. What rats!"

Amelia laughed. "Interesting way of putting it. I see both sides. They want this place to be grand, like it was. The previous owner was here for years and she let it slide into the ruined state it's in now. The historical society would be devastated to see it turned into something modern and out of character."

I began to protest, but she put a hand up. "They don't know you like I do."

"You haven't known me that long."

"But I do know what you want to do with this place. You want to restore it, not totally change it. And I believe you want to incorporate your vision into the historical aspects of the original décor of this home."

I smiled at her. "You do know me."

"And I've already told them that. So, you do have a lot of free rein to do as you wish. But be advised that if you want to seek official federal and state historic designation, you will have to abide by *their* rules from day one of the rehab. You need to decide that soon."

"I know what you're saying and I appreciate it. Just do me one favor."

"And what would that be?"

"Talk to me if you think something won't work. I know you won't like everything I do, but if you think it really won't work whether it's structure, the mechanics or design, tell me, especially if you think the historical society will object. I can't guarantee I'll change my mind, but I am willing to work with them and you to find a compromise if need be."

She extended a hand to me and I shook it.

"You've got a deal. Now come on and take a look at your first temporary renovation."

Like a giddy kid, I jogged up the stairs after her. When I walked into the bathroom, I almost fell over. In one hour, she had cleaned all the porcelain so it sparkled and shone as if wanting to impress, which it did. She had also cleaned the tile floor. It didn't look as great as the fixtures, but it was definitely livable. The metal claws on the bathtub feet were polished and a round shower rod encircled the tub with the shower curtain I had picked out. She had also put together the temporary bathroom storage cabinet so we could put our towels and hygiene stuff somewhere rather than in a box on the floor.

I hugged her. I had to. She had just worked a miracle in one hour.

She stepped back from me, her face flushed and red with embarrassment.

"Amelia," I said. "You are worth your weight in gold!"

She started to say something, but this time, I held *my* hand up. "Don't get any ideas about a raise this soon in our partnership."

It took a few moments, but I saw the recognition of someone teasing her on her face. She burst into loud laughter.

"It's beautiful," I said after she calmed down. "Temporarily beautiful," I added. "I can't wait to see what you do with it when I'm ready to make permanent changes. In honor of your work, come on downstairs and let me get you a beer while we discuss the order of how we're going to do this."

She looked at her watch. "I guess I can have a beer. It'll be quitting time in a few hours."

I giggled. "I said a beer. Not several."

We spent those few hours poring over my designs. I had put all the information in an Excel spreadsheet that when finished, showed the work that needed to be done in order—the first being electric and plumbing. Columns followed with time estimates of how long it would take for each job as well as a list of the supplies needed and the cost of supplies and her labor. The last two empty ones listed the date started and the date completed. I was quite satisfied with the finished spreadsheet. It gave me something else to focus on, which was good because Raeann's disappearance wasn't far from the front of my mind.

After we'd discussed the entire spreadsheet, I walked Amelia to the front door. She was to return at eight the next morning.

Any earlier would interrupt M.E.'s morning routine and I knew from experience that could make for a miserable morning.

As she walked to her truck, I watched her red ponytail bounce with the skip in her step. I wondered what it would be like to be married to someone like her. She was fun, interesting, and smart. She was very attractive—at least to me. She also seemed kind and attentive. However, her childhood memories showed a dark side to her, and because of that, I wondered if she too had deep dark secrets hidden away.

Smiling, I waved as she pulled out.

For a brief moment, I thought about looking up Diane Kensington's information and driving into town to meet M.E. for her meeting.

For a brief moment.

Instead, I went inside and ordered a pizza.

CHAPTER EIGHT

Nothing like comfort food and liquor when you're feeling down. Three pieces of pizza and three glasses of merlot later, I was hunkered down beneath the covers on our bed going over my plans when I heard M.E.'s truck pull into the driveway. The fact that I heard it so plainly told me our house was in desperate need of insulation.

Amelia seemed intelligent in her field, so she probably already knew that, but I wrote it down anyway. Then I set my papers on the floor and turned off the light. Childish, I knew, but it was almost midnight and I didn't believe a first meeting with a lawyer would take seven hours no matter what the subject was.

When M.E. was consorting with Raeann behind my back, she often didn't get home until midnight. Like Cinderella, it seemed to be the magic hour for her. She was almost never later than the stroke of twelve. That and the fact I was in no shape to deal with her lateness nor possessed an ounce of desire to hear what she would have to say, I decided feigning sleep was the way to go. She probably didn't have anything to say anyway.

I listened for the door opening and closing, her footsteps on the stairs. I did not expect to hear a stifled squeal. Not knowing if it was a scream in pleasure or panic, I jumped out of bed and ran toward the sound. In the bathroom, I found M.E. washing her hands and face.

"Are you all right?" I asked.

"I'm so sorry. Did I wake you? I was just so excited at the thought of taking a shower here tomorrow and not at the college. I know it's not the final bathroom, but it sure is a nice surprise. Thank God for Amelia." She put toothpaste on her toothbrush, turned to the sink and began brushing her teeth.

To say I was still a bit tipsy from the wine, tired from a long day that included waiting up for her to get home, and totally agitated that she thought screaming about the bathroom at midnight was okay, would have been an understatement. But rather than engage in an argument, I stormed off to bed.

I knew the real reason I was angry, and even though it was magnified, at this point it *was* unsubstantiated. I climbed back into bed. I would ask her why she got home so late after a good night's sleep and when I was in a better place.

Minutes later, fingers roamed over my stomach. I felt my breasts being massaged, my nipples toyed with, and moist lips sliding over my skin. How could anyone fight that? But I managed to do it. I let out a few snores and soon the caresses ceased. Pleased with myself, I relaxed my body and immediately fell asleep.

When I woke the next morning, M.E. was already out of bed. I wasn't surprised when I heard water running and off-key singing permeating the walls from the bathroom. Yup, insulation was top on the list.

I smiled at the song she sang. If it were alive, it would be so offended by the notes that came out of her mouth. I had no idea what the tune was, but it was the only song I ever heard her sing in the shower. I'd given up asking her what she was singing when she got upset at my question. Let's face it, even though I didn't mean it to be, it was a critique of her musical skills and definitely not a positive one.

Feeling in a much better mood, I took my nightshirt off and made my way to the bathroom. "Care for some company?" I asked, standing naked in the middle of the large room.

I saw the shower curtain peel back slightly and two sparkly blue eyes peer out at me. "Come on in. The water's nice and warm."

"Now this makes it feels like home," I crooned, feeling the warm water rush over my skin as I lumbered into the tub. M.E. had to support me as I tipped this way and that. When I felt stable on my own two feet, I took the loofa from her and soaped it up. I skimmed the sponge over her, lightly caressing her delicate parts. She moaned with pleasure when I moved up and down between her legs, and she leaned into me as she placed her hands on each side of my face and pulled me up into a long, intoxicating kiss. I wrapped my arms around her.

"Yes, this feels like home," she said in a husky voice between gasps of pleasure.

With one hand, she caressed my breasts as the other made its way down my stomach to my vagina. Her fingers circled my center, teasing, implying their intentions. My head fell back and she lavished kisses on my neck just before she entered me.

The motion was slow, but intense. My knees grew weak as she moved deeper, harder, entering inside me and then pulling out slightly, repeating the motion with increasing speed.

I cried out in ecstasy like I had so many times before when I felt my core reaching its orgasmic peak. At that moment, I was grateful for the shower Amelia had given us, even if it was temporary.

"You are so beautiful," M.E. breathed in my ear.

Our bodies were slick with soap and we moved together with such ease, no friction whatsoever. I placed my fingers on her breasts and kneaded the soft tissue, playing with her nipples. My hands moved down to the small of her back and squeezed her buttocks. When I made my way between her legs, she put a hand on mine and stopped me.

"What is it?" I asked, barely catching my breath.

"I have to get going and Amelia will be here any minute."

"What time is it?"

"Seven forty-five."

I continued my sexual assault. "We've got time," I whispered. "I want you. Besides, she has a key."

She gently pushed me away. "I don't want to be on display for your contractor." Her voice was stern, bringing me immediately out of my sensual mood.

I met her hard stare. "Well then, since you've been in here long enough, do you mind if I finish my shower?"

Her kiss on my lips lingered for a few moments. "Only if you promise to pick this up tonight where we left off."

"Will you be home after work or do you have another late night?" I knew how it sounded, but I didn't care. She'd ruined a perfectly good shower.

"Hey now. I always tell you when I've got to stay late at work or if I have an appointment. I'll be done early today, so I'll be home by four. How about we have a romantic dinner and carry that into the evening?" She kissed me again.

This time, I returned the erotic pleasure of her lips on mine with the anticipation of a promise I wanted to her to keep. "I'll hold you to it."

A playful smile teased her lips and she got out of the tub, slowly moving in an animalistic way. I felt my knees grow weak again.

I gasped. "Anything in particular you want for dinner?" I called from the shower, and before she could answer, I added, "Other than me."

"Aww, you know me too well. You choose. I trust your ordering expertise."

I laughed. "Yes, I am rather good at ordering takeout."

I heard her footsteps leave the bathroom and I concentrated on finishing my shower. I wouldn't be ready by the time Amelia got here, but then again, she did have a key.

When I finally finished dressing and got downstairs, Amelia and M.E. were in animated conversation. M.E. saw me first out of the corner of her eyes and their discussion ended immediately.

"Everything okay?" I asked suspiciously.

"Amelia was filling me in on what she's going to work on today. I was also commenting on the fine temporary bathroom. She's a keeper."

"It won't be anything too exciting today. I'm working on the electrical. Nothing beautiful, but very necessary and functional to your living situation."

I eyed Amelia. She wouldn't meet my eyes and she seemed a bit...off.

"Then it will be grand, I'm sure." M.E. winked at me and then grabbed her case and purse. "I'll see you around four. Can't wait to see what is done today." She walked over to me, gave me an unusual peck on the cheek and walked out the door saying, "I'll see you later, babe. Have a good day."

My arms folded, I murmured, "You too, babe."

When the door closed, I turned to see Amelia's red face. But it wasn't embarrassment that showed on her facial features. The look in her eyes was harsher, intense. More like anger. "Is anything wrong?"

She shook her head like she was trying to snap out of a mood. "No, nothing. Just excited about starting the renovation. I'm headed downstairs. If you need anything, let me know."

I was surprised at her abrupt exit. There was no "Good morning," or "How are you today?"

The jovial woman I had gotten to know over the last few days was replaced by someone holding back enmity before it got the best of her. So I let her go, but not without saying, "I'm going to make some coffee. I'll bring you down a cup. Light on the cream, no sugar, right?"

Her eyes brightened a bit, but her lips remained taut and her cheeks appeared to be pulled back by the tight ponytail keeping her red hair out of her face. "Um, yeah, that would be great." She trotted down the stairs to the basement.

I stood in the doorway for a few minutes listening. I could hear her opening her toolbox, rummaging through packages, ripping open plastic and cardboard boxes with supplies she would need for the work she was to do.

I don't know why the next thought entered my mind at that moment, but I needed to ask M.E. when she got home how her meeting went with the lawyer. I also wanted to know if the police had contacted her again. I was bothered that she hadn't talked to me about it at all.

I made two cups of coffee in the Keurig and then put them on the only tray we had. I carried it to the basement where Amelia ran wire along one wall. I handed a cup to her. "So, what can I do to help?"

"You know how to run wire?"

"No, but…"

"Then you can't help." She took the cup and set it down, returning to her work.

I took a sip and waited. She continued to work, ignoring my presence despite the fact I was standing just a few feet from her. "Did I do something to upset you?"

She continued running the wire. She got her drill and made a hole in the wall. Then she fed the wire through. "Did I say you did something wrong?"

"I wouldn't be asking if you had."

Without looking up, she answered, "Then there's nothing wrong."

"I never took you to be a game player," I said.

She stopped what she was doing. "That's low, even for you."

"Really? Even for me? You don't know me. You have no idea how low I can get." I felt the anger from the night before awaken with the sun that was finding its way through one of the small basement windows.

Amelia stood and faced me. After studying me for a few moments, she looked down at her wire cutters and then back at me. "I'm sorry. This is not how our working relationship started, and it's not the way I want it to continue."

"I'd prefer it continue the way it was yesterday," I said, trying to soften my voice and my expression that felt hardened like stone. "You want to tell me what my wife said to you that pissed you off?"

Her eyes widened. "She didn't say anything…"

"You forget. I may not know you that well, but I do know my wife. As a matter of fact, I know her really well. So, what did she say to you?"

Amelia was looking out the window when she answered. "Can I ask you a personal question?"

Her response surprised me. I expected her to tell me what was pissing her off, which was most likely something M.E. said before she left. Since Amelia wasn't ready to tell me, I replied, "Yes. Go ahead."

She looked pensive when her eyes fell back on me. "Is your wife jealous or possessive?"

I rolled my eyes and wondered if looking out the window gave Amelia courage to ask me that very question. So, I looked out the window hoping I would find courage to come up with the right answer. Finally, I said, "I never thought her to be, but my wife is an unusual woman. What might appear to be jealousy or possessiveness is really just her way of loving me."

"That sounds to me like your answer to my question is yes. I may be out of line, but that doesn't make for a good relationship. Or for a good person."

"Understood. I don't disagree, so please tell me what she said to you."

"I need to install a new electrical box and increase the amperage to the house. I put the new estimate on the table upstairs."

"Amelia, I need to know what M.E. said to you."

"Then you'll need to ask her. I've called the electric company and scheduled them to service the pole and add the requested amperage." She walked over to her toolbox and dropped her wire cutters in it. "I can either continue to run all the wiring like we talked about, or I can start on the plumbing. It's your call."

"What's the spreadsheet say?" I asked.

"Since they'll be here at the end of the week, we can stay on schedule with the spreadsheet if we continue with the wiring."

"Then there's your answer. I'll be upstairs if you have any more questions that you already know the answer to but need me to answer for you." I turned and jogged up the steps wondering what just happened. I knew my reply was rude and sarcastic, but I didn't want the first nice person I met in this godforsaken town to treat me like…Like what? Like I had a jealous wife who overstepped a boundary that wasn't even there? M.E. was really pissing me off, and Amelia falling into her games just added disappointment to the possibility of a friendship with her.

I noticed the sun filling up the living room. I stood in front of the window and felt its warmth through the glass panes. Yeah, insulated windows were another must—expecially for the cold winters this part of New York experienced. I never lived in or even visited a state in the winter where there was snow and temperatures below fifty. At some point, I needed to buy winter coats, boots, hats and gloves.

Maybe today would be a good day for that. Shopping therapy always worked for me. Before we left San Francisco, it helped me to forget the negative emotions that had found their way to the forefront of my life. And today, it felt as if they had followed me here, like some supernatural, emotional entity drove with us in the truck and settled inside the house. Now it seemed to be pulling anyone who walked within its walls into its metaphysical embodiment of crappiness.

I grabbed my purse and called down to the basement, "Amelia, I'm going into town. Do you need anything?"

"No, I'm good. Thanks."

"You know where the fridge is. Help yourself. I'll be back, um…whenever."

Outside, I patted Bertha on the hood. "Okay, girl, time to stretch our legs. I've about had it with moody women."

Not only did shopping soothe the beast stirring within me, I found a lot of great deals because, surprise, winter clothing was already out. It was only the middle of August, but winter was just around the corner, for New Yorkers anyway.

I explored every store, strip mall, regular mall, and small, independent retailer that I could find. Needless to say, I didn't arrive home until shortly after five. I wasn't surprised to see that

Amelia's truck was gone, replaced by M.E.'s. I hoped Amelia left before my wife got home.

I filled my arms with the first load of bags. I hesitated before going inside, knowing my wife would chew me out for spending too much money. My argument would be that neither of us owned a winter coat or a pair of boots. That would help for the first trip into the house. I would have to come up with a better excuse to explain the second trip. And an even better explanation if there was a third.

When I entered the living room, M.E. was sitting in a chair, her elbows on her knees and her head in her hands. This wasn't good. She didn't even look up when the door opened and closed, or when I set the multiple bags on the floor.

"M?" I walked over to her, a bit apprehensive at her silence. "What's wrong, honey?"

"They just won't leave me alone." Her words were a mixture of whispers and crying.

"Who?" I knelt down beside her. She still didn't move. "Who won't leave you alone?"

"The goddamn police." She sounded like an outraged customer who had a major bone to pick with the retailer. A really angry bone. But I couldn't blame her.

"I'm sorry, my love. I know we thought this was over when we left San Francisco, but you said you've got a good lawyer. If you haven't done anything, and I know you haven't," I added quickly when her head rose and she directed that angry stare in my direction. "Then we have nothing to worry about."

"*You* have nothing to worry about!"

I almost fell over from the sudden outburst, but instead I put a hand on her arm. "We're in this together. You know that. I've been here with you through it all, so *we* have nothing to worry about."

"Yeah, well you're not the one getting calls and visits from the police, making the college a bit nervous. I could lose another job over this." She stood and walked aimlessly around the room. "For no fucking reason!" she yelled while shaking her fist at the ceiling. Then she glared at me. "And who knows? The police might want to talk to you too."

Even though I was surprised she said that, I answered, "Yeah, they might, but it's you I'm worried about. Please, honey, calm down. Sit down and tell me what happened."

A quick, sharp sigh escaped her lips and she marched over to the couch where I had taken a seat. She sat back, folding her arms like a child pouting.

"The state police showed up at the college. They had the nerve to go to the dean's office and ask to see me. The dean looked up my schedule and sent them over. They waited until my class was over and confronted me at my office. They brought a search warrant."

"Holy shit. Did you call Diane?"

"I did. The cops waited until she got there, even though they didn't have to. She told me exactly what I knew she would. That I had no choice."

"Does that mean you kind of lost your temper?"

"You could say that."

"Oh, M.E., getting angry is only going to fuel their suspicions."

"I didn't do anything," she whined.

"I know, I know. So act as if you didn't do anything."

"I'm acting like anyone would who is being falsely accused. They're stepping on every facet of my life. God, I can't get a break from this. I'm sorry I messed up. Why can't they just let it go?"

"You know they can't," I said quietly. "She's missing, and until they figure it out, you know they will look at everyone and everything that has any ties to Raeann in any way. Including me."

"Great," she spat out. Then she was quiet for a few moments. Finally, she looked at me like someone who wasn't sure they believed what the other was saying. "Why are you still with me?"

"Despite everything, I still love you. Always have, always will. I thought my coming here to this forbidden backwoods town on the other side of the country was enough to prove that to you." I smiled. "I have more proof."

She seemed to soften a bit at my last sentence. Her lips moved in a playful way as if I was suggesting a tryst in the bedroom, or the living room, or any room. Before the idea furthered in her mind, I hurried to the door and picked up the bags.

"I even bought us some winter attire in preparation for the snow and cold." I held them up.

"Uh-huh," she responded with apprehension. The following sound that came out of her mouth was unrecognizable until her face scrunched and she burst out laughing. It wasn't necessarily the reaction I wanted, but it was one hundred percent better than more anger.

She was acting like an Alzheimer's patient obsessing on the subject of Raeann's disappearance, and my "proof of love" in the form of retailing had successfully steered her away from it. I rushed through the purchases as she oohed and ahhed at them. Then I coerced her into helping me carry the rest in without a word about the money I spent with the promise of a runway model presentation of our winter attire.

I went into the dining room and stripped my clothes off, donning the coats, boots, hats and gloves without anything on underneath. After I strutted around the living room, she did the same. We followed our runway show with takeout from an Italian restaurant, a bottle of cabernet franc and then our usual dessert—sex.

The day couldn't have ended any better.

When we were in bed, sleep overtaking us, I remembered something I had wanted to ask her all evening. "Was Amelia here when you got home?"

Her eyes were closed and she murmured, "Umm, she was leaving as I walked in."

"Is everything okay between you two?"

Her eyes remained closed, but her voice was more awake when she answered, "Why do you ask?"

"She was in a really bad mood this morning. I wondered if you two had words or something before you left for work."

"We talked. Well, actually, I talked. I just told her to do her best work because you deserved the best."

"And that's all you said?"

Her eyes were like daggers when they opened and she stared at me. "You don't believe me?"

"I believe you said that. I just wondered if you said anything else."

"What else do you think I said?"

"I'm just wondering if it was a normal mood for her or if something set her off. I don't mean that you purposely set her off, but maybe she took something you said the wrong way."

"And you feel it was me who put her in a bad mood."

"Babe, I don't know who or what it was. I'm just trying to figure out if that's a mood I'm going to see more of. Did she seem in a bad mood when she arrived?"

"Actually, she was kind of short with me."

"Well, then that explains it. Something must have happened before she got here, or last night."

"Are you going to talk to her about it?"

"I don't know. We're not on that level, you know? We don't share personal stuff. It's more like a business relationship."

My answer bothered me. Amelia had already passed the business relationship into forming a kind of friendship by selling me the car and questioning me about my family and my life. However, she didn't seem to want to reciprocate, so the friendship would probably end there.

"Hmm," she sighed, starting to drift off again. "Maybe it's best kept that way."

I kissed her lightly on the lips and snuggled into her. I lay awake for a long time wondering what questions the police had asked her and exactly what they were accusing her of. Then I remembered the questions I had wanted to ask her when she got home.

She answered one of them. The police were still bothering her, but I needed to know more about what the lawyer was going to do for her. I hoped tomorrow would be a better day to ask.

I drifted off to sleep with dreams of love and nightmares of betrayal weaving in and out of each other.

CHAPTER NINE

M.E. canceled her early morning classes. She spent the time in her apartment preparing for her meeting with Melissa. She had already canceled her afternoon classes for a meeting with Diane to discuss the visit by the state police and what to do next.

She thanked whatever god floated in the universe that she had been smarter this time. She stored all of her research in the apartment. She couldn't risk anyone finding it in her office before she was ready to submit it—especially the police—because she knew her focus of study would make them suspicious even though she didn't have anything to do with Raeann's disappearance.

At first, she thought Raeann had been a mistake to her research. She had set M.E. back in her studies for almost a year until she realized the value of the fiasco to her research. Now it was time to finish—to prove her worth to the scientific community. To prove that she wasn't some sicko that had developed her research project only for pure sexual enjoyment.

M.E. hissed as she pulled out her file on Melissa. That's what Raeann had whispered to her the day they were to sign the papers in the dean's office. She was sitting in the waiting room with her expensive lawyer and saw Raeann out of the corner of her eye. Alone. Going into the bathroom. She wanted one more try to convince her to drop the lawsuit, so M.E. told her lawyer she was going to the bathroom.

Despite the lawyer eyeing her with suspicion, she left anyway, pretty sure her legal counsel hadn't seen Raeann. If she had, she wouldn't have taken her eyes off of M.E. She was sure of that.

When she got to the ladies' room, Raeann was coming out. Seeing the look on Raeann's face made M.E. feel as if Raeann knew she was coming to the bathroom and set her up. She glared at M.E., her eyes dark like a demon's. She moved slowly, her shoulder nudging M.E.'s and as she did so, she whispered the words M.E. would never forget. "You are a sick bitch who uses her position as an educator purely for her own sexual enjoyment. You will rot in hell."

M.E. had nightmares about those words, but she never told Adalynn.

Skimming over the papers in the folder, she smiled at the prospect that Melissa could be the subject that would fill the last void in her research that Raeann's turnabout had left. Then she smiled because not only could she actually finish her studies by the end of the school year, but she could add that extra study with Raeann's raving mad tirade. When she finished her analysis, she would present her work to the American Psychological Association. She would finally be recognized for the scholar that she was—maybe get a position at a top university. Hell, Stanford would want her back. She'd have to think about that.

The microwaved dinged. The water for her tea was ready. She sat by the window looking out over a creek and forest. It was peaceful. This was not a town that was on her bucket list. New York City, now that was her first choice. But she couldn't get a position at any of the colleges or universities in the city.

Thanks to Raeann.

The barrage of questions from the police the day before assaulted her mind. They were definitely looking at her as a suspect for the disappearance of Raeann. Part of her wanted to travel back to San Francisco and find that girl's ass and drag her to a police station. And now she had to go into her stash to pay Diane who promised not only to keep her out of jail, but to keep her reputation clean. That meant more to her than anything, since Raeann had already tarnished the reputation she had built for herself at Stanford. There was no way she would let Raeann ruin the one she was building now.

She thought about holding off on her research, but she was so far behind she didn't want to do that. Addy was losing faith in her. She could see it in her eyes. In the way she sometimes kept her distance as if the thoughts of what happened were weighing heavy on her mind, and she was thinking twice about staying with her.

She continued to read Melissa's file. No, stopping her research, even if just until Raeann's disappearance was solved was not an option. They may never find that bitch, but M.E. knew they had to if she was to be cleared of all suspicion.

Yet, part of M.E. hoped they never did.

* * *

When Amelia arrived, I was on my computer looking up different flooring. M.E. hadn't woken me before she left. I barely remembered soft lips on my forehead, but I was finally in that REM sleep after a fitful night of tossing and turning. It felt as if the minute I fell asleep, someone jolted me with a current of electricity to make sure I was awake.

Finally dragging my body out of bed at seven-thirty, I took a longer than usual shower, letting the hot water soothe my soul. Life in Endonford was…I wasn't sure what it was. M.E. was working harder than usual to convince me this place would be our new beginning. Yet our past was following us, poking at us every chance it got.

Then there was the new woman, Amelia. I really liked her fiery spirit that matched her bright-red hair and a smile that would make Garfield, the grumpy cat, grin. Yet the day before, she was as miserable as the cartoon feline. I knew her mood had to do with her brief encounter with my wife before she left for work. Something was said and I hoped to find out what it was.

When I heard Amelia's truck, I went into the kitchen and prepared her a cup of coffee. I was standing at the door when she entered with her toolbelt (I don't know why, but all those tools hanging from her waist made her kind of sexy), and two large toolboxes, one in each hand.

She set them down and took the mug I held out to her. "Thank you. That's very nice of you."

"I understand how a little caffeine can help jump-start you in the morning."

She held up the cup to me in a kind of salute. "I could have used a few of these yesterday morning. I'm sorry about my mood then." She looked down at the cup. "I'm thinking I chased you out of your own home, and I feel really bad about that. It won't happen again."

"I needed to do some shopping anyway. I found a lot of great deals for winter apparel and we're going to need it since coming from San Francisco…Well, you get the picture."

"So, you're saying my mood was a good thing. You got a new coat out of it." She grinned.

I walked to the kitchen and sat down at the card table that seemed to be the most used piece of temporary furniture in the house. "I'd rather your bad mood not be the reason I buy myself a new coat. And boots. And hat. And gloves. And the same for my wife."

Amelia followed me, chuckling. "Oh, boy." She ran a hand through her hair. "I guess I really pissed you off."

"You could say that. You seem better today."

"I am. Ready to get to work." With a toolbox in one hand and coffee in the other, she walked toward the basement. "Leave the other toolbox. I don't need it right away."

"Can you talk before you start or while you're working? Your choice."

Amelia stopped. "Excuse me?"

"You heard me. The reason I hired you was because you seemed like someone I could talk to. Someone who would listen to my plans and work through them with me."

She turned and faced me. "I'm glad you feel that way. Are there plans you want to discuss before I start?"

"No. I also need us to be able to talk about any problems we might have. I need this to be a relationship with good communication in order for this to work. So, we're going to talk about your conversation with my wife yesterday morning that got you so rattled."

"Look, Adalynn…"

"Addy."

She sighed heavily as if weighing her next words. "Look, Addy. We didn't talk about anything that's worth discussing."

"Look, Amelia. I know my wife. I don't know you, but I saw your face when you were talking to her, or should I say, *listening* to her. Your whole demeanor changed." I stood. "What did my wife say to you?" I forced her to look at me.

Her face twisted. She shuffled her feet. She set her toolbox down and looked at me. "It was my fault."

"What was your fault?"

"I asked her about that woman. I overheard you talking about the police questioning her."

"When?"

"Aw, Adalynn. I mean Addy, do we really need to get into this?"

"Yes, especially if you're eavesdropping."

Her eyes widened as did her mouth. "I am not eavesdropping. The day I came here to ask about the job, I heard you ask her as I was leaving. I hadn't even gotten off the first step. I heard you through the door, so that tells you we need to either replace the door or put storm doors on it."

She grinned. I did not.

"The other time was when we went to show your wife your new car. It was kind of hard not to hear. I was standing right there."

"Okay, I can accept that. But why would you talk to my wife about it?"

She shook her head and then settled her gaze on the front door as if she was planning her escape. "Damn it, Addy, I just like you. You hired me without really knowing me. You bought my car. You've been so nice to me. I was just…"

"Just what?"

"Worried about you."

"It's not your place to worry about me."

"I know, I know. I also didn't want to get caught up in something that might make working here…"

I tilted my head. "Difficult?"

Her smile was small, flattened as if embarrassed.

"I can't say I blame you, but could you do me a favor?"

"Sure. Just ask."

"Next time, talk to me. My wife isn't always approachable, especially where I'm concerned, or about difficult subjects."

"Like the police questioning her?"

"Yeah, like that."

"If it really is a two-way friendship you want to start building, then please, tell me what's going on."

I started to protest, but she spoke before I could.

"You don't have to tell me everything. I know it's none of my business. But maybe you can tell me enough to put my mind at ease."

"Fine," I replied in a firm tone. "M.E. had a relationship with one of her students. It ended badly. She got kicked out of Stanford and we moved here to start over. After we got here, the police called, saying the woman was missing, and had questions for her. But she doesn't know anything about it. We were here."

For a brief second, Amelia's face contorted with what appeared to be anger and then quickly relaxed. She took a few steps toward me. "Oh, I'm sorry. I shouldn't have pried. It's just that when you hear the police and you live in such a small town…"

"I understand. It makes you nervous. Please believe me when I tell you there is nothing you need to worry about. She didn't do anything—unlawful, that is. She did do something wrong, but she's sorry for it and is trying hard to make up for it, to do better."

Amelia picked up her toolbox. As she walked past me, she said, "Are you sure about that?"

"Totally," I answered, fully aware of the blunder my wife had created because of her lust for a student. However, I was more aware of Amelia's words and the look on her face when I told her. She was already halfway down the basement steps before I could answer, and even though I couldn't admit it to her, I had to admit it to myself. I, too, wasn't so sure M.E. was trying to do better.

I spent the next few hours making a business plan for my new interior decorating company. I had to come up with a name, how to register it in New York, what room in the house would be my showroom and how I would present my company. I had already decided to focus on historical decorating, but I didn't want that to be the only thing.

I worked to the sounds of a drill, a hammer, and what I believed to be wire sliding through and in and out of walls. At first it was rather annoying. Then it became relaxing, reassuring, except it didn't relieve the stress I was feeling, because I had to know exactly what was said between my wife and Amelia. I decided to go downstairs and try once more with Amelia.

She was tugging on a wire that dangled out of the ceiling. "Damn it!" she said under her breath.

"Do you need some help? I may look like a wimp, but I'm pretty strong when I need to be."

Amelia studied me. "I knew you were more than a pretty face when you helped hoist that heavy desk out of the truck and into the house. Take hold here."

I grabbed the wire where she indicated and waited for her signal.

"Okay, pull."

Together we pulled and I felt the obstruction on the wire that she must have been struggling with resist our pull. So, I yanked harder. Suddenly, the wire freed and we flew backward, our limbs and bodies tangling as we hit the floor. When our movement stopped, she was sprawled on top of me.

My breathing was heavy, but it wasn't just from her weight. Yes, she was a solidly built woman, but her red hair brushed the skin on my face, the scent of her shampoo filling my nostrils. Her laugh was contagious and I found myself laughing with her. Then we had that moment. The one where you feel really good and you look into each other's eyes and you see something…

Followed by Amelia flying off me almost as quickly as she ended up on top of me. She sat on the floor, knees bent, leaning back on her hands, and took several deep breaths. "I didn't see that one coming." She chuckled.

"You've never had wires stuck before?" I asked, a bit surprised.

"Oh yeah, but when I pull on them, they don't totally release like that one did, which leads me to believe it might've broken. And, if that's the case, then there's a bigger problem in the wall that I'm going to have to find before I continue the wiring."

"Can I help?" I smiled.

She hung her head and shook it. "I'm not so sure that's a good idea. You've got some strength." She rubbed her bottom. "You might do major damage to me next time."

I got up and extended a hand to her. She grabbed it and I pulled her to her feet.

"See? Don't take this the wrong way, but to look at you, I'd never guess you were a descendant of the Amazons."

I puffed out my chest and flexed my biceps, grinning all the while. "You Googled me, didn't you?"

"But, of course. Upstanding member of the Women's Amazon Tribe was the first thing that came up." She grinned. "Your smaller stature is very deceiving. Bet it comes in handy."

"How so?" I asked, wondering what she was getting at.

"Well, like if a thug attacks you, thinking you're a pushover. When he does, he'll get a big surprise."

"Very perceptive. It actually did happen to me."

"Really."

"I was walking on Pier 7 in San Francisco one evening waiting for M.E. Some guy tried to grab my purse. I kicked him in the nuts and pushed him over the fence and into the water."

Her eyes widened. "No way."

"Way," I replied. "I called 911 and they came and fished him out." I put my hands on my hips. "So do you want some help finding whatever it was that got ahold of that wire?"

She went over to her toolbox and picked up a crowbar. She held it out to me. "I think you would make a really good demolitions expert."

I giggled. "Women's Amazon Tribe, huh?"

Her shoulders raised, she tilted her head and her eyes looked up to the ceiling. Then she turned and said, "Follow me." At the other end of the basement, Amelia pointed to a spot on the wall. "Go ahead. If you have any frustration or anger, this is a great way to work through it without hurting anyone." She grinned. "Take a swing."

I knew she still underestimated me, so I swung that crowbar and I swung it hard.

Amelia jumped back. "Holy shit!" Then she grabbed my arm before I could take another swing, which I was definitely getting ready to do. The force from her yanking me caused me to stumble back a step. "Okay, okay, I don't need you to do any inside wall damage. Let me take a look before you take another crushing blow to your wall. I need to make sure there isn't anything you might destroy that I don't want destroyed. Like the foundation to the living room or something."

I took a deep breath. "Okay, but that felt good. Don't make me wait too long. I'm ready to take another swing."

"Slow down, woman. It had to have felt good because you put a pretty good-sized crater in that wall, but the important part of demolition is knowing when to stop and check things out." She grabbed a flashlight and peered into the gaping hole I created in the drywall. "It's interesting that the mechanics of the house are in such bad shape, yet they drywalled the basement. Sometimes I can never figure people out," she said as she examined inside the wall. "Okay, I think I see it."

I raised the crowbar.

She stepped in front of me. "Hold on, little lady. You can't smash this one. There's a pipe back there and I need to find out where it leads. I'll have to cut the drywall away and then try to release the wire that way."

"Damn," I said, lowering the crowbar. "How am I supposed to take out my frustrations if I can't swing this thing?"

Amelia chuckled. "There will be other demolition that needs to be completed. Since you really seem to enjoy swinging that crowbar, when I'm ready for it, I'll come and get you."

I hit the metal rod on the palm of my hand a few times. "I could get used to this."

"You're scaring me," Amelia said as she peeled away the drywall to expose the pipe she spotted.

But I could see the grin spreading across her face.

CHAPTER TEN

Amelia's bushy ponytail spread out in ringlets of lustrous red hair down her back as she worked. If it wasn't for the Buffalo Bills baseball cap that she wore backward, partially hiding the curly locks, I might have pulled the rubber band off, allowing it to cascade down her body in a feminine way.

I stepped back when I realized how close I was standing to her. I could explain my intimate position as wanting to see what she was doing inside the wall. I needed to see over her shoulder in order to analyze what it was that prevented her from pulling the wire all the way through. It was my house after all, and I was invested in the work she was doing.

I sighed heavily. Who was I kidding? It was my wife's and my house.

For a moment, I had forgotten about M.E. I silently scolded myself for thinking about Amelia's hair in that way. It would only lead to problems. I loved my wife, but I wasn't one to deny the problems that had plagued our marriage since the "I dos" had been spoken.

Perspective. That's what I needed. I believed I was married to a woman who loved me deeply, but I didn't feel like she was working on our marriage. If anything, she was back to her old self—taking me and our marriage for granted. I, too, agreed to work on our marriage, yet here I was drooling over another woman.

Was that what I was doing?

Of course not. I was making sure our house was repaired and remodeled to the crowning glory it once was. No. Even better. Therefore, I needed to know everything she was doing to get us there, and that meant not only in front of the walls, but behind them as well.

Still, I took another step back before I addressed her.

Suddenly, I was thrown off balance when something solid hit me square in the chest. I landed on my back, feeling the weight of Amelia on top of me. Her head lifted, worried eyes searching my face.

"Oh, God, I'm so sorry. I pulled on the wire thinking it was still hung up." She lifted her hand holding the splayed end of the electrical wire. "Guess I freed it. See? It does happen more than you think." She grinned. "Are you all right?"

I couldn't stop myself. I broke out laughing despite the pain shooting through my butt which obviously hit the floor first. "I sure wish someone had gotten that on film."

Amelia stared at me for a few seconds, a huge yet unsure smile spread across her lips. Noticing she wasn't laughing with me, I stopped.

She lifted her body off mine by extending her very muscular arms, and then climbed off me. "Really, are you okay? You took a lot of weight on you when you hit the floor. Did you hit your head?"

"It's not the weight that got me," I choked out between giggles. "It was the hard floor. God, my head is fine, but my butt hurts."

"Maybe you should consider sitting on an ice bag for a while."

I looked at her. Was she kidding? A freezing cold ass soaking in melted ice water didn't strike me as the answer.

I shook my head when she giggled. "I'm not really sure what you do for an injured butt." Amelia stood and extended a hand to me.

I took it and she gingerly pulled me up. It was then I realized how much my bottom really hurt. "Do you get hazard pay for this job? It can be pretty dangerous." I pointed toward my behind.

"I don't know. Do I?" She cocked her head, another beaming smile brightening her already glowing cheeks.

I cleared my throat. "I know there's a lot of fat back there, but I don't think it did much to cushion that fall."

"Maybe an ice bag isn't such a bad idea after all. Do you want me to get you one?"

"Even if I was to succumb to such a suggestion that inevitably would be one of the most uncomfortable things I can think of, no, I'd rather not."

"Okay, it's your ass," she replied, walking back to the wall and peering into the hole in the drywall. "It's a mighty fine ass, if I do say so myself, but a little bit of swelling would only add to the feminine curves."

I folded my arms and turned my head away hoping she couldn't see the blushing red that was burning my skin with appreciated embarrassment.

She walked over to her tool chest and grabbed what appeared to be wire cutters. I may not have been a contractor, but I had been known to use a tool now and then. She held them up and moseyed back to the wall. As she worked, she said, "I'm not happy this took so long, but I have a better understanding of the guts of this place. It looks as if it's been updated in bits and pieces. A room here, a room there, and then all tied in. I think I can straighten it out so it's not a fire hazard."

"A fire hazard?" I managed to choke out.

"If it stays this way, yes it could be, especially with all the technology we use today. If you draw too much power from one socket, it could set off a spark. Despite the fact there have been upgrades, they're still old. I'll be working on the electrical a little longer than we had planned." She straightened up and looked at me.

"We should revisit my timeline," I said.

"I figured we would. How about before I leave for the day? I should be able to give you a better estimate of the time it will take to complete the electrical by then. That way, I can get the new box and be ready to put it in after the electric company does their thing."

"How about now? I don't know how you haven't noticed, but your stomach has been growling ever since I came down here. I can make an early lunch. Nothing gourmet, just sandwiches, but it should stop those animalistic hunger pain sounds."

"God, that's so embarrassing."

"Not at all. My stomach lets me know when I'm hungry too. I just try to beat it before it makes a nuisance of itself." I grinned, which seemed to take the edge off her embarrassment.

"I'll take you up on the sandwich, but you'll still have to wait until later to visit your spreadsheet." She winked.

"Even better. We can continue our conversations and get to know each other." I turned and trotted up the stairs. I could hear the word "great" escape her lips in a dripping, sarcastic tone. I smiled. "I'll call you when lunch is ready."

Fifteen minutes later (it doesn't take long to slop some mayo and cold cuts on bread), we were sitting at the makeshift dining table, each with a sandwich, potato chips, and a Coke. Not your healthy kind of meal, but as I stated before, cooking was not now nor ever would be on my bucket list, or any list.

"For someone who doesn't cook, it's not a bad sandwich."

"Your comment would lead me to believe you don't cook much yourself."

"Why is that?"

I held up my sandwich. "Really? If you think this is gourmet, well…"

Amelia giggled. "You don't take compliments well, do you?"

"I do when they're deserved. But I don't deserve one for this lunch." I spread my hand across the table like a lawyer presenting their evidence.

"Still, I appreciate you making me lunch."

"Not a problem. I noticed you didn't bring anything today. You know you're not stuck here. If you want or need to leave at any time, feel free. Just let me know."

"Okay. Thanks." Amelia's body stiffened.

"Did I say something wrong?"

She shifted in the metal folding chair. The hinges creaked, which seemed louder than a bullhorn in the midst of an unsettling silence between us.

"So," I drawled, "it's time we even the playing field in this friendly relationship."

"What do you mean?"

"It's my turn to ask getting-to-know-you questions. Like, are your parents still alive?"

Amelia rolled her eyes. "Mom, no. Daddy, yes."

"Seems like we have something in common," I suggested.

"And that would be?" she asked before taking a swig of her Coke. When she set it on the table, the condensation on the side of the glass beaded down her fingers. Possibly one reason for delaying the installation of the air-conditioning. It was intriguing watching the droplets of water play on her skin.

The warm weather was true to the month of August, but thank God, the basement was cool. I had the first-floor windows open, hoping whatever cool breezes might find our little neck of the woods would also come inside.

"Neither of us seems to like our fathers all that much."

"You said you liked yours once upon a time."

"I don't hate him. I'm just not particularly happy with his life choices."

"I never have nor ever will like mine."

"Did you have to deal with it alone?"

"Deal with what?"

I noticed her tone was heading toward annoyance. "Whatever your father did to make you not like him. I mean, was your mother on your side or his?"

I didn't think she even realized the scowl that appeared on her face. I tipped my glass to her. "I hope that look on your face is for your dad and not me." I took a drink and smiled, staring at her, holding her gaze, hoping to break her down.

Finally, she smiled. "I haven't talked about my life to anyone." She swallowed hard. "It's one of those things that if you don't talk about it, you can almost believe it never happened."

"But it did," I said. "Haven't you ever heard about all that psycho mumbo jumbo that says you have to talk about it to get over it? You know, closure and all that stuff."

"The day I walked out of that house for what I thought was the last time and slammed the door behind me was the day I thought I got closure."

I studied Amelia, beginning to see the hurt that was buried deep inside. She was a tough one. You'd never know there was hurt there to look at her. "So you still have some connection to or with him."

"You could say that, but it's not something I want to talk about."

"You never answered my question."

"Which was?"

"Were you alone? How was your mother? Did you have siblings? I mean, I know what it's like to be an only child. There's no one to commiserate with or to when you're mad at your parents."

Amelia made a harrumphing sound and twirled the glass with her fingers. "I had a sister. Foster sister. My parents took her in for the money, which, by the way they didn't spend on her upbringing but on all their nasty habits. She was a long-term foster child with my parents which sucked for her. She was a good kid and didn't give anyone any trouble, which was bad for her because it made her a perfect target for my parents. It was rare, but my parents knew how to work the system. Anyway, she was too shy to tell anyone, including the social worker, how bad her childhood really was. Neither of us talked because we knew what the consequences would be."

"What would they be?" I prodded gently, not knowing if she would answer such a delicate question because I was pretty sure I knew.

Her eyes were on her glass as she twirled it in her hands. Then she looked up. "Beatings, but we also knew that if the system found out, we would be split up. She didn't want to leave me. I was also a foster child. We looked out for each other." Amelia sighed. "I still believe the day they brought her to live with us was the worst day of her life."

"Where is she now?"

"Gone. Away from here. I finally got her out." She stood and picked up her paper plate and cup. "And don't ask me where. It's confidential. I don't tell anyone. For her safety."

I put my hands up in a defensive manner. "Okay, okay." I nodded to her hands. "You can leave those here. I'll take care of them. Just because I don't cook doesn't mean I don't know where the garbage can is."

She hesitated a moment, then set them down on the table. "Thank you for lunch. And I'm sorry. Please don't entertain the thought of getting rid of me because I'm moody. Remember, I'm a pureblood Scot. We tend to get moody. It's nothing personal."

"I thought you were Irish," I exclaimed.

She feigned a knife to her stomach. "Oh, that hurt."

I chuckled. "Didn't mean to insult you. I just assumed."

"It couldn't have been from the accent, since I don't have one. You can tell the difference between them, so it must have been from the red hair."

"You would be correct. I've read that Ireland has a few more redheads than Scotland."

"If you were of Scottish descent, you would agree with me when I say it's not true."

"I've also read that they are stubborn and forthright."

Amelia's shoulders slumped as she folded her arms. "Have you been stalking the Scottish people?" The twinkle in her eye could not be missed. Her lips upturned into a sly smile.

I stood as I picked up the remnants from our lunch. Walking toward the garbage can, I said over my shoulder, "I like to know who my employees are."

I waited a while before I went back downstairs. I worked on my restoration plans but found myself just turning pages without paying attention to anything that was written on them.

I knew the problem. I was bored despite the fact there was plenty I could do. I had to complete my business plan and apply for a license. I had to finish my research on suppliers and I hadn't even decided which room I was going to use for my office.

No, it wasn't boredom. It was loneliness.

I not only left my life, my business, my home, my car, and my stepfather, who continued to exhibit recidivistic behavior, but my coworkers who I spent all day with…and my friends.

I had a lot of friends. Work friends, workout friends, party friends… And even though many of them were more like acquaintances than real friends, I missed them. I hoped that as time passed, I would form the same types of relationships here in New York. But right now, I wanted more. I needed more.

I didn't have to be a rocket scientist to notice that M.E. was falling into the same patterns she exhibited in San Francisco. She had secrets there, and I believed she was forming new secrets here. I had no one to talk to. However, I wasn't sure I wanted Amelia to be the one I chose to confide in. She had already displayed an uncomfortableness with M.E. that bordered on hostility. I wanted to believe my wife was looking out for me, but I felt something else underlying her actions. She was gone all the time and I needed female company. My wife wasn't here but Amelia was.

I brewed a fresh cup of coffee in the Keurig and carried it in one hand with a cold cup of lemonade in the other downstairs.

"You should have brought those down one at a time. Those steps aren't that sturdy."

"Good to know. I don't want to break my neck when I come down here." I reached the bottom step and held out each cup. "I didn't know if you required hot or cold."

A small piece of me melted under her warm smile.

"I'll take both. I always like a good cup of coffee, but this type of work does make me thirsty." She took both and set the coffee down on top of a cardboard box. Then she downed the lemonade.

"I know the jury is still out on me helping and everything, but I'd really like to. Isn't there something I can do that doesn't require swinging a crowbar?"

"Will it take away from my pay if I finish the job sooner?"

I folded my arms. "I didn't think you were all about the money, but no. We signed a contract. I just want to learn and know what is being done to my house."

Her eyes lifted.

"I mean I'm the one who's here all the time and will be running my business out of it. Don't you think it's wise for me to understand its workings so if something fails, I'll know what to do?"

"If it fails, you will call me. I guarantee my work."

"That's great! But you may not always be around. I would hope you take a vacation once in a while."

Amelia opened her toolbox and rummaged through it. She pulled out two hammers and then picked up a box of nails. I waited for a smart comeback, but she was silent for a few moments. Then she totally went off-subject.

"Actually, I could use your help. Your moving truck will be here soon and I need to make an opening in the brace upstairs that was made to shore up the wall and ceiling. Since that room will be one of the last to be finished, I thought we could store a lot of the stuff you won't be able to use or unpack in there, leaving me space to work in all the other rooms."

"I remember we talked about that. We also have space down here."

"Yes, but I don't think you're going to want a lot of your furniture down here. That reminds me...I unloaded some bricks to make temporary risers. Let's do that first. I've got a couple of four-by-eight sheets of plywood in the truck. Help me bring them down?" She set the tools down and trotted up the stairs. I followed.

"Any idea when the truck will be here?"

"I got a text the other day. They should be here Monday."

"Good to know."

We carried the two pieces of wood to the basement. After placing the bricks in a strategic formation, we positioned the plywood to create a support for the boxes that would be stored on top of the two makeshift platforms.

She picked up her hammers and nails again. "Okay, next is that brace."

"Lead on," I answered.

The floors in the stone house were dirty and worn. Much of the wallpaper was too filthy to salvage, peeling in spots, stained in others. The room with the brace was in the worst shape of any room in the whole house. It made me wonder how long the house had been empty and what kind of life had lived in it before we purchased it. What was that saying? *If walls could talk…*

Since they couldn't, at least I didn't think they could, we did. I spent the whole afternoon holding two-by-fours as she expertly pounded nails into them to make a large enough space for furniture to pass through but also kept the ceiling and walls shored up until she could repair them.

She began to open up about her childhood. The more she spoke, the more it sounded like an ugly movie with a crappy ending. Her parents abused them both, locking them in a room without food for days at a time. Her sister found a way to sneak out and raid the kitchen. The first time she was caught, her parents took turns beating her. Then they healed her so they could do it all again. But her sister was a thinker. She had studied their habits and knew the times when they would be out cold from one of their several daily drunken stupors. It was then she would slip out and take small amounts of food so it wouldn't be noticed, sometimes from the garbage.

"They got drunk more and more and often didn't even let us out to use the toilet. So, my sister found an empty mayo jar in the garbage. We used that when we had to." A sad smile washed over her face. "Did you ever try to pee in a small opening? We got really good at it." Her chuckle was sad.

"Where was social services?" I asked. "Didn't you go to school? Didn't the teachers notice anything wrong with either of you?"

"We didn't go often enough for them to see. But when we did, we were really good actors."

"Didn't anyone notice you missing a lot of school?"

"The neighbors liked to keep to themselves, so they didn't care that they never saw us outside, and June and Fred knew all the ins and outs of the system. I don't know how, but eventually they got accredited to homeschool us. At least that's what they had the social workers believing. Our education was one of the biggest jokes going."

"That wouldn't happen here. The neighbors across the street have their noses glued to the window all the time." I let out a small sarcastic laugh.

"In the rural areas, it's everybody's business, but you can find places with no neighbors—no prying eyes. In the city, the rule is, see something, say nothing, except there were several complaints made from people in the neighborhood about the upkeep of our house. My parents sold it before the complaints escalated to social services. They moved us to a house in the country with no neighbors close by. No one could see or hear what was going on. The beatings got worse then and I took most of the punishment. Sometimes when one of them would come after me, she'd step in between us and goad them until they went after her and forgot about me."

"Why would she do that?"

Amelia stopped hammering and sat on the floor, her knees bent, the hammer dangling from her hand between her legs. Her eyes were focused on the tool as if she was forming in her mind how she might use it to beat the pulp out of her parents. "She told me once she thought they hated me more than her. She said she didn't think they'd stop if they got their hands on me." Amelia looked up at me. "You got any more of that cold lemonade?"

"Sure. I'll be right back." I hurried to the kitchen and pulled out the pitcher of lemonade. As I filled two cups with what little ice we could hold in the cubby freezer, I heard the front door open.

"Addy? Addy?"

M.E.'s voice was strained. I stepped into the doorway and saw her turning wildly in circles obviously looking for me.

"I'm here. What is it?"

At the same time, I heard Amelia walk up the stairs.

"You're still here," M.E. said to her, a touch of anger in her voice when my wife saw the contractor.

"I was just picking up," Amelia answered. Then she looked past M.E. to me. "That wall should be good to go until I get to it. Just don't put anything too close to it. I just have to put my tools away and I'll be leaving for the day."

Beads of sweat formed at the edge of her bangs and she wiped them with a bandanna she kept in her back pocket. I walked past M.E. and handed Amelia the cup of cold lemonade.

"Thank you," she said, taking it and going downstairs.

I saw the look on M.E.'s face, but it was one I'd never seen before and that worried me. "What's going on?" I asked in a quiet voice.

"Not until she's gone," my wife answered, directing a thumb in Amelia's direction. Then she stormed upstairs, leaving me standing in the hall perplexed about the two current women in my life.

Fifteen minutes later, I stood on the front stoop and watched Amelia pull out of the driveway. M.E. had parked her truck so close to the back of her vehicle, Amelia had to pull forward and then back up and around through our unmanicured lawn. Since it hadn't been mowed in a while, her tires left two thick lines of flattened grass.

I noticed one of the curtains across the street drawn back and a pair of eyes peering out. I decided at that moment, M.E. may not have had such a bad idea on how to deal with nosy neighbors.

I waved while flashing a "how dare you" smile, and the curtain slowly floated back into place.

I turned. I wasn't ready for what was to come, but I walked into the house anyway to find my wife sitting on the bottom step of the stairway. Even though a part of me didn't want to know what had happened, as I entered the front door, I realized I didn't have a choice.

M.E. held her head in her hands, and I heard quiet sobs.

"They found her."

"They found who?" I walked over and sat beside her, putting a hand on her back.

M.E. looked at me, tears staining the blush on her cheeks. "Raeann. They found Raeann's dead body."

CHAPTER ELEVEN

It was only a matter of time, I thought to myself.

So, how should I have reacted to that news? I wasn't sure in that moment. With Raeann dead, maybe we could finally put the whole noxious mess behind us. Close the door. Leave her and the affair in the dark where it had started to fester, thereby leaving all my feelings right along with it in the blackness. Where it all belonged.

But a woman was dead. So, there was feeling sorry for the ending of such a short life and for the people she left behind who loved her. The dead woman was also someone my wife had slept with and took advantage of. So, there was anger toward my wife for seducing another woman and toward that woman for being so stupid as to fall for my wife's sleazy advances.

But she hadn't known my wife like I did. Then again, I too had fallen for M.E.'s advances once upon a time. So, I did the only thing I could. I wrapped my arms around her.

"Where did they find her?" I asked softly.

"She washed up on shore south from where they found her car, which was at Pirates' Cove north of San Francisco." Her voice was hoarse.

"I'm so sorry. For all of this. How did you find out? Did the police call you?"

M.E. pulled away from me and focused on the front door. "Actually, Diane called me."

"Your lawyer?"

"Yeah. She wanted to give me a heads-up. It seems someone from the San Francisco police is flying here to talk to me."

"Holy shit! Are you kidding?"

"No. I'm not. Diane set the meeting up. She'll be there."

"I'll be there too."

My wife turned to look at me. Her face was that of a person who was just handed a lifetime sentence in jail. (Not that I knew anyone who had ever received that kind of news, but I saw it all the time on television shows. It was always the same face.) M.E.'s usually bright blue eyes sunk, her lids darkened by worry, sadness, and fear. Her skin was pale and even though she had washed her hair and styled it before she left for work, the overwhelming despairing features drained the luster from it.

"You can't be there."

"You're my wife. Of course, I'm going to be there," I insisted.

"I told Diane you would say that. She said they won't allow you in. The closest you can be is in the hall waiting."

I took a deep sigh. "Then I'll be in the hall waiting. Do you know any of the particulars surrounding her death?"

"Diane said I'll find out Monday at the meeting."

"Shit! The moving truck is supposed to be here on Monday."

M.E. walked over to the living room window that looked out on the main road. "Hmmph," she breathed out. "Neighbor nosy body is watching again. You should stay here Monday. Someone needs to be here while the movers unload. You can go through the boxes and find some sheets to cover the front windows. I get tired of seeing those eyes every time I want to look outside."

I went to my wife and slipped my arms around her and laid my head on her back. "I have to be there. I can call the moving truck and have them come another day."

She turned to face me. "Then we'll have to pay storage, and what if they can't cancel? Besides, I'm ready to have our stuff here. This place is so barren and it feels like a desolate, condemned building." She smiled. "Except for the temporary bathroom."

I giggled.

"You can put some furniture around, unpack some stuff and when I come home, maybe the place will look more welcoming than like an empty shell in need of a lot of work."

"I...I can't," I stammered. "My place is with you."

She took my hands in hers. "There is nothing you can do. I'll ask Diane to pick me up and bring me home. She'll take good care of me."

The part where Diane would take good care of her found my jealousy center. I shifted my weight from foot to foot as my eyes drifted up the stairs, then out the window and finally back at her.

"I don't want to do that."

"I know, but honestly, there is nothing you can do there. But you can be here for me before I leave and more important, you can be here when I get home. You can also be here to take care of things since I can't."

"I don't like it."

"I don't expect you to."

"Will we be all right?"

"Of course, we will. I didn't do anything. I was with you. We were driving cross-country."

"What if they think you hired someone to do it?"

I watched her facial features widen in the horror of what I said. "Are you serious? Is that what you think?" She tried to turn away, but I held on to her hands.

"Of course not, but come on. You can't be that blind to think it's not what they'll think. Hell, they might even be thinking I hired someone."

"Neither of us hired anybody. I'm sorry, it's just this whole thing..." This time she pulled away and took a few steps upstairs. She held out her hand. "Come up with me?"

I took her hand and followed her up the stairs. Another one of those sayings I often heard but hated ran through my mind. *This too shall pass.* Seriously, someone had to smack the people who came up with these stupid little aphorisms. *This too shall pass* says nothing about exactly what's going to pass and how difficult it might be. *Deal with it*, was more like it in this situation because that's what we'd have to do.

* * *

Over the weekend, we drove to several different parks and took long walks. Each park had waterfalls and each one was so different, yet just as majestic. Our favorite was Taughannock Park. A one-mile walk led us to the base of the highest waterfalls I had ever seen. By the time we got back to the car, we were ready for a drink. So, we drove to several wineries. One of the advantages of living near Ithaca were the countless wineries, distilleries, and breweries dotting the Finger Lakes region that was home to the small city.

We indulged in wine tastings and dining out, and when we drove home, we made a beeline up to the bedroom and indulged in long, sensual lovemaking.

I didn't want the weekend to end. Never once did we think about Raeann or the San Francisco police. Then again, that was a lie. I was not in denial and neither was M.E. It lurked in the back of our minds because it was not finished. There was no closure and I wondered if there ever would be.

Still, we were able to ignore it and enjoy each other as we discovered what the area had to offer (including each other). We learned how different life was from the one we had in San Francisco. It was quieter, smaller, yet so spread out. It took longer to get to places like the grocery store, shopping centers, or to a movie. But open, airy, beautiful green spaces with lush, crystal waterfalls were certainly closer than they were in San Francisco.

Could I ever get used to it? I didn't know. What I did know was I could get used to every day being like this weekend. The time we spent in each other's arms was closer to what it had been before the discovery of her transgression, and I didn't want it to end. But it was just one more thing I ignored. Had our marriage ever been what I believed it to be? How could it when she was having sex with another woman?

I had made a promise to believe in us once again. Give us a chance. I had to pray that the past two days was the beginning of staying true to that promise.

M.E. came bounding into the bedroom fully dressed. When she had left to go to the bathroom, she'd been naked from stripping off her clothing for another round of lovemaking. I expected her to come back that way. Instead she picked up her work bag and keys.

"Gotta go." She approached me, studying my face. "I told you I had work to do, even though it is Sunday night. I have to call a substitute for my classes tomorrow or get online and cancel them. I also have some class work to finish so I can leave it for the substitute. I don't want to give the administration any reason to fry my ass." She leaned over and kissed my forehead.

I grabbed her hand. "Could that really happen?"

Her eyes grew dark.

I lowered my eyelids. "I understand. I'll wait for you. I wouldn't mind picking up where we left off."

She gently pulled away and walked toward the door. "I don't know how long I'll be. So don't wait up." She turned and blew me a kiss. "I love you. See you later." She disappeared out the door and I sat in bed, naked, listening to the sounds of her footfalls on the steps.

Gotta tell Amelia to fix them. Too much creaking.

Did the weekend mean more to me than it did to her? It was a beautiful time that felt like the beginning of healing in our marriage. I knew that M.E. could have done all that work at home on her laptop, making me wonder if her abrupt departure was more than a need to go to the office.

I began to cry.

When I heard the familiar groan of the wood announcing my wife was home and trying to sneak upstairs, I almost burst out laughing. I knew it was midnight, and now that she was home, it was time for me to go to sleep.

I closed my eyes. I could fake sleep as well as the next person because I had learned that sleep would never come when my mind was so busy scrutinizing every thought that waited its turn to be examined. So, I spent many nights practicing sleep techniques.

I felt the dip in the mattress and the cool air rush under the covers as she slipped into bed. Slender fingers brushed my hair away from my cheek followed by soft lips planting a wistful kiss.

I expected her fingers to further explore my body in hopes of waking me to continue where we had left off. But it wouldn't happen, because when she left me, that possibility had gone with her.

It wasn't long after that I fell asleep. For real.

Monday morning was…I wasn't sure what it was. M.E. had a distant, almost vacant look in her eyes. She got out of bed as soon as the alarm made its unwanted wake-up call, without kissing or touching me. I rolled over and watched her lumber to the bathroom. The water turned on in the shower, and even though I entertained the thought of joining her, I was pretty sure it wouldn't bring those lovely blue eyes back to me. Her mind had to be full of the same kind of scenarios that were running through mine.

I put on my robe and ran downstairs to prepare some coffee, and believe it or not, some kind of breakfast. Me doing any kind of food prep or cooking might be a good enough surprise to jolt her out of the depressing mood she appeared to be in. I knew coffee, toast, jam, and a donut couldn't change what was taking place that day, but it might give her a few minutes of something else to think about.

When I heard her coming down the stairs, I took off my robe and held the hot mug of coffee in front of me. If my attempt at breakfast didn't cause a spark that could brighten her mood, maybe my lack of clothing would.

She stopped in the entrance to the dining room. She looked at me, the mug, and then at the meager breakfast laid out on the card table. A slow, very small grin fought to take the place of straight, hard lips.

"You have gone above and beyond," she said.

"Anything for my wife. I took a quick cooking class online last night while you were gone." I held out the coffee cup. "One cream, one sugar. Just how you like it."

She took the mug and sat down. While she ate the toast, she said, "Did this cooking class also teach what to wear while preparing and serving the food?"

I sat down, crossing my legs, fully aware that my skin was sticking to the plastic cover on the folding chair. Nevertheless, I smiled and drank the cold glass of water I prepared for myself. Coffee and warm weather didn't go hand in hand for me, especially when I was trying to impress with a naked body. Sweat wasn't always attractive.

"As you have probably noticed, it's going to be an unusually warm day today."

She spit out the coffee she had just sipped.

I smiled at her.

After wiping her mouth with her napkin, she held my gaze. "I did see it was going to be hot today. It seems to be a lot hotter in here. Maybe you need to get Amelia going on that air-conditioning unit."

"Maybe if you get going on indulging yourself in a little prework sex with a cold shower afterward, you might not notice the heat."

She stood and walked over to me. Her fingers slid under my chin and lifted my eyes to meet hers. "Not that I don't appreciate everything you've done this morning to keep my mind off the meeting today, but nothing will make that happen. I just want to get it over with." She leaned forward and kissed me lightly on the lips. Her eyes drifted to the window and she released me, walking over to pick up her work bag. "I need to go. Diane just pulled in. Thank you for breakfast. I love you."

She hurried out the door, leaving my naked body sitting at the card table, stuck to the folding chair. I had expected her reaction. I just hoped it wouldn't be the one she displayed, but I understood. At least I thought I did.

When I heard the truck door slam, I ran toward the stairs hoping to get out of sight before Amelia opened the front door.

I reached the top step when I heard her voice. "Cute ass you got there. I know it's hot, but you should put something on to keep from getting sunburned. Or at the very least, if you're going to work with me today, you want to protect your skin from the hazards of contract work."

As I raced to my bedroom, I heard giggling.

Damn Amelia. Still, I smiled.

And that was all I needed to lift my mood that had been squashed by the thoughts of M.E.'s meeting later that day and her rejection of me just a few minutes ago.

I dressed hurriedly and ran all the way to the basement. When I found Amelia rummaging through her toolbox, I stood at attention. "Reporting for duty. Oh, and by the way, the moving truck is arriving today around ten a.m."

She stood, hammer in hand, her lips forming a teasing grin. "I hope I didn't interrupt something."

"Of course not. I was just really hot." I felt my cheeks burn with embarrassment. "I know it's probably wiser to get the furnace working since this heat is temporary and the cold will be here before we know it, but I'm thinking I might go out and get a portable air conditioner for days like this."

She walked over to the makeshift pallets and started hammering a few nails in. "Just for reinforcement," she said to me. "Will you need help with the movers?" she asked in between her swings of the hammer.

"Not with the actual carrying in of stuff, but M.E. requested I get something hung on the front windows. Every time we look out, the neighbors are watching us. M.E. suggested sheets, but there's a box of draperies on the moving truck, so I'm sure I can find enough to cover the windows temporarily."

"What about curtain rods?"

"Well, here's the thing. I don't know what rods I'll use in the final decorating, so I need to measure the windows we want covered and buy cheap rods. Since I need to be here for the movers, if I get the measurements and give you the money, do you think you could run to Wally World and get them for me?"

"I take it you mean Walmart."

"Oh, sorry, yes."

"You're not exactly paying me for doing errands."

"I understand, but I know where I want things to go. I promise I won't fill the rooms so that we have to keep moving furniture, but…"

"But this is going to take a while and I imagine you both want some semblance of normalcy."

"You imagine correctly."

"Okay then. Let me know how many you want and get me the measurements. It shouldn't take me more than an hour to do that."

"And you'll put them up?"

Amelia sighed. "Yes, I will. Now let me get to work or we'll be running behind and I'll have to sit with you to go over that timeline again." She put her hammer away, grabbed a few tools and walked over to the electrical box. "It actually works out well that the movers are coming today. The electric company informed me they upgraded your amperage. Since it's a warm day, I can turn off the electric and get the new box installed." She flipped off all the breakers and began to disconnect everything.

I didn't move, waiting for her to notice I hadn't left.

Without turning her head, she asked me, "Is there something else you need?"

"A measuring tape," I said with a grin.

"Help yourself. Just make sure you put it back where you find it. I'm a stickler about my tools."

"You got it, sir. Ma'am. Boss lady. Amelia."

Finally, she laughed.

By nine o'clock, I had the seven windows measured and sent Amelia out the door. I watched her get into her truck and drive away. Then I went to my computer and continued my work on our plans for the house and for my new business. I felt I had barely begun when I heard the loud noise of a huge truck.

The movers had arrived.

I was glad Amelia wasn't here. I had to grab one box in particular and put it in my car. It was my own private, personal stuff and I was planning on renting a locker somewhere to store it. For now, it would be okay in my little Honda Fit until I could find a place.

M.E. had her secrets. I had kept track of them to protect myself.

CHAPTER TWELVE

When Amelia returned, the movers had emptied about a third of the truck. I felt like a mouse in a maze looking for the cheese reward as I ran around letting the movers know where to put furniture and boxes. I sent boxes of clothes and toiletries upstairs. Most of the kitchen boxes went to the basement. I could rummage through them later for what we needed.

Boxes holding all my tech gadgets went to the living room as well as one television. Of the furniture, only the couch and a coffee table went into the living room, two dressers were delivered to our bedroom, and our dining table and chairs went to the real dining room. I left the card table and folding chairs in the kitchen. It was true that people always seemed to gather in the kitchen. The card table had become that meeting place.

With only a few of our belongings left on the truck, the two boxes of draperies appeared at the foyer in the arms of one of the strapping young men unloading them.

"Just drop them in the dining room. Thank you," I said with a wink.

An hour later, I signed the delivery forms on the dining room table and they left. When I shut the door, I felt a cool breeze wafting across the foyer. I turned to see where it was coming from. A fan had been set up in the entrance to the dining room. Amelia stepped out from behind the wall.

"I didn't take the liberty of purchasing a portable air conditioner, so I bought two fans instead. I put one upstairs in your bedroom. I hope that's okay. I also hung two of the rods on the front windows in your bedroom."

I couldn't help myself. I ran over and threw my arms around her. And then I cried.

She gently pried me off her and held me out at arm's length. "Whoa, what's going on here? I'm sorry if I overstepped my boundaries."

I wiped at my eyes with my fingers to prevent any more tears from falling. "No, no, no. That's not it. You're the best. Thank you so much for doing this. It was very sweet of you. It's a tough day today."

She took a step toward me. "Why? What's wrong?"

"Remember when I told you M.E. didn't do anything illegal, but she did do something wrong?"

"Yes, why?"

"It's coming back to haunt us. There was this college student she got involved with at Stanford. We found out she went missing and they just found her body south of where they found her car."

Then something odd happened. Amelia's face went blank. Her eyes widened, her skin paled. She pulled her phone out of her pocket and began swiping. She tapped on it, put the phone to her ear and went outside.

What had just happened?

A few minutes later she came back. Her facial features were back to normal, but she appeared distraught.

"I'm sorry. I just remembered I had to call someone about my dad. He's in a bad way and a decision was being made today as to whether to send him to the hospital or keep him at his home and put him on hospice."

"Oh," I said, not sure of what else to say. "I'm sorry?"

"Are you asking me if you're sorry or telling me."

"Well from what you said, I thought you didn't have any contact with him anymore."

"I don't. But, he's still the asshole that raised me, if that's what you want to call it, put a rotting, leaky roof over our heads, and tiny amounts of garbage food in our mouths. I'm not like him and I prefer not to have anything to do with him, but unfortunately, I have responsibilities and papers to sign. I need to go."

"Of course. I really am sorry. If there's anything I can do, let me know."

Amelia ran downstairs and was back up in less than a minute. I was still standing in the foyer unsure of what to do. Why had she even come to work? Why didn't she tell me about her dad?

"You're welcome to use my tools if you want to hang the rest of those rods. They're in the dining room," she said as she walked out the door. Then she stopped and looked back. "Thank you. I should be here tomorrow, but if I can't, I'll text you."

"That's fine." I tried to smile, but I wasn't sure it was the right response given the circumstances. It didn't matter. She was in her truck before I could say anything else.

I watched her drive away. How horrible it must have been to have parents such as hers.

But what the hell just happened?

I spilled my guts out to her and she suddenly remembers her dying father whom she hated? I shook my head, deciding I couldn't figure this one out, so I went downstairs. After searching the whole basement to no avail, I found the drill up in the bedroom. I took it and the box of curtains to the living room where I proceeded to hang them. Success with a drill and a curtain rod drove me to the dining room next and then the kitchen.

It was nearly five o'clock when I finished. Two things crossed my mind. One was that it took me longer than I'm sure it would have taken Amelia. I didn't care. I still did it. The other was that it was five o'clock, and I hadn't heard anything from my wife.

The appointment was at eleven. Diane was going to discuss her answers and strategies beforehand, but I knew nothing about how long it would take or what would happen afterward. I couldn't imagine the meeting would have taken six hours, but that was what I had to go with. The thought that M.E. finished earlier in the day and didn't come home or even call me…

I couldn't think that way. She wouldn't. She promised.

My phone. I hadn't checked it all day. Maybe M.E. called.

I'd left my phone in the dining room while I worked. I ran to where I remembered last seeing it, and when I swiped it; I wanted to kick myself. There were two voicemails from my wife.

I didn't even listen to them. I called her, and like the angry, jealous child she often could be, she didn't answer. Payback, I was sure. So, I listened to the messages.

In the first message that was marked eleven thirty, her voice was distraught, worried. She rambled on about the difficult questions designed to trap her into a confession for something she didn't do. She wished she'd let me come to the meeting. The second message was marked two o'clock. In this one, she sounded weary, defeated. "The meeting has finally ended, but it's far from over." That was the only thing she said.

I called her again, and still, she didn't answer. I left a message afraid my voice sounded too frantic. But I was. Partly because I couldn't get ahold of her. More so because I was angry at myself for not having my phone with me while I hung curtains. Could this day get any worse?

I paced throughout the downstairs trying to decide what to do. I could get into my car and drive to her office or Diane's office even though I had no idea where it was. There was always Google Maps.

But what if she came home while I was out looking for her? No, it was best I stay put. I wandered into the kitchen to see what food we had in the tiny refrigerator. Amelia said the electrical was done in the basement. However, I knew it would be a while before every room was rewired. I had told her the kitchen was not a priority. Looking at the nearly empty shelves in the tiny fridge, I wondered if maybe I should revisit the timeline and move the kitchen up toward the top of the list.

Then I chuckled to myself. Why? I didn't cook.

I settled on calling for a pizza. I wasn't sure if anyone would deliver this far out from town, but I was willing to give it a try. By the time my pizza arrived, it was almost seven and there was still no word from M.E.

I called again. This time, she answered.

"M.E., I'm so sorry. Amelia had to leave today for a family emergency and I ended up hanging the curtain rods and curtains. I left my phone on the dining room table while I was upstairs. Are you all right? Your voice mails sounded—"

"Upset, angry, worried?" There was an ugly edge to her voice.

"I would have been there. You know that, but you told me not to come."

"I didn't tell you to ditch your phone."

"That's not fair."

"Do you even know what I've been through?"

"No, I don't. That's why I've been calling you every half hour since five o'clock. When I didn't hear from you, I didn't know what to think until I realized how stupid I was for abandoning my phone."

"It wasn't good, Addy. They pretty much said they believe I was behind Raeann's murder."

"Murder. Is that what they said? It was a murder? Do they have proof?"

"They seem to know she went over the cliff at the parking lot where her car was. They don't have proof of how she went over, but they're assuming she was pushed."

"They can't prove that," I said, confident it was the truth.

"They're going to try really hard. I think the detective on the case doesn't like me. She might as well have come out and said so."

Shit. A female detective. Knowing my wife, she probably tried the flirting thing and immediately gave the detective reason to suspect her. Deciding not to push the subject, I asked, "When are you coming home?"

"I'm not sure."

That was an odd answer, so I asked what I really needed to know. "Where are you? Why can't you come home? I need to be with you. Don't you want to be with me?"

"Sure."

She didn't sound very convincing to me.

"It's just that when I couldn't get ahold of you, I delved into my work. I'm trying to finish up some important research. Why don't you just go to bed and not worry. I'll be home later. I promise not to wake you."

I was shocked and hurt by her dismissal of me and surprised by it. Why wouldn't she want to be with me so I could console her? Then again, I was used to her pushing me away when she was upset with me.

"Fine. I'll be here when you get home," I hung up the phone.

* * *

"Who was that?"

Melissa walked out of the bathroom in a black lace negligee that only covered certain curves, her breasts, and that luscious spot below her navel where M.E.'s eyes were focused. Despite the material, every tantalizing piece of her womanhood peeked through, begging to be touched and fondled.

It was exactly what Mary Ellen needed. More importantly, it was exactly what she wanted, what she craved.

* * *

I waited up until midnight. It was the first time in our marriage that M.E. did not come home by the stroke of twelve. Tears welled in my eyes. Had our marriage come to this? No understanding or forgiveness for a stupid mistake? I understood her anger was fueled by fear, and I wanted to make her realize how sorry I was and how much I loved her. But how could I do that if she didn't come home?

I got out of bed and walked over to the open window. A cool breeze drifted about the room. I looked at the sky, noticing the countless stars that littered a very black background. The contrast of light to dark, black to white was astounding. I didn't remember ever seeing such striking night skies in San Francisco. Too much artificial light, I had read somewhere. I guessed backwoods New York had its advantages.

The sound of a vehicle's motor in the distance grew closer, and as it did, I recognized the sound of her truck. This time, I didn't jump into bed pretending to be asleep. I ran downstairs and waited in the foyer for my wife to enter through the front door. After several minutes, I opened the door and looked out. She wasn't in her truck.

"What are you doing?"

I jumped despite recognizing my wife's voice behind me.

"Oh my God, you scared me. I was waiting for you. Why didn't you come through the front door?"

"I emptied the garbage from my truck, so I came in through the kitchen door. You didn't have to wait up for me. You never do, so why now?"

I ran to her and threw my arms around her. She tensed, but she didn't step back. "You don't seem to understand the depth of my love for you," I whispered in her ear. "I'm so sorry. I should have just gone with you like I wanted to."

Now, she stepped out of my embrace and appeared to be studying my face. "I thought I did know," she answered quietly.

"M.E., I love you so much. To the moon and back. No, to the end of the universe and back. I love you that much. I've stayed with you through everything because of that."

She rolled her eyes. "Are you ever going to let that go?"

"How can we when the police think you killed her? You know I'm here with you, for you. Why can't you forgive that I did a dumb thing today?"

"Because you're not dumb." She walked by me and started up the stairs.

I raced to catch up to her and took her hand and stepped in front of her. While facing her, I walked backward up the steps, pulling her with me. "Then let me show you how sorry I am."

"Sex isn't going to fix it." I watched her eyes grow hard, her facial features not giving way to any emotion other than what was in her eyes.

"I don't expect it to fix what happened. Just to show you how much I love you."

"If that were the case, you would have answered the phone." She walked past me and into the bathroom.

I slumped to the steps, clinging to the worn railing, not caring if it might break from my weight. Tears found their way to my eyes once again, and I wondered how much longer our love could endure the onslaught of the aftermath of her infidelity with Raeann.

I couldn't control my anger. "You always use sex to fix things when I'm mad at you. Why is this any different?"

The bathroom door slammed shut. I didn't care. I couldn't understand how she could be so cold toward me for not answering my phone. Did she think I had nothing better to do than to sit on it all day waiting?

"You always come home by midnight. Did you come home so late just to punish me?" I shouted, letting my anger and hurt fuel my words. "I'd say that's pretty childish. Wouldn't you?"

I sat on the step until I heard her leave the bathroom, and then another half hour afterward. Then I slowly got to my feet and went back to bed. I was relieved to see her asleep on her side, facing the wall. At least, she was there.

The next morning it was so quiet in the house, it sounded as if the singing birds were perched on our furniture instead of outside on tree limbs and phone wires.

I got up as soon as I felt M.E. leave the bed. I had laid awake all night fighting the images and thoughts that wouldn't let the sandman find me—M.E. being tortured by an onslaught of questions in a tiny room, the police finding Raeann's bloated, soggy body on the shore, M.E. in the arms of a faceless woman. I had no idea why I just didn't get out of bed and watch television.

I put a robe on and went downstairs to make another less than spectacular breakfast. I was running out of bread and coffee pods, so today I planned on running to the store. The last thing on my list was to call Amelia to see how she was. It would be more of a selfish call on my end, but I needed to know when she was returning to work. I also wanted to talk about the possibility of hiring a few more people to finish the job sooner.

I was anxious to get our life going. More to the point, my life. M.E. had her work. I couldn't really start mine until I had a decent room with proper electrical to set up my business. I needed at least one room to be finished to feel like I was actually doing something.

"Good morning. Did you sleep well?" I turned to see M.E. fully dressed for work. She sat down on one of the folding chairs. "If you're not careful, I might have to start calling you the official chef of the house."

I placed two pieces of toast, a bowl with sliced banana in it and the last cup of coffee in front of her. "That would be gourmet chef to you." I smiled.

"So did you sleep okay?"

"You should know the answer to that. I never sleep well when we're…"

"When we're at odds with each other?"

"If that's what you want to call it. Look, honey, I'm so sorry." I sat down opposite her. "I want to hear everything, including what's next."

She drank her coffee and I waited until she was ready to speak. "The short version. They grilled me. Hard. They kept telling me how I met her at the park in the middle of the night, we argued because she ruined my career and I pushed her over the edge. They said it in as many different ways as they could. When they didn't get a confession from me, they asked what seemed like hundreds of questions. What's next is I can't leave Ithaca until they tell me I can, and they can call on me anytime to ask more questions. What's next is they're going to try really hard to pin Raeann's death on the lapel of my blazer."

I smiled, wanly acknowledging her feeble attempt at a joke. The blazer she was wearing was one of my favorites—a midnight blue that showed off her glowing eyes.

"What did Diane have to say?"

"She told me I did a great job. She said she believes me when I say I had nothing to do with Raeann's disappearance or her death. We talked at length afterward about different scenarios that the police might come up with, and how I should handle them." She took a bite of toast. "I guess that was longer than a short version."

"I would have sat through the long version. Do you have to take off right away?"

She eyed me warily. "My first class isn't until ten. Why do you ask?"

"Maybe we can go back upstairs and finish talking about it?"

"You want to go upstairs and talk?" Her lips worked to hide a smile.

"I want to go upstairs, but we don't have to talk." I opened my robe and revealed the lack of clothing beneath.

She swallowed hard. "I think I can spare an hour. Or two."

I got up from my chair and walked over to her. I straddled her and sat down on her lap. Then I drew her face to my breasts. After a few seconds, she looked up at me. She placed a hand on the back of my head and drew my face to hers. Our kiss was wet, warm, and full of desire.

It wouldn't be enough, so I took her hand and pulled her up the stairs once again. This time, she didn't resist.

We were in the middle of intercourse, when her phone rang. I wouldn't point this out, except she pushed me aside and jumped out of bed. She looked at her phone.

My mouth dropped open because she had never taken a phone call in the middle of sex before.

Again, what the hell was going on?

"I'll be right back. I have to take this."

"Is it Diane?" I managed to choke out.

"Uh, yeah. Be right back. Don't move. Sorry, babe."

I wondered who my wife was so anxious to speak with that she would stop in the middle of sex to take a phone call. She was always too involved with our lovemaking to care who might be calling. Maybe the fact she was being hounded by the San

Francisco police to confess to a murder she didn't commit could be an exception to that rule. I might be able to work with that. Then again…

I laid back on the pillow basking in the feeling of her inside me, her lips ravaging my breasts and lips, the feeling of our skin touching. The burning feeling inside me was pure and raw sexual desire.

These thoughts made me sit up. Previous feelings crept into my head, making me wonder if that was all that was left between us—sex. Plain and not-so-simple sex.

* * *

"Don't ever call me again outside of school hours," M.E. scolded.

"I'm sorry," Melissa whined. "It's just we had such a great night. I miss you. I want you. Badly."

M.E. cringed at Melissa's words. She would have been flattered if the phone call hadn't interrupted a perfect morning with her wife.

"When can I see you again?"

"I'll call you. I have classes all day and will be grading papers tonight."

"When is your lunch? I'll bring you something." Her voice was like fingers caressing silk fabric, and of course, there was a suggestive undertone.

"I might have some time at noon, but I can't guarantee anything."

"You'll make time for me." Melissa ended the call.

* * *

She walked back in and practically jumped on top of me. "Now, where were we?"

I didn't fight it. I let her mouth consume me, her fingers enter me once again and I drew her in. If that was all we had left, I was going to enjoy it while I had it.

M.E. left for work by nine-thirty. Shortly after her truck pulled out of the driveway, I heard it pull back in again. At least that was what I thought until there was a knock on the front door.

"Did you forget something? Like another round of se—"

"Expecting someone else?" Amelia stood before me, her grin as large as a Cheshire cat's.

"Amelia. I didn't think you'd be back for at least a few days."

She walked past me and turned around. "It turned out to be an easy and quick decision. He's in a hospice facility. Shouldn't be long now."

"Wow," I said, not oblivious to her callous demeanor.

"There's no love lost here. Remember?"

"Yeah, right." Confused by her emotional turnaround, I let her in, closing the door behind her. "Still, are you sure this is the place you need to be?"

"I notice how you said need and not want. The answer to both is yes. I want and need to be here. It keeps my mind free of disturbing thoughts."

"Well, I hope he's at least in a decent place."

"I wouldn't care one way or the other. I need to get to work."

I watched her go downstairs. The fun, friendly Amelia was gone and replaced by a stranger I didn't particularly like. I needed the other Amelia back. So, I followed her.

"Last night I was searching for some food and realized that the baby refrigerator was not going to cut it. So, I wondered if we could rearrange the timeline and move the kitchen electric up. We don't have to redo the entire kitchen. Just get the electric and plumbing done so I can get a few decent appliances."

Without looking at me, she said, "I thought you didn't cook."

"I don't. But there's not enough room in the fridge to keep much. I'd like to have some frozen dinners, pizza, room for more than one can of Coke. Some butter and mayo for the bread. A bottle of white wine. A twelve-pack of beer instead of two bottles. You know, the essentials."

I watched as a tiny giggle escaped her lips. "Only one bottle of white wine?"

"Of course not. I would also need some mixers for the liquor." I answered her with my arms folded. "Did you notice the curtains?"

"I did."

"Well?"

"Well, what?"

"Not bad for an amateur."

"I don't know. I'll have to inspect them closer."

"Geez, you're tough."

She squatted in front of her toolbox and grabbed her drill. "Thanks for putting this back. Let's go inspect your work."

"You won't need that," I said, a little annoyed that she thought she might.

"And why is that?"

"Because I followed every instruction to the letter and it took me from the time you left until five o'clock to finish."

"That doesn't mean it was done right. But it sounds like a good start. Come on."

She trotted upstairs and I followed her, annoyed at her mistrust of the quality of my work. After inspecting every window, she frowned.

"Great," I said with disappointing sarcasm. "What'd I do wrong?"

"Nothing. Absolutely nothing." She grinned and I slugged her in the arm. "Hey. I don't want to have to report you to the worker's union for abuse of employees."

"You're such a turd."

"That may be so, but you did a really good job. I'm looking for some extra help. You want a job?" She laughed.

"Actually, I wanted to speak to you about that."

Her mouth dropped open. "What? Working for me?"

"That or bring in a few other people to move this along more quickly. I need to get my business started and I'd like to have a decent place sooner than later. I'm getting tired of looking at worn boards of wood. I mean, it's everywhere. The walls, ceilings, floors."

"But you don't know anything about being a contractor."

"Maybe not, but I'm a quick learner. I have a good memory. You only have to show me something once. You can give me all the mundane jobs that don't require a professional. I can run to the store to get supplies, hammer nails into boards, hold something for you. Whatever." I looked at the floor and then out the window. "I just need something to do. And I really want to be a bigger part of this renovation. I want to say I helped bring this stone house back to life. Back to its glory. You know…a love project."

The whole time I made my little speech, her eyes were intently watching me. "This is a situation I've never been in before. Usually, I don't hire my employers." She chuckled softly.

"I won't cut your salary, if that's what you're worried about. We made an agreement, signed a contract. I promise I won't go back on it. Call it hazard pay for training me."

"And do I get extra if you mess something up and I have to take extra time to fix it?"

"Not that that's going to happen. But, yes."

She stuck her left hand out. "Then you've got a deal. We can shake for now, but I'd like a revision to the contract."

I understood her request despite the itty-bitty stab in the heart I felt. "Agreed." I picked up a hammer. "Now, where do we start?"

Amelia's green eyes sparkled. "Just promise me you won't do any demolition without my approval."

I gently put the hammer back in the toolbox and held up my three fingers, making the Girl Scout sign. "Scout's honor."

After she instructed me on the tools to gather up, I heard her mumble under her breath, "Don't tell me you were a Girl Scout because I'll never believe it."

"I saw it in a movie." I grinned.

"Oh, thank God."

We both laughed.

CHAPTER THIRTEEN

M.E. came home early that night. I took her to dinner and was so excited by what I had accomplished with Amelia that I chattered through the entire meal, not once asking M.E. how her day was. I was so immersed in the renovations of our beautiful, historic stone house that I was blind to much of anything else.

Of course, it was something new for both of us. And despite the fact my wife displayed an apathetic behavior toward me and my ramblings, I remained totally wrapped up in the excitement of building, repairing, and creating, I ignored her reaction.

I didn't care. I was too excited—for me. For the first time in months, I didn't care about the affair, or Raeann missing, or even her death. Today was the first day in a long time that I was free of those thoughts because I was working with Amelia. It was the medicine I needed to cure the sickness that had been taking control of my physical and mental well-being. Working with Amelia allowed me to start healing from the disaster that had come to be our life.

We didn't make love that evening. We didn't make love for the next few weeks and I didn't care. I didn't miss feeling like that was the only reason she was with me. I had purpose.

I ignored M.E.'s growing displeasure and resentment toward my working relationship with Amelia. That was probably because it was turning into a genuine friendship. Amelia finally opened up to me. We talked about our childhoods. I told her stories about my college years and when my mother died. She told me about her training to be a contractor and the man who hired her as an apprentice and expected more than a lackey. She told me that when he was done training her, he offered her a job. Instead, she went off on her own.

We laughed all the time, and it felt so good. When I told her about my father going on a drunken, pot-smoking binge with his young chick, she cracked a joke.

"I've got a math problem for you."

We were working in the bedroom. We had finished the electrical in the kitchen as well as the plumbing. The next day, I bought a new refrigerator, and just that one appliance brought such joy. When it was delivered, I was giddy like a little kid on Christmas because this one thing allowed me to imagine the finished project. I actually began to feel like the house was coming alive. I could see it puff out its chest as the old was replaced by the new. I couldn't wait till we got to the walls, ceilings, and floors. Then, I could decorate and my dream would finally become a reality. I imagined standing on the front lawn beaming with pride as the house breathed in new life.

I stopped screwing the cable clips to a two-by-four. "What does a math problem have to do with my father and his blond bimbo that could be his great-granddaughter?"

"If your dad is sixty-six and his girlfriend is twenty-one, how much money does your dad have left?"

It took me no longer than two seconds to burst out into uncontrollable laughter. That was how it went until the day she told me how her parents abused her and her sister.

"What was your sister's name?" It was the one question I hadn't asked in all the conversations about her family, the one I didn't think would bring up bad memories. Or so I thought.

"Sunny. I called her Sunny because she was like a ray of sunshine." Amelia looked at me. Her eyes were misty and her shoulders had slumped.

"That's beautiful," I said. "But why do you look so sad?"

"I miss her. That's all."

"It must be hard staying here while she's somewhere living a life without your parents. Without you. I hope she's doing well and it's everything you wanted for her." When Amelia didn't say anything, I added, "I just wish you could get away from your dad. If that's what you want. He's been hanging on for longer than I thought he would."

"Oh, he's gone." She stopped what she was doing. "I mean he's still in hospice and totally out of it, but for me, he was gone a long time ago."

I found her reply odd, but I didn't know how I'd be if I was raised by parents like hers. "Why don't you take some time off and go see your sister?"

"I can't!" she practically barked at me.

"Whoa, what did I say that's got you pissed off?"

"Sunny is a closed subject. That's all."

"Why?" I found it hard to understand where all her anger was coming from. I could understand why her parents would be a closed subject, but she was free with the information where they were concerned. She seemed to be the same with her sister. Until now.

"I have to go downstairs and pull this wire. I'll be back in a few." She left without answering the question.

My jaw dropped as I watched her leave. Weeks of laughing with a friend had just been stamped on by something I said, but I had no idea what I said that was so wrong. That pissed me off. So, I stomped downstairs and found her sitting on a large cardboard box. Crying. Maybe she was crying because the box was collapsing in the middle and she was slowly sinking into its contents. The sight made me want to laugh. Then I wondered what was in that box, hoping it wasn't anything breakable and maybe that was why she was crying.

She looked up at me and when I saw her drooping expression, tearstained face, and misty eyes, my heart crumbled with the sadness I saw written all over her face. I quickly took her in my arms, which only made her cry harder. As she sobbed, the box gave way and we both fell inside. I hung on to her, her shoulders shaking with the intensity of what she was feeling (which I couldn't fathom) and then an odd noise escaped her, followed by another. When I could finally make out what the noise was, I realized she was laughing. Really, really hard.

I let go of her and tried to get out of the box. I didn't join her emotional release because I had no idea which emotions were making her a lunatic. But when I stood and looked down at her, I smiled. And waited.

Finally, she sat up and wiped her eyes with the bottom of her T-shirt. It was a good thing she didn't wear mascara because her light blue shirt would have had large black stains on the bottom. I imagined imprints of her eyes and eyelashes on the material and I giggled.

I extended a hand to her and pulled her out of the box. "Okay. Here's the thing. Working relationship aside, I think we have developed a really great friendship. So trust me when I say you can tell me anything."

She let her head fall back and took a deep breath. "Can we get something to drink and sit outside? I'd rather not talk about it in the basement. Just seems…well this isn't the place I want to have this discussion."

I looked at the box. "Looks like blankets and towels. As for the drink, you just said the right thing. I love opening the door to our new fridge. It's a promise of what's to come. I've got beer, wine, and lemonade."

"A lemonade would be great."

I pointed to a pile of our stuff that we were storing in the basement until it had a place in the house. "There are two outdoor chairs over there. If you would, please take them out back and I'll get the lemonade."

She smiled. "Still got some big prying eyes?"

"Every time we step out front. I'd be lying if I said I would've bought the place even if I had known about the neighbors beforehand."

"Then I'm glad you didn't know about them." She winked and went to get the chairs.

Ten minutes later, we were sitting outside in the shade of the house sipping, lemonade. I waited, which was hard because I still wondered what I'd said that triggered her outburst.

As if reading my mind, she said, "I'm sorry. I got angry at you for something that wasn't your fault. You're just closer to it than you think."

"What are you talking about?"

"Sunny is dead."

I wasn't sure I heard her correctly. "Excuse me?"

"Sunny is dead. She was murdered."

"Oh my God. I'm so sorry. Did your dad do it?"

"No," she said with conviction. "He had no idea where she was."

"Then what happened? When did it happen?" I sat up in my chair. I had to wriggle to a more upright position.

"Sunny was a nickname I'd given her when we were young. I would tell her that all we needed to survive was her sunny disposition. No matter what, she always made the best of our horrible living situation, which was something I couldn't do. One day she was staring out the window when it was raining. She said it made her feel better. She said the water cleansed the earth, and every time it rained, she wished it would do the same inside the house." Amelia sighed heavily and I could tell she was struggling.

"Are you sure you don't want a beer or a glass of wine?"

"Probably not a good idea. I don't like to drink any alcohol when I'm working. Even a little amount can lead to mistakes."

I stood. "I'm getting us both a beer. We don't have to work the rest of the day and if that makes you feel guilty, we can go into town and get the supplies you have on your list for next week." I went into the house and returned with two very cold beers. Two Coronas with a wedge of lime in each. "Now I have room in the fridge for limes." I winked.

She twirled the bottle in her hands and then took a drink. "I didn't want to tell you. I still don't want to."

"Why not? I thought we were past that. Besides, it's obvious you need to talk to someone."

"It shouldn't be you."

"Amelia, please stop with the confusing generalizations and tell me what is going on." I hoped she couldn't sense the frustration in my tone, but if I felt it, I'm sure she did too.

"No. I can't. You need to drop it. It's none of your concern."

"Amelia, you're my friend. You've helped me so much. Let me help you. I can tell there is something that's really weighing on you."

Amelia was silent for what seemed a very long time. She gulped her beer and then wiped her mouth with the back of her hand.

"Amelia, what is it? It can't be that bad. Tell me. I want to help."

"Raeann. My sister's name was Raeann."

The weight of her proclamation shut down my lungs and my heart and I felt like I would need a defibrillator at any moment. "That's not a very common name." I struggled with my sentence.

Amelia took another long swig of beer, then turned to face me. "The same Raeann your wife had an affair with back in San Francisco."

"Wha…what are you saying?"

I was pretty sure I knew what she was saying. I didn't know what to do. I didn't even know what to think until one question popped into my mind. Did Amelia know that when she came looking for the job? After that, my mind flooded. Was that the reason she came to us offering her services? How did she know? How did she know who we were? How did she know we were coming to New York? To buy a house in the same town she lived in? Did she really live in Ithaca or did she follow us here?

I stood so fast I knocked over my chair and dropped my beer. I positioned myself directly in front of her but far enough away to get a head start…if I needed one.

She spoke when I moved, as if knowing the impact her words had on me. "I'm sorry. Really. I should have told you sooner. I know what you're probably thinking."

"No, you don't." I glared at her, angry and hurt by the betrayal.

"I didn't know it was you and your wife who bought the stone house. When I heard it was sold, all I knew was that the new owners were from out of town. I also didn't know my sister was missing at the time I came and asked for the job. I was just so excited that the house would finally get its due. It's a magnificent historical structure. I wanted to be a part of bringing it back to life, and I knew from the moment I met you that you would be the person to do it."

I began to pace side to side in front of her. "So, did you know who we were when you saw it was us who purchased this place?"

"I didn't know your names when I came here, but I recognized your wife from the pictures Raeann sent me."

"So, you've known all along about my wife and your stepsister, but you kept quiet. And now, Raeann is missing. What'd you do? Formulate a plan to make sure M.E. was implicated in her disappearance?"

"No, of course not! I'm not going to lie. I hate what your wife did to my sister. Raeann went to San Francisco to get a degree, a career, a new life. She got caught up with Mary Ellen and it ruined her. She's dead because of it. She'll never get that chance for a better life."

I stopped pacing. "I'm sorry," I said quietly.

"It's not your fault. I blame your wife for…"

"Wait a minute," I interrupted her as my mind tried to put the pieces together. "When did you find out your sister was dead? When I told you in the basement?"

"First off, why is that even important to know?" Her anger spilled out into her words. "She's dead, goddamn it!"

I glared at her. "Is that why you left so quickly that day in the basement? It really wasn't about your father, was it?"

"That would be correct."

"So you've been lying to me all this time. About everything."

"Really? You want to talk about semantics? Were you hoping the police wouldn't contact her next of kin and let them know? Duh, they did, and I'm her next of kin. How do you think I found out? When I looked at my phone, there was a message from the San Francisco Police Department. I went outside to call them. They told me she was dead." Her eyes were rock solid as she stared at me.

Shame bubbled inside me and my stomach started doing handspring double pikes. I thought I might lose the half bottle of beer I'd drank. "Why didn't you tell me? We've been working all this time together, forming what I thought was a really great friendship and you never told me."

Amelia stood and took a tentative step toward me. "I didn't know how. Raeann was my sister," she choked out. "Mary Ellen is your wife. You're my…my friend."

"M.E. didn't kill her. She didn't have her killed. I'm certain of that. She may not be the best wife, or person for that matter, but she's not a killer."

"How can you be so sure? The way she treats you. She uses people."

"Other than what your sister most likely told you, how do you know? How do you know your sister didn't paint an evil picture of my wife because she didn't want to leave me for your sister? Instead, she broke things off with her. What makes you think you can believe what Raeann told you?"

I stared hard into Amelia's eyes, daring her to challenge me.

"She never lied to me. She was my sister."

"Foster sister. And M.E. is my wife."

At that moment, Amelia broke down into emotionally wounded sobs. She shrank to the ground, and I went to her, taking her into my arms, holding her up.

"I'm sorry," I whispered in her ear. "I'm so sorry."

We sat there for several minutes, an autumn breeze loosening the dead leaves on the trees, allowing them to waft effortlessly to the ground. A few birds chirped out a song that sounded unusually sad to me, making me wonder if they could feel Amelia's pain.

Finally, her crying subsided and she stood, wiping her eyes with the bottom of her T-shirt. She looked up to the sky when she said, "I guess this puts us in an awkward situation. Where do we go from here?"

She returned to her chair like she was too weak to hold herself up anymore and I followed her lead and went back to my chair. "I'm not sure. I really need your help and I've been so happy learning your trade. I don't want to become a contractor, mind you, it's just so gratifying to know that I'm a major part of bringing this beautiful stone house back to life. However…" I leaned forward to look her in the face. "If it's too hard for you to continue, I'll understand. If that's the case, I would hope you could recommend other contractors that you trust and might be able to finish the job. It's really up to you."

"I don't know."

"Look, Amelia, I can't imagine what you're going through, but you've known for over a month and you've seemed to do okay with it. You come after M.E. leaves for work and are gone before she comes home. If I promise you won't have to deal with her at all, will you at least consider it? I've come to value our friendship; I depend on it being there, but as I said, I'll understand if you can't continue."

"Can I think about it overnight?"

"Sure. But you need to promise me one thing."

"What?" she said with a hard edge.

"That you'll keep an open mind. Don't be the judge and jury for your sister's death. Wait for the police to find the culprit."

"What if they don't? What if whoever did it is so cunning that they've permanently covered any way they could be discovered?"

"I don't believe that to be true. Everyone makes mistakes. It's just that if you continue to believe my wife did it, it will be hard to work together. I can't stop you from feeling that way, I just ask you keep it away from here."

"Are you going to tell her?"

"Hell no," I scoffed. "Definitely not a good idea."

"She'll probably find out sooner or later."

"Let's hope for later. Better yet, not at all."

"Okay. If you don't mind, I'd like to go home."

"Of course. I'll walk you to your truck."

We strolled to the front yard silently, yet I questioned everything in my life and everything between us. I was pretty sure she was doing the same.

She opened the door and took me in her arms. She hugged me tightly. "Thank you for understanding. Thank you for being my friend." She kissed my cheek, got in the truck and drove away.

I touched the spot where her lips left tingling skin, wondering why, if she had known, did she even want to be my friend? Feeling the softness of her lips on my cheek, I didn't care why. I was glad she had.

CHAPTER FOURTEEN

Per usual, M.E. came home long after dinner time. Knowing this would happen, I drove to town after Amelia left and bought some frozen dinners and a few other staples. I decided when I got home, I was going to start ordering meals online again. Even though we had a side-by-side, state-of-the-art refrigerator with a bottom freezer, I still had no desire to cook, but now I had room to store the food.

I stopped at the liquor store and bought a few bottles of wine and then drove my little car home through the backcountry of Ithaca. It truly was some of the most stunning scenery I had seen. Ithaca was nestled in between hills of trees and dotted with farms, homes, and state parks. And in those parks were breathtaking waterfalls—some large, some small, but all with their own character and beauty, as my wife and I had discovered.

If I hadn't been such a city person, I could get used to it. But…my goal was to get back to San Francisco. Someday. If M.E. proved herself, she might be able to get back on the good side of the academic world and possibly find a position at one of the other twenty-plus colleges and universities in the fifty square miles that made up our favorite city.

It could happen. It would happen. I was sure of that. Until then, I would make the best of this place. Actually, it wasn't as bad as I had thought it would be, so I could live here for as long as it took, as long as that wasn't *too* long. I had made a five-year plan. I would be willing to extend that on a yearly basis if need be, but ten was my limit. It gave me more than enough time to create an interior designing empire that I could take back to San Francisco.

But if I lost Amelia's friendship...I hoped it wouldn't come to that.

I had prepared a frozen dinner for myself and exnayed the wine. Instead, I got my drill and continued affixing the wires to the two-by-fours inside the walls of the bedroom where we had left off before Amelia's revelation to me.

I finally knocked off about eleven o'clock and went to bed only to wake at the sound of M.E.'s truck pulling into the driveway long after midnight. It appeared she was extending her usual return home time past twelve a.m. A brief flash of me telling her about Amelia being Raeann's sister was image enough for me to feign sleep. I didn't have to pretend. I was asleep before she came into the bedroom.

When I woke, I looked at my wife to find her fast asleep. A few locks of her brown tresses fell in disarray across her face. She looked beautiful. And she looked so peaceful. I wondered why. She'd told me during our previous dinner, after I rambled on about working on the house, that the police were still maintaining contact with her, asking her the same questions over and over again. They now wanted to know her whereabouts over a period of time before we left San Francisco.

She had to be getting scared. But if that were the case, why weren't there creases of worry on her forehead while she slept, just like there had been for months after her cheating with Raeann came to light?

I wondered if it was time to address the fact that she had been coming home late for weeks, with each week later than the one before. She was falling back into the same pattern she had when she was having sex with Raeann. Had she found someone else? Again? Another college student?

I had promised myself if it happened again, it would be the last time. So, why hadn't I asked my wife what kept her out so late every night? Away from me? Probably because I knew she would lie and I wouldn't be able to distinguish between a lie and a truth. The only option would be to spy on her like a woman who had become blind with jealousy and did stupid things like following her, sneaking peeks at her phone (if she ever let it go and walked away long enough for me to get a glance), or smelling her clothes for the scent of another woman. Stupid detective work that usually exposed the lie.

I wasn't ready to stoop that low.

I got up, showered, and went downstairs to the kitchen. I began to fix breakfast for both of us as I had for the last several weeks, but stopped. This time, I only prepared my breakfast. I was finishing up my toasted bagel with cream cheese and coffee with Starbucks creamer (I found it at a grocery store in town and now had a large enough refrigerator to keep it in. Yeah!) when M.E. hurried into the kitchen, showered and dressed.

She glowed. Her smile was tantalizing until she got to the table. "Where's my breakfast?"

"Where we keep all the food. Cupboards. Fridge. I did put a K-Cup out for you for your coffee." I continued to drink my coffee while I worked on my computer. I was updating the timeline with the work Amelia and I had finished. I had also been searching for other contractors, all the while hoping I wouldn't have to make those calls.

She walked over and kissed me on the forehead. "Well, thank you, but I'm going to pass. I don't have enough time to make my own breakfast. I'll get something at the college café on my way to class."

She picked up her briefcase that had been sitting on one of the chairs—most likely where she had left it after she got home.

Damn. That could've been a perfect opportunity to snoop. I guessed I really wasn't ready to go that far. But as I watched her walk out of the kitchen, the thought of the possibility of another betrayal was no longer nagging at me. It was shouting. Ignoring it, I called after her, "Will you be home for dinner? I thought we could go out."

She stopped but didn't turn around. "I'm not sure. I've got papers to grade. I'll text you later today and let you know."

"Of course. I understand. Have a good day."

Her head turned and she flashed me that smile that always made me weak in the knees. That morning, my knees didn't go weak, my heart did.

I watched her truck pull away. I needed the only friend I had in this backwoods town. I hoped she needed me too. I had pulled up Amelia's contract on my computer and got her address. I typed it into Google Maps but decided to wait an hour or two and see if she would show up. After an excruciating two-hour wait, I was locking the front door, purse and keys in hand, when I noticed a familiar truck driving down the road. I sat on the front steps and waited for it to pull in.

My heart raced with the anticipation of the decision Amelia had come to. I couldn't assume that just because she was coming here meant that she was going to continue working. She wasn't the kind of person who would send a text that she was breaking up with me or quitting a job. I was unsure of whether or not I wanted her to stay. I needed to finish the refurbishment of the stone house, but I was leery of Amelia being the contractor to do it. She had lied to me, and I'd be a fool if I didn't wonder what her motives were behind keeping those secrets.

I held my breath as she got out and walked up to me. "Hey," I said.

"You going somewhere? I kind of need my assistant today. We're going to hang drywall. Can't do it myself."

I blew out the breath I was holding, feeling a sense of relief that I had only felt once before—the time M.E. lost her job and reputation, just not her freedom. "Damn, you caught me. Thought I might have to do some more shopping."

"If you'd prefer…"

I stood and unlocked the front door. "I've been anxiously waiting to learn how to hang drywall, so shopping can wait." I smiled at her.

She laughed and I laughed with her.

A half-hour later we were hanging the first eight-by-four piece of Sheetrock in one of the spare bedrooms. Up until now, our conversation was about drywalling. But I couldn't take it anymore. I started crying. At first, the sound of Amelia's drill drowned out my quiet sobs, but as they got louder, she looked at me and stopped.

"What's wrong? Are you upset that I'm here?"

"No, no, not at all. I'm glad that you're here." For whatever reason, I cried harder.

"Oh, damn, maybe this is a bad idea." She put the drill down. "I've got names of other contractors. I wasn't sure you'd want me back."

"Oh, that's not it," I cried. "Of course, I want you here. You're my friend. My only friend in this godforsaken place."

"Then what is it?"

I sat on the floor and Amelia did the same, taking a place opposite me. "Talk to me."

"You asked me once if I was so sure that M.E. wouldn't cheat on me again."

"You said you were."

"Aw, damn, Amelia. I was lying. I'm not sure."

Amelia's eyebrows raised and the look on her face said guilty. She believed my wife was cheating and was also behind her sister's murder.

"I'm positive my wife is not a killer or someone that would plan to have another person murdered. But a cheater she was and what's that saying? Once a cheater, always a cheater."

She tilted her head with a small grin. "You like sayings."

"Not really. They just seem apropos most of the time."

"So, you think she's cheating again?"

"Yeah. I'd like to say I'd bet this house on it, but I can't risk losing the only home I have right now." A small, defeated laugh escaped my lips, and I shrugged my shoulders. "Know what I mean?"

"I do. You want to believe her when she said she wouldn't do it again, but your heart and/or your mind is saying otherwise. So, why do you think she is?"

"Her patterns are the same as they were before."

Amelia's eyebrows dipped. She took a short breath and crossed her arms around her bent knees. "Okay, what patterns or signs are you seeing?"

"Mostly coming home late almost every night."

"How late is late?"

"Used to be midnight. Always by midnight."

"And now?"

"Much later."

"That's odd," she mused.

"For a typical person, maybe, but she's not typical."

"I notice you used the word typical instead of normal."

"Are any of us really normal? No one can profess to know what the true definition of a normal person is."

She smiled. "Very psychologically academic, but true. It's interesting, though, that we seem to know the meaning of abnormal."

I ignored her brief theoretical instruction. "She's also pulling away from me again. We've always had a great sex life and a very physical relationship. Now, she's so distant."

"It was like that before?"

"The last time? Yes."

"You need to find out. She shouldn't be allowed to treat people this way!"

I scooched away from her and tensed, waiting for the fallout.

Her eyes widened. "Oh, I'm so sorry," she said in a quieter voice, as she realized the extent of her outburst. "It's just that, it's…"

Feeling the tension that had taken over me, I took a deep breath and relaxed. "It's what?" I asked, wondering what had gotten her so worked up. I mean, it wasn't her wife that was cheating. But as she spoke, I knew I wasn't the only one affected by the byproduct of my wife's indiscretions.

"You don't know everything," she said quietly.

Okay, maybe I was being an ostrich with my head in the ground when it came to my wife's shenanigans, but that comment angered me. Amelia didn't really know me or my wife and she had never met us until we moved here. She knew only what I had told her (and that would be the apathetic part of me talking).

"Look, I didn't want to be the one to tell you."

"Tell me what?"

"Your wife was using my sister in a sexual experiment. She was part of the research."

Despite the fact my legs didn't want to unbend from a cross-legged position, I clambered to my feet. "You have no idea what you're talking about."

Amelia remained seated. "Raeann told me. She really loved your wife and Mary Ellen led her to believe she felt the same way. When Mary Ellen told her it was over, Raeann got angry. They had an argument and in the process of throwing things at each other, a file was knocked off the desk. Raeann picked it up and got a quick look before Mary Ellen grabbed it from her. Raeann was the subject of her sex research."

I turned and ran downstairs. No way. No way was my wife that twisted. Raeann made it up. I was sure of it. I heard footsteps behind me and I spun to face my wife's accuser. "It's all hearsay. Just because Raeann told you this doesn't make it true."

She eyed me with a mix of sympathy and determination. It was an odd mix of emotions.

"Did you know she had an apartment in San Francisco?"

"No, we lived in a townhome."

"She had her own apartment. That's where she and Raeann would meet and have sex. Lots of it," Amelia spat out.

"I would've known."

"Really? Did you ever bother to check things out when she started these patterns?" She used her fingers to make air quotes around the word patterns. "There are records, you know. You could find out about the apartment if you really wanted to."

I walked into the kitchen and pulled four beers out of the refrigerator. I set them on the table and sat down in one of the folding chairs. I needed something to keep myself from cracking.

Amelia followed me. "Are you expecting company?" she asked, a suspicious tone in her voice.

I opened one of the beers and took a long swallow. I nodded to the other chair. "One for you…" I slid the beer across the table toward her. "…and three for me."

Her shoulders slumped as she sat and opened the beer. "You're right. I'm telling you what Raeann told me. But don't you think you should check out a few things?"

I didn't answer. I just kept drinking.

"Look, Addy, I really like you. I enjoy our friendship and even though I wasn't sure working together was a good thing, you've turned out to be a pretty good apprentice. We'll be finished ahead of schedule and you've saved yourself some money. I hope we can continue the friendship past this love project."

I wanted to smile at that, but I couldn't. "Even though we will finish early, I will still pay you what we agreed upon," I said dryly.

"I expected that since we signed a contract." Her smile made her face shine, her freckles more pronounced. Her green eyes glowed and she snorted a quiet laugh. "Raeann got hurt. Really bad. And I don't mean just emotionally. She's dead. You can't get hurt any worse than that. I just don't want it to happen to anyone else. Including you. You need to find out if Mary Ellen is cheating and anything else that she might be doing. You need to protect yourself."

I opened the second beer. "I'm sorry about your sister. And I appreciate that. But what am I supposed to do?"

"Has your wife noticed that we're way ahead of schedule?"

"No, she comes home, goes to bed. Gets up and goes to work. She doesn't look at anything we've done. She probably won't notice anything until the rooms begin to look like real rooms. You know, window treatments, furniture, accent pieces."

Amelia smiled. "Ah, she'll only notice the finished product."

"If it keeps going this way, yes."

"I want to help you, but I don't want her to catch on that I am. If you don't think she'll notice we're taking time off from working on the house, then I'll help you."

"Trust me, she won't. Besides, it probably won't take that much time." I looked out the kitchen window. "Will it?"

"Can't say. Depends on how well she hides whatever it is she has to hide."

I took another long swig of beer. "Where do we start?"

"I think you need proof that she had an apartment in San Francisco. If what Raeann said was true, your wife could be doing the same thing here. So, we should also try to find out if she has an apartment in Ithaca."

"All right. How do we do that?"

"Through detective work. We follow her."

"First off, I'm not really comfortable doing that, especially if she sees me. Second, it makes me feel like I'm a jealous wife who is stooping to the lowest of lows."

"I understand that you don't want her to catch you following her. You could hire a private detective to do it for you."

"Great. How expensive is that going to be?"

"I may know someone who won't be too expensive."

I opened the next beer and tipped it toward her. "Then make it so." I stood. "If you don't mind, I'd like to take the day off. You can continue your work, of course. But I need time to think…" I lifted the beer into the air. "And drink."

CHAPTER FIFTEEN

I spent the rest of the day in my bedroom drinking, napping, thinking, and then thinking some more. If Amelia wanted to help me discover if my wife was up to something, then why should I stop her? In my most hopeful state, I didn't want it to be true. I wanted to find out that M.E. was staying late at her office grading papers, meeting with students, making phone calls, and strategizing with Diane on how to field the questions from the detectives assigned to Raeann's murder investigation.

The only thing I could do was wait. Wait for the detectives' report and wait for my call from the detectives to question me. I knew they would call. I just didn't know how long it would be before they did. But as I laid in bed, one thing Amelia had said to me was eating me up inside. M.E. had actually told me that she was doing psychological research to gain respect in her field. Most of the time I ignored her work discussions. Psychology bored me. Her work bored me. I think she knew that.

But there was one night…Tiny snippets of a discussion we'd had were coming to the forefront of my mind. She'd never told me the subject of her research, but she'd been so excited about it at dinner one night, that I stopped inspecting the Italian Renaissance décor of the restaurant where we ate and looked at her.

She was beaming—bright and shiny like she looked after we had one of our wild and delicious sexual encounters. I remembered wondering for a moment if she was having sex with someone else because we hadn't in a few days. But she would never do that. Or so I thought.

Now, the question was had she learned her lesson? Did she mean what she kept telling me over and over again—that she loved me and only me and she would spend the rest of her life proving it to me? She promised we would regain our position in the professional worlds we had existed in…

I sat up. I never lost face in my line of work. My company was disappointed that I had to leave but I was assured a position if I ever wanted to go back. M.E., on the other hand, was told she would never get a position at Stanford again. I thought that was because of her affair with a student. Had it really been because they found out about some sexual experiments she was conducting for her research? If that were the case, it couldn't have been an approved research project. I found it hard to believe that Stanford would approve sexual research when their students were the subjects.

"Hey, Addy."

I heard Amelia's voice come from downstairs.

"I'm done for the day. Can you come down here and I'll show you what I did?"

I didn't answer for a moment. I wasn't sure I could get myself down the stairs. Three-plus beers later and a head full of vexing thoughts made me wobbly.

"Addy? Are you all right?"

"Yeah. I'll be right down." I lumbered out of bed and brushed at my clothes in hopes of looking, at the very least, presentable. I walked along the wall for support and when I got into the hallway, Amelia was waiting at the top of the stairs.

"I hope it's okay, but I thought you might need a steady arm to help you down the stairs. I'm thinking they should be next on the timeline. Make them safe and sturdy. I know I don't feel secure when I go up and down them."

I knew what she was doing. Amelia was making excuses for my beer binge. And I was grateful. I walked over to her and took her arm. "Thank you. It's been a rough day."

Her smile was sweet and uplifting. "I'm sure it was, but I'm hoping when you see the progress I made today it might cheer you up."

"I'm already cheering up. Lead the way."

She guided me down the stairs and into the kitchen. All of the drywall was up and had a first coat of mud on it. I was amazed because I never heard a hammer or a drill, or any grunting on her part for that matter.

"Oh, my God. It's amazing. How did you do this all on your own? I thought that drywall was heavy when the two of us carried it!"

"I went to Home Depot after you went upstairs. I bought enough to do the kitchen, and I had a friend help me—the one who is going to do some detective work for you. I hope that was okay."

"Sure. So, you explained everything to…"

"David. My roommate. Not everything. It's up to you how much you want to tell him. I just asked him to look into your wife's possible apartment rentals in San Francisco and Ithaca. And I told him to find out if she's…cheating. It's pretty typical stuff for him. Most of his clients have been spouses wanting to find out if their wives or husbands are cheating. He's gotten pretty good at it."

"You didn't tell him anything about Raeann or what happened in San Francisco?"

Amelia dropped her eyes and took a deep breath. "He's my roommate, my best friend, so he knows Raeann was having an affair with her professor. We tell each other everything. Except for this. I didn't tell him everything about you and what happened in San Francisco, but he's not stupid. He put two and two together. I didn't confirm it nor give him any details about it."

I opened the fridge and took out another beer. In my mind I was thinking—the hair of the horse? The dog? Didn't matter. I needed another beer. I sank into the folding chair once more. I found myself sitting in that chair a lot lately.

"I appreciate that, but from what you're saying, I guess it doesn't really matter what you've told him. Can I trust him not to gossip?"

"His main source of income is his private detective business. Being discreet and keeping secrets is a big part of it. And as I said, he's my friend. He won't say anything." She leaned forward and said in a quiet voice, "I'd get really pissed if he got me fired."

I choked on my beer and almost spit it out.

"Hey, I'm not saying anything about the amount of beer you've downed today, but would you like to get some dinner? Or we could order takeout and eat in this beautiful kitchen. I never heard you come downstairs so I know you haven't eaten anything all day. Food would do you some good."

I smirked. "Despite the fact it's looking more and more like a room, it's still far from being a kitchen. I think I'd like to go out to eat. But I have one stipulation."

"Oh, a stipulation," she mocked while rocking back and forth on her heels with her hands clasped behind her back.

I stood and poured my beer in the sink. "Glad this is still hooked up." I turned to face her. "You pick the place. I don't want to think or make any more decisions today."

"Agreed. Get your purse, jacket or whatever. I'll be out in the truck."

I knew why she said that. She was giving me time to call or text my wife and let her know I was going out to dinner. Rather, she assumed I would do that. But I was so mad at M.E., I had no intention of doing that. Until I did.

When my wife starting coming home late again, I did try to call her. She never picked up, but she always sent a quick text. I decided I would do the same. I found my phone and texted that Amelia and I were getting a bite to eat. One of two things would happen. She would want to know where we were going, giving her the opportunity to show up if she so desired. Or she wouldn't respond.

One thing I knew for sure. I would have to prepare myself for the fallout of her jealousy. Either way, there would be consequences. I knew this because I had come to the realization that M.E. thought of me as a kept woman. I was hers and only hers. It felt as if we were both prisoners in our marriage, except she considered herself a prisoner with a Get Out of Jail Free card whenever she wanted it. I was locked in a jail cell with no way out and getting madder by the minute.

As I walked out the door, I wondered how I had put up with it for so long.

I learned early on that you can't let life's miseries knock you down. And if you have to talk about it in the future, laughing is the best medicine. It keeps you from falling back into those helpless feelings, but gives you the power to take the lessons learned and apply them to the future you.

And laughing is what Amelia and I did. She chose a Mexican chain restaurant for dinner. Over margaritas, nachos, and tacos, we laughed nonstop while we told each other stories of our warped childhoods. If an outsider had been listening, they would have thought us two very pathetic women as we giggled about Amelia and her sister going through the garbage cans looking for food and ending up with most of it covering their arms and clothes.

"You should have seen her," Amelia laughed. "It was the first time we decided to play thieves and scrounge for something to eat. She was so low to the ground she could have been a snake. She wriggled her way across the kitchen floor and almost made it to the garbage can when we heard a loud noise."

"Oh my God, did she get caught?"

"No. It was our evil stepfather falling down the stairs in a drunken stupor. We grabbed what we could and scrambled out of the kitchen, through the dining room, and into the living room. When we saw him go down the hall to the kitchen, we ran upstairs. We ended up with more wrappers than dinner, but we were so pumped with adrenaline, we knew we would try again."

Amelia's eyes dulled and her face sunk.

"I'm sorry you had to go through that. But you did what you had to do. In the end, it's what we all do to survive."

She forced a smile to her lips. "Thanks for that and for making me laugh. I hadn't thought about our struggles until now. It always seemed to rip a hole in my heart, especially now that she's…"

I reached across the table and covered her hand with mine. "No child should have to go through what you and your sister did. I'm sorry for your loss."

I started to pull away, but Amelia slowly turned her hand and held on to mine. She squeezed as small drops pooled in her eyes and then trickled down her cheeks.

Something in the warmth of her hand and her body language screamed of a heavy heart. I gave her hand one more squeeze and then pulled away. I motioned to the server to bring our check and treated Amelia to dinner.

"Please, let me pay half," Amelia said.

"You can leave the tip. Ten should do. I need to get home."

Our ride back to the stone house was quiet. What could I say to a woman who suffered a childhood like a caged animal? But what I really felt about it kept me from saying anything. We all went through shit. It's what we did with the shit that counted.

When the stone house was within sight, I gasped. The one time my wife came home early had to be the time I went to dinner with Amelia. And the only reason she was home was because she got the text. Making a decision that could put you in a difficult position while feeling angry isn't the smartest thing to do, but I didn't care. Dinner with my contractor got me out of the funk I had been in all day.

Still, I swallowed hard.

"Do you want me to go in with you?"

I leaned my head back as she pulled into the driveway. "Not a good idea. You need to leave."

She stared at the house as if waiting for a jealous maniac to barge out the front door. "I don't think you should go in alone."

"I'll be fine." I spoke as I got out of the car so it would appear I was simply saying goodbye to a friend. If I lingered or turned back to say something, it would only fuel whatever emotions would greet me at the door. "Thanks for going to dinner. I'll see you tomorrow." I didn't give her a chance to reply. I shut the door and strolled toward the house, holding my breath. I needed to hear the truck pull out of the driveway. She couldn't hesitate. *Please, Amelia, don't hesitate.*

I sighed when I heard the wheels on the dirt-and-stone driveway and the engine switching gears as it went from reverse to drive. I didn't look back.

The door opened before I could grab the handle.

"Where have you been? I've been so worried! Your car was here and you were gone."

I felt a bit of the tension in my shoulders release from the concern she was showing until I realized she hadn't seen my text.

"A phone call, a text, hell a note would have been nice," she said angrily, then turned and walked away.

I closed the door behind me. So many things ran through my head. Why did she choose to be home on this night? Did she see my text? Or was she lying about it? She had to have seen it because she wouldn't have come home early otherwise. What game was she playing? Whatever it was, it was a good one. She pretended to let her concern escalate over time into anger. Maybe I would tell her that Raeann was Amelia's sister? Really piss her off.

That last thought was a definite no.

I followed her up the stairs to the bedroom. I decided to try the nonchalant attitude in hopes it would calm her.

"I went to dinner with Amelia. You've been so busy lately, when she asked if I wanted a bite to eat, I thought I'd be home before you. I mean you haven't been home for dinner in weeks." I knew it was stupid to add that last sentence, but it was the truth.

She stopped in the bathroom doorway. "I've been working." Her monotone reply made me shiver. It was the way she said it—all the implications those three little words exuded in the tone, her body language, her refusal to turn and face me—that chilled my blood.

"I sent you a text. Did you ignore it?"

And then she turned.

I couldn't read her. Her face was blank, her eyes hard as they took me in. And in a single moment, everything changed. Her blue eyes softened, the tense muscles of her cheeks, forehead, and jaw relaxed. She took a step toward me.

"I'm sorry. I'm so sorry. I was so busy, I never checked. I finally finished up with some research and I wanted to come home and celebrate. When I saw you weren't here, but your car was, I got so worried."

She took another step. I didn't move. In front of me was my wife. The one I had loved for so long. The one who swore to love me for the rest of my life. When that woman showed herself to me, I melted and everything else that happened between us, all the bad and the ugly, melted into the softness that was being presented to me right now.

Her fingers reached out and stroked my cheek. My head leaned into the touch and I closed my eyes. I knew she was moving closer as her hand stroked my hair and cupped the back of my head.

I sucked in a breath, waiting for whichever way the next moment would play out. Relief washed over me when I felt her lips on mine, her tongue teasing me to open my mouth to let her in.

I reciprocated, and the simplest of responses was enough to land us in each other's arms, then onto the bed tearing at our clothes. It had been a while since we'd wrapped ourselves in each other's arms, and that single fact made the familiar return. I couldn't fight it. I didn't want to. So, we made love to each other like we always did, and when we fell onto our backs after that sexual, primal instinct had been satiated and from the exhaustion of lust, my emotions sunk to a new low.

I was to blame as much as she was. We had built ourselves a life that resembled the movie *Groundhog Day*. We loved deeply, mutually. Then we…we loved with trepidation, mistrust, and fears. Then we loved deeply, mutually. And then we loved with trepidation, mistrust, and fears. Our life could be a sequel to the movie.

But in doing so, we never really solidified the relationship into what it should be. We just kept going back and forth. The only good thing was our sexual connection softened the blow that would come with the ugliness.

The rhythm of M.E.'s breathing slowed, growing deeper, peaceful. I got out of bed and threw a robe around my sweating naked body. It chilled me to my core, and I wondered if it was from the sweat or the growing angst.

I grabbed my phone and went down to the kitchen. After brewing a cup of hot tea, I sat at the table with my computer and phone and started to work. The house was coming along and it was time to finish the business plan for my interior decorating company. I also continued to search for news on Raeann. I needed to know what the San Francisco police were thinking. And I needed to know what, if anything, my wife was up to.

Hours later, I felt hands slide inside my robe and find their way to my breasts. I tilted my head back and allowed the fingers to caress my nipples.

"Shouldn't you be in bed sleeping? With me?"

"I couldn't sleep. I'm sorry."

M.E. removed her hands and sat opposite me. "Why not?"

I shrugged. "Just one of those nights where my mind can't turn off."

"Huh. So, what's keeping you awake?"

I straightened my back and smiled. "Amelia is getting to the point where I'll be ready to start decorating rooms. The parlor is almost finished with the drywall. Then she'll paint and refinish the floors. The living room will be next. She's making good progress. I just need to be ready to do my part so I don't fall too far behind. Now, I'm choosing draperies, accent colors, trim, and accessories. I'm getting really excited about it. We're getting so close to the part that I love doing, and it will be important that I do my best work since it will not only be our home, but a showplace for my business."

"So, it's probably been a good thing that I've had to work late. It's given you time to get this done quicker than we originally planned."

I stared at her. *We.* She said we. She had not put any work or input into the plans because she had no interest in doing so, and she definitely hadn't helped with any of the renovations. So, if she felt that staying away to do her "research" was her contribution to the rehab of our new home, then who was I to argue with her? Because I would never win.

"Yes, my love. You've given me the time to work on this place without feeling like I'm neglecting you." I stood and placed my empty cup into the newly installed farmer's sink. Then I turned around. "I'm so grateful for that. And for you." I walked toward the stairs. "You're right that I should be in bed sleeping. With you." I smiled the best seductive smile I could muster. "Are you coming?"

She jumped up from the chair and took my hand. I started to lead her upstairs, but she passed me and pulled me up.

I went with it.

CHAPTER SIXTEEN

Sun poured through the windows of our bedroom. When I opened my eyes, the light was blinding and I threw a pillow over my head. M.E. had pulled the curtains open and I wondered if she did it absentmindedly or if she was sending me a message. Either way, I got out of bed and was about to take a shower when I heard the water running. I decided to wait until she finished, even though the message she was sending me with the open curtain was to get up and join her.

"I'm not falling for that. I'll shower later," I said to the window, accusing the sun of waking me up before M.E. was done. I quickly dressed and made my way to the kitchen to prepare breakfast. This morning, I would make breakfast for two. Some way, somehow, we had to find our way back to the decent relationship we had before all this mess happened. But if she was repeating her cheating patterns, was that even possible? Would I be able to turn the other cheek to another transgression? I didn't know.

As I toasted some bagels, selected yogurt containers and gathered together the makings for coffee, I heard footsteps on the stairs. My shoulders tensed once again, waiting for my wife to appear in the kitchen.

"This is a nice change."

"Since you didn't get up and just leave like you've been doing, I thought you might like some homemade breakfast instead of café food at the college."

I tried not to make it sound like another accusation, but I wasn't sure I succeeded until I felt arms around my waist and a whisper kiss on my neck.

"That's very sweet of you. I was beginning to wonder if you didn't love me anymore."

I fought the cringe that wanted to turn my body into a rigid response. "What would make you think that? I've been here waiting for you to be here." I pulled away from her and got the Starbucks creamer out of the fridge. I turned and looked at her. She was seated at the table.

"I'm not sure what you mean by that." Her reply was curt. Then she swallowed and said, "Why do you always have to do this?"

I leaned against the refrigerator, the creamer in my hand. "Do what?"

"I've been working really, really hard. I'm trying to build a life for us, bring home the bacon. God, I always hated that saying, but you know what I mean. I have to put in the overtime to rebuild my reputation. I thought you understood that."

I relaxed a bit, but not entirely. "I do." I didn't say anything else because I really didn't want to get into a fight.

"You're not showing it. I was so surprised that you weren't home for me last night."

"M.E., do you really expect me to be a kept wife? Besides, I never know when you're coming home. And I sent you a text." I waited for a response. When she didn't say anything, I continued, "While I'm here restoring this home, I'm also preparing *my* business plan to start *my* company. I've been busy too, but I've been here, in this house, every day, every morning and every night except last night because I was sick and tired of waiting for you, which seems to be what I'm always doing.

You expected me to text or call or leave you a note, and I did. But you never do. You can't come home and expect me to be here when you finally show up." I walked over and slammed the creamer on the table and then sat down. I fixed my coffee and then stared at her. "I expect the same. We both know that hasn't been the case." I picked up my cup and held it in both hands, feeling the warmth of the liquid on my fingers and palms.

"You're right. I'm sorry. I've just been so busy and worried. More worried than busy. Part of that is what I wanted to talk to you about."

Now what? I put my mug down. "Okay, I'm listening. What is it?"

"A detective from San Francisco is coming to interview me. I've been spending time with Diane preparing. They still have me on their suspect list despite the fact they have no physical evidence whatsoever."

"When?"

"Today. I'm scared, Addy. They seem to really want to pin Raeann's death on me."

"They can't. You didn't do it."

"But they'll harass me until I break. Diane said the police try to do this all the time and that's why there are so many false arrests."

"Why haven't you told me this before? It's been over a month since all this started."

"I know. I'm sorry. I didn't want to worry you, and I honestly didn't think it was going anywhere. But the last week has been bad. Calls every day."

"Are you going to let me come this time?"

She stood. "I'd really like that. I've left the time and address of Diane's office next to your purse upstairs. I'll see you later." She kissed me on the top of the head and left for work.

Instead of being happy that she was finally including me, I wondered if she might have taken that opportunity to snoop in my purse and phone. God, paranoia was beginning to take over my life. Even if it was true, there was nothing to find. No, by putting the information near my purse, she was trying to do what she should've done from the start—include me, her wife, in proving her innocence.

When I heard the front door shut, I put my head in my hands. For so long I wanted to be on this train ride. I loved every stop along the way, every adventure, excursion, and experience, but now I was beginning to see that every station we stopped at was the same. The scenery was blending together like a modern art painting of colors on a canvas that flowed into each other, and I was unable to tell where one ended and the other began.

Worse, I had growing thoughts in my mind to derail the damn thing. If I was to save my relationship, we had to get off this train. I decided then and there that after her meeting with the San Francisco police, I would take her to dinner where we could sit at a secluded table. It was time for a serious talk.

I ran upstairs to shower and change for the day. Amelia would be here soon and I looked forward to working with her. I began to feel lighter thinking of her smile that came along with a sense of humor that often presented itself through sneak attacks. Whoever said *laughter is the best medicine* definitely knew what they were talking about.

The front door opened just as I got to the bottom step. Amelia's thick red hair lay on her shoulders, and her eyes were shining like emerald stones. Her smile. It said so much to me. Like, "I'm so happy to see you. You look beautiful today." (Maybe I was hoping she was thinking that. It had been a long time since M.E. gave me any compliments and meant it in a way other than sexual.) And if Amelia was thinking the same thing I was, the next words out of her mouth would have been, "I can't wait to start working with you. It's so much fun!"

I hoped my smile spoke the same language as hers. She was my friend, my confidant, and my employee. Most importantly, she had become an anchor in my upheaved life that felt like a boat adrift on wild seas.

She bounded forward and gave me an awkward hug. Then she stepped back, her smile still dazzling like it was the only thing in the room the sun had found. "Hey, girl. Sorry. I just wanted… Well, I'm kind of a hugger and I thought our friendship was to that point. Unless…" She spoke the words in an all-thumbs kind of way and it was so cute.

"Like Olaf, I like warm hugs."

She stared at me. "Who?"

"No effin' way. You've never seen *Frozen*?"

"No."

"Ever heard of it?"

"No."

"OMG, girl. It's a Disney film about two sisters in Norway or something like that. One has magical powers and makes a snowman that comes to life. You need to watch it." I stopped, realizing I had hit a very tender and sorrowful nerve. "I'm sorry."

"It's okay. Really. If I can watch it with you, I'd like to."

That request sent my body into flight response. *What are you doing?* I ignored my internal thoughts. "Since we're so far ahead of schedule, I think we can find a morning or afternoon to take a few hours off and have movie time."

Again with the brilliant smile. "I didn't know you were into Disney."

I started down the stairs to begin the workday, hoping she followed. When I heard her steps, I answered, "We've only known each other for a short time. Still lots to learn."

We carried what we needed upstairs. Today was a day of sanding and mudding since we had installed drywall in the kitchen. It was a messy business and after a while of sanding the walls, I turned to look at her. I started to laugh. "You could be Olaf's twin."

A thin layer of white dust covered her face, mask, and hands, and only her eyes peeked out from under white-coated eyelashes. She had donned a baseball cap so her red hair was spared.

She pointed to me. "I think we'd be triplets." She went back to putting what she said was the last layer of mud on the walls. "One more day of sanding and we'll be ready to paint. Have you chosen your colors?"

I put my hands on my hips. "Uh-huh. I can't believe you would ask an interior decorator that question. That was one of the first things I did after buying the place."

"Then we should go get the paint today when we're finished. I also need some border tape and more plastic tarps. I have enough to cover the furniture but not the floors. I don't mind vacuuming the dust up, but I don't want to clean paint off the floors."

"But you're going to sand them."

"Yes, but some paints can leave stains especially if the floors soak it up real good. And these babies are drier than the desert sand."

I chuckled. "Okay. It's a plan. How about going now? We can get the paint, then bring some lunch back and watch a movie?"

She stood and put her hands on her hips. "You really want me to see this movie."

"More like I want to see the movie. I think I need a distraction from life and what better way to do it than to watch a Disney film? Let me get my purse and we can go."

She started down the basement stairs. "I've got to get a few things. I'll be up in a minute. Don't forget to bring the information for the paint colors."

"In my purse." I ran upstairs and located my purse on the table in our bedroom. When I grabbed it, I stopped. "Shit. Damn. Fuck." (I didn't usually use that last word, but I felt it was appropriate.) Holding the small piece of paper, I jogged back downstairs. "Amelia?"

Her happy face appeared in the kitchen door and my face fell. I wondered if she would be as disappointed as I was.

"Yeah. I'm all set."

She walked toward me as my voice rang out in frustration. "Don't bother."

She stopped and looked up at me. It was a few seconds before she asked, "Is everything all right?"

"I forgot I have to be somewhere at one o'clock. Can we do this tomorrow?"

If she was disappointed, I couldn't tell.

"Sure, there's plenty of other things I can work on this afternoon. I'd like to get some minor plumbing done so we can finish that state-of-the-art kitchen that you're never going to cook in. And I heard you say the other day that you needed more closet space." She chuckled as she turned and walked out of my view. "I know the perfect spot for a closet. I'll work on that too."

I sighed. She remembered me telling her I would use the stove for storing sweaters. She listened to me. She made me laugh. It was refreshing—different from what I had become accustomed to. She made me smile and I did so as I prepared to leave for Diane's office.

I hadn't met the woman who was helping my wife stay out of jail, but I was positive there was no way they could pin this on her, so I hoped the money we were spending on Diane Kensington was worth it.

When I walked out the door after shouting goodbye to Amelia, who was busy in the basement banging and drilling, my smile faded.

I could only hope this would all end soon.

I parked in the only parking garage on the north side of the city and walked to Diane's building. Her office was on the third floor and I contemplated taking the stairs. I knew taking my time was avoiding the meeting, but that was stupid because I had already committed to showing up and hell...I was there. I pushed the elevator button for the third floor, sucked in a breath, and stepped inside.

Diane's office took up the entire third level. Oak hardwood floors, neutral wall color, and lots of accents in subtle browns, tans, and blues made the space appear as if she was trying for a homey feel while maintaining a business atmosphere. If that was the case, she erred on the side of too homey.

I found myself at the receptionist's desk staring at a young blond woman who was talking into her headset at the pace of an auctioneer. At that rate, she'd be off the call shortly, so I stood and waited.

When she ended the conversation, she looked up at me, frustration in her eyes and a forced smile on her lips. "Can I help you?"

"I'm here for the meeting with Mary Ellen Montgomery."

She studied me as she said, "You are." It sounded more like a challenge than a confirmation. "And who are you?"

"Ms. Montgomery's wife, Adalyn Pious," I replied in a huff, responding to the receptionist's cool attitude.

Her eyes immediately shifted to look at me and I thought I saw a look of shock and surprise that left as soon as it appeared. "Oh, one moment, please." She pushed a button. "Ms. Kensington, there's an Adalynn Pious here for Ms. Montgomery's meeting." Pause. "Uh-huh. Yes. Okay. I'll let her know."

I couldn't help myself. "Let me know what?"

"They'll be with you shortly. Please have a seat."

I looked at my watch. I was ten minutes early. Damn, so much for taking my time. And why did I have to wait anyway? And I definitely wasn't liking the blond bimbo at the desk who obviously didn't like me either, for whatever reason that might be.

She went back to her work, and I grudgingly took a seat in the brown leather couch that felt more like a wooden bench. Luckily, only five minutes passed when I heard a door open down the hall. M.E. appeared in the waiting area. I stood and took her in my arms, but she gently pushed away from me and to my surprise, glanced at the receptionist. I wondered if the girl behind the desk was another homophobe, so I let it go. I knew my wife was struggling with this visit and I wanted and needed to be here for her.

She turned without a word and I followed her into a meeting room with a long wooden table and matching chairs. There were folders in a neat pile in front of one of the seats. She closed the door and faced me. Then she took my hands in hers.

"I'm sorry, but Diane said you can't be in here."

"Then why did you ask me to come?"

"I thought you could sit in on the meeting, but she said…" M.E.'s eyes roamed the office and then settled on me again. "She said it's not an informational meeting."

"What does that mean?"

"She's not sure, but she has her suspicions."

"Which are?" I was getting angry. I knew I shouldn't, but I couldn't help it.

"That they might have something to incriminate me."

"That's impossible. You didn't do it."

"I know. I just have to wait and see what they've got. Will you wait for me? You could go shopping or to a restaurant on the main drag. You've wanted to do that. I can call you when it's over and then you can meet me here. That way you won't be far away." She wrung her hands, as if she needed to get every drop out of a dishrag. Then she whispered, "In case I need you."

My heart sank with the heavy feeling of seeing her in such a vulnerable state. I took her in my arms, not caring if the homophobic receptionist walked in on us or not. "Of course. I'll check out some shops and get a coffee. Promise you'll call me as soon as it's done."

"I will." She kissed me quickly and then opened the door for me. "See you soon."

"Yeah, sure." I squeezed her hand. "Good luck, babe."

Her smile was weak, and I left not knowing what else to say or do.

This time I took the stairs and I hurried to the street that was lined with shops and restaurants. It ran east/west and was closed to traffic for a few blocks, allowing pedestrians to stroll leisurely down the main drag and window-shop or simply sit on a bench and take in the ambiance of the small city.

A huge part of me wanted to go home—to work on my future even if the current project was the kitchen. To be with someone who made me feel good, who didn't make me feel like we were always in turmoil or a state of flux.

Walking down the sidewalk, I didn't feel like shopping, but I forced myself to go into stores and browse, waiting for the text or phone call.

Three hours later, I was sitting in a small coffee shop reading the local newspaper when my phone buzzed. I pulled it out and saw it was my wife.

"Hey, hon? Are you okay?"

"Can you pick me up?"

"I'll be there in ten minutes."

M.E. was pacing back and forth in front of the building when I arrived. She walked with such ferocity, I half expected to see a rut in the cement. When she caught sight of me, she ran and threw her arms around me.

"They have video of Raeann's car in that parking lot before we left. Because of that, I've now become a person of interest. They want me to tell them where I was every minute of every day the week before we left."

I stepped back from her and took her hand, leading her to the parking garage. "You can do that. We can work on it tonight. It was only a few months ago and I'm pretty sure our minds still work fairly well. We'll make a timeline."

She leaned her head on my shoulder. "Thanks, hon."

"By the way, where's your truck?"

"I left it at the college. Diane picked me up before lunch. I can leave it there. I don't mind riding home in your tin can." She flashed a weak smile. "You can take me to work tomorrow."

I squeezed her hand. "Maybe you should take the day off tomorrow."

"I can't. I'm at a crucial part of my research, and I have some classes I have to attend to. Grade time."

"Okay. Let's grab some takeout and go home. We can have a quiet evening and brainstorm the timeline for you."

"Why don't you tell me exactly what was said at the meeting?" I asked on the drive home. "It was pretty long. Did they grill you the whole time?"

"Actually, it was only a little over an hour. I stayed with Diane to go over some things. She tried to help me figure out where I had been and what I had been doing, but I was too upset."

"So, what did they say?"

"They have footage from a person that shows Raeann's car in the lot before we left. They've been searching the area looking for clues. They said they found DNA in her car that doesn't belong to her. They took a sample from me."

"Can they date how old it is? I mean, I wouldn't be surprised if you were in her car. You had an affair with her."

She lifted an eyebrow, clearly disturbed by what I just said. "From what Diane said, if it was in her car, I'm a suspect. It wouldn't matter how old it is."

"Shit. We need to do that timeline. Do you have the dates you need to remember?"

"Diane said to go as far back as a week before we left."

When we arrived home, Amelia's truck was still in the driveway, I pulled onto the grass to go around it and park in front.

"What is she still doing here?"

M.E.'s question was legit since it was past five o'clock, but I hoped the tone she used was merely a result of her fear from being a possible suspect in Raeann's disappearance and subsequent death. And that solidified my decision not to tell her about Amelia and Raeann's sibling bond.

"She's employed by us. Remember? She was working on plumbing in the kitchen and I'm sure she just lost track of time."

"Fine," M.E. mumbled as she got out and slammed the door.

Just as we reached the steps to the front door, it opened and Amelia exited with one of her toolboxes in hand.

"Hey there!"

"How'd it go today?" I asked before M.E. could say anything.

Amelia glanced at my wife and then kept her eyes on me. Her face was bright and cheerful, but she stiffened when she spoke. "It was a good day. You should put our order in for the rest of the appliances we talked about. I think we're ready to paint in the kitchen. We can get the paint tomorrow, like you said."

Her last sentence sounded like a challenge—to my wife—and I felt heat from M.E.'s body despite the fact she stood a foot away from me.

Then Amelia did something that was sure to make M.E.'s blood boil, resulting in a catastrophic jealous explosion. She winked at me as she walked past, making sure her steps were hurried and she would be far enough away from us for any physical retribution from my wife. She called goodbye as she opened the door to her truck.

I turned to look at her and her smile was filled with…Well, I wasn't sure. I thought I saw desire, then a flicker of challenge, as if to say "I will expose you for who you are." I was pretty sure that part of her smile was not for me. At least I hoped not.

I returned her smile and watched as she shut the door and backed out of the driveway. Then I turned to see the pot ready to boil over.

CHAPTER SEVENTEEN

M.E. stormed through the front door. She spun and faced me as I closed it behind me. "Is that what you do while I'm working hard at my job and trying to stay out of jail?"

"If you mean am I working on refurbishing the house, then yes. Anything else would be a no."

"I don't think so. I saw the way she looked at you. *Winked* at you. Hell, she practically had spittle dribbling out the side of her mouth!"

I took a small step backward, realizing the door was behind me. "Jesus, M. There's nothing going on. She works for me. I've been helping her get this done quicker so I can start my business. It's been good for me because I'm learning how to build things and fix things so I can do it myself. You've been able to live your life. To work. I want that too. I miss it, so this has been good for me."

She took a step toward me and said in a low growl, "That's not what I saw."

I sidestepped her and headed toward the kitchen. I heard her hard footsteps on the wooden floors behind me. With each heavy footfall, I cringed, and I felt a bit afraid. I thought I knew who my wife was, but this, this was something I had never seen before. There had always been a certain amount of jealousy that coursed through one of her veins, but it was the "teasing" kind, warning me to stop or I'd get the "mad" kind.

At this moment, M.E. was past that kind, and I was getting nervous about the kind I was about to get. I had to nip it in the bud. Once I was in the kitchen, I walked over to a makeshift cupboard where we kept plates, silverware, pots and pans, bowls—and knives. I leaned against it with my arms crossed.

I didn't know if my wife figured out what I was thinking, but she stopped at the doorway.

"I am not having an affair." I took a risk and added, "You were the one that had an affair. Remember?"

Her mouth twisted and her eyes roamed the kitchen. Her chest expanded as she took in deep breaths followed by continual swallowing, as if something was stuck in her throat. Maybe it was the words she wanted to say and I was glad at that moment that she was trying to keep them down.

But she didn't succeed.

"You spend every day with that bitch. You two giggle, exchange glances, go to lunch and God knows what else. I don't even want to think what else," she sneered.

I tensed. My risk hadn't paid off. It was only making her more upset as her unfounded suspicions took hold of her mind.

"You're being ridiculous. Amelia and I are only coworkers, friends. That's it. End of statement."

M.E. marched up to me and did something I never expected her to do in my wildest dreams. She raised her arm and slapped me in the face. Hard. "Don't lie to me."

The horror of my wife's actions did not produce fear in me. Instead, anger bubbled to the surface. My hand immediately went to my face, hoping it would dull the pain that exploded in my cheek, mouth, and eye.

We faced each other for a moment as the implications of her action played out in my mind, and from the look on her face, was also playing out in hers. Her eyes were fixed on me and her lips spread in a hard, thin line. I watched her facial muscles twitch as if a myriad of emotions were fighting each other to reach the surface. I had no idea what was going through her mind, what she would say or do, but I could tell she was struggling with her next words and/or her next action. We stood motionless, face-to-face, our eyes not leaving each other.

I reached my other hand back to the drawer that I knew held the knives, keeping my eyes on her. I pulled the drawer open and said, "I will never let you do that again." I knew M.E. was aware of what was in that drawer. I hoped she got the message.

"Oh my God, oh my God. Babe, I'm so sorry. I didn't mean to do that. I'm just so afraid of this whole mess with Raeann. It's got me doing crazy things." The words fell out of her mouth in a crazed rambling.

Slowly, I pushed the door shut and then walked to the freezer. I took an ice bag out that I had purchased after the first time I hit my fingers with a hammer. The whole time I kept my eyes on her. "You can sleep in the spare room tonight. Don't you dare come near me." I went upstairs as she called me to come back followed by uncontrollable sobbing. I felt nothing except the pain in my face. After locking the bedroom door, I lay on the bed and fell asleep, never waking until the following morning.

I stumbled into the bathroom to look in the small mirror hanging above the pedestal sink that was useless for two women who need counter space for their toiletries. I wasn't surprised to see swelling and bruising. I hoped makeup would cover it.

I dressed and before I went downstairs to get something to eat, I stopped by the closed door of the spare bedroom and listened. There was no noise. Either M.E. was asleep or she was already downstairs. My stomach rumbled from the lack of food.

I lifted my head, preparing to face her in the kitchen, but when I got there, she was nowhere to be seen. After a sigh of relief, I made some tea and heated up leftovers from the food we had brought home the previous evening. M.E. must have put it in the refrigerator at some point. I noticed she had also eaten some of it. Knowing the way I felt, I was surprised she could eat anything.

I decided to work on my business plan until Amelia arrived.

Amelia.

She couldn't see me like this, especially if M.E. was here. I wasn't sure I'd be able to stop a female cat fight. I found my purse in the living room. My phone and a folded piece of paper sat on top.

My mouth went dry knowing, *knowing* it was a note from my wife. I sat down and opened it.

Addy,

I'm sorry for last night. I'm under so much stress. I didn't wake you to take me to work, so instead, I called a coworker. I'll be home for dinner tonight. I hope we can talk and spend some time together.

I love you, M.E.

I ran up to her room to make sure she was gone. The spare room was empty, the gray sheets on the lone bed rumpled. I closed the door and went back downstairs, debating what I wanted to do when the front door opened.

"Hey, girl, you ready to go get some pa…?" Amelia stopped and stared at me. "What happened?"

I took the last few steps at a hurried pace and walked into her open arms. I didn't cry. I had no more left in me, but what I did need was the warm hug that I knew she would give me.

"I thought about telling you I walked into a wall because after working with me for the last several weeks and seeing how clumsy I am, you'd believe it."

"But that's not the case, is it?" she asked quietly.

"No." I pulled away from her. "How about a cup of coffee?"

She gently cupped my chin and examined my face. "That looks like it really hurts. You should have some ice on it."

I went to the kitchen. "I've only got one ice bag. I had to put it back in the freezer this morning. It should be pretty hard by now." After I prepared two Keurig cups of coffee, I got the ice bag. I added a bit of sugar and creamer, picked up my spoon and stirred, and stirred, and stirred.

"You going to tell me what happened?"

I sighed. "I think you know."

"Why did she do it?"

I cocked my head and gave her an expression that asked, *Are you kidding?*

"We didn't do anything."

"You winked at me. We appear closer than friends—the smiling, giggling, the happy, friendly way we are with each other. She doesn't like it and it pisses her off."

She hit the table with the palm of her hand and rolled her eyes. "Oh, come on, now. That's what friends do."

I took a sip of my coffee. "Normal friends, yes. But not her friends," I answered, my words dripping with sarcasm.

"No, her friends just sleep with her." She slammed her mouth shut and then was silent for a few moments. "I'm sorry for that." She got up and went outside, appearing in the kitchen a few minutes later with a manila envelope in her hand. "I'm not sure this is the time to give you this, but you asked me to do it. David gave it to me last night. He said this should be all you need to answer the questions you have."

I raised my eyebrows. "Yeah? What questions are those?"

"Just look at the information. I'll be in the basement finishing up some electrical. Come get me if you still want to go get paint. Or if you need me." She left me and went downstairs.

I stared at the envelope that she had set on the table. Did I want to know what David had found? For years, I wondered where my wife was in the evenings she didn't come home until midnight. Why hadn't I simply asked?

Because I didn't want to know the specifics. I was afraid of the answers. I always knew something wasn't right. I always knew my wife was far—very far—from perfect. I just never wanted to know why. Now, lying on the table in front of me was the answer to the one question I avoided for many years. Who was she really?

My wife had slapped me. Physically assaulted me. I put my hand to the tender side of my face and swallowed hard. Then I picked up the envelope. After turning it over again and again, I finally unclasped the flap and pulled out what was inside. I began to shuffle through the papers, glancing quickly at each. Copies of two rental agreements stared back at me. One was for an apartment in San Francisco. The other was for an apartment in Ithaca, both signed by Mary Ellen Montgomery. Behind these were two photographs of buildings. I turned them over to see each was labeled as to which apartment it was. The next picture stood out like a flashlight beam piercing a dark night.

"Fuck!" I slammed the papers and photos on the table.

"What is it?" I heard Amelia call as she ran up the stairs and stood in the kitchen doorway.

I held up the photograph. "This is the lawyer's secretary. I met her yesterday. Now I know why she was such an ass to me."

Amelia shook her head and sat down.

"Have you looked at any of this?"

"It's not for me to look at. If you want to share it with me, I will sit and read and listen to you. That's up to you."

I pushed a few of the papers over to her as I continued to study the pictures and peruse a few other documents. When I couldn't look at them anymore, I set them down on the table and looked at Amelia. I wanted to run from the pity that had turned her usually bright green eyes to the color of muddied grass.

"I think I always knew in the back of my mind she was having sex with other women. I just never considered there would be more than one. But after…your sister, what you told me…Whatever she's researching, she believes it will repair her reputation in the academic world once again. If they know what her research is, how can that even happen?"

"I don't know," Amelia whispered. "But how can you even consider staying with a woman who hit you?" Then her voice got louder, harsher, angrier. "Who treats you like a piece of meat—like one of her research subjects?"

I glared at her. "She doesn't treat me like one of her research subjects," I shot back. I took a deep breath. "She hasn't always been that way. I wouldn't have stayed if our relationship wasn't good." I turned away. "It's just not good anymore."

"Did you know she had an apartment?"

"Nope. Had no idea."

"Do you think she had one in San Francisco?"

I sat back down. "Never thought about it."

"Until now?"

"Yeah, until now."

"The report says she takes women there. It sounds like that's where she does her research."

I dropped my head in my hands. "God, this is sick. Worse than I ever thought it would be." A thought struck me and I looked up at Amelia. "How did David find all this out?"

"I told you. He's a good detective. Knowing him, he followed M.E., observed her at the school. He looks like a college kid. He probably saw her hanging out with women—maybe one more than another. He might have talked to them. He's a good talker and a good listener. He knows how to interrogate nicely to get the information he wants."

And then it hit me. I wasn't the only one disturbed by what my wife was doing. Amelia was finding out what my wife had done to her sister. I knew that was true when she asked me, "What do you want to do about it?"

I stared at her. "I'm not sure what you mean."

She started to collect the papers off of the table. "Do you want to go to the apartment? Catch her in the act?" She held a handful of papers in the air. "Do you want to wait until she gets home and confront her with all of this?" Then she stood and placed them back on the table. She sighed heavily. "There's something else you need to see. I wasn't going to show you because you didn't ask for it."

"What is it?"

"Some information he got without permission from Diane Kensington's secretary's…off her desk when she stepped away."

I rolled my eyes as I searched for a picture on the table. I showed her. "Her secretary."

"Yes. Melissa. I thought…rather he thought…you might want this information. As I said before, I didn't look at or read anything. He just briefed me on what this particular piece of information was about, so I don't know the specifics."

"And what is it about?"

"The results of yesterday's inquiry with the San Francisco detective."

"How did Melissa get this information?"

"Probably the same way David acquired it. By snapping a photo on his camera when she was away from her desk."

"Did she steal it to protect my wife or to turn on her? God, if they were fucking…" I looked at Amelia. "Then why would she want to turn on my wife?"

"Most likely because Mary Ellen did what she always does. She used Melissa and was probably going to discard her like she did with Raeann."

I waited for her to continue. When she didn't, I said, "So, M.E. told Melissa she was leaving me."

Amelia cringed. "Yes. Your wife told Melissa that you two were separated and heading for a divorce."

I swallowed. "It sure seems like you know a lot for *not* looking at any of this." My eyes dropped to the mess of papers strewn about the tabletop.

"If you do read this, you should destroy it afterward or hide it really well."

I extended my hand.

"It's in the truck. I didn't bring it in just in case…Well, I'll go get it." She scurried out of the house and was back again in a minute. Then she handed me another official-looking envelope.

I took it. I looked at Amelia. She smiled wanly at me and started to leave the room.

"You can stay," I said.

She sat down as I opened the envelope and took out copies of the transcripts for M.E.'s meeting with the San Francisco police, Detective Joseph Remming. I would have to do some of my own research on this person.

He grilled my wife with tactical precision. Reading it, I felt like I was in the room as the questions were thrust at my wife at the speed of a racing train never giving her time to explain herself. She appeared to trip over her words, and who wouldn't with such an onslaught of interrogation?

I jumped to the end where there was a one-page conclusion. Most of it I already knew from speaking with M.E. The police determined the date and time of when Raeann's car was abandoned in the parking lot. It was in the middle of the night on July fifth. That was two days before we left for California. Therefore, she was a suspect. They would give my wife a few days to come up with her alibis, proof of her whereabouts for every minute of the week prior to when we left for New York. They, of course, would do their own research and then match the results of their investigation with her proof and alibis. It didn't take a rocket scientist to know if it didn't match up, M.E. was in trouble.

They also found my wife's DNA inside Raeann's car, but they couldn't determine how long it had been there, despite my wife informing them she hadn't been near or even seen Raeann since they settled the case. However, the fact that it was there added to their suspicion.

I couldn't read anymore, so I thrust the paper into Amelia's hand. "I can't do this. Just tell me what it says."

Amelia read for a few moments and then began to summarize. "It says someone came forward with a video of a woman who appeared to be looking for something inside Raeann's car. The person was videoing her friends and caught it in the background just inside the frame. The image was the back of a woman who was approximately the same height and stature as your wife in blue jeans and a dark-brown jacket, but not much else could be made out as the woman wore a dark-brown baseball cap and was partially hidden by the car. The video was taken the day of July sixth."

The next thing they would do would be to get a search warrant to go through my wife's clothing looking for the blue jeans, a dark-brown jacket and a dark-brown baseball cap. They wouldn't find any of that clothing here. M.E. not only didn't own anything like that, she would never be caught dead in it. I also knew we would be able to account for most of the time the week before we left. Most of it, but not all of it.

I sighed. "It's all circumstantial evidence. But I've heard of people being convicted on less. She didn't do it," I said with conviction.

Amelia started to say something, hesitated and then said, "Are you sure? Absolutely positive? I mean you had no idea she was having sex with students claiming it to be for research. You had no idea she had an apartment that she used for her sexual encounters. What makes you think she didn't kill my sister?"

I felt anger rise in my throat along with the bile that was a result of admitting the atrocities my wife was committing and had kept from me...for how long?

"She's not a killer. She's a sex addict. That part doesn't surprise me. We've always had a very physical relationship and a lot of the time it was initiated by her. I never thought much of it until we moved here."

"Why?"

"Because she seemed...Oh, this is uncomfortable. She seemed hungrier for it than she usually was. And it often felt more like wild, savage sex than making love."

"Maybe that was because of Raeann. Maybe that was how she dealt with what she did."

I glared at Amelia. "She didn't kill Raeann."

Amelia's voice rose. "How can you be sure? Look in the mirror, Addy. You're telling me sex between you two has been animalistic and now you've got a bruised face. I've heard her yelling at you and I've seen her jealousy. How. Can. You. Be. Sure?"

I broke down and cried. "I can't," I whispered through sobs.

Amelia jumped up and took me in her arms. "Then I ask again. What do you want to do about it?"

CHAPTER EIGHTEEN

"You're wrong, you know."

We were sitting on the couch having a beer. Strike that. Several beers. At either end of the plush, microfiber sofa we each tucked our legs underneath us. Our bodies were inches away from each other and I could feel the pheromones between us heating the temperature in the room.

"Wrong about what?" I asked after a long swig.

"It's not enough to convict her. She'll get away with it. You'll be stuck with her and you could be next."

"She wouldn't hurt me. Besides, I can divorce her."

"You really think she's going to let you divorce her? God, Addy, open your eyes. The woman is out of control. She needs to be stopped before she hurts someone else." Amelia took an even longer swig of her beer, then added quietly, "I don't want it to be you." Her eyes were shimmering like emeralds and I could see the emotion in them. "I really care about you."

I didn't know how to respond. What to do? But she was right. I knew deep inside M.E. would never divorce me. I also recognized that she was getting out of control. She had never hit me before until last night, and I wasn't sure I would be able to defend myself against her. I never felt more like her slave than I did now.

Amelia leaned toward me, her mouth still, but her eyes studying my body. I didn't pull away; instead I waited for her to come closer. And she did. Slowly with balletic movements, her lips found mine. She kissed me lightly, her eyes open the whole time, as if waiting for my reaction so that she could respond in kind.

I didn't kiss her back, but I allowed her to kiss me. She ended the kiss with a light peck and then sat back. "I'm sorry. I shouldn't have done that."

"Don't be sorry," I said, smiling. "It was nice. I'm just—"

"I know. But I needed you to know how I feel. I'll help you. I'll stand by you. Whatever you need." She took my hands in hers. "You just can't live like this."

"No, I can't, but I don't know what I can do about it. I can't leave her. She won't ever let me go."

Amelia took another swallow of beer. She sucked in a breath as if tentative about her next words. "What if she were to leave?"

My laugh was that of a defeated person who knew better than to believe in something that just wasn't going to happen.

"I can make it happen," she said.

I stared at her. "What do you mean?"

"Do you want her gone?"

"What kind of question is that? I don't know. Of course, I'd like it if she'd just up and leave, send me divorce papers and move into her apartment with that whore Melissa. I'd be grateful to the bitch to take her off my hands, but that's not going to happen. I'd give anything to go back to San Francisco—without her." I shook my head and tears formed in my eyes. "I can't believe I just said that."

Amelia sat forward with her elbows on her knees, the beer bottle turning in her hands, condensation from the glass dripping down her fingers. "She could disappear," she said in a barely audible whisper.

My head snapped in her direction. "No," I said sternly. "I can't do that. That's not me. I can't."

"You don't have to. You just told me it's what you want."

"No, I didn't. I told you I'd like her to divorce me and leave me alone, not for you to make her disappear."

"She killed my sister. I was supposed to protect her and I didn't because your wife had her claws so deep in her, Raeann couldn't get away. There was nothing I could do to save her. Now I can."

"You can't save her. She's dead."

"I can save her soul. I can revenge her, and I can keep you from the same fate."

I got up from the couch and took another two beers out of the refrigerator. When I handed one to her, I said, "Let's go for a walk."

We went to the backyard and wandered into the woods. Our pace was slow, almost deliberate. Then Amelia grabbed me, turned me around and planted a very demanding kiss on my lips. I felt a different kind of desire than I ever had with M.E. It bore into me with need, yet gentleness and…protection. And because I felt protected, I kissed her back. And then I jumped away from her and threw my hands to my lips.

"Amelia, I can't do this. I'm married. I won't be like her. I won't cheat on my wife. I'm sorry." I turned and ran to the house. I paced back and forth in the living room trying to think of what I would say to her when she walked in. But she never came into the house. Instead, I heard her truck start.

I hurried to the front door and opened it in time to see her backing out. When she was on the road, she looked at me, her smile bitter and sad. She put her hand up and performed a small beauty queen wave. I waved back. I picked up my phone and texted her. *Paint tomorrow. Okay?*

There was no reply. Of course, there wouldn't be. She was driving. At least I hoped that was the reason. So, I continued to check my phone for an answer until I heard a truck engine pull into the driveway. I ran to the door, swinging it open ready to say, "Didn't you get my text? We're painting tomorrow." I stopped dead in my tracks and closed my mouth when I recognized it was my wife's truck and not Amelia's.

My shoulders slumped and I went into the kitchen to prepare myself a cup of coffee. At first, I thought of making it to mask the smell of beer, but then I didn't care. Now I just needed to be clear in my head for whatever and whoever walked through the front door next.

As it brewed, I quickly picked up the papers and stuffed them into my briefcase. I couldn't keep them there. I didn't trust my wife now. Thank God, she hadn't come home before we returned from the woods. I would have to find a better hiding place before she went snooping. There was never any reason for her to do so, but I no longer knew the woman who would walk through the door at any moment.

It was several minutes before M.E. came in. When she did, she walked slowly, with apprehension. Good, I thought, maybe she's a little scared of me. *She damn well should be.* Who was I kidding? What was I really going to do?

I sat at the table sipping my coffee, not meeting her gaze, and waiting. I looked at my watch and I realized I hadn't had lunch. That thought made my stomach rumble, and the beer headache that was forming in my temples started to pound.

My wife made herself a coffee and sat down not saying a word.

Finally, I couldn't take it anymore. "You're home early."

"I took your advice. I called a sub to take over my afternoon classes. I stopped at Diane's office to discuss what comes next and then came straight here."

Oh, you mean you didn't bother to stop at your apartment and service Melissa or some other college student?

She looked at the side of my face that was still gaining color from her slap the previous night. "I'm so sorry. I don't know what got into me."

I took another sip of coffee and peered over the top of my mug. *You were an out-of-control asshole.*

"Can you ever forgive me?"

That seems to be all I do lately. I continued to stare.

"Addy, say something. Please. I can't take this silence. I need to know what you're thinking, feeling."

You don't want to know. I'm thinking I'm done with you and your lies and your out-of-wedlock escapades.

"Please, Addy. You're my wife. I love you."

That one made me spit out my coffee. I grabbed a napkin and wiped my face and then the spittle on the table. Despite the fact I loved coffee, I hated the smell of it on my hands so I got up and washed them. With my back to her, I said, "I'm not sure what you expect of me and I'm not sure what I'm willing to give."

"I expect you to be my wife."

I turned around to face her, nauseated from the lack of food, too much beer, and my wife's words. "I am in name and on the marriage license. The rest is yet to be decided."

"Addy, I need you," she pleaded.

"I thought that too. And then I found out about Raeann." I watched her shoulders slump, and before she could say anything, I added, "And Melissa. And only you know how many others."

Now, she snapped into military attention mode. Her eyes grew larger and they appeared cold, as if iced over. She stumbled on her words. "Wh…What are you talking about?"

"Are you going to lie to me again? Probably not a good idea since I know it all."

"Know what?" she challenged.

I started to leave the kitchen. "Everything you've been doing for, well, I don't know for how long. You've made your bed, M.E. Now you're going to have to lie in it."

As I walked by her, she grabbed my arm. She only pulled hard enough to stop me. I waited.

"You best let go."

"You don't know anything. Give me time to explain, to fix all this. I love you. You love me. You can't walk out on that."

I yanked my arm away. "Right now, I'm only walking out of the kitchen."

I picked up my briefcase and walked upstairs. I had to hide the papers quickly, and an idea of where to keep them came to me. I listened for her footsteps. Relieved I didn't hear her following me, I shut and locked the bedroom door. Then I sat on the bed and realized how sad it was that I had to lock the door of the bedroom I shared with my wife—from my wife. I surveyed the room. The flowered wallpaper on the plaster walls was old, dirty, and tearing in places. But the walls, like the stained and worn wooden floors held stories of others who'd slept in this room. When the walls were replaced and the floors refinished, those stories would be sealed forever. I hoped ours would be too.

A few hours later I went downstairs and found M.E. on the couch sleeping, which was odd. She never took afternoon naps. She was never home long enough to take one. Even on holidays and weekends she was always on the move.

I left her a note saying I was going out to pick up dinner and would be back within the hour. I hoped she would join me. When I returned, the lights were dimmed in the house and I found her in the kitchen with a candle on the table, two place settings and a bottle of wine.

I wasn't surprised and I wasn't impressed, but I obliged her and only for the moment.

We ate the Italian meals I brought home. I had a glass of wine, she had three full glasses—emptied the bottle. And despite every subtle hint I could come up with that she needed to pace herself, she downed every glass. She told me about her classes and the college, which she hadn't done in a long time. Not surprising, she stayed off the subject of her research.

At one point she got up to get another bottle of wine, but she stumbled and fell against the table. I jumped up, righted her and took the bottle, setting it on the table.

"I think you ought to go to bed. You could use a good night's sleep."

She looked into my eyes, hanging on to me and said, "Will shou helper me uptairs?" The slurred words didn't hide the lust in her eyes.

I sighed. "Sure. Come on. I'll clean up after."

She threw her arm around my shoulders and leaned against me. I got her to the stairs and took her other hand, placing it on the railing. We lumbered up, all the while she tried to plant kisses on my neck. I pulled away, but she held on, her lips making weird smacking noises. Some of the steps creaked, a result of untreated, dried-out wood, and I was afraid our weight might cause one to crack. The only thought going through my head was I couldn't wait until Amelia showed me how to fix and refinish them.

When I finally got her to the top, I turned toward the spare bedroom. M.E.'s body stopped suddenly, making her feel like a stone pillar.

"Where are we going?" Realizing I wasn't taking her to the master bedroom appeared to have sobered her up instantly, but her surprised reaction allowed me to step away from her.

"I'm taking you to bed."

She pointed to the master bedroom. "That's my bedroom."

Rather than argue with her, I immediately decided to let her have the master bedroom. I would wait until she fell asleep and then retire to the spare room. Upon seeing she was heading to the bedroom she wanted to sleep in, she regressed to her drunken stupor. At this point, I had no idea which of her physical states was the real one and which was fake. How many other times had M.E. lied to me. Tricked me? Deceived me? I realized in that moment I didn't care. I just wanted to get her into bed, alone, and get out of the room.

When we reached the bed, she plopped down with her fingers grasping my shirt. She pulled me with her. She was fast. Her lips found mine and their intention was undeniable. She fumbled with my clothes, but I kept pulling back and twisting this way and that to stay dressed.

Finally, she bolted to a sitting position. "What the hell, Addy!"

I stood and backed away. "There is no mood here. No desire. No nothing."

"But I want you. I need you," she pleaded in a pathetic tone.

"Well, M.E., tonight we're going to do what I need. You're going to get a good night's sleep and we're going to talk about everything tomorrow."

"There's nothing to talk about," she whined. Then she shifted to look sexy, inviting. "Besides, I'm not tired. I took that long nap."

"And a few minutes ago you were drop-down drunk, that is, if you really were. If you want sex, go find Melissa. I'm sure she'll service you. I have some work to do. If we both get a good night sleep, we can get that timeline done. Maybe talk about things."

Her expression soured. "I think the only important thing is that we are married. We love each other. We stick by each other through better or worse."

I picked up my work bag, phone, and purse and walked over to the door. "We seem to have the worse down pretty good."

Her smile was small and unconvincing. "And we'll get through it. Then it will be done and all we'll have left is the better, the good parts of life, of our marriage."

"Get some sleep."

I closed the door half expecting her to run after me and pull me back in or yell after me. But only silence came from the room. I sighed heavily and went into the spare room. I put clean sheets on the bed, and it wasn't long before I fell asleep. It wasn't long after that my phone dinged with a text from Amelia.

I hope everything is okay. I drove by in the afternoon and saw M.E.'s truck. Are you sure you want to paint tomorrow?

Panic struck me. She was going to back off. I would lose the only other person I knew in this godforsaken, backwoods, empty, too-far-away-from-any-major-city town.

M.E. wasn't feeling well, so she came home early. Absolutely I want to paint. We will need to go get paint. Can you be here at ten in the morning?

Sure. If anything changes, let me know.

THANK YOU!!!!! Will do. Have a good night.

You too.

Relief washed over me. It would be easier to deal with M.E. if Amelia was around. I knew it might look like I was using her, but we had bonded over my stone house. I wasn't stupid, though. Now, I was painfully aware of the two facts that would make my relationship with Amelia like walking a tightrope. First, Raeann was her stepsister. Second, I was pretty sure Amelia had feelings for me. Or...I sat up. *Is she using me to get to my wife?* For the revenge she sought over Raeann's death at the hands of my wife? I worried I couldn't trust anyone.

I set my alarm for seven in the morning and planned on waking M.E. early to make the timeline over coffee. It had to be done. The lawyer needed it to help prove her innocence. She was still my wife and I would not be put in the position where everyone thought I was married to a murderer. It wouldn't just ruin M.E. It would ruin me. Worse, if word got out that she was running psychological, sexual experiments for research that no one was going to acknowledge, it would be a double whammy.

I had hidden the report David supplied me in a safe deposit box at a bank. I stopped there when I picked up dinner for us the night before. I had to decide what I was going to do with the information, if anything. The problem left was that Amelia knew the truth and so did David. Did he have copies? That fact alone could make the decision for me.

I needed Amelia.

I fell asleep once again but I was restless. I awoke several times, my mind fighting the much-needed sleep. I finally dragged myself out of bed at five-thirty and took a shower. I took my time reveling in the warm water as I reviewed again and again the different scenarios that could happen with my wife. I wondered if we'd be able to get through all this and find ourselves on the side of happiness.

The water turned cold, as if a sign that it would never happen. Maybe I could help my wife to beat the murder charges that seemed likely to come her way, but I couldn't help our marriage. At some point, I needed to end it.

I spent the last bit of time before the seven o'clock hour arrived making an Excel spreadsheet for the week prior to our leaving San Francisco. I filled in the times and places when M.E. was with me. The times she was off on her own she would have to fill in herself. I also realized that I would most likely have to provide an alibi for those times as well. I remembered some of the places she told me she had gone, but I wouldn't fill those in. I needed to hear it from her. I would, however, make a list of alibis for myself during those times.

I walked upstairs to the master bedroom to wake my wife.

CHAPTER NINETEEN

Nine o'clock and four cups of coffee later, we finished the Excel spreadsheet. I stared at my computer screen, willing it to fill in the blanks. There were too many, and I was afraid my wife had dug a hole she couldn't climb out of. Despite everything that had happened, I didn't want her to go to jail for something I believed she didn't do. She was a cheater, not a killer. What bothered me was that she couldn't—or wouldn't—account for the empty time slots.

"Look, M.E. I already know you've cheated on me. So if these times you say you can't remember are times you were cheating, so be it. You have to fill them in. You need their alibis or you could rot in a jail cell for the rest of your life. Please."

"Can you print this out for me?"

"Of course."

"I'll take it to Diane and see what she has to say about it. I need to get going or I'll be late for class."

I pushed the print button then got up to get the copy for her. I knew what she was going to do. She would fill it in without me being able to see what she was entering into the blank time slots. If I didn't see it, I couldn't accuse her of anything or add it to the list of cheating I already knew about. And even though filling it in without me seeing it would deny the San Francisco detectives ammunition against her for a murder wrap, it would also deny me ammunition for a divorce. But it didn't matter. I already had enough.

And then it hit me. When had I become so suspicious of my wife? I couldn't answer that, except to wonder why I had become that way.

I stood behind her holding the sheet of paper against my chest. "You know, it doesn't really matter what you did during those times you won't account for. I already know you cheated at least twice on me. That's enough for a divorce."

"You're not going to divorce me," she said, not so much matter-of-factly, but it sounded more like a statement of power and control.

"I will, if I want to. I never signed on for a cheating wife."

M.E. slowly pushed her chair back and faced me. "And I didn't sign on for a self-absorbed, money-hungry, social-climbing sycophant." She glared at me. The anger in her eyes looked as if at any moment she would shoot lightning bolts from her pupils.

Shocked beyond belief, my jaw dropped. Never had she verbally assaulted me like that. She was always chasing after me to get me in bed, always complimenting me on my looks and my sexual skills.

A part of me was scared of her, but it was a very small part. More than anything, I was angry. How dare she? And that's exactly what I said.

"How dare you say those things to me! Through all of this, I have stuck by your side and not once said anything remotely cruel to you. I have never belittled you or insulted you!"

Her face came within inches of mine. Her eyes darted up and down my face and then finally settled on mine. "Threatening to divorce me is all that and more," she hissed.

"Hey, everything okay here?"

My heart sunk when I heard the familiar voice. Now was not a good time for Amelia to show up.

Without shifting her gaze, my wife said, "Aww, here's the skank. And you said you weren't cheating. Really, my love? She's here all day and even has a key. You're just better at hiding it."

I couldn't believe this was my wife speaking. "Nothing is going on between us," I whispered to her, but Amelia heard me.

"She's right, Mary Ellen. Nothing is going on between us other than a friendship and a working relationship. That's all."

M.E. looked around me. "Of course you would say that. You're fucking my wife."

Amelia took a step toward us and M.E. responded with a threatening step of her own after she pushed me aside.

I saw Amelia's eyes flare.

I quickly positioned myself in between them. "Let's not act like two hormonal males. Fighting is not the answer."

"And just what is the answer?" Amelia said, keeping her eyes on my wife.

"To fire your ass," M.E. said before I could respond. "You need to leave my house."

"It's not just your house," Amelia tossed back at her.

"Stop it, both of you." I thrust the paper to M.E. "You should get to your classes and you need to get this paper to Diane. We'll talk when you get home. That is, if you're coming home tonight." I knew it was stupid to goad her, but I was consumed with anger. She could explode at any moment, but she didn't.

She ripped the paper out of my hand and said in a hushed voice, "Yes, I'll be home." Then she looked back at Amelia. "This wench better not be here."

When she walked by Amelia, she jabbed her with her shoulder. I waited for the door to slam, ready to tackle Amelia if she decided to chase after M.E. Even after the sound of the door closing, I still remained motionless until the noise of the truck engine roared to life and the tires squealed on the asphalt road.

I began to pace the kitchen. "Shit, shit, shit." I glared at Amelia. "You shouldn't have pushed her."

Amelia approached me, but stopped when she got close enough to touch me, as if debating what the right thing to do would be.

I made the decision for her by sitting at the table. I motioned to M.E.'s chair and she begrudgingly sat down.

"How much of it did you hear?"

"Pretty much everything."

"Why didn't you go back outside or stay outside when you heard us?"

Amelia looked down at the table and traced her index finger around a coffee spill. "I was worried she'd hurt you. She's already hit you once, and she sure was building up to it again." She paused a moment. "I wouldn't be surprised if you said she'd already hit you again before I arrived."

"She didn't." I wanted to say she wouldn't hurt me, but we already knew that wasn't true.

Amelia's palm slapped the table. "God, Addy, she's already hit you, and she hasn't just hurt you physically, but socially, professionally, and emotionally as well." She looked up at me. "Should I go on?"

"No," I exhaled.

"Why do you put up with it?"

"I'm married to her. What do you want me to do?"

"I told you. Divorce her ass. Get away from her and go on with your life with someone who would love and take care of you. Not use you."

"You mean someone like you?"

"Would that be so bad?"

I couldn't answer. I really didn't know the answer. Instead, I said, "We need to get paint. I need to do something…else."

Amelia's eyes softened. "There are other things we could do."

That one suggestion made bile from the morning's coffee start to make its way up my throat. I swallowed hard to keep it down. "Painting is what I need," I mumbled. "Be right back." I ran upstairs and into the bathroom. It was bad enough I had a wife who seemed to just want me for my physical attributes and sexual prowess. Now here was another. I thought of her as my friend, my coworker. Nothing more.

She wanted more. I saw it in her eyes, heard it in her voice. I couldn't cross that line. Not now. Maybe not ever, but if I told her how I felt, I wasn't sure what that would do to our working relationship.

I splashed cold water on my face, grabbed my purse and then ran downstairs to where she waited in the foyer. I forced a smile on my face. "You ready?"

She opened the door and motioned for me to exit. "Off to the paint store," she replied, an amused expression on her face.

When she pulled out of the driveway, the only thing I said to her was, "I loved her. I still do."

She didn't answer, making the drive to the big box home store and the walk inside as silent as a monastery during prayer. When we reached the paint section, I pulled out the sample cards I had taken weeks ago and laid four of them on the counter.

"I'll go get the ceiling paint. Meet you back here," Amelia informed me.

I put my order in for satin finish and leaned against the counter while I waited. I watched as people milled about looking for the items they needed for home repairs, building, and renovations.

This was all so new to me. In San Francisco, we had the money to hire people to do these things. My life was one of a socialite—parties, dinners, meetings, and redecorating affluent people's homes, not my own.

How did I get here? No, strike that. I knew how I got here. How was I going to get out?

I noticed Amelia toting a five-gallon bucket of paint down one of the aisles. Her biceps tightened and bulged under the strain of the weight.

"Maybe a cart is in order?" I grinned.

"I can carry this," she answered, setting it on the floor.

"Believe me, I can see that. But there will be four other cans of paint and I can only carry two."

She leaned into me and murmured, "Wuss." Then she smiled and said, "I'll be right back."

Within minutes, she returned with a cart and lifted the five-gallon container, making it look like me lifting a one-gallon can of paint. I rolled my eyes and turned to the counter. Amelia stood next to me.

"I'm sorry," I whispered. "I'm sorry for my wife's actions and what she said this morning."

"I've got a hard shell." She shifted her weight as if uneasy about the conversation. "Do you really want to stay with her? I'm so afraid for you. She's out of control. Can't you see that?"

The paint associate came over with the first can. He opened the lid, put a spot of paint on top of it and then sealed it.

"Not here," I hissed.

Amelia stiffened. I hated scolding her but I sure didn't want my business known in a home improvement store filled with everyone in Ithaca who had a home improvement project.

I plucked the first can off the counter and put it in the cart. When the man returned with the next three, I put them in the cart and thanked him. We checked out in silence and remained silent with each other until she pulled out of the parking lot.

"I'm sorry. I don't want to upset you, but my God, her behavior isn't normal."

"It might be for someone who's been targeted by the San Franciso police as a murderer. One that she didn't commit."

"How can you be so sure?" Her question sounded more like pleading.

"I know her. I've known and watched her throughout the last twelve years. We've been together since college. She wouldn't kill anyone. She might be guilty of some other crazy things that neither you nor I would ever think of doing, but she is not a murderer."

"Addy, she thinks my sister ruined her life. Because Raeann came forward about your wife's actions, your wife lost her prestigious job at a top university, you had to sell your home, your expensive cars, you lost a lot of your friends, a great position in a very upscale interior decorating business, you were practically run out of town...to here, and..."

My head snapped in her direction. "How do you know all that?"

She paused. "You told me." She had a sheepish grin on her face.

"No, no I didn't. I told you some things. But I didn't tell you everything."

"Okay, so maybe I'm assuming some of it. I'm sorry, but after everything I've heard and seen, I'm pretty much correct, aren't I? I mean, let's face it. If, or should I say when, the police question you, they're going to say the same things. They might already be looking at you as a suspect."

I neither confirmed nor denied her assumptions, but I wasn't going to let her last statement go without a response. "I am not blind to the fact that Raeann was not the one who fucked up our life. My wife was totally responsible for that. I can't believe you said that."

"I can't believe you keep defending Mary Ellen. I'm just so angry at her for everything she's done to you…to my sister."

I eyed her with suspicion. I wasn't blind to the possibility that Amelia had her own modus operandi where my wife was concerned. Exasperated by all of this, I asked, "Can we just start painting? I need something good right now and seeing a finished room would really help."

She looked at me, smiled, and sighed. "Sure."

There was nothing more to say, so I turned on the radio and stared out the window, part of me wishing this would all end. But I was actually dreading the ending because I didn't know how this would all play out. And that worried me.

Three hours later we stood in the middle of the kitchen. We had worked together to prep the kitchen, taping the woodwork, and laying down the drop cloths. It also took the two of us to move the refrigerator into the next room. Then Amelia painted the ceiling while I painted the walls.

As I turned in circles examining our work, it was the first time I felt elated. Finally, one room looked fresh and new and so close to being finished. Next, Amelia would install the recessed LED lights in the ceiling above the counters and the other light fixture that would be above the table followed by the flooring and then the cabinets. The counter would be installed by the granite company. Then the rest of the appliances would arrive. As much as that sounded like a lot, I was ecstatic that we were close to having a real kitchen, even if it would only be for show, because I still wasn't going to cook.

"Living room," was the only thing I said to her. We picked up the paint supplies and coverings and moved it all to the living room. We were close to finishing when I heard the front door open.

I looked up to see M.E. standing in the entranceway to the living room, a scowl on her face. Her expression forecasted the upcoming events and my shoulders dropped. I had to nip it in the bud or I would be refereeing a major boxing event.

I jumped up from the floor where I was trimming along the baseboard and ran over to her. I grabbed her hand and dragged her to the kitchen. When we got there, I spread my hand around the room.

"What do you think? Do you like the color?" I was forcing such a large smile on my face, my cheek muscles ached.

"What's she still doing here?" M.E.'s eyes were sharp and fixated on the living room where I was sure Amelia was close to the entryway, listening. She looked like someone who was about to turn to the dark side in a horror film. (God, I hated horror films.) I resorted to desperate tactics. I took her in my arms and kissed her full on the lips. I put what little sexual emotion I had left toward her into it, hoping she didn't feel the difference from our normal passion. Then again, after everything, how could there be any normal passion left between us? I felt as if I was doing a free solo climb on El Capitan. I hoped I didn't fall. There were no ropes to hold me, no net to catch me.

"Does it matter?" I whispered in her ear. "You're home. With me. That's all that matters."

I was startled when she pulled away. She had never done that before. When I was the one who initiated an intimate moment, she was never one not to take advantage.

"I want her out of here before I come back downstairs." She leaned forward and hissed in my ear, "If you remember, I said I didn't want her here when I got home. That's a really good way to keep me from coming home." She turned and left the room with me following her.

I shook my head and watched her take the steps two at a time. I knew Amelia was watching. As hard as I tried to put on my big, bad rock face, I was failing, and if I didn't find solid footing soon, I'd fall to the ground. Splat.

I walked over to Amelia and put my hand on her shoulder. "Please. I'll be fine. You need to leave."

"You won't be fine," she said with an edge to her tone. "That woman is nuts. It's not safe here for you."

I gently directed her toward the front door. "I'll pick up. I have your number if I need help. But I won't," I quickly added. "We'll be fine. I suspect it didn't go well at the lawyer's. Please, just let me deal with this."

She grabbed both my arms and forced me to look at her. "You won't be okay. This is not okay."

I shook her hands loose. "Amelia. Stop it. This is *my* life, my marriage. Let. Me. Deal with this. I know you think she murdered your sister, but she didn't. She wouldn't. How many times have I told you she may be a self-serving, dominating… rough woman, but, she's not a…"

Amelia was staring at the stairs. I turned to see M.E. standing halfway up, meeting Amelia's glare. I shook my head. This wasn't good.

"M.E.," was the only thing I got out of my mouth before she spoke.

Ignoring me, she addressed Amelia. "Raeann was your sister?" There was a warning in her voice. If I didn't get Amelia out of here fast, I wasn't sure what would happen. I couldn't risk things getting worse.

I looked at Amelia and mouthed the words, "Leave now."

"Answer me, bitch."

I spun around and glared at my wife, mouth opened. "Uncalled for," I scolded. "Please. Go upstairs. I'll be up in a minute." I hardened my gaze and tightened my facial muscles in hopes she would recognize my request was not a request, but a demand.

"Did you know about this?"

"If you love me, please, go upstairs. Now."

She turned and walked upstairs in a slow, deliberate pace.

When I looked back at Amelia, she was shaking her head.

Without thinking, I pushed her toward the door.

She wriggled her arm free from my grasp and exclaimed, "What the hell has gotten into you?" She pointed up the stairs. "That one is bonkers. She's going to hurt you."

"She already has, but not like you think," I growled. "And if you don't leave, it will be you that gets hurt and I can't let that happen." I opened the door and continued to push her through it.

She planted her feet to the ground to stop her momentum. I saw her eyes soften and a small grin tickled her lips. "You really do care for me."

"Yes, you oaf. You're my friend. I care for you a lot and I don't want this to get out of hand. You need to leave."

The grin left as quickly as it came. "And I don't want you to be alone here with her. Addy, she's getting nuttier by the day. This whole thing is making her crazy. You have no idea what she'll do now that she knows Raeann was my sister, and that you knew."

"She doesn't know that," I spat. "As far as she knows, I just found out when you said it."

"Yeah, but what you said about her. You don't think she's not gonna be hurt by those insults? Add that to the anger already coursing through her veins and who knows what she'll do."

"Look. I've always been able to calm her."

"Yeah, with sex."

I hit her in the arm.

Then I immediately regretted it. "I'm sorry," I said softly.

"No, I am. That insult was supposed to go toward your wife but it hit you instead. I'm sorry. Really. I'm just so worried about leaving you here alone with her."

"I'll be okay. I'll text you. Every hour if that will help."

She grabbed me and hugged me, but the thought of M.E. watching us from the upstairs window made me pull back. I nodded toward the upper floors.

"Sorry," she said. "I'll stay away. You can't help those that don't want it."

I grabbed her arm to stop her from trotting down the stairs to her truck. "I don't want to lose you. I need you. I'll call you tomorrow. I need your help. I have to figure out what to do about all of this, and I can't do it on my own."

Amelia said nothing.

"Please," I pleaded, gently squeezing her arm. "I need you." I hoped that playing on her need to be needed would convince her to leave now and return the next day.

She leaned in, kissed me on the cheek and whispered in my ear, "I'll wait for your call. Be careful." Then she left.

I stood on the step with my arms folded to protect myself from the cold. It wasn't so much the cold breeze making its way through the leaves that chilled me as the icy feeling left by two very important women in my life.

At that moment I wondered if I would ever be warm again.

CHAPTER TWENTY

When I walked into the bedroom, M.E. was sitting on the bed, her legs tucked up with her arms around them.

"Is she gone?"

I remained in the doorway. "Yes."

"What does she think I'm going to do? Kill you like she thinks I killed her sister?"

If sarcasm could drip, she'd be drooling. I straightened as I put my guard up.

Noticing my movement, she said in response, "Oh, come on, Addy. I haven't killed or hurt anyone and you know I would never hurt you."

"But you have," I retorted.

"You look pretty much alive to me."

"You know what I mean."

"And you know what I mean."

I took a tentative step into the room, realizing that her anger was growing again.

"I do. I'm sorry. I know you would never hurt me," I said, trying to placate her.

And just like someone with a split personality, she literally turned the other cheek. She reached a hand up to me. "Of course, I wouldn't. I love you. Let me show you how much."

I wasn't scared to take her hand in fear that she would hurt me. I was afraid that we were going to have sex and she would see right through me. There wasn't much left for her in my heart and making love to her right now would be a lie that I wouldn't be able to hide.

She dropped her hand. "Aw, come on, Addy. We've slept apart enough. It's time to get our life back on track. In every way. This will be a good start, you know? We've always been able to fix things."

"With sex," I said.

"And it's always worked for us. Nothing needs to change. You know I didn't hurt Raeann. You *know* it deep in your heart."

I did know it, but it wasn't Raeann's disappearance and subsequent death that kept me from taking the few steps forward to meet her on the bed. It was the affairs—the numerous affairs that I knew were too many to count. The lies and omissions of the truths, and the research. The sick research.

I was so tired of it all and I wanted—needed—to get my life back on track. Not ours. Mine. But if I didn't satisfy her insatiable need for sex right now, would she explode? And if I did it just to keep the peace until I could find a way out of this, would I be able to walk away for good?

She slipped her shirt over her head and I caught a glimpse of the hardened muscles of her abdomen. She reached behind her back and unclasped her bra, letting it fall to her lap. Her breasts shimmered in the low light of our bedroom as the sunrays had slipped behind the trees. Her nipples were hard. She got up and walked over to me, keeping her eyes on mine, her face melting into the expression that I knew well. Pure lust.

My mind raced. Should I? Shouldn't I? What would happen if I did? What would happen if I didn't? I had seconds to make the decision and even less time to muster up the strength to stick to it.

Her fingers on one hand played with strands of my hair while the other found its way to my breast, slowly caressing, kneading, fondling. I closed my eyes, trying to fight the desire within me. Our sexual attraction was something I could never deny, but now, I realized I had to. If I didn't break the cycle, I would never be free.

But...

It felt so good.

Her lips found mine and our desires met with such intensity that our tongues wasted no time reacquainting our stalled passion. My body shook with such ferocity that I felt as if I might lose control at any minute.

But I already had.

I found myself clinging to the toilet bowl at two a.m. I told myself over and over that I did what I had to do, yet despite that self-proclamation, my physical actions had made me physically ill.

I dragged my ravaged body down to the kitchen for a hot cup of tea. I leaned against the counter waiting for the Keurig to heat the water as my mind replayed the sexual encounter I had with my wife. I shuddered thinking in earlier times I would call it making love like most married couples who really were in love called it. But I knew I was no longer in love with M.E. I realized I had lost that loving feeling (wait, wasn't that a song?) a long time ago, and even though I tried with everything I had to hang on to it, I couldn't. It slipped through my fingers like a greased pig in a rodeo competition (which in my eyes was an event that mistreated the poor animal) and no matter how hard I tried, I couldn't hang on.

And I never would.

I pulled my cup from the Keurig and plopped a tea bag in it. While dipping, I looked around the kitchen. It looked so good; I couldn't help but smile. There didn't seem much in my life lately that made me smile. That had to change.

I sat on the couch looking out at the night sky and the trees that lined our backyard. It was peaceful, there was no denying that, but I actually found the occasional late-night city headlights and streetlights much more soothing than fireflies and twinkling stars. A nature girl I was not. A city girl, I was.

I couldn't remember how long I had been sitting there when I heard movement upstairs. The shower was running, so M.E. must have been getting ready for work. She would have no idea how long I had been out of bed, at least I hoped she didn't.

I waited for her to come down, and when she did, she was dressed in a black, tailored business suit. It fit her like a glove, a very sleek, shiny, skintight glove. A cream-colored collar peeked out from the neckline of the suit coat. Her makeup was flawless, and I suspected part of it was because of how rested she looked.

At least one of us slept.

She leaned over, kissed me and then smiled. "Where's my coffee?"

"Mug on the counter, K-Cup in the Keurig waiting for you to push the button," I said, working hard to return her smile.

"I'll be right back."

When she left the room, I mimicked her question to me. "Where's my coffee?" I said in a dour tone.

She returned a few minutes later with two mugs and handed me one. Then she sat next to me on the couch. "How long have you been up?"

"Not long."

"You don't look so good. Didn't you sleep? I mean, that sex was mind-blowing. I slept like a baby."

"Not much. Just feeling a bit under the weather."

"Then you should take it easy today. I expect you to tell that she-devil to stay away from now on after the way she treated me last night." She stood. "You'll have to find another contractor so you can finish our home. I didn't think she was all that good anyway. It seems to have taken a long time. I haven't checked her work yet, but I'm sure I'll find some shoddy things."

The entire time M.E. was speaking, I felt my blood boil, causing a major category ten hot flash. I wanted to shout that Amelia had done a fine job and taught me so much. The house was ahead of schedule and I believed no one could do a better job than she had so far. I also wanted to tell her that if I wanted Amelia to come over then she had my permission to do so, and it didn't matter what anyone thought, including my wife.

So, why didn't I?

Instead I sat in silence, biting my tongue so hard I expected blood to drip down my chin. The only thing I could think of doing was to look at my watch. "It's getting late. Don't you think you should get to work?"

She feigned a look of concern on her face. I say feign, because I knew she lost concern for me the moment Raeann entered her life, followed by Melissa and whoever else she was screwing.

She began to unbutton her suit coat. "Maybe I should stay home. Take care of you."

"No!" I jumped off the couch. "I'm fine. Really. I have a lot of work to do to prepare for my company. I promise I'll lay low and just sit here on the couch feeding my face and working on my computer."

"Is she coming here?" M.E. challenged me.

"What the fuck, M.E. Let's not get started on this. I just told you what I was going to do today. Since when did you stop trusting me?"

"Since you got really defensive when I suggested I stay here to look after you. I think that was pretty nice of me, and you acted like it was the worst thing ever."

I sat down next to her and put my hand on her leg, running my fingers up her thigh under her skirt. "I'm sorry. I didn't mean for you to think I wasn't appreciative of your offer, but if you stay to babysit me, you'll miss your classes and I won't get my work done." I took her empty mug. "The only thing you'd be doing is babysitting me and we both know I don't need a babysitter."

"Ain't that the truth." She grabbed my hand as I stood to go to the kitchen. She winked at me. "But that's not all I'd be doing. Maybe you need some more loving. It makes me feel better. I know it does the same for you."

I gently pulled my hand away. "Of course, but as I said, I'm feeling a bit under the weather. Stomach upset, so sex is not going to help that. Tums are what I need." I walked away quickly, but not too quickly. "I'll be right back to kiss you goodbye."

I listened for her movements and finally heard footsteps. I could only hope she was getting her coat, purse, and work bag.

Sure enough, when I returned to the foyer, she was standing with her coat on, bag and purse in hand.

"I'll see you tonight. Rest up, my love." She planted a slow, sensual kiss on my lips and then took a step back. "You can make it up to me tonight when I get home. You know how voracious my sexual appetite can be." With a literal shit-eating grin on her face, she turned and went out the door.

I wanted to smack that grin right off her lips.

I sucked in a breath, waiting for the sound of her truck leaving the driveway. When I heard the squealing tires on the road, I braved a look out the window to see if it was my wife who left or Amelia who showed up.

Thank God, Amelia's truck was nowhere in sight. I almost passed out from lack of air before I let out the breath that was disintegrating in my chest.

I couldn't call Amelia. It was best she stayed away that day, and I yearned for a day without either my wife or Amelia ambushing me every chance they got. I grabbed my phone and texted her instead.

My wife just left. I'm okay but didn't sleep last night so I'm going to bed. I'll call later.

I didn't wait for an answer. Instead, I went to bed. I fell asleep fast and hard.

One of the few things that was actually working when we purchased the stone house was the doorbell. I remembered that when I heard it buzzing incessantly in my dream. And then I woke. I took in my bedroom, processing the daylight. It was as if a filter was on the sun dimming the light in the room. It had to be clouds because there was no way I had slept the whole day away.

I jumped up and looked out the window, noticing two things. Several clouds were indeed filling up the sky. The other was Amelia below me pressing the doorbell nonstop.

I threw open the window. "Enough already. I'll be right down." I slammed the window shut, hoping it wouldn't break. The glass was thin and the wooden frames were worn and fragile to say the least. I had to be careful, reminding myself the windows weren't slated to be replaced until the following week.

I ran downstairs, ignoring how I must have looked. I was still in my robe and then realized I had nothing on underneath. I turned to go back up and put some other clothes on, but I knew the added time would make Amelia attack my doorbell again.

I threw the door open and pulled her in.

"What the hell?" she asked. "What's going on? Is everything okay?"

I shut the door and turned to face her. "M.E. doesn't want you here. Today, or any day. And I don't want those nosy neighbors to tell her you were here."

"They're going to see my truck, and besides, does she even speak to them?"

"Yeah, but not very nicely. I wouldn't be surprised if they tell her your truck was here just to see if they can stir up trouble."

"They're busybodies, gossipers, not antagonizers."

I walked toward the kitchen with Amelia in tow. "You can't be too careful."

"Are you okay? Did she hurt you?"

"Stop it, no. She's just an angry bitch."

Amelia grabbed my arm and spun me around. "Girl, you are paranoid. But you've got good reason to be that way, even though it's not your neighbors you should be afraid of. Are you ready to discuss your options to get out of this mess?"

My shoulders sagged from the weight of *this mess*. "I don't know if there's anything I can do."

She pulled me close and hugged me. I fought the urge to pull away, and then I fought the urge to cry.

Her fingers stroked my hair while she whispered soothing words to me. "Not you. *We*. We'll find a way. We can do this. Together." Then her arms wrapped around me tightly, engulfing me like a caterpillar in a cocoon.

It hit me then that even though I had hoped to keep Amelia out of this, there was no way that was going to happen. I wriggled from her embrace and went to the refrigerator. I took out two beers.

"I know it's early, but strategizing something like this is going to take a little bit of alcohol." I held one out to her.

She took the bottle and sat at the table. I tossed the bottle opener to her and after catching it in one hand, she opened her bottle. Then she held the church key out to me. "It's closer to lunch than you think."

I sat down and opened my bottle. We performed the habitual clinking of the bottles and drank in silence.

"Guess I slept longer than I thought. So, I'm all ears if you have any suggestions."

"I've already told you to divorce her ass."

I gave her a disgusted sideways glance. "Saying I'm going to divorce her and doing it won't solve this right now. I get you don't like her. And I get she doesn't like you, but all this animosity from both of you isn't going to help me."

Looking down, she fingered her bottle. "I'm sorry. I promise to keep it under control."

But I could see the rage and desire for revenge bubble inside her. She still believed M.E. murdered her sister, and just thinking it made my own blood boil. How many times did I have to say my wife was a cheater, a user, an asshole, but she was no killer? Then again, did I really know that? She had hid so much from me, and she had struck me. I no longer had any idea of what she was capable of.

"As I told you before, I can't divorce her. It's a financial thing. There has to be another way."

"Can you access all your"—she air quoted the following words—"financial sources?"

"I'm not sure. I think she has a few hidden ones and those are the ones I'm most concerned about."

"Would it help if my guy did some digging to find out if there's anything else she's hiding and if so, what?"

"I don't know, Amelia. I don't want to involve anyone else."

"He's already involved."

"Yes, I know, but I shouldn't have even done that. Let me do some digging on my own." We drank again. "If I find out what I want to know, then what? Why did you ask if I can access everything?"

"If you can do it without Mary Ellen knowing, maybe you can empty those accounts, move money, change names on the accounts, deny her access…Then there's nothing keeping you from divorcing her."

"I'm not sure that would be possible, but I'll look into it."

Amelia took another swig of her beer, emptying the bottle as if it would give her strength to say the next thing. "Unless you don't want to divorce her."

I did. I really did. But I didn't know if I was ready to admit that to Amelia. She would pin her hopes of being with me on that one answer.

Suddenly, an appropriate answer came to me. "It's not whether I want to or not. It's something I have to do."

"I understand that. You've been together for a long time. Hard to let go of those feelings right away despite what they do."

I sighed heavily, knowing the digs were going to continue no matter what I said or did. "God, I'm so tired." I felt like a sixteenth-century witch tried and convicted and now laying on a platform with hundreds of pounds of stone piled on top of me. And then I thought, *what a freakish thing to think about.* It was probably because my mind was a bit foggy from lack of sleep.

Amelia seemed a bit on edge. She was shifting in her chair, as if weighing the gravity of what she was to say next. While I waited for her to speak, I got us each another beer, telling myself there would be no more after these. The last thing I needed was to do something I would regret in a drunken stupor in my house with the remote chance that M.E. could come home and interrupt us with a gun in hand…or something.

Before the animosity between my wife and Amelia had increased, I knew the chance of M.E. coming home early was meager at best. Now, I couldn't be sure of anything my wife did anymore, not that I wanted to find myself in any uncompromising position with Amelia. Thus, no more beer.

I opened one bottle and set it in front of her, waiting for her to speak. I didn't open the other one. She moved again in her chair, so I said, "Well if there's nothing more to work out right now, how about we get some more painting done? Just for a few hours. Then you'll have to leave."

"Are you going to fire me?"

"Of course not!" I exclaimed, a bit shocked she would ask that. Then again, why wouldn't she after everything that had happened? "I expect you to help me finish this house so I can launch my business. It's just going to take a bit to get this all sorted out."

She locked her gaze on me. "What if…What if something happened to her?" She looked down at her bottle and began fingering it once again.

"I don't understand what you mean," I said slowly, but I was pretty sure I did.

"Anything can happen," she hurried on. "I mean any one of us can get in a car accident, or fall…get hurt. What if by some miracle something happened to her? If she…um…if she died, everything would go to you. Right? You'd be free of all this."

"That's horrible!" I exclaimed. Amelia remained still with no reaction to my outburst whatsoever. I took a deep breath to calm myself and then said, "But let's be realistic. The odds of that are slim, wouldn't you say?"

"You never know," she answered with a wink.

That wink made me nervous, scared, and worried.

She got up from the table and poured the rest of her beer in the sink. "Don't want to paint outside the lines," she joked. "M.E. would get pissed."

I would have laughed at the first sentence, but the second one was not a joke. Just another dig.

"So, off to the living room?"

"Great," I answered and opened my beer.

A few hours later, the living room was done. The soft ivory color would bring out the different tones in the wood floor when it was finished. At least, that was what Amelia told me. But I could picture it in my mind, and I couldn't wait for the man Amelia had hired to replace the floors to get it done. He would do one at a time, closing off whatever room he was working on from the rest of the house. It would take a while, but I didn't care how he did it or how long it took. I just wanted it done.

I took a deep breath and surveyed the room. She'd already finished the ceiling, and it was exquisite. She was a master at antique plastering. She textured the ceiling, adding medallions at strategic points, including around the central light fixture. When the floors were done and I could do my magic, I'd make it the showplace my mind had imagined for so long.

I turned to face her. Forgetting the complications of our relationship, I threw my arms around her and squeezed her tight. "Thank you so much for everything you've done for this house." Remembering the complications of our relationship, I jumped back. "Sorry. I got carried away. We're on the homestretch. I have something I can get excited about."

Amelia's cheeks flushed. "Don't be sorry. I'm happy to see you excited about something. Especially since it involves me."

I hated walking fine lines. It wasn't one of my fortes. I had no balance.

CHAPTER TWENTY-ONE

Amelia convinced me to start on the dining room. I protested, but finally gave in. We said nothing while we prepped the room, but when she began to stir the five-gallon can of ceiling paint, she said, "Don't you worry. I'll take care of you. You won't have to put up with this much longer and I won't let her take anything away from you, you hear me?"

I sighed heavily and looked out the dining room window. "There's nothing you can do," I said, looking back at her.

"Maybe, maybe not."

Ignoring the voice that screamed inside me, I took her hands in mine. "I don't want you to do anything. Promise me you won't do anything."

She leaned forward as if to kiss me and whispered, "I can't promise you anything."

"Please, Amelia. You said you'd give me time to do some investigating on my own. You need to let me do that before I make any decisions about my marriage."

"I know what I said."

"Fine. You should leave now in case M.E. comes home for dinner."

"When was the last time she was home for dinner?" Amelia tilted her head and raised her eyebrows.

"Please, Amelia. I'll see you tomorrow morning. Okay?"

"Okay, fine."

Just then, my phone rang. I hurried to my purse and yanked it out. I expected the screen to say Wife (my call sign for M.E., of course), but my heart jumped and my armpits began to sweat when I saw it was M.E.'s lawyer, Diane. Why was she calling me?

"Hello?"

"Ms. Pious?"

"Yes, this is she."

"This is Diane Kensington, your wife's—"

"Yes, I know who you are. Is there something wrong?"

"I received a call this morning from a contact of mine that they were putting a warrant out for your wife's arrest in the murder of Raeann Wilson. I've been trying to get ahold of her, but she's not answering her phone. The police have also been searching for her. She never showed up for her morning classes. Is she there?"

"No."

"Have you heard from her?"

"No!" I practically shouted into the phone. I took a deep breath. "She left for work this morning and I haven't heard from her all day, but I expect her to return home sometime this evening. I just don't know when."

Amelia came over to me and put an arm around my shoulder. "What is it?"

I wanted to shrug it off, but instead I stiffened.

"If you hear from her, please tell her to come to my office."

"Why? So she can get arrested for something she didn't do? I thought they didn't have enough proof," I said as my stomach began to crawl up my esophagus.

"They didn't, but they've found something. I haven't been told what it is, so I need to find your wife before they do. The biggest problem will be the few places on that timeline she gave me where she doesn't have an alibi. I've had someone checking them out and we've been able to find concrete collaborations that prove she was where she said she was—except for one. I believe that one is part of what they're basing the warrant on."

"Which one was that?" I asked, going through those few times in my mind that I knew only M.E. could fill in, and likewise, would be hard to prove.

"July sixth at night from ten p.m. until two thirty a.m. You had marked that she came home at midnight. We found security cameras in your neighborhood that show her coming home later."

"I really thought it was midnight. It was just the time she always came home when she had things to do in the evening, so I never looked at the clock." I knew how lame that sounded. "Now that I think about it, I never heard her come home. I was sleeping."

"I understand. Just please, if you hear from her or if she comes home, call me immediately at this number. Don't call my office. I'll be in and out and I gave Melissa a few days off so there's no one to answer the phone."

"I will. Thank you, Diane."

She hung up and I stared at the phone.

Amelia's face was crinkled with worried inquiry. "What is it?"

I walked into the kitchen and got a beer out of the fridge. Even though I had sworn off beer for the day, the call from my wife's lawyer warranted it. I sat down in one of the folding chairs. After taking a long drink, I answered, "That was Diane Kensington, M.E.'s lawyer. The San Francisco police have a warrant for her arrest. She thinks they're basing it on one night when M.E. said she was running errands and she had no alibi."

"Maybe this is it," Amelia said coolly. "It's about time."

I shot her a look. "What do you mean by that?"

"It's finally going to happen. You know I've believed all along that she did it. Besides, if she's convicted, you can finally divorce her, get everything and go on with your life."

I stood abruptly, knocking my beer off the table, and shouting at her, "How dare you? How many times do I have to tell you? She. Didn't. Do it!"

Amelia rushed over to me and attempted to take me into one of her *I'll make it better* hugs, but I pulled away and leaned against the fridge with my arms folded. "Leave me alone."

"I'm sorry. I can't change the way I feel. About anything, and that includes you."

Looking at the floor, I answered, "I never asked you to feel anything about me."

"You didn't ask, but you can't deny it's just been happening between us. You can't deny it," she hissed, and it made my head snap to look at her.

"Amelia, I'm not denying anything. I hired you without knowing you and we became friends. I care for you. It's just that…I'm married and I've known my wife for so long. She would never…I'm just so torn."

She took a step toward me.

"I have to stand by her. I have to see this through. You understand that, don't you?"

"I do. Maybe she knows the police have a warrant for her arrest and that's why she hasn't come home yet."

She didn't take another step. Instead, her eyes roamed as if she were studying me, looking for a response, waiting for me to say something she wanted to hear, but I was pretty sure I wasn't going to say it.

Her hand reached for me, and I let her fingers enclose around mine. She squeezed and then turned to leave. As she walked out the door, she said loud enough for me to hear, "I won't let anything happen to you."

Midnight.

M.E. still hadn't come home, and I was still sitting at the kitchen table. Alone. Shortly after the lawyer's phone call, something inside me said M.E. wasn't coming home at the usual time. She hadn't been home by midnight the last few days and I wondered if it was because of her research with her latest concubine.

Melissa. Surely Melissa knew what was going on. She was Diane's receptionist and I'd bet our stone home the lawyer didn't suspect the relationship between her receptionist and my wife. Melissa struck me as sneaky. She probably listened in on Diane's conversation with the San Francisco detective and ran straight to my wife. My insides ripped apart because I had hoped I'd be the one my wife would want to be with on the night before she got handcuffed and dragged away to prison.

But no…M.E. was off somewhere, and I had no idea where.

I decided it was time to go to bed and not worry about what M.E. did anymore. I hadn't been able to stop her when she went after Raeann. I wouldn't be able to now. As I changed into my PJs, I wondered what had changed her. I had been a good wife, a great wife—except for not cooking, but she never cared about having a personal chef. She had always wanted a personal lover— one at her beck and call. I filled that position. I was successful, and together we presented a professional, upstanding couple in both our work worlds.

So, why did she have to search for more? Why wasn't I enough?

My mind was exhausted from trying to figure everything out, let alone what to do with it, and I fell asleep almost immediately. But even in my dreams, those questions repeated over and over like some kind of mantra that lulled me to sleep.

It was the loud banging on the door that woke me. I grabbed my alarm clock to check the time and saw it was three a.m. The pounding on my door persisted, so I threw on my robe and headed downstairs. I was apprehensive about answering the door, being alone in the house, but maybe M.E. forgot her key.

On my way downstairs, I checked the second bedroom just to make sure M.E. hadn't come home while I was sleeping. She wasn't there. No lights were on downstairs and I quickly checked the living room and kitchen. My wife still wasn't home. I stopped at the front door and called out when the knocker took a break.

"Who is it?"

"It's the police, ma'am. We're looking for Adalynn Pious."

They were looking for me. Why?

"Adalynn, it's Diane Kensington. It's okay. Open the door."

I took a deep breath and undid the chain and deadbolt. Then I opened the door. Two policemen and Diane were standing on the battered concrete stoop. I sighed, thinking the first people to visit our home had to see the sad state of the outside of the house that wouldn't be landscaped until the inside was done. But now I wondered if the front steps should be repaired sooner.

I knew why I was thinking about that at a most inappropriate moment. It was avoidance in the most generic way.

"I'm pretty sure you know it's three in the morning. You better have a good reason for pounding on my door and scaring the shit out of me."

"Ma'am…"

Diane put a hand on the cop's arm and stepped in front of him. "We've been looking for Mary Ellen. Can we come in?"

"I don't usually take guests in the wee morning hours, but since you're the police, sure, come on in. Let's have a party," I answered with as much sarcasm as I could muster at this time of the night. "And just so you know, she's not here."

They walked past me into the house and I closed the door turning to face them. "Go ahead. Search the house. Just please don't make a mess, and if you do, put it back." I folded my arms and glared at them. They didn't move. "Go on, search."

The policeman that first addressed me looked at Diane. Then she looked at me. "Do you know where she is?"

"All I know is she's not here. I already checked before I opened the door. That's why it took me so long."

"Aren't you worried?" the second officer—a female—asked.

"I would've been if I had woken at a normal hour and noticed she wasn't home yet, but as I've stated before, it's three in the morning and I'm not quite awake." I glared at her. Her eyes drifted downward and the expression on her face told me she understood.

"Before you ask anything else, no I haven't texted her. Yet. I would have when I woke up. I waited up for her until midnight and fell asleep shortly after that."

"Is that usual for her? Staying out all night?" the first cop asked.

"No, it's not. It is usual for her to come home around midnight. She stays at work a lot, grading papers, preparing lectures, working on research."

"We checked her office," Diane said. "She wasn't there all day today, and she missed all of her classes, or rather it's now yesterday."

I flinched at what she said. That was not typical. M.E. was very dedicated to her classes and her work. Of course, I now knew her work consisted of sleeping with her research subjects, but I wasn't about to tell them that. I wondered how much Diane knew and if I should tell them to check with her newest girl toy, Melissa.

Melissa. Diane had told me she gave her a few days off. I fought the urge to roll my eyes at the possibility that M.E. was, in fact, with Melissa.

Still, I decided against saying anything.

I hurried to the kitchen and grabbed my phone off the charger. There were no messages or texts from my wife. It really wasn't like her. I could count on two hands the number of times she came home past midnight, and almost always, I had a text on my phone informing me she would be home soon (unless she was mad at me like she had been of late). Otherwise, it was always by midnight.

I looked up to see Diane watching me. I held up the phone so she could see the screen. "Nothing," I said.

"Do you have any idea where she might have gone?"

I dropped my hand to my side. *I might take a guess that she's at her secret apartment with her paramour*, my mind wanted to shout out loud. But if Diane didn't know her secretary was boinking my wife, I wasn't going to be the one to tell her.

"No, none. It's too early to contact the college," I said, reaching for straws.

"Do you want to report her missing?"

"I thought you had to wait twenty-four hours for that."

Diane leaned forward and said in a quiet voice, "I think in this case, the police will take the report."

I looked past her to the two cops still standing in my foyer. "I want to report my wife missing."

At nine o'clock in the morning, I was once again sitting at the table drinking coffee. The police had taken my report, asked me all sorts of questions, inquired as to what places she might have gone, things she liked to do (maybe a late-night hike at one of the many parks in the surrounding area), any favorite hangouts, any friends or coworkers she spent time with. I didn't know the answers to any of their question, and if I really thought about it, that wasn't surprising. I knew nothing about my wife's life away from me until Amelia's friend investigated her. And even with that information, it didn't fill in all the time M.E. spent away from me.

By now, I knew the difference in sound between Amelia's and my wife's truck, so when I heard a vehicle pull into the driveway, I knew it was Amelia despite the text I sent her asking her to stay away. Of course, she ignored it. Still, I ran to the front door and flung it open almost wanting it to be M.E.'s truck.

My shoulders dropped.

Amelia emerged from the driver's seat and stood by the front hood as if waiting for an invitation. I didn't want to give it, but I didn't want to her to leave, so I turned and went back to the kitchen, leaving the front door open.

The old wood creaked and the rusted hinges groaned, signaling me she had closed it. Part of me didn't want to install a new door or even replace the hinges and refinish the wood surface. This one had character and it was a good alarm. Besides, the wretched sounds of the front door had become soothing, familiar.

Amelia opened the refrigerator and put a six-pack of beer inside, taking two out. She opened them and handed one to me. "It feels like I've been drinking a lot of your beer. I thought I'd bring some."

"Thanks. It does seem like we sit here a lot and drink beer."

"It does, doesn't it?"

"Do you know?"

"Know what?"

"M.E. is missing."

I watched her face for any sign that she knew. If she did, she hid it well.

She took a long drink and then said, "That's too bad. I'm sorry."

"Hmm." I dragged out the word. "Not the answer I expected."

Now Amelia's face changed. Her eyes dipped together, making her eyebrows almost meet in the middle. "What did you expect? For me to jump up and down and scream hallelujah?"

The image of her rejoicing in that way over the disappearance of my wife made me laugh. It came out raw and sad, but the image struck me as funny. "Actually, yes," I answered.

"I'm not that bad of a person. Any idea where she might be?"

"No. I waited for her to come home and fell asleep sometime after midnight."

She was quiet and appeared to be contemplating her response. "Are you going to look for her?"

"I put in a missing person report with the police, who were here looking for her. They've already checked the college. They also asked her coworkers for places she might hang out. They checked those. And of course, they searched the house."

Awkward silence filled the kitchen. I knew what she was going to say next.

"Did you tell them about the apartment?"

"No, of course not."

"How do you know she's not there?"

"I don't."

Amelia shifted in her chair. "Don't you *want* to know?"

"That's why you're going to take me."

We parked Amelia's truck two blocks down from my wife's secret apartment. This part of the city was run-down with empty buildings, overgrown lawns littered with garbage, and rutted parking lots. The area was slated for revitalization, but it had failed several times. No one wanted to be the start of something they believed would fail again. M.E.'s apartment was an example of how owners of run-down buildings could at least pay their taxes.

By sticking close to the buildings, we could stay out of view of any stray passersby. The last thing I needed was to be seen near M.E.'s hidden apartment when they found out she had one.

Once we entered the building, I asked Amelia how we were going to know if my wife was there. Her apartment was on a second floor, and of course, I had no key. To my surprise, she pulled a key out of her pocket. "David swiped it from the office downstairs. The owner uses the rest of the building for storage and keeps a bunch of keys in a desk drawer. He took them and tried each one until he found this one."

"And he didn't get caught?"

"He watched the area enough to know when no one was around."

"We can't just unlock the door and walk in. What if she's in there?"

"To quote you, that's why you're going to stay at the end of the hall around the corner. I'll knock. If she's there, I'll run. David informed me of a way to get out of the building without being seen. If you hear me coming, go back down this hall and wait for me at the door." She stopped and put a hand up. "Stay here."

I did as I was instructed, except I leaned forward to peek around the corner. She knocked on the door and waited. After a few seconds, she rapped again. A few minutes went by before she signaled me to come down. I wasn't sure I wanted to, but I had to know.

I made my way down the paneled hallway with brown indoor/outdoor carpeting, unsure if the brown was its actual color or a result of the filth. I was relieved to enter the small living room, but the interior wasn't much better than the hallway. The paneling extended into the apartment, but thank

God the carpeting was newer, a thick, short shag. Except for the clean, almost spotless room, I didn't recognize anything.

An overstuffed couch sat in the middle of the room with a small wood coffee table in front of it. At the far end of the room was a large entrance to the kitchen. The appliances were in relatively good condition, but the almond color gave away their age. Off the kitchen were two doors. I opened the first, finding a bathroom typical of an apartment of this type—plainly furnished in order to reap a higher profit. White fixtures sat on tan tiles.

I closed the door.

When I opened the next door, I cringed upon seeing it was the bedroom. The blankets and sheets on the bed were ruffled, reminding me of the aftermath of the sexual romps M.E. and I often had. But no one was in the bed. I shut the door quickly and marched toward the front door of the apartment, saying to Amelia who was standing in the living room as I passed, "I need to get out of here." I felt as if I was about to throw up all the beer I'd been drinking.

Suddenly, I felt a hand grab me. I jumped and saw it was Amelia.

"God, girl, you scared the shit out of me."

"You've got the advantage," she said, staring hard at me.

"What the hell are you talking about?"

"No one knows about this. Clean out the incriminating stuff. Take her files. Make the apartment just look like a place she kept away from you for whatever reason other than her sick and twisted research. That way, it can't come back on you."

She had a point. "Fine," I spat out and began to search the desk, the one file cabinet and three bookcases that were against a wall in the living room. Amelia immediately joined me and when she found something incriminating, she put it in a pile. We worked quickly.

I didn't realize Amelia had stopped searching when out of the corner of my eye I saw her wiping things with a cloth. I gritted my teeth. We had left fingerprints She was wiping them down. Great. Now I felt like I was committing a crime. In a way

I was. We were in my wife's secret apartment that as far as she was concerned, I didn't know about. We were basically stealing her research. On the other hand, she was my wife and she was missing. That had to count for something.

When I felt I had everything that could point to her sick and twisted research, I looked around for something to put it in. I found some cloth sacks used for shopping. M.E.'s work filled two of them.

"I think I've got everything clean of our prints. I'll take the rag and wipe down the door when we leave. We should get going."

I was in total agreement, knowing that if M.E. showed up while we were there, it would not be good. Then I wondered where my wife was hiding because at this point, I assumed she was running from a murder conviction. I actually hoped she would be here with her research subject, her love slave, but I was relieved that she wasn't. I was, however, even more relieved that I had been replaced in that capacity. I understood now that it was all I ever was to her, and I wondered how much of her diluted research had been performed on me.

I glanced around the room one more time and shook my head. My stomach rumbled with beer and my anger was making it a time bomb. I honestly never saw this coming. In the back of my mind, I had always known that M.E. was unfaithful, but this...this was beyond my comprehension. I walked out the door before I could trash the contents of her apartment.

I watched Amelia feverishly wipe the door, the frame and the knob. Then we hurried out of the building and back to her truck. As I got into the cab, holding the two bags of papers on my lap, I knew I was done with our marriage, with M.E. However, I was afraid of M.E.'s reaction and subsequent actions to this news and to her missing research.

CHAPTER TWENTY-TWO

Amelia pulled into my driveway and turned off her truck. "We need a drink."

"I'd like to be alone," I said, hoping to deter her from staying any longer than for one glass of wine. "Would you mind?"

She put a hand on my arm, and I tensed. "You shouldn't be alone. Your wife is missing. And I think you shouldn't read those papers by yourself."

"I don't want to sound rude or ungrateful, but *you* shouldn't read these at all, and what I do with my wife's research is no one's business but mine and my wife's."

Flinching at my words, she withdrew her hand. Her facial muscles shifted from eyes hard with anger to her mouth dipped in sadness. They changed as fast as someone channel surfing with a television remote. Then her cheeks pulled tight in confusion while her eyes softened with tears. It was almost humorous because her face was totally unreadable and I couldn't tell what state of mind she was in from one moment to the next.

Her eyes were focused on the windshield when she spoke with a deep, dark voice. "Have you been playing me?"

"Excuse me?"

"I really like you. I thought you liked me the same way."

"Of course, I like you, and you know that, but I can only think of you as a really good friend right now."

She scoffed. "I don't know what you want from me. I've been nothing but kind, understanding, supportive, protective." She turned to face me. "Loving."

"I didn't ask you to be those things."

"You wanted those things!" she shouted.

I pressed against the door and wrapped my fingers around the door handle. I swallowed hard. "I need to go. Thank you for helping me."

She rolled her eyes. "I'm sorry. I'm just so emotional about all of this. My sister is dead and the person who killed her is your wife, and she's missing. So, we may never find out the truth—if she really did do it or not."

"Then you admit it may not have been her."

"No. I totally believe it was. I'm only saying that for your benefit, because you're so stuck on her innocence."

I squished my body against the door from the feeling of uneasiness that was creeping inside me.

"What do you want from me?" she asked in a childlike voice.

"I could ask you the same thing."

A tear slowly trickled down her cheek. "I did it all for you," she whispered.

"Did what?" I asked.

She ran her hand through her hair. "I thought..." she mumbled.

"Thought what?" I prodded, hoping she'd say something that was coherent.

"She's never coming back, you know."

"Who?" I was getting concerned. Amelia appeared to be losing her shit.

"Your wife. Your wife is never coming back."

"You don't know that. My wife will be home. Probably soon, so maybe you should go."

"She. Is. Never. Coming back!" Her voice rose in volume, but it was controlled like she had evidence to back up her words.

And it was because of her inhibited reaction that my stomach flipped as I asked, even though I already knew the answer, "How do you know that?" But I needed to hear it from her.

She said nothing. Then she opened the door and got out of the truck. She walked up to the cracked concrete steps. I gathered the bags of papers in my arms and fumbled with the door. When I reached her, I pleaded, "Amelia, please. Answer me."

"Not here. Inside," she ordered. Then she stood on the stoop, obviously waiting for me to unlock the door. I held the sacks of papers in my arms while fumbling for the keys. When I pulled them from my pocket, she reached to grab them from me but I yanked them away. I glared at her and then clumsily unlocked the door as I hung on to the paper sacks to prevent them from spilling to the ground. She pushed the door open and held it for me. Her expression was still unreadable and I worried about the subsequent conversation. Amelia was not herself. She was becoming unhinged.

When we were inside, she shut the door so hard, I thought it would break off the hinges, but the old, dried wood held. Still, I jumped when it shook from the jolt of her slamming it shut. Like so much in the house that hadn't been attended to yet, it would need a good overhaul when all this was over.

I took a step toward her and then stopped, noticing the angry emotions playing out on her face. I spoke softly, hoping I could calm her enough to be reasonable and get her to leave. "I've got a bottle of red in the kitchen. Let's go have that drink you said we needed."

I placed the bottle, two glasses, and an opener on the table. "I'll be right back. How about you pour us two glasses?"

"Of course," she said, her face stoic almost as if she knew she had to fight a raging battle within and win in order to stay. She fuddled with the aluminum cover and then put the opener into the cork.

I picked up the sacks, but not before I saw her twisting the opener with a deliberateness that sent chills up my spine. I went upstairs and put the papers under the bed and then hurried to the bathroom thinking I might throw up from the betrayal that came in many forms—a blond college student, a hidden apartment, my missing wife, and a woman in my kitchen who didn't particularly seem in her right mind.

I splashed cold water on my face and knew what I had to do. I went back to the kitchen. Amelia was sitting at the table, nursing her glass of wine. Another one was on the table. I picked it up and took a long swallow.

"You're right." I tried to sound a little cheerful, then I sighed. "I needed this." I held the glass up.

"You don't believe me," she said quietly.

"If you mean about my wife never coming back, then no, I don't. She always comes back," I said, tipping my glass toward her and smiling.

She looked up at me. "After everything that woman has done to you, why do you still stick up for her?"

"I'm not sticking up for her. I'm just stating the truth. Besides, she's my wife, and she's been in my life for a very long time. I truly loved her. A part of me still does. You just don't give up on real love like that."

"You call that love?" She spit out the words and I scanned the floor, looking for the spittle I'd have to clean up.

"I'm not denying it's turned out to be a warped kind of love, but it wasn't always like that. She's missing, goddamn it. If it were just a friend, I'd be as concerned for them as I am for her. It's one thing to know she might go to jail and I'll have to deal with that. It's another not to know where she is. I'm worried. Is she hurt? Did she leave me? Run away so that she doesn't have to face a trial? I'm a need-to-know kind of person. I need to know where my wife is!"

Amelia didn't budge. "I thought you'd be happy she was gone?"

"Relieved, maybe, but not happy."

I studied my friend. There was something behind her blank face, something boiling inside, just below the surface, and I could tell she was working really hard to keep from exploding.

A sudden thought raced through my mind and I struggled to grasp it. I needed it to take form because there was something important lurking within a question I needed to ask. I sank into the other chair at the table. Then I took a deep breath, let it out and swallowed. "What did you do?"

"I don't know what you're talking about. I didn't do anything. I've just been trying to help you."

I wanted to scream. Plain and simple, because I didn't want to argue again. I wanted an answer to my question. I understood at that moment another disagreement about my wife's innocence would never make a difference with her. Not anymore. Amelia did not understand, and it appeared she never would.

"Then what is wrong with you?" I asked in a calm, but solid voice.

Amelia's shoulders began to shake with what appeared to be rage. When she looked up at me, her face was dry, but her skin was pale and her eyes were wide. She shrugged. "She killed my sister and now she's gone. She may never have to answer for what she did. She probably ran away."

"Maybe. Maybe not. But no matter what, I *need* to know what happened to her. Until then, all I know is that she will come back. I know her. She's my wife."

"She *was* your wife."

My weight shifted in my chair with the turmoil I felt in my bones. I swallowed before I spoke. "She still is my wife, but I am not blind to everything she did." I reached out and touched her fingers with mine. Even though she flinched, I caressed them as I spoke. "You have to understand everything I've gone through and ev—"

"I know what you've gone through! But I don't know what my sister went through. The agony that evil woman put her through. The pain she felt when she was pushed over a cliff, hitting the rocks on the way down, breaking every bone in her small…" She sobbed. "Frail…" It was as if her body buckled, as she slid off the chair and fell to her knees. "…body." Her cries were uncontrollable.

I knelt on the floor beside her and took her in my arms. I stroked her hair. "I'm so sorry. So sorry. I know how much you loved her. I loved my wife that way too. The word is loved. Even though that feeling has faded with all that she did, that part of you never goes away. You just learn to live with it."

"I can't live with that," she cried. "Don't you see? That's why I had to do it."

"Shhh, it's okay," I crooned, stroking her back, hoping that talking to her and comforting her was enough to get her to tell me exactly what it was she did. She sank into my body like a small child afraid of the monster under their bed that woke them up from a peaceful slumber.

I knew from here I had to tread lightly. "What did you do?" I asked in a quiet, soothing voice. "It's okay, I'll understand, but I need to know just like you needed to know what happened to your sister."

Her sobs quieted, but she continued to cry. "I loved my sister. I never stopped. You can't go on not knowing what happened to someone you still love, but you don't love Mary Ellen anymore. You said so yourself."

I hugged her closer to me. "But I did love her. For a long time. I won't be able to go on if I don't find out what happened to her. I need to close that chapter of my life. And if M.E. finds out I took her research, she might blame me for ruining her. I'll always have to look over my shoulder. Please, Amelia, I need to know. What did you do?"

"I didn't do anything." Amelia pulled away from me and got up off the floor. She walked to the kitchen door and opened it without looking back, but she stopped, her hand on the knob. "Will there ever be a chance for us?" she asked with choked words.

Still on my knees, I answered, "Amelia, I'm still in the chapter of my married life. I need answers to end it before I can move to the next."

"You'll get your answers." She walked out and shut the door behind her.

I got to my feet, ran and opened the front door to see her walk around the corner of the house. I had no idea what I expected to see or hear. She didn't look at me. She said nothing. She got in her truck, backed out of the driveway and drove away without a backward glance.

My head pounded, yet I felt like I would topple over from heavy fatigue at any moment.

Why? What? When? How did I get to this point in my life? I sank onto the couch and took in the interior of the stone house I had lovingly and painstakingly worked to transform into a showplace.

The living room was beautiful with freshly painted walls and would be even more so when the new wood floors were installed. The rich grains and natural colors, refinsihed wainscoting and moldings would elevate it to elegant. Beyond that was a new kitchen that soon would be complete with the latest in everything an expert chef would want outfitted in their workspace—even though I would never use it in that capacity.

Hell. Depending on how things developed with my wife, who was currently missing, would I stay here? I already knew the answer to that. No. I never planned on making this my forever home. It was an interim. Somewhere I had to be until everything else fell into place so I could go back. Back to San Francisco. I just always thought my wife would go with me.

From day one, I had always wanted my old life back—my home, my job, my friends and family and the plush life we had built together. Now, I was definitely stuck in this wretched place not knowing exactly what happened to my wife and wondering if that damn Amelia did something to blow my chances of ever getting back to California...

I had to think. If M.E. was gone for good, where did that leave me? How much of a mess would I have to clean up? And how was I going to get Amelia to admit that she killed my wife because I was pretty sure she did? In Amelia's eyes, I had scorned her advances—I was sure of that. Was it enough to make her mad? If she did do something to my wife, would she leave a trail in my direction because I scorned her?

My head still pounding, I was clear enough to know I needed to protect myself. But how? What or who did I need to protect myself from and did I even have to? Either way, I believed that preparation was the key—anticipating anything that could happen and having a plan for it (which always included Excel spreadsheets).

I found a pen and pad of paper and turned on the television that I hadn't watched since the movers put it in the living room. I began to write down my thoughts, but I passed out before I got one solid idea written on paper.

I woke with a start when I heard a loud knock on the front door.

"Damn," I spat, trying to sit up. "Not again." I felt groggy with a dull pounding that lulled in the back of my head.

The knock grew louder, faster, and for a moment I pictured Amelia standing on the other side to plead her case of us being together. I hesitated until I heard a familiar voice.

"Ms. Pious, it's Diane Kensington. Open up please."

I stumbled to the door, hearing the urgency in her voice. The room spun a bit and I thought I might pass out from the dizziness. When I opened it, she pushed me out of the way with her body and went directly to the television.

"Where's the remote?" she asked.

"Excuse me?"

"The remote."

I pointed to the small black box on the floor where it must have fallen when I passed out.

The volume rose, filling the room with reverberating angry sounds, and drew my attention to the flat-screen. There, I saw my wife's secret hideaway burning, reminding me of the devil's eternal fires of hell. The blaze engulfed the part of the building where her apartment stood. It was as if I could feel the heat through the television, but the heat I was actually feeling was coming from the lawyer standing next to me. Anger filled her next words. "Did you know about this place?"

"I, I, don't understand," I stammered. Of course, I knew about it, but even in my fogged state, I knew better than to tell her, "Yes, Amelia and I were just there today and I stole my wife's research." Instead, I watched the intense, flaming colors of red, orange, and yellow take over the television screen, filling me with horror. It was just a building, but why did my guts feel like they were being cut out of me? My wife's house of assignation where she conducted sick, sexual research burning to the ground was the payment for her wrongful deeds. So, why should I care if her den of iniquity was going up in flames? My head felt light like a balloon floating in the air and my body seemed to follow suit swaying side to side as I watched.

I don't remember asking, but I heard the words, felt my mouth move. "Was she in there?"

* * *

When I woke, I was in a darkened room that smelled of hospital antiseptic cleaners. It took me several seconds to distinguish the tiled walls, linoleum floor, and the bed with an obvious plastic cover over the mattress that made sounds as I adjusted my body to sit up. The IV stand next to me confirmed I was in a hospital room. My gaze rested on a woman sleeping in a recliner next to the window. Thick red hair fell down and around her shoulders. Rough hands lay across her lap. She was dressed in fresh clothes—at least I thought they were fresh because it wasn't her usual work apparel.

Amelia's black jeans, black boots, and white waffle shirt looked more dress-casual than down and dirty work clothes. Her hair was never down, but always pulled back.

I stared at her and not just because her attire was something I wasn't used to. Why was she here? I shut my eyes, trying to remember what had happened and how I got in a hospital bed. Her lids opened, her head lifted, and a smile appeared on her lips. "Well, it's about time, sleepyhead."

Sleepyhead. If I had truly been asleep, why was I in a hospital bed? I lifted the sheet and looked down at my body wrapped in one of those disgusting hospital gowns—definitely on the bottom of the fashion style scale.

"What happened?" My throat was raw, making my voice sound ragged, rough.

"I believe they called it a meltdown."

I wracked my brain to remember my so-called "meltdown," but the only thing I could remember was starting to make a list (a list of what, I had no idea), and then hearing a knock on my door.

"I don't remember."

Amelia got up from the recliner and pulled a metal chair over to my bed. When she sat, she took my hand in hers. I didn't withdraw.

"Diane Kensington went to your house." Then she lowered her voice as if someone might be listening to our conversation and she didn't want them to hear us. "The building where M.E. had her apartment was set on fire. She was looking for M.E. Something about a warrant."

"Did they find her? Has my wife come home?"

"There's more," she said with a look of pity on her face. "Melissa overheard Diane on the phone talking to the police about bringing your wife in. I'll bet she was going to alert Mary Ellen, maybe run away with her because she asked Diane for some time off."

I breathed a sigh of relief. Maybe M.E. wasn't dead from a fire like I assumed, and had just skipped town. "Does Diane know about them?"

"I think she does, but not about M.E.'s research, however, she knows now about the apartment. When the apartment was on fire, they found Mary Ellen's name through the owner of the building. The police called Diane and she went straight to your house. You saw it on the television and asked her if your wife was in the apartment. Then you passed out. You've been out for over eight hours." She squeezed my hand. "I've been so worried. They ran blood tests to make sure there wasn't any underlying cause for your passing out."

"I passed out because I've been stressed with everything that's going on and the thought of my wife dying in a fire just pushed me over the edge. Amelia, how do you know all this?"

"I have my ways." She winked. "But there's one more thing you need to know. Earlier in the evening, Melissa's apartment was also on fire. I heard Diane in the hall say the police have a lot of questions for you."

The door opened and Diane walked in just as my stomach dropped and my heart began to beat faster. I didn't have time to process everything Amelia said because Diane jumped right in.

"I'm so happy to see you awake." She glared at Amelia. "Will you please wait outside? I need to speak to Adalynn." She waited for Amelia to do something or say something. When she didn't, Diane added, "Alone."

Amelia squeezed my hand. "I'll be in the hallway if you need me."

"She won't," Diane replied for me.

I watched the exchange between them, wondering why Diane felt animosity toward Amelia.

When she left, Diane turned to me. "Why were you taking antidepressants? Do you know you almost overdosed on them?"

"Excuse me? What do you mean I almost overdosed? I'm not, nor have I ever taken antidepressants."

"Adalynn, I'm not accusing you of anything. It's just what they found in your blood. The doctor will be in to tell you, but I overheard a nurse inform him you had antidepressants in your system. Desipramine to be exact. They believe that's what made you pass out because your blood pressure dropped."

"So, someone's been drugging me, is that what you're saying?"

"If you say you haven't been taking any pills, then yes, someone has. Any idea who that might be?" She glanced toward the door.

"There's no reason for anyone to give me pills," I answered.

"Well, let me go check with the doctor and see when you can get out of here."

"What about the fire? My wife?"

"The police will be in to speak to you about that. I don't know any more than you. I'll be right back."

As soon as she left, Amelia slid in.

"Did I hear correctly? Someone drugged you with antidepressants?"

I cocked my head and raised an eyebrow. "Listening in, huh?"

"That's because I care about you. You have to know it was most likely your wife that was slipping pills into your liquids."

That was the last thing I needed to come out of Amelia's mouth. "You need to leave. I can't deal with this right now."

"Addy, come on."

"It's bad enough you've been accusing my wife nonstop of killing your sister. Now you're accusing her of drugging me."

"You can't deny what that bitch has done." Amelia's voice rose.

"Shhh," I scolded her. "Keep your voice down. We're in a hospital, for God's sake. And yes, I can deny it." I looked at the door for a nurse or doctor to come running in to see what all the ruckus was. When no one appeared, I turned my gaze back on Amelia. "Let's agree not to talk about that. The only thing I need to know right now is if my wife was in either apartment when they were on fire."

She took a deep breath. "The police and fire investigators are still on the scene. They haven't released any information except that both fires started inside the apartments. That's all they've said."

I was about to ask Amelia to leave again when the door opened. Diane Kensington stood in the doorway with two policemen behind her. This was becoming a déjà vu I didn't want to repeat. My stomach contents rose up into my throat that was already burning, and it made me wonder if they'd had to pump my stomach. *It's crazy the way the mind works in difficult situations.*

Seeing the three of them, I came to the conclusion that the news couldn't be good. Now I was glad to be in a hospital bed. I wouldn't have to worry about falling to the floor. Again.

Amelia walked over to the recliner and sat down, leaving room for Diane to stand next to the bed and take my hand.

"Are you feeling all right? Are you up for this?"

"I'm all right. But I have a feeling that's going to change." I almost laughed, knowing Diane was putting on a good act. I never got the sense that she liked me.

I watched her swallow hard and then glance back at the policemen. One of them nodded and Diane stepped aside for me to get a better view of them as they approached my bed.

My eyes drifted from her to Amelia and then settled on the policemen. There was nothing in the expressions on Diane's and Amelia's faces that revealed why the cops were here. Their faces were stoic, almost blank.

I waited for one of them to speak.

"Miss Pious," the shorter man began.

"Ms. It's Ms. Pious."

Diane stepped into view. "Adalynn, this is Officer Canner. Please listen to him. He's only trying to help."

I didn't feel as if anyone was helping me—more like I was being ambushed.

"I'm sorry to have to tell you this, Ms. Pious," the smaller officer began again, and to my surprise without any animosity for me correcting him. "There were two bodies in the remains of an apartment fire. That apartment belonged to Melissa Blaken."

Shock went through me, igniting my nerve fibers as if I stuck my finger in an outlet. I felt like I was on fire. Flashbacks of flames swallowing an apartment that I saw on the television were of M.E.'s apartment. Why was he saying the apartment belonged to Melissa?

"We believe the other body to be your wife, Mary Ellen Montgomery. Did you know she was there?"

I took several quick breaths. Did I hear him correctly? I swallowed and took several more breaths—deeper and faster. *Can't hyperventilate, can't hyperventilate. Stay in control.*

I pulled my hand from Diane's and folded both in my lap. I stared at my fingers. "Are you sure? How can you know so fast?"

The officer shifted his weight, obviously uncomfortable with the answer he was about to give me. "The, um, bodies were recognizable. They didn't die from burns. They were in the bedroom. The fire started in the living room, and the firefighters put the blaze out before it destroyed the bedroom. Autopsies are being done to determine the cause of death."

I took a deep breath. "Are you telling me one of the bodies fits the description of Mary Ellen? That my wife is dead?"

"Yes ma'am."

My wife was dead. M.E. was dead. Why? What happened? Who killed her? Why was she in Melissa's bedroom? Well that was a stupid question. "Do you know what killed her?"

"I'm sorry, ma'am, but as I said, the autopsies are being performed to determine the cause of death. We have not other informationn at this time."

I raised my voice. "Who killed my wife?"

Diane took my hand again and stroked my hair with her other. "Shh, you need to stay calm. They don't have all the facts yet." She watched me with more sympathy than I could stand.

I began to cry. "Why? Why would someone do this?"

But I knew why.

CHAPTER TWENTY-THREE

I sat alone in the hospital room, repulsed by the sanitary odors weaving in and out of the stench of sickness. The doctor had ushered Diane, the police, and Amelia out of my room to let me process the news they had brought me.

My wife was dead. I never saw this coming. I hadn't prepared a backup plan for this. I had plans for when she went to jail and plans for if she was incarcerated for a year or ten. But for her death, I had nothing, even though there were so many scenarios I could have made. Now I would have to deal with her death and no plan in place. I had no idea what to do, and trying to sort it out in a hospital made my head pound. Guess it was a good thing I was in a hospital.

What made my head spin even more was that my wife died in Melissa's apartment—not hers. I remember Amelia telling me that Melissa's apartment was on fire earlier in the evening, but the only one I saw on television was M.E.'s, and it looked like that one was totally destroyed. What had happened?

After examining me, the doctor suggested I try to get some sleep. He said I would need rest for when the police returned in a few hours to question me, and because of the pills I had somehow ingested, he couldn't give me anything. He told me I had desipramine in my system—a drug used for depression. It wasn't enough to be an overdose, but since I had never taken antidepressants before, it was enough to lower my blood pressure, make me dizzy, and thus, cause the fainting spell.

I promised I would sleep. It was the best I could do to get the doctor to leave, but I made him promise if my vitals were good when I woke up, and the tests showed my kidneys and liver were doing okay, he would discharge me. He said he would, but he didn't know how long it would take for the test results to come back, and that we had to wait for them to make sure the drug was leaving my system.

I wanted to discharge myself, but thought twice about it, wondering if it would make the police suspicious of me, despite the fact I didn't do anything. I rolled over and looked out the window.

I just wanted to be done with all of this. It wasn't supposed to happen this way. We moved here to start a new life, to end the chapter of her cheating in San Francisco, but no, she couldn't stop. Why had I been so stupid? I believed when Raeann was no longer in her sights, she would come back to me. We would build a life here that would eventually take us back to San Francisco.

However, I had come to understand that no matter what I did, what changes we made, no matter how big or small, M.E. couldn't help herself. No one could help her. And now because of her rapacious need for sex, resulting in sick research that she obsessed over to become accepted by her colleagues, she was dead. She would have been better off doing research on people who had voracious appetites for sex and how they ruined their lives because of it.

Dead.

I didn't want her dead. In jail, maybe. Out of my life, most likely, but not dead. I had loved her. I married her. What was worse was she took me with her. I was dead too. Dead inside. Numb of all emotions.

The doctor was right. I was exhausted and needed sleep so I could answer the cops' remaining questions. After that, I would find a way that would make it possible for me to return to San Francisco and put all of this behind me.

* * *

"And you knew nothing about the apartment."

"Officer, how many times are you going to ask me that? Do you need hearing aids?"

Diane shot me a warning look.

"No, I did not know anything about the apartment and that is the last time I'm answering that." I wasn't angry at the officer for asking the question over and over again. I was angry at my answer.

Diane put a hand on my shoulder. I was sitting on the edge of the bed fully dressed, about to get the hell out of the hospital when they showed up. I would have felt much better doing this at home and I told them, but they were in a hurry and wanted to interrogate me now. So, I complied.

"Was your wife having an affair?"

"If you mean here, in New York, not that I knew of. I did know she was having one in San Francisco, but that ended. It was part of the reason we moved here."

"Once a cheater, always a cheater," I heard Amelia say under her breath from the hall. I wasn't surprised that she was out there. I suspected she had been waiting for me to wake up.

Hospitals needed to soundproof their walls better.

The officers looked at each other. The taller one went over and shut the door.

"She's my ride home," I answered their exchanged looks of annoyance. "So, can I go now?"

"We'll need you to come down to the morgue and identify the body."

I swallowed and almost choked on my spit when the officer said that. I would have to look at my dead wife? On a metal slab in a morgue?

At that moment, I really hated her.

One of the officers cleared his throat. "When was the last time you saw Ms. Montgomery?"

"I'm a little foggy on what day it is, but I think two days ago. She left for work and didn't come home that night. I waited until the usual time, midnight, then I fell asleep shortly after."

"Was it usual for her to come home at midnight?"

I rolled my eyes. "That's what I said. The usual time. She often worked late and was always home by midnight. I didn't know she wasn't home until your comrades knocked on my door in the middle of the night." I looked down at the floor. "God, don't you people talk to each other?"

"Adalynn, please, they're just trying to get information to understand how M.E. died. Don't you want to help them?" Diane asked.

I stood. "I am more than happy to cooperate, but I don't have any information that's going to help them. I don't know anything about her apartment or her affair. Nothing, nada. Zilch. Zero." I looked from Diane to the two policemen waiting for the next question. I wanted to point to Diane and say, "She probably knows more about it than I do," but I knew it wasn't true. Finally, I asked, "Can I go now? I need to make arrangements for my wife."

"If you would ask your ride to follow us to the morgue, you can go after you identify the body. And then we'll need you to come to the precinct for more questioning. An officer will call you to set that up."

"Of course you do," I said under my breath. Then I called to my ride so she could hear me through the closed door, "Hey, Amelia, did you hear that?" I wouldn't be surprised if she had because I'd bet my tiny Honda that her body was glued to the wall just next to the doorway.

Amelia slipped inside. Smiling, she asked, "I heard nothing. What can I do for you?"

"I need a ride to the morgue. I have to identify some remains."

"Of course. I'll drive you there and then home. You'll need someone to be with you. It's not a pleasant thing to do."

I didn't say anything. Instead, I walked out the door and toward the elevator. Only Amelia followed me. When we were on the elevator, I asked her, "Did you have to identify your sister's remains? Is that why you said it's not pleasant? By the way, I think the word 'remains' is an odd word for describing identifying a loved one's dead body."

The elevator stopped on the ground floor. "Yes and yes, and I agree with you on the word 'remains.' I had to do it by a Zoom call. They couldn't wait for me to fly out to San Francisco. I imagine it's worse in person. You have to smell all those obnoxious morgue smells."

The doors opened. "Oh God, I can't stand the hospital smells. I don't know how I'll do with death smells." I stepped out and I felt a hand clasp mine.

"I'll be there to hold you up if you pass out again."

I pulled my hand away. "Gee thanks," I answered, knowing that's what she thought I would do. Then I said, "I'm sorry. I appreciate it. I really do."

Still, I wondered what was going on with her. She was acting so weird—almost like she was bipolar. It was so out of character for her. She was always cheerful, but the day before, she was adamant my wife was not coming back to the point of being crazed about it. Then she showed up at the hospital, as if she were my better half watching over me like a hawk. Now she was giving me a ride to the morgue, ready to hold me up in case I fainted at the sight of a dead body that was most likely M.E.

I wondered if she heard all my answers to the police. I didn't think she could through the closed door, but I wondered if she was really on my side or if she would rat me out for the lies I'd just told. I didn't know about the apartment, her research or her affair with Melissa—until Amelia told me about them. I imagined that in her eyes, she would say I had just committed a crime by taking the papers out of my wife's apartment, but she wouldn't rat me out since she'd gone with me and wiped down the fingerprints. She'd also known what was going on, and she'd known longer than me.

We walked in silence to her truck as I waited for her to point that fact out to me. But no words were spoken. I climbed in and she started the motor in silence. We drove to the morgue without another word to each other and I thought I was going to burst a gasket if one of us didn't say something soon.

"Thank you for agreeing to take me to the morgue and then home."

Very slowly, Amelia rested her hand on mine. "When will you believe in my feelings for you? I would do anything for you. Anything."

There it was. The one thing I didn't want to happen. The one thing I didn't want to deal with. Those few words made me tense, because now as I anticipated seeing my dead wife, I had to figure out what to do about Amelia.

She pulled into the parking lot of the morgue and I got out of the truck. I felt as if my stomach had joined the American gymnastics team. It flipped, did somersaults, cartwheels, and dismounts. I swallowed, hoping to keep the contents of my unruly organ where they belonged.

We walked into the morgue and I gave my name to the receptionist—if that's what you could call the male attendant sitting at a desk outside the room where all the dead bodies were kept.

He got up and went inside. A few minutes later, he returned with the coroner, Dr. Janet Cortana, who explained the process to me. She'd pull a white sheet off a dead woman's face in hopes that I could officially identify her.

I didn't want to identify the dead body. Crap. Shit. Fuck. (There was that word again. Oh God, I was going to be sick.) I followed the female coroner into the dead body containment room. The linoleum floors, mottled from years of scrubbing, were in stark contrast to the stainless-steel decor. Everything was stainless steel and if it was a home, it would be stylish and the feature of a home improvement makeover show. As a very reputable San Francisco interior decorator, I would know.

But this…this was morbid, except this line of thinking quieted the gymnastic stunts in my gut; it just didn't calm the shaking in my body. I clasped my hands, hoping to quell the emotional response to the corpse smells filling my nostrils. I couldn't even take a deep, calming breath.

"Can we get this over with, please?" I gulped.

"Yes, of course," Dr. Cortana said as she led me over to a stainless-steel gurney.

The white sheet covering it had bumps and curves in all the right places for it to be a female body. Part of me was hoping for a dead male body. She took hold of part of the sheet, obviously near the head, in her fingers and held on to it.

"Are you ready, Ms. Pious?"

I sucked in a breath. If my wife, the woman I had believed to be the soul of my life, the woman who had once fulfilled me sexually and intellectually, who was there for me (oh yeah, until she cheated on me over and over again) and now was truly dead as the police insisted, it would be her body under the shapely stark white sheet.

I couldn't look. I never wanted her to die. I just wanted her to be my wife—to love and respect me in the way she had—until…I couldn't remember when she started living our relationship in a way that only worked for her and not for us or especially, not for me.

When had that all changed?

I felt like fainting, and I put my hand back to steady myself. I instantly realized I had put it on the dead body, and I felt myself starting to drop to the floor. Amelia put her arm around me and took my hand. The good doctor's eyes were soft and patient as she waited for my answer.

It made me want to scream at her. *Don't make me do this. How the hell would you feel if this dead body were your husband, or wife, or worse, child?* Finally, I nodded.

Dr. Cortana gently lifted the end of the crisp, white sheet and pulled it down below the neck. Her neck. M.E.'s neck.

I had no tears. I had no screams. I was numb from head to toe. My brain was numb. There were no emotions rolling around in my head. Either that or there were just too many all jumbled together and no way to pull them apart.

"Ms. Pious, do you recognize this body?"

I cleared my throat. "Yes, that's my wife," I whispered.

"What is your wife's name, please?"

"M.E." I cleared my throat again. "Mary Ellen Montgomery," I said louder and with more conviction. I had to force out the next sentence in a whisper. "Do you know what killed her?"

"I'm sorry, Ms. Pious, the autopsy hasn't been completed yet."

My gaze couldn't leave M.E.'s face. There was no million-dollar, perfectly white, full-lipped, toothy smile. Her lips, appearing as if they were glued together, gave a stoic expression on her face. Her lids were closed, preventing me from taking one last look into those brilliant blue eyes, and her usually soft, dark-brown hair and thick, velvety lashes lacked the luster they always had, now dirty with ash. Still, I needed to touch her, so I leaned over and kissed her forehead. Then I gently stroked her hair and recoiled. It felt more coarse than silky.

She was truly gone. I would never be able to run my fingers along the muscles of her stomach or down her slender hips. I would never again feel her inside me, sending me to a sexual climax I had never experienced with anyone else but her.

I would no longer have to wait for her to come home, wondering where she was, what she was doing and who she was doing it with. More importantly, I would no longer have to wait for the M.E. I fell in love with to come back to me, even though I knew she never would have…dead or alive.

I felt a pull on my arm and realized Amelia was gently moving me away from the gurney. The whispers in my ear became louder. "Come on, Addy. Let me get you home."

It was soothing yet disturbing.

I allowed her to take my arm and lead me out of the morgue. I got in her truck feeling almost as lifeless as the bodies in the metal drawers that lined one sterile wall of the morgue. I didn't speak on the way home and Amelia didn't pressure me to. When she pulled into my driveway, she opened my door and helped me out. Then she guided me into the house and up to my bedroom.

She helped me undress and got me into bed. I was too desensitized to feel anything, to react to anything. That was the only thing I could come up with when I felt lips on mine and the weight of a body on top of me.

I gave in to the warmth of moist lips pressing on mine. I gave in to the curves of the body moving up and down my torso. My hand raised to pull her head closer, allowing our mouths to open. I stroked thick, bushy hair and…

I shoved as hard as I could. Amelia rolled off and onto the floor with such force, I felt the bed move when she hit the floor. There was a loud "umph" followed by an agonizing groan.

"What the hell do you think you're doing?"

Amelia scrambled to her feet, a horrified look on her face.

"Good God, woman. I just identified my dead wife's body at the morgue."

Amelia moved to the bed. Slowly, she sat down. "I'm…I'm so sorry," she whispered with a shaky voice.

I jumped out of bed, pulling the comforter with me, and wrapped it around my body. My first instinct was to yell at her to leave, but something stopped me. "Why don't you go downstairs and get us two beers? I could use one right about now. I'll be right down."

Amelia stood. "Are you sure you don't want me to leave?"

I took a deep breath to hold down the anger, frustration, and sadness that were fighting to take over. "No, no. I need time to…to process. A beer and some company will help me to relax. If you don't mind staying a while. Then I'm pretty sure I'll be able to sleep. I need rest to deal with all of this. I'm tired, but I can't sleep." I turned so she couldn't see me roll my eyes. What I just said made no sense to me. Why would it make sense to her? But when I looked back, she had left the room.

I dressed so fast, I was tripping over myself as I pulled on a pair of pants and then my socks. I hurried down the stairs to the kitchen and saw Amelia sitting at the table nursing a beer. Another opened one sat on the table.

I sat down and took a long swallow. It didn't taste all that great, but I needed a buzz for the conversation I hoped to have with her.

"I want to thank you for, uh, being there for me the last few days."

"I wouldn't have been anywhere else. It's a lot for anyone to handle."

"You know, you're always saying that, but this can't be easy for you either. I mean with your sister's death and the connection to my wife."

"You mean her killer."

I studied Amelia. Underneath her gleaming green eyes and bushy Scottish red hair was an indelible anger produced from a deep-rooted belief that my wife murdered her sister.

"I'm sorry," she blurted before taking another drink.

"It's all right. I accepted a while ago that I can't change your mind."

"Why would you want to try? The police believe your wife did it."

"But they haven't proved it."

"Yeah, now they'll probably just close the book on my sister's murder. Just like you can't get blood from a stone, you can't get justice from a dead body." She looked at her beer. "Then again, maybe you can."

I wasn't sure which question to ask. *What do you mean* floated around in my head but whenever I asked her that, the conversation took a nasty turn. So, I tried a different approach. "How?"

Her eyes peeked out from under eyelashes darkened with mascara. "She's dead. She doesn't get to live her cushy life with a beautiful woman by her side, come hell or high water. I still don't think it's good enough for what she did to my sister, but at least it's something." She pushed her lips together like she was going to spit on the floor—more like on the memory of my dead wife, but she refrained.

I didn't say anything, but I focused on her face that was full of emotion. I couldn't seem to relate, because once again, there were too many emotions all at once to understand exactly what she was feeling. There was something beneath her exterior that she was fighting internally. The struggle was evident in her wretched moods and her feelings for me that went up and down with the speed of a roller coaster with twists, turns, and inversions. Because of that, I didn't know what to do next.

How was I going to get Amelia to admit any wrong doing, if she did indeed, know how my wife died. I swallowed hard, understanding the only way I was going to get her to open up truthfully was to step into her emotional lair. In doing so, I needed to choose the emotion I wanted to capitalize on. I had to tread carefully, not being able to identify what state of mind Amelia was really in, and what she might do if I pissed her off.

It would be a huge risk on my part because the image of us being in bed together was the one that first came to mind and it wasn't something I wanted to do. Still, I knew it was the only way I would be able to get her to open up. So, I had to do, what I had to do.

I extended my hand across the table and touched her fingers, running my thumb softly over her skin. She didn't move, but once again those green irises raised and took me in. "I'm sorry about upstairs. I'm just so confused and sad and angry. I never expected anything like this to happen when we left San Francisco. I was hoping for a quiet life, one where we could work to return to our former selves."

She eyed me suspiciously. "You really wanted to be what you were in San Francisco?"

"Not that part. I'd hoped she would redeem herself, become the woman I fell in love with. I could have a successful business once again with a happy home life. I wasn't a fool. There was a chance it wouldn't happen, but I had hope."

"Good thing you don't gamble." She chuckled softly.

"Yeah, I would have lost big time."

She sniffed and then wrapped her hand around mine.

"How about we get some dinner and then come back here for a night of drinking." I held my empty beer bottle up. "I'm going to need a better drink than this."

Amelia took a moment before she answered. "I'd like that. Italian or Thai?"

I wanted to say truth. Instead, I answered, "I'll get my purse and coat and meet you at the front door."

I was actually happy I took this route. For now.

Amelia's night and day attitudes had settled into the light of day. Dinner was more than pleasant. It was as if we both secretly decided to ignore the elephant in the room and return to the friendship we had developed over time. We enjoyed our meals, talked about the house, her work, my work, my life in San Francisco, hers in Ithaca, all without any mention of my wife and what had just happened.

It wasn't until dessert when I realized I was out in a restaurant with another woman, enjoying myself, laughing and drinking the same day I identified my dead wife's body. I choked on the swallow of wine that passed through my lips.

"Are you okay?" Amelia stood and was about to come over to me, most likely to hit me on the back.

I put my hand up. I knew the other people in the restaurant were watching, knowing full well what it felt like to have a dry red wine go down the wrong passageway. I quickly took a sip of water and tried to speak. In a hoarse voice, I answered, "I'm fine. Really. Can we get out of here?"

I wasn't fine. I thought I was going to be sick, but I couldn't back out of my plan now. I had Amelia in a good place and I needed her to stay there. I needed her to admit to what I believed she had done and explain how my wife had died.

When we left the restaurant and she took my hand, I felt confident this mood of hers would last long enough for me to get the truth out of her. If her mood began to tank once again, I would make it last until she told me the whole truth and nothing but the truth.

CHAPTER TWENTY-FOUR

After sharing a bottle of cabernet sauvignon at the restaurant, I suggested we go to the stone house, where I immediately opened a bottle of merlot. I brought two full glasses and the bottle with me to the living room and stood in the doorway.

In my most seductive voice, I suggested, "We'd be a lot more comfortable upstairs. The alcohol I'm about to drink will make me very sleepy and I won't have to worry about making my way up to my bed."

Amelia's smile was one I'd never seen before. It played at the corners of her lips, but there was a mild twitch. She looked at me, her eyes dancing with anticipation.

I swallowed hard, because my anticipation was not even remotely close to what Amelia's was. She anticipated a great evening of sex. With me. I anticipated throwing up during an evening of sex. I didn't want to, but I knew I'd have to perform to keep Amelia where I wanted her. It took everything I had to put all that had happened in the last months back in the recesses of my mind and focus on what I was about to do.

I handed a glass to Amelia and helped her off the couch. She followed me upstairs where I set the bottle down on the nightstand. After fluffing the pillows, I settled onto the bed and sipped from my glass. Without looking, I felt the mattress depress next to me.

"I've heard of people going into shock, but I never understood what that meant until now." I moved, adjusting the blankets beneath me. "There's a numbness in my body, my heart, my brain, in every muscle, vein, artery, and cell. It's as if I'm not processing anything."

Her hand moved to mine. She gently covered my fingers, touching each one.

"Is this what you felt like when your sister died?"

"Yes, but we don't need to talk about that." She reached for me and pulled me close so I rested against her with my head on her shoulder. I put an arm around her chest. "You need sleep. I'll be here with you and we can talk about whatever you need to in the morning. I promise you'll feel better."

How could she say that? She still didn't feel better about her sister, and I knew I would never feel better about M.E.'s death, only that she was out of my life. The lies and cheating, the emotional abuse would now be over, but instead of her being alive, possibly in jail, she was dead lying on a metal gurney in the morgue.

So, how was I supposed to feel? Debilitated by sorrow? Overjoyed? Angry? Relieved? Grateful for this woman holding me? A woman that by rights should not want anything to do with me since she believed my wife killed her sister. A woman who I believed killed my wife. Should I be mortified? Or... obliged? But here she was, and if I'd let her, we would be having sex—or in her mind, making love. How screwed up was that?

I sat up. "Why are you here?"

Amelia propped herself up on an elbow and stared at me. "You know why."

"No, I don't. Why are you here?"

"Don't you want me here?"

"I'm not saying that. I'm asking why are you here? After everything that's happened. I mean you believe in your heart that my wife killed your sister. I know in my heart that she did not. That thorn is always going to be between us."

"Not anymore. The thorn is rotting in hell." She smiled and then leaned forward, placing a soft kiss on my lips.

I felt sick. What was happening with Amelia? It took every bit of strength and resolve I could muster to return the kiss, but I held back, not allowing it to escalate.

She pulled back and smiled again. "She had to go. Otherwise, there would never be room for me," she said as she touched my chest with her finger, "in that lovely heart of yours. Now she's gone and we can be together." She kissed me again, this time pressing her lips harder into mine, playing with my mouth, enticing it to open.

I held her off by speaking. "What if M.E. wasn't dead? How—"

"She would be in jail for her crimes. Eventually, she would be out of your life and eventually she would seep out of your heart. I thought I could wait for that, but I couldn't. Besides, she needed to pay for her crimes, not just be out of your life. Jail was too good for her because she'd still be alive and you would never let her go. So, don't you see? Your life would have been ruined waiting for her and never being able to have her. Why would you waste your life like that when I'm here to love you the way you should be loved? I knew once she was gone, you would give yourself to me. It was the only way."

Her lips pressed against mine once again, and she forced her tongue into my mouth. I felt sick. It was all wrong. Her taste was wrong. Her words were wrong. She drew me close and her hands roamed my back and sides, making their way to my breasts.

I let her feel me, but I kept talking. "I don't understand. What was the only way?"

She continued to caress me, running her hand under my shirt. She kissed my neck, nibbled my earlobe and in between advances, she said, "To make her go away, to disappear. She had to die."

This was the delicate part. I allowed her to feel me, consume me, all the while holding my innate sexual responses in check. I hoped that she didn't sense me holding back, that by giving her what she wanted, she would get lost in her desires, allowing her to open up to me.

I moaned under her touch and kisses. "How did you do it?"

Her breath was ragged. "You…" she breathed. "Don't really…" Another deep breath escaped her lips. "Want to know."

I pulled her lips back to mine and kissed her hard. "Yes, I do. I need to know how much you really wanted me."

"My friend…"

"David?" I asked, keeping my hands on her back.

"Uh-huh. He…"

She was going for the button on my jeans. I took her hand and put two of her fingers in my mouth. She moaned. After she took a deep breath, she said, "He, uh, tapped…" More heavy breathing as she began to knead my breasts. "…Melissa's phone." She pulled her fingers out of my mouth and replaced them with her tongue.

I pulled my lips away and planted kisses down her neck to the top of her shirt. She arched her back as I inserted my fingers under the top of her jeans and slid them along her skin at the waistband.

She forced the next words out. "Mary Ellen and Melissa were going to meet at Melissa's apartment in the morning before her classes. That was all I needed."

I flipped her over and crawled on top. "For what?"

Amelia's eyes opened and she stopped.

I knew I wouldn't get the answer if I didn't pull her back in. So I rubbed my pelvis against hers, kissed her, and caressed her body. "What did you do for me? For us?" I whispered in her ear and then teased her earlobe with nibbles.

She grabbed my hips and guided them while she thrust against me. "Poison. In their coffee."

And there it was.

I knew I couldn't just stop. I needed her to still want me. To trust me. I continued what I was doing with her for a few more minutes and then gently rolled off her, falling to my back and breathing hard.

She immediately perched up on an elbow. "Are you all right? Did I hurt you?"

I put an arm over my face. "No, no, no. I think the drugs that were in my system are still there and I'm feeling faint. My head is throbbing again."

"I'm so sorry. I'll get you a cold cloth for your forehead and some aspirin." She jumped off the bed and hurried to the bathroom. I heard her rummaging around, most likely looking for aspirin, but it had me wondering if she was also looking for the pills everyone believed M.E. was giving me.

When she came back, I took the aspirin and she placed a cool washcloth on my forehead.

"Amelia. Thank you for everything today, and I hate to say this, but…"

"I know. You need some sleep. I'll stay here in case you need anything." She covered me with a blanket and then laid down beside me.

At this point, I believed there was nothing more I could do but fall into the deep sleep that really was calling to me. Until that happened, I rolled over on my side away from her and closed my eyes. As her arm pulled me closer, I felt an overwhelming sadness. My wife was dead and Amelia had killed her. With poison.

Soon, I heard lumbered breathing, and I relaxed. My only hope was that she wouldn't wake.

Despite the turmoil in my brain, I soon fell asleep and remembered nothing until the morning light filtered through the blinds. Dreams had plagued my sleep, telling me what I needed to do when I woke. I opened my eyes and checked to see if she was still sleeping.

I slipped out of bed and quickly dressed. I found Amelia's truck keys in her coat pocket and hurried downstairs. I needed to look in her truck. I wasn't sure what I would find, if anything, but I had to start somewhere. I actually hoped what Amelia finally told me was just a dream, a nightmare. Wasn't denial one of the stages of grieving? Did that apply to finding out someone you thought was your friend killed your wife?

I was taking a big chance, but if Amelia really did poison M.E. and Melissa, the poison might still be in her truck somewhere. I slowly opened the front door, careful to reduce the possibility of creaking hinges or groaning dry wood. I kept my eye on the bedroom window as I unlocked the door of her truck and rummaged under the seats, in the glove compartment and then in the work bag she always kept in the foot well of the back seat.

My hand swept around the bottom of the bag and stopped. My fingers felt something familiar. I grabbed a paper sack, pulled it out and found two pill bottles inside. I did not expect to be so lucky and find something on my first search. I really believed Amelia would hide anything incriminating much better than this. I sucked in a breath when I read the prescription on the first—desipramine. On the second, cyanide. I grabbed a rag on the seat and picked up the bottles. I emptied a few of the pills from each into my pockets being careful to keep them separate. Then I put the bottles back into her work bag and closed it. I took another look at the bedroom window while I closed her door as softly as I could. Not seeing any change in the closed position of the blinds, I jogged back to the front door.

I found two small containers in a box and put the pills in them, labeling each one with a marker. I hid them in a box in the basement. Then I went to the kitchen and made coffee. I put bread in the toaster and placed a jar of raspberry jam on the table. Soon, I had two cups of coffee and a few pieces of toast with sweet raspberry goo. While I prepared the sparse meal, I wondered how many times I had tried to please M.E. with breakfast and what it would be like to do it for someone who would really appreciate it. I sighed as I placed it all on a tray and took it up to the bedroom. To my relief, Amelia was still sleeping and that gave me the upper hand.

Her red hair against the white silk pillowcase and her pale skin and pink lips reminded me of the picture of Sleeping Beauty. For a moment, as I stared at her, a peaceful feeling filled me. How did we get here? Could it be any different between Amelia and I? Could we really find real love like she kept telling me we could? I placed the tray on the small table and sat down, touching her cheek. As I waited for her to wake up, I knew the answer to my question was no. I couldn't be with a killer. How ironic was that. Amelia believed my wife killed her sister and Amelia killed my wife. I was with one and now I was with the other. I had to walk away from all of it.

And then out of the corner of my eye, I caught sight of a business suit M.E. had worn the day before she disappeared. She had left it on the chair and asked me to get it dry-cleaned.

After a few seconds, her lids fluttered and green gems stared up at me. "Good morning," she said in a husky voice.

"Good morning. I brought you some light breakfast, you know, me not being a cook and all."

She smiled. "I can work with that. You don't know it yet, but I'm a pretty good cook myself. I'll have that kitchen working in no time, and when I do, I'll make you one of my specialties." She sat up and received the cup of coffee I held out to her.

I stood and looked down at her. "I'd really like that, but it's going to have to wait. There's a lot of things I need to do today. Phone calls, paperwork, lawyers, and the police want to speak to me again."

"And I'll be with you through all of that."

"No, Amelia," I said. I picked up my cup from the tray, trying to sound comforting and positive. "You can't. I have to do this alone and you showing up to the police station with me isn't a good idea." I leaned forward. "If you know what I mean."

I almost burst out laughing when Amelia shook her head. She looked like a dog who had mites in their ears and shook relentlessly to expedite their exit. But then I saw her expression and realized my teasing seemed to trigger something within her.

"Oh, my God." She put her hands on her face. "I'm… what…I'm so sorry. I…"

The old Amelia was back, and I had hoped for that. It would be easier to do what I needed to do.

Her shoulders shook with gut-wrenching sobs. I put both our mugs back on the tray, sat on the bed and took her in my arms. Why? I didn't know. I sure as hell didn't feel sorry for her. She murdered my wife and my wife's slutty girlfriend (that one

I could thank her for, but not my wife). M.E. didn't need to die, just to pay for her mistakes. Death never gave you the chance to make amends for your transgressions.

I let go of her when her cries subsided. "You should go home. I'll call you later when everything is done."

"But what I did…" Her eyes searched my face.

"You did what you had to do so we could be together. That just can't happen today." I smiled reassuringly at her.

"Wha…What are you going to do?"

She shrank back into the pillows, reminding me of a child who just lost their parents and was unsure of their fate. In a moment of anger, I felt satisfied, because that was exactly how she should have felt—mortified by what she did. Yet, seeing this woman who had become my friend, had kept me sane and happy, falling to pieces on my bed, my anger passed as quickly as it had come.

Now, I felt sorry for her.

"I'm going to do exactly what I told you. I have to make preparations for M.E.'s body and her funeral, call friends and family, go to the police station…" I looked away.

"Are you going to tell them?"

I smiled which might not have been the best reaction because her expression turned to fear. It made me wonder what kind of smile I'd given her. So, I sat down and took her in my arms again. I couldn't have her running off. "No, why would I do that? We wouldn't be able to be together." But I wasn't so sure of that. Why wouldn't I tell them?

Amelia sat back and looked at me, her eyes wide. "Really?"

"Yes, really. We're both kind of in this together. I did lie to the police already." Then I sealed it with a light kiss on her forehead and stood up. "Now, you have to get going. Diane will be here soon to prep me for the police interrogation and go over some papers with me. No idea what they are, but you can't be here when she comes."

"Yeah, right," Amelia answered as she got off the bed, her clothes looking as if they were put in the road and run over repeatedly by passing vehicles.

"Not a good look." I giggled. "Wrinkled left the fashion industry back in the eighties."

She looked at her clothes and wiped her hands up and down, as if that action would iron out the wrinkles. Then she grabbed her coffee and a piece of the toast. "Looks pretty good. Who says you can't cook?" She winked. "Call me later when you're all done?"

"I will. We can have dinner and maybe take a moonlight walk and talk about things."

She kissed me. "I'd like that."

"Good. Drive carefully."

"I love you."

It was something I didn't expect to hear, and to say it took me by surprise was a really big understatement. How did I respond to that? So, I said the first thing that came to my mind.

"I know."

By the look on her face, I knew it wasn't what she expected, but she smiled and left without another word.

Now, I had to hope I hadn't made a mistake.

I shut the door behind Diane after two hours of grueling questions and paperwork. M.E.'s death (or as I knew it, my wife's murder) had totally screwed up the police investigation on Raeann's death (or as Amelia knew it—Raeann's murder by my wife).

I kept asking Diane what any of this had to do with me, and she kept responding that I was M.E.'s wife and I must have known something. Anything.

"Raeann?" she asked.

"No, not until Raeann went to the college board and my wife was called up on charges of coercing a student into a sexual relationship."

"Melissa?"

"Nope. Not until the fire. Not until the police told me there were two bodies in Melissa's apartment and that one was hers and they believed the other to be my wife."

"And you knew nothing about the affair?"

"Knowing about Raeann, any stupid female would come to the conclusion that the fact my wife was dead next to Melissa in her bedroom kind of alluded to an affair. Did I know before that? No. But I will admit that I wondered what she was up to on the really late nights. Despite the fact that I had hoped my wife changed, what's that saying? Once a cheater, always a cheater." This seemed to be my standard aphorism lately.

"But you knew it was Melissa."

"No, I didn't. However, she called one night to speak to my wife about her class. Not many students do that, but at the time, I didn't think much about it because my wife acted normal."

As Diane closed the folder with all the papers in it, she told me she would keep me informed on any new developments. "I feel I need to tell you that the police are going to drill you more than I did. Your wife had an affair in San Francisco and she was having one here. They're going to wonder how you didn't know that."

"Did *you* know that?" I challenged her. "You were working with M.E. and Melissa was your secretary."

Her hard stare pierced through me. She sighed. "They are still going to look at you as a suspect. Mary Ellen's extramarital affairs would make any woman angry. They also have their suspicions about your wife. I believe they have enough evidence to pin Raeann's murder on her. Be prepared."

I thanked her and showed her out the door. Then I grabbed my purse and coat to drive to the police station. I hoped this would be the end of it. I needed to execute M.E.'s will, call her family, although her siblings probably wouldn't care what I did for a funeral. Her family had disowned her when they found out she was a lesbian.

M.E. wanted to be buried in San Francisco and I would honor her wish. Thank God she wanted to be cremated. Getting an urn of ashes back to San Francisco wouldn't be so bad. Hell, I could snail-mail it. A dead body would be another thing altogether.

The police grilled me with the exact questions Diane said they would. And I answered them as I had to Diane. No, I didn't know anything about Melissa or my wife's spare apartment. No, I didn't know where she'd been for the two days she was missing. No, I didn't kill her, and no, I didn't set the building on fire. I wasn't sure they believed me when I said I wasn't a raging jealous wife, which I really wasn't. I was just fed up with M.E.'s life the way she lived it. I wanted out of it. I think they believed that. Why wouldn't they? All of it was true.

I just didn't tell them everything.

CHAPTER TWENTY-FIVE

I spent the rest of the afternoon going over the important papers M.E. and I kept in a small but very heavy safe that we carted with us from San Francisco. I made lists and more lists: who to call and decisions to make, which pretty much encompassed everything from submitting death certificates to the appropriate institutions to what I was going to do when all was said and done. There really was no question about my next move. I just needed a lot of lists to get it done quickly and efficiently.

When it got close to dinner time, I called Amelia. "Hey there. It's been a long day. I'm ready for some food and drink. What about you?"

I heard her exhale. "I was so worried. I didn't think you were going to call. I was afraid…" She stopped.

"That the police were going to show up at your door? I told you that wouldn't happen."

"I know. I'm sorry. I'm sorry."

"Stop. Look. I want to thank you. For everything. I'd like to bring dinner and wine over to your place. I've got paperwork all over the place, and I want to get away from here—you know? Too many memories. And I don't want to go to a restaurant. I don't want to be with other people. Only you. Then after dinner I thought about taking a walk. Does that work for you?"

"That would be wonderful."

"Text me your address and I'll be over in about an hour. I have to pick up some things. See you soon."

"I'm looking forward to it! Oh, things have been so crazy. I forgot to tell you I've moved. I'm still in Newtonfield but not in the apartment anymore."

"No problem," I replied.

* * *

Amelia ended the call. Then she jumped up and down shouting a joyful "Yes!" and "Finally!" All day her stomach had churned, wondering if Adalynn was really in the same place she was. After all, she hadn't said I love you back to her.

She had cleaned her house, put her paperwork in order and written letters in case the woman who had stolen her heart turned her into the police. But Addy hadn't. She was on her way to Amelia's home bringing dinner and wine with her. And she was alone. She no longer had a roommate. When Amelia made plans to end the life of the woman who had murdered her sister, she moved out of the apartment, leaving it to her friend David.

She couldn't risk her friend finding out what she had done. She also couldn't risk Addy finding out that it was she who had done all the detective work, not David. It was the only way she could carry out her plan of convincing Addy that Mary Ellen was no good for her and to rid the world of the woman who killed her sister. She didn't want to involve her best friend in any of this and she was pretty sure their friendship wouldn't survive the truth.

Tonight would be the romantic night she'd always wanted with Addy. Tonight, they would make love. Tomorrow, they would talk about their future. Amelia imagined herself moving into the stone house with Addy where they would build a life together. Addy would have her interior decorating business and Amelia would remodel homes that met her clients' desires.

It would be perfect.

She looked around the shoddy house her foster parents called home. The never took care of it. They made Amelia and Raeann do all the cleaning, but eventually they drank so much, they would just forget to make them do their chores. So, they all lived in filth.

When her father passed, she came to the house. She wasn't sure why except it ended up being a free place where she could hang her hat until she knew what avenue her life would take. Now she knew. And after she moved in with Addy, she would burn the place to the ground.

With Addy's phone call, Amelia's mood took a one-hundred-eighty-degree turn. She hadn't felt this great since the day she first laid eyes on Adalynn Pious. She took a quick shower and changed into fresh clothes with the anticipation of being with the woman she loved.

Mary Ellen was a fool. She had the perfect woman and she blew it with her narcissistic, ludicrous needs. Amelia knew it was a marriage headed for disaster the first day she met them. Addy had left the room and Mary Ellen grilled her about her qualifications all the while flirting with her. If she hadn't wanted the job so bad, she would have walked out.

She was glad she didn't.

Now she ran about the downstairs, cleaning, straightening, and lighting candles in the very old and very small farmhouse in the middle of nowhere on fifty acres. She stopped at one point, remembering when her father moved them from the Ithaca slums to the tiny house he bought, primarily because there were no neighbors. Despite the fact Ithaca was a small city, the neighbors were just as nosy as those in New York City. But in the tiny house in the middle of nowhere, whatever he did to his wife, or his foster daughters would stay within the tiny walls.

She hadn't told Addy that when her father died, she'd moved into the house. It was as if it was meant to be because she didn't want David to find out what she had done. So, she moved back into the den of iniquity to protect her friend from the decisions she had made and the things she had done.

But now, none of that would matter. Addy loved her. Amelia was sure of that. Addy hadn't called the police on her and she was coming over to dinner—to spend time just with her. All of Amelia's work was coming to fruition—the detective work, manipulating Addy by showing her the worst of Mary Ellen, poisoning Mary Ellen and her whore, setting the fires to cover up her transgressions and…crimes, positioning herself to be Addy's confident, supporter, comforter. When she told her, Addy would appreciate how Amelia had looked out for her, protected her, saved her from a life that would always be full of pain. Now, Amelia could fill Addy's life with love. Yes, everything worked out. Tonight, after they made love and sealed their life together, she knew everything would be all right. If Addy asked, she would tell her what she wanted to know about Mary Ellen's death. However, she wouldn't tell her that she gave her a few of the pills slated for Melissa to help her sleep. She'd been so tired. *I almost lost her because of my stupidity*. She felt deep down in her heart that Addy would forgive her, if forgiveness was needed.

* * *

I pulled into the dirt driveway of the gray, decaying clapboard house. I knew Amelia had moved here because I'd done a little digging myself. When she was working, I found her wallet in her work bag and looked at her license for her address. Her apartment address was crossed out and on the back was her new address. Then I looked up the property on Google Earth. It was as she had described it—no neighbors, totally remote…and rundown. The worn roof looked more like a feeding ground for moss, making it almost impossible to tell the color of the shingles. Paint had peeled off the door and window frames and the lawn was a field of weeds. Being an upscale interior decorator, I was totally repulsed. I would have rather seen a brick building on a yard made of concrete littered with garbage—citylike.

I could only hope the inside looked better.

I followed the driveway to the back of the house where I parked in front of a building that, except for the shape of it, was almost a carbon copy of the house. I assumed it was a garage or barn. The back door opened before I reached the front step. Made of wood that was rotting on one side, I might be taking my life into my own hands if I tried to navigate up the steps to the door where Amelia waited.

She reached down and took the bags from me and said, "Let me put these inside the door, then I'll help you up."

I handed her the bags and waited, surveying the backyard. It looked the same as the front. All weeds. She made her way down and extended her hand, pointing to where I should place my feet as she led me up the stairs and into the house.

"A little embarrassing, but I haven't been here long enough to fix those steps. Sorry," she explained as she shut the door.

"Why would you move out here to this, when you had a nice apartment with your friend?"

"Remember when I told you my dad couldn't stand the prying eyes, so he moved us out here?" She swept her hand around the room. "You can't get any more private than this place." She smiled. "There's fifty acres with no neighbors. I've thought about knocking this house down and building. But maybe I'll just hang on to the land." She winked at me and then she picked up the bags. "Come on, this way. We can sit in the dining room. It's the nicest room in the house." She laughed nervously.

We passed through the kitchen. I couldn't help it, but my interior decorating expertise ran amuck. If there was one room that needed a total makeover, this one did. Decorated in typical 1970s avocado and ugly orange, the room shouted, "Help me!" The stove and refrigerator were avocado. The floor was paisley orange linoleum (that is, where you could see it). Most of the flooring was old, worn, and in some places, rotted. The cabinets were painted white with orange knobs, and when my eyes took in the counter, I moved away from them. There was clutter consisting of small rusty appliances, empty food containers, piles of paper and in the spots where I could see the Formica, the original avocado color was more like a dark green from years of dirt and grime. I focused on Amelia's back as she led me to the next room because that kitchen hurt my eyes.

She set the bags down on the table and we started to unload them. I pulled out a bottle of wine.

"What, no beer tonight?"

"No beer. We're celebrating, remember? Beer is for misery. Wine is for celebrating. Do you recognize this?" I smiled. The bottle still had the white ribbon on it.

"Oh, my God, yes. It's the wine I left on the front seat of Bertha." She looked at me. "But, aren't you mourning?"

"That too." I kept the smile on my face, but inside my stomach was churning with the remnants of my broken heart. "Do you have a working oven?"

"I'm a good cook, remember?"

"That doesn't mean the stove in this, um, house is working."

"It is."

I handed her the bag with the cartons that needed to be heated. "These need to be warmed," I said, noticing the bottle opener and two glasses (not wine goblets) on the table. "I'll open the wine so we can start drinking while we wait."

"On it," she said while picking up the food and taking it into the kitchen. I didn't follow her because I thought I'd pass out if I stepped into the kitchen again. I was satisfied sitting in the nicest room in the house, the dining room—if you could call it the nicest room in the house. It was cleaner and plainly decorated with old, garage sale furniture. I just hoped she wouldn't want to give me the whole tour.

I returned the bottle with the white ribbon to the bag and opened the other one. I poured two glasses, took a sip, and then waited for her return.

"It should take about fifteen minutes," she said when she sat down. She picked up her glass, extending it across the table, and said, "To us," when I clinked it.

I didn't want to say it, but I did. "To us." I knew my voice sounded weak and unconvincing, but I didn't care. I said it.

"How was the interview with the police?" she asked and I wasn't surprised that she went directly to the topic that could end her life.

"Exactly like I told you it would be. Did I know about the apartment? Did I know about Melissa? Did I know where my wife was before her death? What happened in San Francisco? It lasted three hours and I think they were pretty frustrated that they didn't get out of me what they wanted."

"And what was that?"

"They want to know who killed my wife and Melissa, but I think they believe it wasn't me. The other thing I think they wanted was a confession, that I knew my wife killed Raeann. Basically, any dirt I could give them on anything concerning all three. I had none to give."

"But you do…have dirt to give."

I set my wineglass down. "But I didn't give it." I met her eyes. "How did you do it?"

"I really don't want to talk about it," she said and then took a long drink of wine.

"I think you owe me that. And if you really want to be with me, you need to understand that I will not enter another relationship with secrets. Been there. Done that. And look how that went."

She scrunched her face as if in pain. "I have a friend at Cornell in the prepharmacy program. We talk about her research sometimes, which is working on antidotes for poisons." She sighed. "Growing up in the slums, I became an expert in the five-finger discount. You get my drift. I told you that Melissa's apartment was tapped. I heard her call Mary Ellen and insist she come to her place before her classes. Then she ordered two cups of cappuccino from the coffee shop on her street. I know the shop well. I do deliveries for Uber Eats when I have downtime."

"Did David record any of this?"

She squirmed in her chair as she answered, "No. There are no records, audios, or pictures of what he did. You have all that is left. Anyway, I waited for the coffee to be delivered and slipped the poison into the cups. I was lucky because Mary Ellen showed up a few minutes after. She picked up the bag off the floor and knocked on Melissa's door. I waited for two hours and then went inside. They were dead. After that I came to your house."

"Did you start the fire?"

She didn't answer. She drank more wine.

I opened the bottle and filled her glass. "Did you?"

"I had to."

I heard a ding and knew the fifteen minutes was up. Amelia went into the kitchen. I refilled our glasses. Then she came out with the food, silverware, and plates. "This looks delicious," she said, but her eyes were downcast.

"I'm glad. I got coconut curry for you and pad Thai for me." I pushed the container with her meal toward her and grabbed for mine.

"Don't you want to share?"

"I'm not in the mood for the coconut, but you're more than welcome to take some of mine."

"Are you sure?"

I smiled. "Absolutely."

She returned my smile without looking up and spooned some of my dinner onto her plate. We ate, but our conversation was minimal, commenting on the flavor of our favorite foods and other trivial topics. I wasn't sure if she trusted me, but her smile was soft and her eyes sparkled like someone who was longing to be with their love.

"You think M.E. was slipping me some pills, don't you?"

Her eyes blinked but she kept eating. It was as if I could see the wheels in her mind turning, identifying and evaluating the thoughts I'd just said.

Finally, she answered, "Yes. I do."

"It makes sense."

"What does?"

"You believe my wife killed your sister. And the way you feel about me, I can imagine if you found out she was drugging me, it would send you over the edge." I took a drink of wine to help me stay calm.

Amelia joined me and took a much longer swallow, emptying her glass once again. "I did and it did. Mary Ellen Montgomery was an evil woman. She used my sister, she cheated on you, and then when my sister tried to bring her to justice, she killed her." She picked up the bottle and refilled her glass. "When I met you, I couldn't believe someone like you—this beautiful, smart, kind, and funny woman—could actually be in love with such an evil person. Yes, I developed feelings for you, and I know I shouldn't have. But you can't help what you feel. Mary Ellen could see that. Remember the morning you left us in the room alone?"

I nodded.

"She warned me to keep our relationship totally business. She didn't want us to become friends. She kept an eye on me and I—" She took a drink as if she had to rethink what her next words would be. "I kept a close eye on her. I didn't trust her, so I watched her closely when she was home and sometimes I followed her at the college."

"You did?" I didn't know what else to say or what I even felt about that. Then I asked, "Did she notice?"

"No. But remember that day you were so tired? You didn't seem right. I went to the apartment before I took you there to look around and found a pill bottle in a drawer. Melissa's name was written on it in marker."

That surprised me. "Do you know what was in the bottle?"

"Antidepressants."

"I don't know why my wife would give me pills without me knowing, but I read in her research that she did put them in the drinks of her subjects. I haven't read all of the papers, so I don't know why she did it or for what research outcome."

"Because she's a fucking asshole," Amelia spat. "She probably gave them to my sister." She took a long drink.

"It would seem likely."

"Good riddance," she said as I watched her empty her glass. Then she held it up and smiled.

I reached down into the bag and pulled out the other opened bottle with the white ribbon on it. She grinned as I filled her glass and waited.

"I wanted to save this bottle for last, so we could really enjoy it." I still had wine in my glass, so I didn't refill mine. I was drinking slowly in order to stay sober.

"Why did you start the fires?" I was curious as to why she would burn both apartments.

After taking another drink, she answered, "I burned M.E.'s apartment to protect you—to get rid of any evidence that you were there. You never know if a strand of your hair dropped, or if we missed anywhere you touched." Then she fixed a hard stare on me. "I also burned Melissa's apartment for you. I was angry at what Mary Ellen was doing to you. Again. When I found them, they were naked in her bed." She took another drink.

I cringed at her words. I knew my wife cheated, but the vision Amelia just painted of M.E. naked in bed with another woman was too much to bear.

Then she shifted in her chair and scrunched up her face in a look of pain.

"Are you all right?"

"Yes, just a stomachache." She looked at me seductively. "But it won't keep me from spending time with you. How about we take this somewhere we can get more comfortable?"

If the bedroom was anything like the rest of the house, there was no way, even if I wanted to. And I didn't want to. So, I didn't answer.

"I have a question of my own."

"Of course. What is it?"

"How did Mary Ellen get the job at Ithaca College? David told me with her record, even if the college couldn't say anything, it would be almost impossible for her to get another professorship position."

This time I took a long drink. "My father. He's on the board of directors for Stanford University. He knows people. I asked him to find her a position. This one was open."

"I thought you and your father weren't on good terms?"

"I never said that. I just don't like what he's become. Kind of disrespectful to my mom."

"Huh," she slurred. "Then I guess, if we're being honest with each other, I should tell you that David didn't do the investigative work. I did. I moved out so he wouldn't find out what I was doing." Her smile at me was lopsided. "And so we could be alone."

My smile was wide. "I'm not mad about that. In fact, I'm glad it was you who did the investigation. Noble of you to protect your friend."

She let out a small grunt. "I need some coffee. Want some?"

I nodded, leaning back in my chair.

Amelia started to stand, but then she dropped back into the chair.

"Did you know I was a twin?" I offered.

Her mouth opened and her eyes narrowed, obviously surprised by my change of subject. "No. I didn't."

"Did you know Raeann was a twin?"

Her lips pursed, and I couldn't tell if it was from confusion about our conversation, or if she was still in pain.

"Are you okay?" I asked.

"Yeah, I don't think the coconut agreed with me tonight."

"You knew that Raeann's adoption records were closed, didn't you?"

"Yeah, of course. My parents never looked into either of our adoptions. To put it bluntly, they wouldn't have wanted us to find out we had family out there. It would have killed the good thing they had going." Another gulp of wine. "I helped Raeann search for her birth parents, but we never found them. What's this got to do with us getting comfortable?" She reached across the table and took my hand.

I pulled it back as I wondered what kind of drunk Amelia was.

Then her eyes opened wide. "How do you know she was a twin? She didn't know." A small groan escaped her lips.

"Are you all right? You look a little peaked. Do you need me to get you something? Tums?"

"I'm okay. How do you know Raeann was a twin?" she repeated, obviously getting frustrated, and I wondered if the kind of drunk she was would soon make an appearance.

I leaned forward and smiled. "Because she was my twin."
Surprise.

"What do you mean?" Her eyes widened. "She wasn't your twin. You're lying."

I sat back. "You see, my mom was really young when she got pregnant. She was talked into keeping the baby by her parents who were not well-off, but they were devout Catholics. Didn't believe in abortion. But when she had twins, they knew there was no way they could take care of their daughter and her two babies. So, they took one of the babies and put it up for adoption. They didn't tell her until after the fact, and they didn't tell her which one."

I pushed Amelia's glass toward her. She just glared at me.

"My mother named one Adalynn, obviously me, and the other Raelynn. However, her parents changed the name on the adoption papers to Raeann and made it a closed adoption so my mother could never find her. I always wondered why my mother was a drunk. Now, I know my mother was devastated over the loss of her other baby. So, she packed me up and left New York for California as a punishment to her parents. You know the rest of that story. My mom worked at a movie studio, got in bed with the owner and married him. But she was never right—a true alcoholic, mostly because of her guilt over what happened. It all makes sense to me now. Did I ever tell you my mom died of liver cancer?"

Amelia shook her head in stunned silence.

I nodded to her glass of wine. "That's what drinking too much alcohol can do to you. It can kill you."

A low groan came from her lips. "Why didn't you tell me?" Another moan. She shifted in her chair and gripped her stomach.

"I never planned on you. You were a total surprise, one I never expected and absolutely didn't want. But there you were staring me in the face. You fucked up every plan for every scenario I had made. I had no idea how I was going to deal with the wrench you threw into my life." I noticed her struggling. I also noticed her glass was empty. I poured more wine into it. "Drink, baby. You look like you don't feel well. Wine helps stomachaches, but if you have some antacids anywhere, I'll get them for you."

Amelia stared at me.

"Sex will be much better with a good buzz. You know what I mean?" I winked at her.

"I'm okay. Just some bad gas. Must have been something in the curry. I should know better than to eat spicy. It doesn't always agree with me."

"Are you sure?"

She adjusted her body once again and as worry lines appeared on her face, she mangaged to say, "I'm good."

"Anyway," I said, waving my hand nonchalantly, as if I was talking about the weather and the likely chance of showers and how it wouldn't ruin our outdoor plans. "You only have yourself to blame for all of this."

"What are you talking about?" She hadn't really absorbed the information I was giving her because she had been fighting the pain in her stomach. But now I had her attention.

"I told you over and over again that my wife did not kill your sister, but nooooo, you wouldn't listen. I tell you again, M.E. did not kill your sister, who really isn't your sister. She was mine, my twin. And you know what's really comical about all of this? I had no idea I had a twin either. You know, Amelia, if you had just have left it alone, let the police deal with Raelynn's death and stayed out of our lives, none of this would have happened. I had it all under control."

"Addy, what are you talking about? I love you." She groaned and bent over clutching her stomach once again. "Oh, I don't feel so well."

"It appears Raelynn looked into her own adoption without you knowing. She found out everything. She even approached my rich stepdaddy and threatened him in some way. She never told me with what and my stepdaddy wouldn't return my calls. She told me he gave her some money, but more important, he gave her valuable information. He told her everything about my mother, her parents, and me. He felt so bad about it afterward, that's why he got M.E. the job for me.

"She couldn't take revenge on her grandparents because they're both dead, and unfortunately, so was her mother. So, she targeted me instead. She planted herself in M.E.'s path. She seduced her and found out about her research. She used it all against her and ruined our lives. When it was all said and done, and we were getting ready to leave California, that's when the bitch called me and asked me to meet her at Pirates' Cove. She wanted to revel in her revenge. She was angry that I grew up having everything, and she grew up in this…" I spread my arm around the room. "…in this real crappy life. I said I was sorry for that and that I had no idea. My mother never told me anything about her. But she was so filled with hate that it didn't matter what I said or how much I apologized." I leaned toward her and said slowly, "Your so-called sister took everything from me. Everything!" I shouted. "She was so filled with hate. She said she wouldn't be done until I was left with nothing, until I was alone and life abused me as it had done to her. She wanted M.E. to herself, but M.E. only wanted her for her research. That sent her over the edge. So, she decided to ruin both of us."

I watched Amelia's face twist with not just pain, but the reality of what I was saying. Her skin was pallid and sweat beaded down her brow. She was breathing fast, but shallow. I couldn't tell which pain was gripping her more—physical or emotional.

"That's really fucked up, don't you think? I knew nothing about her. I had no say in how my life or hers ended up, yet she decided to take it all out on me."

I let out a long sigh.

Despite the obvious agony she was in, Amelia's face lit up with sudden comprehension. "What did you do?" She echoed the question I had asked her the day before.

"I made sure she slipped on the high cliffs. I stayed for a bit and watched her body twitch until she grew quiet. It wasn't long before the waves pulled her into the ocean."

Now Amelia's face was a picture-perfect visage of horror with a good dose of a nonbeliever who just found out the ghost that was haunting them was really real. "You…you killed my sister?" Her voice was weak; her energy was draining.

I leaned forward again. "*My* sister. And yes, but not really on purpose. She just kind of slipped and I left her there. I knew they would find her car and her body eventually. I set everything up to look like M.E. did it. You should've listened to me. I tried to tell you. M.E. didn't do it. Maybe then you wouldn't have poisoned my wife. If you hadn't appeared on our doorstep, none of this would have happened. I was taking care of it, setting my wife up to take a fall she'd never recover from. Except, I didn't want to kill her. I love her—or should I say I did love her. I just wanted her to rot in jail so I could divorce her and go back to San Francisco with everything we had and everything she didn't think I knew *she* had. Then here comes Saint Amelia riding in on her white horse to avenge her fake sister's death. It took me a lot of lists, a lot of plans, but I figured it out. Especially after I found the two pill bottles in your work bag."

"You...you went through my truck?"

"Of course. I'm not a stupid woman, but I'm kind of insulted that you thought I was." I took a sip of my wine. "I suspected you murdered my wife the minute I heard she'd gone missing."

Amelia clutched her stomach and her head dropped. I wouldn't be wrong if I said part of the pain was physical and the other was mental—an emotional reaction to what I just said.

"You killed Raeann. You set me up, not Mary Ellen," she struggled to say. Then she lifted her head. "How could you do this to me after everything I did for you!"

"You did nothing for me but make this a whole lot harder than it had to be." I kept my voice even and stern.

She groaned louder this time. "Addy, something's wrong. Please help me. Some...some...thing's wrong."

I shook my head. "Shh, shh. I know something is wrong. One pill bottle had the antidepressants in it, but the other one, well, it wasn't the same, was it?"

"No." She was crying now.

"It was the leftover poison you used on them, wasn't it? You put all the antidepressants in one bottle and the poison in the other. Didn't you?"

Her face contorted with pain. "Oh God, oh God, oh God," she moaned. She was sweating more profusely now, most likely because her heart was racing, her blood pressure was tanking. Her breaths became short and ragged.

"You ruined everything. There was no way I could be with you, especially after you killed my wife. I wasn't sure how I was going to do this and get away with it until I found the bottles. So, thanks for that."

Amelia gasped as she fell off the chair.

I donned a pair of gloves and pulled a folded piece of paper and a pen out of the bag. "I wrote a suicide note for you. I'd like you to sign it. You need to own up to what you did. It says you poisoned my wife and Melissa and why. Oh, and that you set the fire in both apartments."

"Are you cr...crazy?" she whispered between labored breaths. Her skin was cold, clammy, and pale. Convulsions would come next. I had to hurry.

"No, really, I'm not. Just a woman who has been scorned by every female in her life. But"—I knelt down next to her—"if you really love me, and you're sorry for killing my wife and that poor girl, you'll sign this. After all, you did do those things, didn't you? Come on, Amelia. You know this is better than going to jail for the rest of your life for murder. Besides, believe me when I tell you they will never find out who really killed Raelynn. I made sure everything was targeted toward my wife, and you know I was successful. You believed it. The police believe it. Hell, even her own lawyer believed it—for the most part."

"I could tell them," she said in a dying whisper.

"But you can't. You'll be dead. Please, if you love me…"

I moved when she began vomiting. I waited while the grips of the poison took hold. Then I put the pen in her hand and placed the paper beside it where she could sign.

Amelia stared up at me. "I loved you. I did it all for you," she wept. "For us. Addy, please help me. We can fix this."

"I *am* helping you, and I am trying to fix this, and the only way that will happen is by you doing this for me. You will die with a clean conscience."

"You'll…never…get away…with this."

"Aw, honey, I already have. If you don't sign, I'll find a way to do it for you. Please know if things were different, if you had kept out of it, if we had met later, there might have been a chance for us. I really did like you. I might have even been able to love you, but not after what you did. Please. Sign."

And to my surprise, she did. She scribbled her first name after which her hand fell limp and then she started to seize.

EPILOGUE

I learned many things from plotting Raeann's death to look like M.E. murdered her. One of those was to always clean up and wipe away any fingerprints or DNA that you left at a place where you shouldn't have been. I didn't touch anything when I entered her house except for the glass and bottle opener. I put the glass in my bag. I left her containers of food, but I picked up mine and my used silverware and put it in the bag as well.

I wiped the bottle of red wine that Amelia had left on the Honda's front seat, leaving it on the table—with the white bow. I took the other one and anything else that would have pointed to the fact that another person was here. I wiped anything down I thought I might have touched, including the bottle and the bottle opener. I would dispose of all evidence, including the leftover pills.

Then I left Amelia's confession, the pen and the pill bottle with the poison in it on the table and picked up my bags.

"Goodbye, Amelia." I kissed her on the forehead. "I really am sorry." Then I wiped her forehead with my cloth and tossed it into the bag.

I made my way out of the poor excuse for a house and down the steps, carefully avoiding a broken ankle. I had checked the forecast before I left and saw it was going to rain. As I walked across the dirt driveway, large drops began to fall and I was glad they would wash away my footprints and hopefully my tire marks.

I pulled out of the driveway looking left and right. It really was in the middle of nowhere. There were no cars, no houses, no people in sight. It would be a while before anyone found her and if I was to stay safe, I would have to help that along.

I stopped at the town dump and disposed of the remnants of our meal and the other wine bottle. Then I drove home. I would call the police in a few days, saying my contractor hadn't shown up for work and wasn't taking my calls.

If no one reported her missing by then, they would find her. But David might report her missing and I was okay with that because Amelia had made that easy too. She had done all of the investigative work, not David. She moved out of the apartment to keep him from finding out. So, he knew nothing. My hope was her suicide letter admitting her crime would be enough to satisfy him over her death.

When I pulled into my driveway, I felt that feeling you get when you think someone is watching you. I got out of the car and whipped around to see a face peering at me from the front window of the house across the street. The neighbors watching. Again. They were always watching. I felt just like Amelia's parents had when they lived in the city. But I had an alibi for being out.

I picked up the pizza on the front seat that I had also purchased when I went to get the dinners for Amelia and me that I paid cash for. I lifted it up and nodded toward them, smiling and waving with my other hand to my neighbor. She smiled and threw me a quick wave. Then the curtain fell back into place.

It was time to leave.

* * *

I stood in the middle of the empty living room in my stone house. M.E.'s stone house. Amelia's stone house. The movers had left, and I felt…I felt…I didn't know what I was feeling.

The events of the last year floated in and out of my mind. It was both David and I who reported Amelia missing on the same day. He said he hadn't heard from his friend in three days and she made a habit of calling or texting him at least once every day. I told the police she hadn't shown to work in three days and wasn't answering my calls or texts. David called me looking for his friend. I told him what I told the police, but he grilled me anyway saying Amelia would have told him how depressed she was. He said he knew she was running into trouble with my wife. I told him I didn't see any signs of depression in her. Then I had to console him over the phone while he sobbed. He apologized and ended the call.

The police found the scene as I had left it. I didn't want to think of the state of Amelia's body. Thank God they asked David to identify her remains and not me. I wasn't sure I'd stand up for that one.

Of course, I was pulled in for questioning. While I sat in the interrogation room, M.E.'s lawyer, Diane, came in. She told me I might have information to corroborate the police investigation as to what happened. She was given permission to show me Amelia's suicide note, and of course, I acted surprised and sad when I read it despite the fact I typed it.

My stomach actually rolled with each word as it brought memories back of everything that had happened since Raelynn approached me in San Francisco. Finally, I looked at Diane. "She had told me several times she thought my wife killed her sister. She was so distraught over that. Has that case been settled and closed?"

Diane folded her arms as she glared at me. "There's no definitive evidence to solidify proof that your wife murdered Raeann, but most everything points to her and they haven't found any other leads." Diane sighed. "I feel like there's something you're not telling me. I can't prove you were involved in any way, but if there is something, the police will be sure to find it. It would be better if you confided in me."

I tried to look sad, not smug. I looked down to hide my surprise and worry. She was right. The police might eventually learn that Raelynn was my sister. I tried to clean that up as best I could. For now, it was my secret. "There's nothing. I've told you everything." I uttered a small cry and then sniffed. "I can't believe you would think that."

"I'm sorry, Adalynn. This must be so hard, but I say it like I see it."

"So, Amelia poisoned my wife and your secretary. Has the medical examiner determined the poison?"

"The same one Amelia took. Cyanide. I find it odd that she would take that. It's rarely taken for suicide because it's such a horrible way to die."

I gasped. "How awful. Maybe she took it because she felt guilty giving it to my wife and Melissa." I managed a tear. "In this note, Amelia says she killed Melissa because she was the woman my wife was cheating with. She was angry at both of them for hurting me. She loved me." I choked in a sob. "I had no idea."

"That's what the police want to speak to you about. Are you ready to speak to them?"

"Yes, yes of course."

Diane left the room and soon after the same two policeman that showed up in my hospital room took her place, asking me countless questions.

Yes, Amelia and I were friends. Yes, she was also teaching me how to do home improvement projects. No, I had no idea she was in love with me. Yes, I knew Amelia believed my wife killed her sister. We talked about it two or three times but agreed to disagree. I believed in my wife, Amelia did not. Now I knew why.

I was very convincing. How could I not be since there was a lot of truth to my answers—just not the whole truth, but it was enough for the police to believe my answers. Even though there were some small lies and definitely a lot of omissions, it was best for everyone to let it end the way it did. Besides, I fully believed in lying by omission because some people just couldn't handle the whole truth and nothing but the truth. However, I could tell the police were suspicious of me when they asked me how I could be so naive, so blinded to what was going on around me. I told them I was too involved with my own life and I trusted what M.E. told me. She was my wife. They accepted my explanation and, well, they had no proof. Raelynn's tie to me was the only thing that could throw a wrench into my life. I hoped they would never find out. Raelynn owed me to keep this secret in her grave. I had to believe that's where it would stay.

Tears flowed down my cheeks, and I realized that it was the sadness speaking. I could feel the sorrow trying to take hold of me. So much sorrow. But…there was happiness too. *So much* happiness because I was finally going home. It was over, although not the way I had planned. In fact, I hadn't made any plan that even remotely resembled the true facts of what had happened.

The house was completed by another contractor I hired (a male this time—I wasn't taking any more chances). He finished the few things Amelia didn't get to, and when I gave my seal of approval, I called a realtor who put a for sale sign on the front lawn. The house sold in a little over a month, giving me time to get back to San Francisco before the snow and freezing weather hit hard.

I spent a lot of time finishing M.E.'s affairs. I was given permission to clean out her office and claim anything that wasn't related to her teaching. I hoped that was where M.E. kept her personal files and I was right. I was able to find the money I suspected she had and never told me about. I found her will, and I already had her research. Until I left, I kept all of it in my safe deposit box.

The police no longer had any reason to keep me in Ithaca, so there was nothing and no one keeping me at the stone house. I sold M.E.'s truck and packed Bertha for the long trip home. The Honda Fit and I were going to drive cross-country alone. I would be able to relax and think and plan for the next phase of my life, and I wouldn't have to spend most of the drive in the "platitude seat" feeling miserable. Instead of contemplating what vegetables were planted in the next field that blurred as I passed it, I could contemplate all that had happened, where it had left me and the future I was embarking on. Because... I would be in the driver's seat.

When David, Amelia's friend, arrived in her truck to claim all of her tools I offered him a cup of coffee. We sat at the table in the beautiful chef's kitchen. He stirred the creamer into his coffee longer than needed before either of us spoke.

"I'm so sorry for your loss. She was a wonderful person. I know I only knew her a short time, but she was funny, full of life, thoughtful and so kind." Of course he didn't know the half of it and I didn't tell him, and we discussed how neither of us could understand why she would do what she did.

His dark-brown eyes seemed hollow, broken. "She never would have committed suicide." His voice had a sharp edge to it. "Did something happen here that upset her?"

"No. She worked hard and she also taught me how to fix things and do some of the work myself. She always seemed happy."

"She didn't like your wife, you know."

"I know. I'm sorry."

"She liked you. A lot." He put his coffee cup down and studied me a moment. "From everything Amelia said, I wouldn't be surprised if your wife had something to do with all of this."

I knew then that the police and Diane weren't the only ones who suspected there was something more to all of this. So, I said to him, "We formed a great friendship. Sometimes we confided in each other, but this house was our main connection. That was all. I can't speak as to what part my wife may have played in all of this because I have no idea." I stood. "I can help you load your truck," I said, hoping it would bring him peace and keep me out of it.

I had already brought Amelia's things up from the basement. We carried them out to Amelia's truck. I could see the powerful sadness in his eyes. I knew it would take a long time for him to get over her death. I hoped the fact that she left her truck, business, and that despicable house to him in her will might ease his pain, if just a little. (It was a good thing she hadn't changed it to me being her benefactor. That would have been bad.)

When he hugged me, I felt a twinge of regret, but quickly sent it on the cold breeze that was filling the air as we stood on the front step saying goodbye. After all, we were like two friends mourning the loss of a loved one by looking for the strength to get through it with the physical connection of a hug.

Now, don't go getting your panties all in an uproar. I told you the story as it happened. I just didn't include all the details— only those that I felt were pertinent to the events that happened. I'm not a bad person. I just ended up involved with bad people, and I knew…*I knew* the only one who could help me to get out of it was myself. So, I did what had to be done and that was to wrap it all up in a single box with a bow on it so I could give everyone the closure they would need, including me.

You see, I am a survivor.

I picked up my purse and walked out the front door, listening to the familiar creak of the wood and the squeal of the hinges for the last time as I shut and locked it. I didn't look back. I would never look back.

I got into the car and addressed the ornately colorful urn on the passenger seat next to me. I found it humorous how the only way I could get M.E. to take a ride in my tiny Honda Fit was in an urn.

"Ready to go home?"

Also By Nance Newman

Self-published books

Whisper's Series (paranormal mystery)
You're Not Alone
Bad Man, Bad Ghost
Dirty Wrong
Sound Travels
The Structure of Lies
Bad Man, Bad Daddy

Heartwood Series (young adult magical realism fantasy)
Heartwood
Fractures
Dubiety

Nonfiction
Journaling Through a Heartbreak

Lesbian Fiction
The Stonewall Railroad (science fiction dystopian novel)

Bella Books, Inc.
Happy Endings Live Here
P.O. Box 10543
Tallahassee, FL 32302
Phone: (850) 576-2370
www.BellaBooks.com

More Titles from Bella Books

Hunter's Revenge – Gerri Hill
978-1-64247-447-3 | 276 pgs | paperback: $18.95 | eBook: $9.99
Tori Hunter is back! Don't miss this final chapter in the acclaimed
Tori Hunter series.

Integrity – E. J. Noyes
978-1-64247-465-7 | 228 pgs | paperback: $19.95 | eBook: $9.99
It was supposed to be an ordinary workday...

The Order – TJ O'Shea
978-1-64247-378-0 | 396 pgs | paperback: $19.95 | eBook: $9.99
For two women the battle between new love and old loyalty may prove
more dangerous than the war they're trying to survive.

Under the Stars with You – Jaime Clevenger
978-1-64247-439-8 | 302 pgs | paperback: $19.95 | eBook: $9.99
Sometimes believing in love is the first step. And sometimes it's all
about trusting the stars.

The Missing Piece – Kat Jackson
978-1-64247-445-9 | 250 pgs | paperback: $18.95 | eBook: $9.99
Renee's world collides with possibility and the past, setting off a tidal
wave of changes she could have never predicted.

An Acquired Taste – Cheri Ritz
978-1-64247-462-6 | 206 pgs | paperback: $17.95 | eBook: $9.99
Can Elle and Ashley stand the heat in the *Celebrity Cook Off* kitchen?

9 781642 475845